KISSES IN
Heartache

VANESSA LUISA

Kisses In Heartache
Cover Design: Lori Jackson
Cover Photographer: Daniel Jaems (Paperback Model)
Editor: Rebecca's Fairest Reviews, Emily A. Lawrence, Kelly Allenby
Proofreader: Emily A. Lawrence, Gemma Woolley
Formatter: Stacey at Champagne Book Design

ISBN: 978-0-6450535-9-3, ISBN: 978-0-6450535-8-6

He's forbidden, a blue-eyed daydream, and... *my gorgeous childhood rival.*

The first time I locked eyes with Tate Meadows, I drowned in an allusive game of *he loves me, he loves me not,* and I haven't recovered since, no matter how deeply he hates me now.

Tate wasn't only my first love....
He's my first heartache.
Frenemy
Regret.

He's the broken rebel with a cause who saved me.
I'm the pink-obsessed good girl, riddled in depression.
Together, we're forbidden, forced into our elite parents' Manhattan feud.
But I would have loved him till the end of time, only... *I ruined us instead.*

When we were younger, Tate promised we'd escape to the moon.
Now, his heated gaze only promises one thing... *complete and utter carnage.*

And if it's anything I know, it's that he always wins.

Always.

Until he doesn't...

To that vintage rock 'n' roll, drive-in cinema, and heart-shaped candy kinda love...

And to Mamma, Nonna, and Nonno,
My love for you all is infinite.
<3

"Is your heart filled with pain?
Shall I come back again?
Tell me dear,
Are you lonesome tonight?"

ELVIS PRESLEY, 'ARE YOU LONESOME TONIGHT?'

Playlist

Theme Song: "Wish You Were Here" — Pink Floyd

"White Mustang" — Lana Del Rey
"Cinema - Acoustic" — Gary Go
"Black and Blue" — Ramsey
"Are You Lonesome Tonight?" — Elvis Presley
"Them and Us" — Pink Floyd
"Nights" — Makk Mikkael
"Enough" — Fornicras
"Kiss Me Harder" — Jordan Fiction
"Smells Like Teen Spirit" — Nirvana
"Sad Sex" — Ängie, Tail Whip
"Are You Filming Me?" — twst
"Are You Even Real?" — James Blake
"Surrender" — Elvis Presley
"My Girl" — The Temptations
"Crazy" — Patsy Cline
"Pixie Hollow and Purgatory" — Alexis Munroe
"Boys Like You" — Tanerélle
"Fade to Blue" — Roniit
"Silver Lion" — Tsar B
"Terrible Thing" — AG
"Heat" — L.A. Rose
"Can't Stop" — Red Hot Chili Peppers
"Somebody Else" — The 1975
"To Build A Home" — The Cinematic Orchestra, Patrick Watson

PART ONE

ALMOST TO THE MOON

past

Chapter
ONE

London

PAST.
Seven Years Prior.
London and Tate are ten.

Thundery pearl-sized raindrops have always been my escape whenever I want to run away from the world as I know it. Daddy and Mommy say nothing good can ever come of it, but for me, it's hope, and after every wintery storm, the kaleidoscope of colored rainbows warms my soul.

They're my favorite parts of every Manhattan storm.

The rainbows.

Every time, I run up to the window so fast, I slam my nose against the cold glass, fogging it up with my every breath. My little hands spread against the glass as I stare out. I love the way my baby-blue eyes sparkle back at me through the reflection as I look out at the wonderland of colors.

Violet is my favorite, but I do desperately wish there were pink.

Or soft rose.

Or magenta.

Or anything other than blue.

I hate blue.

It reminds me of the blotches of the dark blue marks my daddy leaves on my skin whenever he drinks too much. They hurt and make salty tears rush down my cheeks. But Mommy never stops him. Never stops him from hitting me.

He says he's not happy. Not happy with me.

That it's all my mom's fault. That it's all mine.

But I don't know why.

I don't know why they don't love me. Why they never hold my hands like the other kids' parents do. They never tell me they love me. They never rock me to sleep.

Mommy says it's because I'm a bad girl even though I eat all of my vegetables, brush my hair every night before bed, and never ask questions when I have nightmares and run out of my bedroom to find strange men in suits kissing my mommy.

Nothing makes sense.

I'm all confused.

But my teddies make it better.

Teddies and storms and rainbows.

Except for tonight. Right now. Here on this bench in Central Park.

Because there are no beautiful colors. Just nothingness. Just me, midnight, and heavy rain the size of golf balls. It's just dark, black, and depressing. Bleak and empty.

Lonely.

Lonely like my heart.

As I clutch my fluffy teddy closer to my chest, a ruffle in the bushes behind me has me shutting my eyes. *Who is it?*

Who's there?

I do my best to ignore the strings tightening around my heart and focus ahead. On the gorgeous observation point at this park. At the silvery moonlight grazing over the lake behind the barbed wire. Then the lit-up city skyline a few hundred feet away that looks so pretty.

"You stole my spot, blondie." A boy's deep, defeated voice who sounds my age echoes behind me.

And then my heart stops.

Everything does.

Truly, I don't care who it is. Boogieman or some daydream. All I care is that it's somebody. Anybody. Because suddenly, I'm not alone… *not anymore.*

While part of me wants to turn around to put a name to the face, I know I'm not brave enough to glance over my shoulder and stare at him. Wherever he is.

I tighten my grip on my fluffy teddy bear, holding it closer to my chest while heat gushes across the back of my head at the stare I feel. It takes everything within me to block out whoever's watching and the way my teddy shivers in my grip because my ice-cold hands tremble with callous nervousness.

It's a habit I hate.

A habit my parents always pick on me for.

But I can't help it.

Staring down at my teddy, I do everything to swallow down the large knot at the back of my throat, which only thickens with every awkward passing second.

"Blondie, I said you're sitting in my spot."

"My name isn't blondie."

"Then what is it?"

Curiosity itches up my spine, but I don't dare look over.

Grazing the pad of my thumb over the teddy's ruined button eye, which is hanging on by a bare thread, I shrug. "Mama says I shouldn't say my name to strangers."

"Mine says I shouldn't sneak out the window at night, but I still do."

I let his words sink in.

Marinate.

He shouldn't be here, either.

I can't help it. My agitation wins, and I glance at my mystery shadow boy and… *wow.* He looks like a wonderland. The perfect dream for a fated Disney princess like me. The moonlight creeps down, glazing over his baby-blue eyes, which are so bright and mesmerizing. They stare through me like lasers.

I know boys don't like the term *cute*, so I'll use something more fitting instead—*beautiful.* He is beautiful with that boyish smirk that brings heat to my cheeks, thick long lashes, and a sadness to his gaze that has me questioning if his reasons for being here are as sufficient as mine.

To escape.

I decide I hate him for it. Hate he's hiding in Central Park at midnight because this was supposed to be *my* place.

My escape.

My safe haven.

Not *his.*

The second reason I hate him is that his smirk slips, and without reason, a slight frown takes its place. He dives his hand into his dark rain jacket and slowly slides into the seat beside me.

He's close now.

Real close.

And it gives me the chance to study him without any barriers as the twinkling stars skim the part of his beautifully tousled hair sticking out from his jacket's hood. It's the mix between a dark sandy brown and ultra-light toffee. The kind of color that reminds me of gingerbread and all things him.

I hate how he's staring out at the water, giving me the most perfect perspective of his straight nose and full lips.

I hate how hot my entire body feels in the Manhattan winter and how wildly my stomach floods with bad kind of butterflies at the sight of him. Or how his minty, sandalwood blend becomes all I breathe.

But most importantly, I hate that I know exactly who he is. And although we've never met before, my parents have crucified his family since the beginning of time and vice versa, conditioning me to believe that this boy is complete and utter sin.

Just like his last name.

Meadows.

Tate Meadows.

The boy with the cold heart that I've spent many nights thinking about. Wondering if he could really be the troubled boy my parents brainwashed me to believe he was just because of their feud with his father.

In my ten years, I've never seen a boy so up close before. Seen the softness of their skin. Been witness to the lightening heat surrounding my heartstrings.

"I know who you are," I whisper into the night, wishing he could just get up and leave me alone. "I know who you are, Tate."

Tate stares and stares and stares until I'm sure my stomach is eating itself alive. I've never stared at a boy this long without getting that inevitable itch to look away... *until tonight.*

As much as I know I shouldn't like him, I can't look away from him. From his mesmerizing eyes. From his steady stare that aches for me to drown in his oceans and forget all else. Until he speaks, and *gosh*, his voice becomes my escape instead.

"That makes two of us," he says, and when he turns to me, there's a melancholic strain in his eyes that tells me he regrets his words. "Your voice is so much softer than I thought... London."

Chewing on my bottom lip, all I'm left to do is stare with a tightness lacing my entire body. I hate to admit he looks exactly how I imagined him—an angel's dream. Only because I've searched him up one too many times online.

He's popular.

Beautiful.

Why does he come to this park alone at night? Don't his parents ever catch him?

My parents don't check on me at night; in fact, they're hardly home. I wonder if his parents check on him and wonder if he's all right. If they know their son sneaks out the window for midnight therapy. If they know he smells like heaven.

White noise coats the space between us as honking horns from a far distance cut into my late-night daydream.

I should walk away.

I should hide from this boy.

I should hate him like I want to.

But then I remember the true reason why I'm here. *That rainbow.* So I stay still and stare down at the teddy, not caring how long I feel Tate's eyes on me, burning through the left side of my head.

That is until my bones jump out of my skin at the sudden unearthly lightning bolt and following thunder that rumbles beneath the muddy grass my white Dr. Martens are stationed in.

Three.

Two.

One.

Heavily pounding rain casts down on us, its velocity reckless, and I can't help but grimace.

Why didn't I bring a jacket? Anything?

I glance between Tate's waterproof jacket and my pink fleece Barbie pajama set, getting wetter by the second.

You're a loser, London Héroux. A loser for getting drenched like this when you own five million umbrellas at home.

Okay, maybe not *thaaat* many, but you get it.

I should have been more attentive. But I was just so in my head when I snuck out of my parents' penthouse apartment after my nanny—who is taking care of me while my parents are in Dubai—rushed out of my house just before midnight to see her boyfriend.

I know because when she came to check on me, I pretended I was asleep.

Not even ten seconds later, I heard a barely audible ringtone and her soft mumbles telling the person on the other line, "*She's asleep, and I'm fucking bored. Let me see you, baby. I miss you and want you to fuck the brains out of me.*"

Whatever that last part means, it sounds like trouble. Anything that includes brains out of their intended space—the cranium—sounds problematic. And like it should be in a full-on sci-fi movie.

No, thanks.

Within seconds, the apartment door slammed shut, and I shot my eyes open, staring up at the super high ceiling of my very lonely, quiet, and freezing penthouse.

And then I started to cry. I don't know why, but it helped ease the pain in my chest a little. Until it didn't.

Here I was, alone and abandoned on a school night. A night that should have been filled with happy thoughts, my parents tucking me into bed, and a bedtime story.

But my parents were never that kind. I don't think they'll ever be. Work is where their loyalty lies. Work. And money. And reputation.

Definitely not me.

I know that big *R*-word because it's all they ever talk about. Being rich. Staying rich.

Rich.

Rich.

Rich.

Reich in German.

I hate that we are—*rich*, that is—because ever since I learned that word, I've been spiraling in an endless pit of doom filled with Brontë, Pink Floyd, and sad thoughts.

Sad thoughts that only manifest lying on my king-sized bed alone at home. That's when I decided the park was a good idea.

Tate—my enemy, or whatever he may be—is also rich. Well, his parents are. I can tell from his expensive haircut, that YSL raincoat, and squeaky-clean sneakers that he is. *That* and the fact that every day I take the bus from elementary school, his driver passes me.

Every.

Time.

Tate goes to a different private elementary school than me, but I've seen his baby-blue eyes stare out from the passenger seat with a soulless expression one too many times.

Wandering.

It's as if he's spacing out, wanting anything else but this as he leans his elbow against the armrest and his clenched palm balances his head. I know because every day I watch him—even if it's a fraction of a second before the car speeds off and turns left in the street while the bus goes straight—it ain't his parents driving him, it's his driver.

And every day it's a new car.

Maserati.

Ferrari.

Audi.

Always sleek black with glossy wax. Tate never sees me. He's staring out at the world too much. Dreaming. But I always see him. See the agony in his eyes. The frown on his lips. The stiffness of his light olive skin and taut physique from all the sports I know he does.

Next year is middle school, and we may not take the same route. I don't know why that thought makes my heart hurt. I don't care about Tate. I don't care about Tate Meadows at all. But something about possibly never seeing him again, even for a few seconds at a time every morning, sprays sadness all over my body.

He's become a habit.

A secret habit.

A daily routine.

And I'm not sure why I'm thinking about it so hard when he's sitting right next to me and my honey-blonde waves are sticking to my face as the thundery rain soaks my clothes, but I am.

I'm thinking about Tate while glancing at him.

I'm thinking about the way it feels like he saves me from drowning every time I look at him in the mornings through the bus windows and right now while he stares right at me.

I'm thinking about why it doesn't hurt to breathe so much now that he's near while we're looking at each other, and it's a mess.

We're a mess.

Broken.

A broken soul.

That's what I see looking back at me.

Gulping down the intensity of him has me focusing on my hands for a minute. I don't know why he's looking at me like that, but I don't want it to stop.

I hate myself for it.

I do.

I hate myself for acting pretty normal while my entire body trembles from the rain. Water is everywhere and gliding down my lashes into my eyes.

But here I am, leaning over and acting normal as I pull a white daisy from the field of flowers just by my feet. I swirl it around with my pointer and thumb, then hover it under my nose and breathe to anticipate the sweet scent. Instead, cold rain is all I smell.

Ugh.

Large drops fall on the petals, making them bounce back and forth but never tearing. That makes me smile. Smile because I'm trying to act all normal and ignore Tate, so he doesn't have to see the warmth across my cheeks. Warmth he brings.

I've never felt like more of a little girl as I slowly pull off each petal of the daisy. With each tug, I mutter in my head the nightmare that is, *he loves me, he loves me not...*

I know Tate doesn't love me. He'd have no reason to. But hate— hate, he has a reason. And yet my little heart beats like crazy as I continue tugging, knowing Tate will never love me and I'll never like him because he's not someone I could ever know.

And yet... I play the crazy game.

I softly whisper the words this time, through the pouring rain where I know he can't hear me—not through heaven's roar.

"Tate Meadows loves me..."

Pull.

"*Tate Meadows loves me not...*"

Pull.

"*Tate Meadows loves me...*"

Third last petal.

Pull.

"*Tate Meadows loves me not...*"

Pull.

"London, what the hell are you doing?"

My breath goes all funny—thicker.

I ignore him.

"*Tate Meadows loves me...*" I whisper, tugging the last petal free, and I feel nothing but numb as I stare at the bare stem.

He loves me.

I roll my eyes and throw the stem far, watching as it kisses the water's surface and skates across each ripple like it's ice.

Yeah, right. Tate could never love me.

I'm a Héroux. A Héroux could never mix with a Meadows. It's sin. Straight up sin.

"London," Tate slightly shouts through the rain because it's the only way I can hear him. "London, look at me."

My teeth are jittering, slamming together again and again and again due to the cold chill seeping through my pajamas, skin, and bones.

I don't.

I don't look at him.

Instead, the fresh smell of rain is all I breathe.

"I'll swap you with my coat!" Tate yells, but it sounds as if it's with a frown, like it's the last thing he wants to do.

Wait, what?

That has me swinging my head toward Tate.

Piercing light blue eyes motionlessly stare back at me in waiting. The only hint of any sort of expression is his tight jaw and the clench it does twice before he gestures at my teddy with his chin.

I knit my brows in confusion. *Is he serious? He wants my teddy bear?*

It takes two seconds for me to weigh up my options between

freezing to death and separation anxiety. In the end, I choose to sacrifice the latter.

Tate Meadows unzipping his raincoat for me is a sight I thought I'd never see.

I pout. "But it's blue..."

"What is?" he asks, pulling his coat off.

"Your coat. It's blue."

"So?"

I grimace, feeling the bile rush up my throat, just like it always does when I think of the color blue and what it means for me. "I don't like blue."

Tate scrunches up his nose. "Well, that's stupid. Blue is the best color in the world."

I poke my tongue out. "I hate it!"

"My parents say I should hate *you*."

I don't know why I struggle to breathe for a moment. Of course he should hate me. That much, I know. I guess I've just never heard those words out loud before. *From him.*

"My mama and daddy say I should feel the same way about you too."

"Good."

"Huh?"

"Good," he hisses through his perfect pearly whites. "I said *good*. It's better this way."

Better this way?

Our stare down ends with a scoff on my behalf and a glare on his. I thrust my teddy bear at his chest. "I hate you."

Tate practically throws his raincoat in my face. "I. Hate. *You.*"

Slipping on his raincoat, I almost want to laugh at how oversized it is. Tate is already so much taller than me, causing the raincoat to end by my ankles, and the sleeves cover my hands, even rolled up. But it's okay. It's okay because it keeps me warm. And safe. And it smells like him, which makes my stomach flip with butterflies.

Good butterflies this time.

I glance over at Tate and can't help but notice how drenched his cashmere sweater and jeans are already. His dark caramel brown hair seems even darker in the rain, and I watch as he slicks it back with one hand, but one or two cheeky strands remain and fall over his eyes like he's Superman.

The rain seeps into my teddy even more, soaking it through so much that I'm sure if he squeezes it hard enough, a waterfall will escape. But his grip on my teddy isn't hard. Not at all. It's soft and gentle and almost like... almost like he wants to protect it.

I don't know if Tate's mommy or daddy and stepmom ever give him any toys or teddies, but right now, it's like it's the very first time he's holding something other than empty space.

"Bye, bye, Mr. Bunny." I sigh, waving over at my teddy with a frown.

Tate looks at me as if I'm crazy. "Why is it called Mr. Bunny if it's a bear?"

"'Cause, it just is."

"Wellllll, that's stupid."

My brows rush together. "You can't say that! Mommy said that's a bad word!"

A slow, boyish smirk rises up his lips. "Stupid! Stupid! Stupid!"

I roll my eyes into the back of my brain. *Ugh. Why are boys so annoying?*

"I liked it better without you here."

Tate's stare remains as he parts his lips as if he's going to say something, but he pauses. And seconds later, they're closed again.

I look up at him, confused.

What was he going to say?

Did I hurt his feelings?

I shrug to myself and face my body toward the lake again, glancing up at the moon.

Boys...

Moments pass with the thundery rain being our only friend. I don't know what Tate is thinking, other than the soft sigh that escapes him, almost as if he's bored. Not of me. Not of this moment. But of life.

Tired.

Tired of life is what I mean.

Gosh, the moon is so pretty. Even through the heavy rain, it's so bright and big and perfect. How did it get all the way up there? I've heard some people say it's made out of cheese, but I don't think so. It couldn't be. I don't know what it's made of, just that it's pretty, lights up the waves of the lake, and sparks such happiness to my heart that I smile slowly into the night.

"Did you sneak out?" Tate's voice lingers in my chest for a second too long.

I nod without facing him. "Yeah, my nanny left to see her boyfriend. She thinks I didn't notice, but I did. My parents are away... in Dubai. Did you sneak away too?"

"Yeah. My parents aren't away, but they never check on me at night. I come here to hide."

Hide from what? I want to ask him. But I know I can't.

I'm not supposed to know anything about Tate Meadows.

Nothing at all.

My parents would ground me if they knew where I am right now. Which is why I can't tell them. How I know Tate won't tell his.

This is our secret.

Only ours and nobody else's.

I gulp down thickly. "Tate, this is my first time sneaking out..."

Tate Meadows scoffs.

Scoffs.

Obviously, this isn't his first time and definitely won't be his last either. And there's that same ol' smirk again. "Wanna run away from earth one day together?"

My heart skips at the way he's looking at me... so deeply.

Shrugging, I stare at the shimmery moonlit body of water. "I dunno. Where we gonna go?"

Silence greets me.

Swinging my legs, I count to ten. Then again. And again. When I reach a full minute, I glance over my shoulder at Tate, who's still holding my teddy like it's his prize, his smirk long gone.

Tate chews his lower lip softly, concentrating before those blue-eyed wonderlands flicker up to the bright full moon above us.

He scoots closer to me and gestures to it. "*There.* We'll go *there.*"

To the moon.

"But..." I whisper, all confused. "But... you can't live there!"

"Why not?"

"Because... Nobody lives on the moon."

Hopeful blue eyes meet mine, and everything else just fades. "Then it could be just ours."

Chapter
TWO

London

PAST.
Seven Years Prior.
London and Tate are ten.

<u>Entry One: The moon, raincoats, and you.</u>

Dear Tate,
    I could never say this to your face...
but yes, yes, I wish we could run away
to the moon together. When you told me that
the moon "could be just ours," I think I
blushed a little. Okay, maybe I actually
blushed a lot. You probably didn't see me,
though, because I looked away.
    I do that sometimes... look away, that

is. I don't like people looking at me for too long, so I always look away. Like when I get in trouble with Daddy, and I see the anger bubbling up. He always gets that popped vein in his forehead that I hate. It makes me feel sad. He makes me feel sad.

I thought I would feel sad when you kept on staring at me tonight, but I didn't. For the first time, a stare didn't scare me. Your perfect blue eyes made me want you to stare into mine forever. Do you believe in forever? That something could last that long? I do. I only looked away from you because I thought if I didn't, I would cry.

Why?

Because nobody has ever wanted to go somewhere with me before. My mommy and daddy are always busy, and I ain't got nobody else. I think that's why I ran. Why I sneaked out from home and found myself at that lake—to not be alone. The rain calms me, but it isn't human, so I was still alone.

And then came you.

My gorgeous rival.

Tate Meadows.

I could finally breathe when you sat

down next to me, no matter how many times I rolled my eyes at some of the things you said.

Just to be sure, stupid is a bad word. And now I hate you more because you made me write that word in this journal. (A journal you will never see, read, or know about).

But it's okay.

My parents won't find it.

I'll hide it somewhere they'll never find.

I've never written in a journal before tonight, so you better not be tough on me. I was going to use this notebook to write songs, but using it to fill it with you sounds much better.

I don't know why I'm writing here, but you made me feel so much, so I wanted to write it down. My mommy and daddy always tell me so many bad things about you and your family. That you're monsters. Those that hide under your bed and crawl out while you sleep. But monsters don't give you raincoats when you're freezing to death. Right?

So why did you? Give me your raincoat, that is?

I know I gave you my teddy (Mr. Bunny, I miss you), but why did you want to swap to start with?

Or perhaps, the better question is, why did you choose to take my most valuable possession?

I still have your raincoat on. I don't think I'll ever take it off. I like it too much.

I like you.

All the raindrops on the raincoat haven't dried yet, and it's creating a patch on my pink silk bedsheets that I'm currently lying on, but I don't care.

I wonder if you're still taking care of Mr. Bunny. Did you take her home, or did you lose her? I hope you took her home, wherever home may be for you. (And yes, Mr. Bunny is a girl).

My eyes are getting tired, and I just want to dive into my bed and fall asleep with sweet dreams. But before I do, I have three questions for you, Tate Meadows. Just three.

1) What were you hiding from when you sneaked out to Central Park tonight?

2) Why did you stand up and leave

seconds after you said, "then it could be just ours."?

3) ~~If~~ I sneak out tomorrow night, for the second time in my life, will you be there by the lake?

Because I will be. I'll wait for you. I'll wait for you forever until the day I hate you, because right now I want to run away with you. To the moon. To anywhere you like. So long as I'm with you.

Until we reach the moon,
London

Entry Two. Midnight madness

Tate,

I waited in our spot until midnight... but you never showed. I hope nothing bad happened. I hope Mr. Bunny is okay. I wore your raincoat again because it was storming again, and here in Manhattan, when it storms, it's like heaven coming undone.

Truth is, I'm kinda sad you weren't

by the lake tonight. I really thought you would have been. My hands were sweaty all day just thinking about seeing you. That and the fact I didn't sleep a wink last night. I couldn't stop thinking about what I would say to you tonight. What you would say to me. I also hoped that you could give me Mr. Bunny back. I can't sleep without it. I need to hold it tight to feel all right, and without it was torture.

But I guess it'll be another night without Mr. Bunny...

Why didn't you show, Tate? Did I say something wrong?

Are you not coming to the lake anymore now that I know your secret escape?

Will you ever come back to the lake? Ever ask me if I want to run away again?

I wish we went to the same elementary school just so I could ask you without worrying if you'd be there or not.

The moon didn't seem as beautiful tonight. The dark clouds wouldn't let go of the quarter moon. I liked it better last night. When I was with you. Today my nanny said my parents are going to come back from Dubai in three days. That means

I have two more nights to sneak out to the lake without getting in trouble.

Please be there tomorrow night.
Or the next.
Or both.

Until we reach the moon,
London

Entry Three: Pinky Promise me...

Tate,

I'm starting to think my parents were right about you, no matter how badly I wish they weren't. I waited on our bench until sleep consumed me, and I woke up with the twinkling stars staring right back at me. Yes, that's right, stupid. I fell asleep in the middle of Central Park.

And yes, I'm saying stupid now. It may be a bad word, but it's exactly what you are.

How can you take Mr. Bunny from me and give me your raincoat and never return?

Did I really make you upset? What did I even say?

It's like you're doing this on purpose, Tate. Made me get lost in your eyes, and now you're gone... Where did you go? I don't want to go to the lake if you won't be there tomorrow night. I feel foolish, and I'm pretty sure a police officer was going to ask me a few questions when I entered the park alone. Thankfully, I've watched one too many comedy shows and pretended to blend in with a random family. When the officer began walking in another direction, I bolted toward the lake.

I waited, and waited, and waited.

For a ruffle of the bushes behind me.

For a reason to feel my heart thump so fast again.

For your honeyed sin voice to say, "You're in my spot, blondie."

But it never came.

You never came.

And I'll hate you if you don't show up tomorrow. I really will, Tate Meadows.

I pinky promise.

Be there,

London

<u>Entry Four: Monster.</u>

StupidFace,
    I. Hate. You. So. Much. Goodbye.

    Sincerely,
    Blondie.

P.S. I should have never given you Mr.
Bunny.

PPS. You're like Manhattan snow, beautiful
but cold.

PPPS. I'm going to shred your fancy YSL
raincoat into a million little pieces. You're
welcome.

Chapter
THREE

Tate

PAST.
Three and a Half Years Prior.
NYE London and Tate are turning fourteen.

It's been one-thousand, two-hundred, and seventy-seven days since
I last saw London Héroux.

I know because I've been counting.

Yeah, I know. I'm fucked.

I didn't have it in me to return to the lake the night after the thunderstorm. I didn't know what to say to her. How to act. How to simply
be. So I didn't return until a week later. The nights by the lake without London feel different. I don't know *how* exactly, but they just do.

Colder.

That's how they feel.

It's crazy how one single night can change your life forever...
Like tonight.

The piercing echo of crashing glass has my heart jolting up my throat. It scares me so much that the sewing needle slips from my hand, getting lost in the sea of my bedsheets.

God.

That broken glass.

I always know it's coming, especially this late at night. I just never know when…

That's the part that startles me the most.

In fact, it all does. But I just have to put on a brave face.

My father is an alcoholic, and there's nothing in the whole world I can do to change it.

My stepmom always pleads with him to stop. To not hurt her. To not hurt me. But when he's in one of his violent outrage moments, anything can happen. Just ask the scar on my forearm.

It's why I wish I could see London every night, to ease the hurt my father supplies.

Except… *she never returned to the lake.*

Not since the very first night.

Three and a half years ago.

I thought it could be our hideaway. Our secret. Our escape. I was wrong.

"Oh my God! What is wrong with you, Mirko?" My stepmom's scream echoes through the walls of our luxurious Manhattan brownstone.

Everything echoes.

We moved in last week after less than six months of living in our previous house. Unopened boxes are scattered everywhere. I'm in middle school now, and my father was supposed to be better in this district. *Everything was supposed to be better.*

But it's New Year's Eve, and everything seems to be the same.

My birthday is in less than an hour, and my parents locked me in my bedroom so I wouldn't ruin *their* New Year's party. The one they hold every year to keep up appearances and create a fake fantasy that the Meadowses are perfect, when the truth is, they're not.

We're not.

Champagne. Caviar. Millionaires. It's all happening outside my bedroom wall.

The lives of the New York City elites.

My father and stepmom don't care about me. They never did.

They never will. All they care about is golf, diamonds, and the latest Rolex. Sometimes, I even question if my father remembers he has a son, and my stepmom a daughter. It's why I find myself sitting on that bench by that lake every night, wishing upon a freaking star that London Héroux will appear and save me.

I'm terrified to admit I've held onto Mr. Bunny for more nights than I'd ever thought I would to ease the pain in my chest that comes with every one of my parents' arguments. My best friend, Levi, would kill me if I told him that a teddy bear belonging to London Héroux is my comfort. As much as I love him, he'd tease me for being the upcoming star quarterback holding a bear that belongs to a forbidden blonde angel to sleep.

It doesn't matter how much time has passed. I can still smell the hint of rosy vanilla submerged in its fur. The same scent I caught a whiff of the night I told London the moon could be ours.

I've gone to sleep for the past three and a half years staring outside my bedroom window at the moon, wondering if London ever does the same. If she replays that night as much as I do.

Gulping down, I find the needle in my bed with the chocolate brown thread and continue sewing the little button on Mr. Bunny. His eye.

When London gave the bear to me, he only had one button eye, and I was going to keep it that way until the other came undone this morning. I managed to find two antique buttons at a thrift shop and thought Mr. Bunny deserved a facelift.

Smiling softly, I finish off his last eye and hold Mr. Bunny back, satisfied with the results. My room is dim, the wall sconces I have on above my bed providing little light, and just as I pack my grandma's sewing kit away and set it on my bedside table, breaking glass pierces the air again.

And then the shouts resume.

"Are you serious, Mirko? What is wrong with you?" My stepmom gasps as the lively music comes to a screeching halt. "I'm so sorry, everybody. I think my husband has had one too many for one night... and it isn't even the New Year yet."

The guests laugh.

Laugh.

Because the Meadowses are perfect, and nothing could break us. Right?

Wrong.

There have to be at least three hundred and fifty people out there. My stepsister, Maddie, is sleeping over at one of her friend's houses, which leaves just me to witness the carnage that is my parents' broken marriage. A marriage holding on by a thin thread of rehab, therapy, and lies.

They think I don't see anything. They're wrong. I see it all. Every. Single. Thing.

So I do the one thing I always do whenever it feels like too much...

I switch off my light.

Slip out of bed and smooth out the sheets.

Get dressed and tuck Mr. Bunny into my raincoat's deep pocket.

Slowly, I climb out of my first-floor bedroom window with steady hands.

And when crushed rock rumbles beneath the soles of my canvas runners, I *run*.

I run through the front porch. Through the streets. Through the city that never sleeps. Until my lungs are burning and my heart floods with the hope that perhaps tonight will be different.

Rushing past the crowds of people already partying the incoming year, I finally make it into Central Park. I feel calmer here. Safer with the smell of fresh greenery, holistic plants, and warmth of the familiarity of this place, no matter how violently the chilly winter air kisses my face.

It feels like all the air has been knocked out of my lungs as I come to a stop, inches from my bench.

Oh.

My.

God.

My grip on Mr. Bunny tightens.

Honey-blonde.

Honey-blonde is all I see.

I know how wrong it is. How wrong the relieved grin on my lips is, because for a little while, I believed something bad had happened to her, so seeing her tonight feels like a miracle. A real-life miracle.

That is until I step closer, snow flattening beneath my feet, and the soft sounds of sobs have my grin falling.

London has her back to me on the bench and hasn't seen me yet.

Tension clenches around my heart at her hands, which rush up to her face as she cries out to the cold, cold, world.

There's not a soul who passes by that notices her.

That cares.

Nobody but me.

It takes three strides, and I'm right behind her. Without thinking, I do the only thing that comes naturally and round the bench. The second I sit beside London and pull her into my arms, her entire body tenses up.

And mine? My body?

Well, it goes into shock.

Complete sugary shock.

I've never touched a girl before. Never hugged a girl who wasn't my stepsister or mom or stepmom. Never wanted to—*until London.*

"Get off—"

"Shhh, it's okay, it's me," I murmur against the side of her head, and it's as if my voice—my presence—is enough to loosen every muscle in her body and simply give in to me.

Give in to my warmth and comfort.

No matter how badly I can feel my frantic heartbeat in my ears, I give in to the foreign feeling and embrace London tighter.

My lips brush against her freezing cheekbone, and it takes all of me not to feel an ounce of something as I dive my nose into her hair. That all-familiar rosy vanilla blend is all I breathe.

She is all I breathe.

I don't know what it feels like to have a crush, but London Héroux could be something like it.

"You never came back." London trembles through her sobs, suddenly struggling in my grip as if she wants me to let go. I hold on to her tighter. "I hate you, Tate. Get off me!"

You never came back.

My brows knit in confusion. "I *did* come back."

"No, you didn't! You made me look silly; that's what you did! Get OFF!"

I panic. "I'm just trying to help. Stop screaming, London. Somebody's going to think I'm hurting you!"

"You are," she cries, slipping out of my hold. "Get off me before I scream for the police!"

I raise my hands up to my head in defense and slide away from her on the bench, instantly missing her warmth.

I thought this was where it would begin.

Where the real fight would start.

Where all the reasons why she hates me so much would escape.

Instead, London looks at me, like *really* looks at me, and I get lost in those darkened baby-blues that scream fear. Not of me, but of something that was.

My brows furrow, and I attempt to work this out. Attempt to understand the reasons behind London's sobs, which have now mellowed down to whimpers and hiccups.

The reason there's pain written all over her face as she tightens her pink trench coat and scarf.

The reason there's a dark blue blotch forming just under the right side of her lip.

It's highlighted by the silvery moonlight and dim lighting from the art deco lamp two feet away. The bruise is huge and raised, causing that side of her lower lip to be swollen and a tinge redder than her candy-floss-colored plump lips.

Those I seem to stare at more tonight.

I don't know why I'm feeling so protective of her; all I know is that I don't want her hurting. I don't want her in pain. I want to know who did this to her.

Who made her black and blue?

Who made her cry here tonight as the stars twinkle down, hitting the surface of the lake and reflecting up into those baby-blue delights?

Unable to stop myself, I give in to temptation and reach out a hand to her. Gliding it over her cold chin, I cup her jaw, and my thumb automatically rushes up to brush over soft lips.

Whoa.

I need to gulp down as I explore her lips with my thumb ever so slowly. A slight gasp escapes her when I begin tracing the outline of her lips, making me wonder if she likes it. If she likes me touching her lips like this.

She's so beautiful...

She's older than when I last saw her. *Less of a little girl.*

The tension eases, and her shoulders drop as I continue. My touch seems to calm her down, and I decide I like that. I like seeing her relax around me.

My thumb slows just before I reach her swollen bruise, and so many questions rush to my head. One, in particular, stands out. And it's all I think about as her eyes squeeze shut, and her face scrunches up when I lightly graze my thumb over the mark.

"When did this happen?" I whisper into the night.

A moment passes. "Four nights ago."

"Does it still hurt you?"

Eyes still closed, she nods.

"Who did this to you?"

Nothing.

She gives me nothing.

I hate the way her lower lip trembles like that, in sadness.

I slip my thumb away but keep cupping her face. I think I like the way my heart skips a beat when I do. And the way she looks at me, like I'm the only thing that matters.

Swallowing thickly, I slip my hand away and study her pretty face. The tip of her nose is so red from the cold, but I think it's the cutest thing ever. That same coldness seeps into my bones.

"London?"

She opens one eye. "Mhmmm?"

My heart is in my throat.

Thump. Thump. Thumpppp.

Chewing my lower lip, I play with my hands and pray to God she'll say yes to what I'm gonna ask.

"If I press my forehead against yours, promise you won't get mad at me and scream again?"

Both of her eyes open wide at my question, and I'm pretty sure diving face-first into that freezing lake feels better than the extended silence between us.

My stomach flips, and I don't know if it's because I'm going to be sick or because I like the way that scarlet blush works its way up her tear-stained cheeks.

"Okay," London whispers back, her breath creating a fog in the air. *That's* how cold it is. "I promise."

I shut my eyes and do just that. I lean in and press my forehead against hers.

We inhale at the exact same time.

All I feel is her when her hands come to rest on my knees. And even though it's one of the coldest Manhattan winter nights, right now—with *her*—this unspeakable warmth wraps around me that feels like the heat of hell. Because perhaps that's exactly what I am, a devil for going against everything my parents have ever warned me about the Hérouxes.

That they're untrustworthy. Cheats. Worthless.

And while that may apply to her parents, London isn't worthless. Or a cheater. Or untrustworthy. She seems smart. And important. And beautiful.

And hurt, so freaking hurt.

But by who?

I catch a glance of her two bracelets. The first is a Hello Kitty one, and the other, a soft pink pearl bracelet. She's such a girly girl. A true sucker for anything pink and sparkly.

When I kiss away the tears on London's cheeks, my lips burn from the sparks that fizzle despite the wetness.

A noise escapes London's throat that I've never heard before, and it's something half between a silent sob and a moan.

I like it.

My lips linger on her cheeks for what feels like forever.

I wish we could have spent the last three and a half years like this at night. *Every. Single. Night.* I'd take anything with London instead of my father's screams, the alcohol bottles shattering against the wall, and all the hospital visits after he gets so drunk that he gets into fights and becomes concussed.

As I rest my forehead against hers again, I catch a flicker of her eyes, which look up at me and gently fill with tears, creating a beautiful glimmer.

Okay. London Héroux is my crush.

"You look pretty when you cry..." I murmur and scratch the back of my head before adding with a sad smile, "Not that I want you to cry because nobody would want that. It's just that… well, you look pretty when you cry. That's, uh, that's what I'm trying to say."

I don't expect London to giggle, but I'll take it. "You literally could have said that *paragraph* in six words."

Back to the sarcasm, I see.

I smirk. "I get like that when…"

"When what?"

I suck in a sharp breath and smile. "When I get nervous, I say a lot of words… like, like I am right now, you know. Crap."

"I do, too, so don't worry."

London shuts her eyes, so I do too. I'm cupping her face, so I can feel the smile that etches on her lips. The one that has me reach up and feel every groove of her smile line like it's a cure. A cure to the madness crawling up my skin and into my veins whenever she's not around.

"You're nervous?"

"Mmhmmm. *You* make me nervous."

London gasps cutely. "Me? Why me?"

I shrug even though I know. "You just do."

Her warm breath tickles my lips. We're inches apart. *Inches apart from heaven…*

"Tate?"

"Yeah?"

"You…" she begins, her voice a sugary dream. "You make me nervous too, Tate."

My heart clenches.

You make me nervous too, Tate.

"Good." I press my forehead even harder against her. "I've come to this lake every night to try to find you again."

"I came the first three nights, and you never showed. I thought you hated me or something."

"I could never hate you. I'm not my parents," I admit. "I came back to this lake a week later after we met. I waited a week because I didn't know what to say to you. So… yeah."

London sighs. "Oh."

"Yeah… you make my heart feel funny."

"Really?"

"Yeah. It's weird."

"Boys *are* weird."

A boyish half-smirk works up my lips just as a thought crosses my mind. "I have something for you, but you gotta hold your hands out, close your eyes, and promise not to peek!"

"But I hate surprises!" She laughs.

"I promise, it's a good one."

London dramatically huffs and holds out her hands, seeing as her eyes are already shut. "Okayyyyy."

Unable to wipe the grin from my face, I pull back from London and slip Mr. Bunny out of my raincoat pocket. I'm fast to hide the teddy behind my back when she pops an eye open.

"Hey! I said no peeking!"

London pokes out her tongue and re-shuts her eyes with a glowing smile. "Hurry up!"

My gaze drops to that bruise, and my grin is instantly replaced with a frown.

Who did that to her?

Why doesn't she want to tell me?

I give London a countdown to three, and on *zero*, I pull out Mr. Bunny from behind and hold him up like he's Simba, and this is a *The Lion King* remake.

London's eyes open wide, and the gasp that escapes her is like no other. Alongside the pretty grin that follows.

"Oh! My! Gosh!" London squeals and snatches her teddy from me. "Mr. Bunny!"

She hugs it to her chest, stands to her feet, and spins around in circles to the point where she flattens all the snow. *That's* how happy she is.

She jumps around.

She giggles.

She does everything I expected her to do with the soundtrack of my laughter. And just knowing *that*, knowing I've made her *happy* and *brightened* her mood makes me the luckiest boy alive.

"I, uh…" I scratch the back of my head. "I tried to give him some new eyes. It's not perfect, but it's still Mr. Bunny."

I keep my gaze on her.

On Mr. Bunny.

On her bruise.

London notices. She notices me staring and cups a hand over her bottom lip, covering it. Her timid gaze roams everywhere but me. When those baby-blues finally meet mine again, there's a light in them. A warmth. And all I really want to say to London is...

Something doesn't have to be perfect to be beautiful.

Be beautiful. Be London. Be London with all of your hurt.

You can look like whatever. You'll still be London Héroux. You'll still be the prettiest girl I know. But that doesn't mean I won't kill whoever hurt you. So, who did it? Who hurt you?

London steps forth and slowly stands between my thighs. She slips Mr. Bunny into the pocket of her trench coat, and I find myself staring at his golden button eyes before London calls my name.

Breathe.

I glance back up at her, my hands slowly find hers. Our fingers gently intertwine like a dance of death, and seeing as I'm still sitting down, I tug her closer till our thighs are brushing. *Sparks.* Sparks lace my skin in ways I never know existed, exploding fireworks come alive inside.

I'm addicted.

I'm addicted to her, and I can't stop it.

Helloooo, sleepless nights.

I literally have to clench my jaw because I hate how much I like it. How much I like London's hand in mine.

I nod toward the bruise. "Who hurt you?"

"Nobo—"

"I don't believe you. Who did this to you?"

London shakes her head. "I said nobody, Tate. I'm okay. I promise. It was an accident."

An accident?

I don't believe her.

"Are you not saying who it is 'cause you think it'll get the person in trouble?"

London parts her plump lips, but no words come out.

She just keeps staring as a light wind passes, making her long honey-blonde hair sway a little against her coat. It's like she's in slow motion, like this is the part of the movie where the girl tells the boy why she ran away, and the boy holds her tight.

Except it isn't.

It isn't at all because London doesn't say a word.

Her fingers tremble in my hold, and I bring them closer to my lips. They're so frozen, coldness pierces through my hands and a shiver rushes up my spine.

"You're freezing," I say and box her fingers against my mouth before blowing warmth into her hands.

Never once do I stop looking at her. Stop looking at the way her mouth curls into a soft smile despite the pain. And right here, it's as if we're wrapping ourselves in our own little secret. One I know I'll remember forever.

I'll remember *this* night forever.

The night London Héroux let me warm her hands.

"Who hurt you?"

She sighs. "Just some girls from school…"

I give London a look that says I don't believe her.

She slips her hands out of mine and sits beside me, staring out at the lake.

Darn it. That's what I get for asking too many questions.

Bringing her knees up to her chest, she wraps her arms around her legs, rests her cheek on her knees, and then turns to me. She smiles. *Smiles.* And I'm happy I didn't make her upset.

"This isn't how I thought I'd spend my birthday eve…"

Huh?

My heart stops beating. "Wait, what did you say? It's my birthday tomorrow too."

London's jaw drops. "No way! Same!"

"Oh my God!"

We stare at each other until we're laughing like we're crazy. The laughter rumbling up my chest feels so good. *London* makes me feel so good.

I wipe the happy tears from my eyes and smile back at her. "Do you think being fourteen will bring us more luck?"

"Maybe. I mean, I already got the best birthday present ever. *This.*" London waves around Mr. Bunny. "So, I'd say turning fourteen will be special."

Holding your hand was my birthday present, LonLon.

Just as I'm about to say something, cheers from a distance break me out of my thought. There are people laughing before, "*Two minutes to go!"* is shouted in unison by voices so far it could be from around the skyscrapers. Those we can only see from a close distance are all lit up and pretty.

And then it hits me.

Two minutes.

They shouted *two minutes.*

It's going to be midnight in *two* minutes.

It's going to be the New Year in *two* minutes.

It's going to be both of our birthdays in *two* minutes.

Suddenly, two minutes feels like too long. Or too short. Or whatever it may be. I'm so lost in London's eyes to even notice what I'm really feeling. I'm just glad. Glad I'm here with her.

I want to start the year fresh, which is why I say, "I'm sorry I didn't come back the night after."

"It's okay." She blushes. "You're here now."

I am. I'm right here. And I'm never leaving.

My fingers slip back into hers because I like the way it feels. She lets me.

"Would it be okay if..." I gulp down and glance at our intertwined hands. "Would it be okay if I held you until midnight comes—"

"Yes," she breathes before I can even finish.

I scoot closer to her and pull her into me. My right arm wraps around her shoulder, almost as if it's a half hug, but my left hand is still intertwined with hers on my lap. London nuzzles into my chest, and we lean our heads together.

I've always spent New Year's Eves alone in my bedroom due to my parents' rowdy parties. This year, I'm with her. And I'm holding her hand.

Holy crap.

I'm holding London Héroux's hand!

"Do you have any wishes for the New Year, or your birthday, or both?" London whispers.

"Just one."

"What is it?"

I look down at London in the solace of my arms, and we smile in unison. "I can tell you, but you have to promise not to tell anybody else..."

"I promise."

I glance between her eyes, and something in my chest shifts. "I want to spend every New Year's Eve like this with you. Think you could sneak out of your house once a year for me?"

London curls her body to me as we keep each other warm. "Only if you sneak out of your house once a year for me."

"Deal."

"Deal."

"So… we can't meet here any other night? Just in three-hundred and sixty-five days?"

I gulp down, knowing how much this next year is going to be torture. "Once a year. I think that's the best thing to do, you know, because…"

I don't need to continue; the look in London's eyes tells me she's already figured out why.

Our parents.

Their bitter feud.

The forbiddenness of us.

"Okay."

"What's your wish for the New Year, or your birthday, or both?" I ask.

"Aside from really wanting to see you here next year too?"

I can't help my slow, cocky smirk. "Yeah, aside from that, because that's an obvious one."

London cutely rolls her eyes before thinking long and hard. "Earrings. I really want to get my ears pierced."

"Oh cool, they'd look really pretty on you."

Giggling, she turns back to the lake with flushed cheeks. "Stop making me blush, Tate."

"But I like it when you blush."

"You like it a little, or you like it a lot?"

"I like it a hell of a lot."

London turns back to me with a grin. "Will you ever stop saying bad words?"

"Mhmmm." Tipping my head back, I pierce my lips shut and pretend I'm concentrating really hard before bursting out into laughter. "Nah, I like the way you tell me off about it."

"You're so annoying!"

"You steal my bench, and now you're stealing my birthday? Tsk, tsk, tsk," I tease. "*You're* the annoying one, Héroux."

"Shut up, Meadows."

I put on my best *London Héroux* voice. "*Don't tell me to shut up. Mama says it's a bad word!*"

"You think you're *so* funny..." London full-on glares at me, so I give her my best straight face, which instantly fails, and we're both bursting out into laughter. Again. She playfully punches my chest with her free hand, and it just makes me hold her shaking body closer.

The laughter settles down, and we simply stare at each other, but it isn't just a stare; it's so much more. I feel it all through my veins, and I'm sure London does too. It must be the reason she squeezes our intertwined hands right in that moment.

I squeeze back. Harder. Longer. Slower.

We stare.

And stare.

Then stare some more.

Until people cheer, "*Happy New Year!*" and loud screeching explosions of fireworks have us both glancing toward the lake and above the Manhattan skyline at the wonderful mix of red, green, and blue fireworks.

They go wild.

Again and again and again.

Every single explosion feels like the fireworks going off inside me. Those that match my every heartbeat because of her.

"Wow!" London gasps in awe and gestures toward the fireworks. "Look at them, Tate!"

That's when I stop looking at the fireworks and focus on her instead. On her face, which flickers every single color of the rainbow, including that pot of gold. Because as stunning as all those colors are, she's so much more stunning, and I want to do everything to prove it to her.

London Héroux is beautiful.

Through her pain.

Through her loneliness.

Through her darkening bruises.

She's beautiful.

"Happy New Year, Tate!" She grins, finally looking back at me.

I grin back and don't miss the hitch in her breath when I lean closer. I kiss the side of her head, letting my lips linger again, and murmur back, "Happy Birthday, LonLon."

Moments later, I'm walking her home in silence, but I never let go of her hand. Not until we reach Madison Avenue, where she tells me it's better if I let her go here in case someone sees and people talk.

Her family must live in one of these lavish apartments. A penthouse, nonetheless.

London looks up at me, her hair smoothly blowing in the wind, and slowly smiles. "Thank you for making my night better. I'm glad we found each other again, Tate."

"Me too." I smirk. "Don't miss me too much this year, all right? You'll see me soon enough."

"A year is never enough." She laughs, but there's sadness to it, and I know why.

It's too long.

A year is too long, but this is how it needs to be.

Bringing our interlocked hands together, I press my lips against her hand and smile against her skin. "You're not freezing anymore…" I let go of our hands, and I instantly miss her touch. "Good night, London."

"Night, Tate," she whispers before tucking Mr. Bunny further into her trench coat and spinning on her heels.

I stand back and watch her walk away with my hands in my pockets.

We were just two fourteen-year-olds walking through Manhattan hand in hand. The city is crazy with people on this New Year's early morning, where darkness still blankets the sky, but I focus on her. Only her. I want to make sure she makes it home all right.

London is about twenty feet away before she stops in her tracks.

Oh.

My breath halts.

Is everything okay?

All the worry is replaced with a huge grin when she turns and begins running toward me with a girly smile. It's only when she's inches away that she slows down.

"I forgot to give you a goodnight kiss!" London pants, and I think

I straight-up die when she rises on her toes and plants a long kiss on my cheek. She pulls away, grinning. "Good night!"

I chuckle. "Sweet dreams, LonLon."

London jogs backward with that goofy smile I love until she turns around and runs home. When I see her slip inside an apartment lobby, I wait a few seconds before turning around and walking toward my own brownstone.

She's safe. She's home.

Yet my jaw clenches because I still want to know who hurt her, but maybe next year she'll tell me. Maybe, just maybe, she will.

With every step I take, I feel that rosy vanilla blend still with me. My cheek burns with her sweet kiss. *I'm never washing my freaking cheek again. I swear I'm not. Ever.*

I smile into the night, never wanting to let this feeling of such happiness go.

And suddenly, I'm not cold anymore. Not in the slightest.

Because London Héroux is all I feel... *still.*

Chapter
FOUR

London

PAST.
Six Months Later.
London and Tate are fourteen.

With my fifteenth birthday in only six months, I know what's also coming… *Tate.*

Dreamy, beautiful, real-life James Dean—Tate Meadows.

The thought of seeing him has made me giddy for the past one hundred and ninety-eight days. My palms get all sweaty just thinking about him.

I've spent the past six months reading back the journal entry I wrote last New Year's, every single word making me relive the moment my hate for Tate Meadows melted into like. I really like him. Like I like *like* him… *a lot.*

A lot has happened in the last few months—for one, I advanced to being a level seven gymnast. Challenging myself on the bars, beam, floor, and vault has always consumed my life. Apart from being the perfect A+ student my parents force me to be, gymnastics and ballet are all I ever do. But it's been good. A good distraction from missing Tate so much.

So yeah, I miss him.

A heck of a lot.

Especially on nights like these when I'm in bed alone and bored at 7:00 p.m. because that's my bedtime. *Yeah, you heard me right.* I just graduated from middle school. It's the summer break before ninth grade. I'm turning fifteen in a few months. Seven o'clock is my *bedtime.*

Insert eyeroll

Oh! And I'm finally growing bigger tits. *Halle—freaking—lujah.*

So, on lonely nights like these, my only option is to either write more in my journal or read past entries. I do the latter. I go back and read about everything I wrote down the night Tate found me crying in Central Park. And how the worst night of my life turned into the best…

All because of him.

Entry Five: The fireworks were for us.

Tate,

I haven't stopped grinning since I said good night to you and sneaked back into my apartment not even five minutes ago. I think I've blushed so hard tonight my cheeks are about to explode from just how red they still are. I thought I hated you. I was wrong. I like you a lot, Tate Meadows.

And I don't know if that's a good or a bad thing. But I want to think it's good.

I like the way you comfort me.

The way you kiss the side of my head.

I like the way you kept holding me so tight.

And the way you clasped my hand all the way home.

I like that we share the same birthdays because the fireworks were for us.

But most of all, I like that you told me I make you nervous because you do the same to me.

There's something about you that makes me feel different. I don't know what is, but I wish I knew. Maybe it's because I don't really know how to act around boys. All my friends are girls, and the ones I do see at school, ballet, or at the gymnastic center, I rarely even speak to. It's why sometimes I look away or don't know what to say because this is all really new to me.

You challenge everything for me... and I like it.

You did that thing again, Tate, that thing where you stare deep into my eyes until I forget to breathe. You did it a lot, and every time, I just wanted to melt right there in your eyes. You've got a stare that could kill... in the best, most possible way.

We didn't talk about the moon tonight,

in fact, I don't even think I glanced up at it because I was so obsessed with you instead. Actually, wait, I did look up at the moon... but that was before you came.

How did you know I was there, Fate? How did you know I needed you?

I ran away from home because it was all too much. I know you kept on asking me who hurt me, and maybe I was wrong for not telling you, or maybe I was right, but either way, I know I would have cried if I told you the truth. And I don't want to cry in front of you.

Not again.

You told me I looked pretty when I cried (which made me blush again), but I don't want to be that in front of you. A crier. I want to be strong. And confident. And independent.

I guess that all comes with growing up, right?

Ugh. I just wish I could be eighteen already. That way, I could find you by the lake anytime and any way I like, not just one night out of an entire year. It's going to be torture... complete torture not seeing you for that long...

But I guess replaying the sparkle in

your eyes when I kissed your cheek will be worth it.

Until we reach the moon,
London

P.S. Thank you for Mr. Bunny!

<u>Entry Six: You fit me better than my favorite sweater...</u>

Tate,

Okayyy, so I lied. I never did shred your coat in a million little pieces like I said I would over three and a half years ago... I kept it. I caught you looking at my trench coat all those months ago when we met for the second time. It was almost as if you were expecting me to have your raincoat on instead. Did you?

If I'd known you were going to show, I would have.

Truth is because you were so tall for ten, it still fits me.

It still fits me now that I'm almost fifteen.

The raincoat still smells like you, but part of me wishes it were a sweater. That way I could wear it to bed instead. Yes, I would have to take it off in the morning before I stepped out of my bedroom or else my parents would notice it's not mine, but it would be worth it. Besides, my parents are rarely home anyway.

I like that we don't talk about our parents when we're together. The thought alone makes me so sad. I guess you could say my relationship with my parents is... crazy. So it means a lot to me that we don't talk about them.

What are your parents like? Are they as scary as my parents say they are?

There are only a few months until I see you again, and there's already so much I want to say to you. I just hope you don't forget our deal to meet by the lake on New Year's Eve because that would be depressing.

Until we reach the moon,
London

P.S. I wish we could meet sometime in

the summer too. Summer is my favorite season.

Entry Seven: Wish you were here...

Tate,

When I began this journal dedicated to you all those years ago, I did it to express all my emotions. But right now, tonight, this journal means so much more to me than that.

Do you remember that night all those months ago? The night you found me crying in Central Park, held me tight, and brushed your thumb over my bluish bruise right by my lip? Do you remember how you couldn't stop asking me who hurt me? How all I did was sob until you fixed my hurt with your warm touch alone?

Well, it happened again.

And again.

And again.

So many more times than I can count in the past few months.

I have bruises. Cuts. Even a small little scar between my left thumb and pointer finger. It happened two months ago. The night after my last entry. That place between my left thumb and pointer finger... that's where the glass seeped into my skin. The glass from the whiskey bottle my father threw at me when I was trying to help my mother. My mother, who fell down against our fancy white marble floors when he struck her. The white marble floors I thought would stain with crimson red blood. Blood that didn't stop dripping from my cut lip for three hours after he punched me in the face because I received a B+ on my English paper.

He said I'm a poor excuse of a daughter.

That I'm ungrateful and undeserving.

A "bitch" for not getting an A.

And then he pulled me out of cheer, dance, and gymnastics for a week to prove his point.

To punish me.

I love gymnastics, Tate. You have to understand, it's all I breathe. Besides you of course. I love it so much I'd die for it. One week may not seem like forever to you, but it does to me. It feels like my whole life slipping away.

But what hurts is that the person who

is supposed to love me the most is hurting me the most, and my mother... she doesn't even tell him to stop. She cares more about her "reputation" and fresh manicure.

Yes, Tate. My father physically abuses me.

He abuses my mother too, but only with words. Verbally. Aside from that one night he hit her.

Then blackmails us into keeping it all a secret.

I wish I could tell the world.

I wish I could tell the world who the real Sterling Héroux is.

I wish I could have told you that night you asked me, but I couldn't.

I couldn't and still can't because it hurts too much to admit. The hits he gives me always get harder when my mom threatens to leave him. He calls her a "selfish bitch," and that he'd ruin her reputation. That she won't get a dollar out of him. He also says she'll find me at the bottom of the Hudson River if she dares try to leave, but she doesn't care about that one.

He would kill me, Tate. He would kill me if I told anybody else, and I don't want to die. Sometimes, when I can't sleep at night, my mind wanders, and whenever I think of death, my throat closes up, and my heart begins to beat slower. I think too much about it that I convince myself I'm going to die, so I spend the entire night staring at the glowing red light of my bedside table clock with tears streaming down my cheeks. It's like when I think about breathing too much, and all of a sudden, the room starts to feel dizzy because just like that, I forget how to breathe.

Does that ever happen to you?

Do you ever feel like you can't breathe?

It often happens to me. Every time my daddy is about to strike, I lose my breath.

I know you can't see them, but I'm sorry for all of the tearstains dripping onto the page and the messy blotches of ink. I really wanted to make this journal pretty, but it's all ruined.

I also hate how now that we're in high school, we don't seem to have the same route like we used to. Well, we didn't seem to have the same middle school route either. So I haven't seen your driver pass by my bus in the mornings for years.

I'd do anything to see you before winter. Anything to be in your arms again while you kiss the side of my head. Anything, Tate. I'd do anything to run away with you to the moon, so long as my father is all the way down here on Earth.

I know you'll never hurt me, Tate. You'd never leave me all bloodied and bruised like my father does. I just want a normal life.

A normal life without all the chaos and noise.

A normal life without rich parents who don't care about me.

I just want a normal family who loves me. And I swear, I'll love them back. I will.

I... (Sorry for the teardrop again, the knot in the back of my throat is burning)

I just want you, Tate.

Forever.

Just you, the moon, and Mr. Bunny.

That's all I want.

Winter, please come fast,
London

Entry Eight: It's getting worse.

Tate,

I miss you.
I don't think I can do this without you.
The fighting is getting worse, and I
really want to escape to the moon with you.

Endlessly missing you,
London

As my fingers graze over the last entry I wrote, a knot forms at the back of my throat. The same knot that always reappears whenever I think about my father and everything he's put me through.

I wish I were the type of girl who could rebel. Who could spiral into a world of trouble just to escape my parents, but I'm not that type of girl… *at all.*

I'm London Héroux.

The good girl with the good grades and the pink silk ribbons in her hair.

Ribbons I pull extra tight every night because my mother doesn't want my hair to be a mess in the mornings.

Mornings I sometimes wish would never come because I know exactly how they'll end… in hell. Except the morning of New Year's Eve—that's when my heavenly prince will come and save me. Save me and take me to a faraway land I'll never want to escape. *Ever.*

My heart jolts at the loud thumps slapping against the marble floors outside my bedroom door.

Shoes.

Expensive leather derby shoes—shiny—nonetheless.

Shoes that belong to my father.

I know they do.

I always know when he's coming. I feel it deep inside my bones, like when New York's winter seeps into my skin.

I hate winter.

But it's summer now.

My favorite season.

Manhattan's type of warmth and pretty flowers and fluttering butterflies.

The summer's here, and I'll be all right. I will. I have to be.

In a panic, I shut my journal and slip it under my pillow. Just as I lie back down in the bed and shut my eyes as if I'm sleeping, my bedroom door swings open with such force, it slams against my wall. Twice.

"Get up, London! Get up!" my father grits, and I haven't even opened my eyes yet, but I can imagine the grimace on his face. That evil kind of grimace I know I'll always hate him for.

Sorry, Sterling Héroux, I'm sleeping.

It's 7:00 p.m. My bedtime.

Remember?

Ugh.

I slip deeper under my bedsheet.

"London Mila Héroux. Get. Up."

"Dad," I groan as if he's just woken me up from the best beauty sleep of my life. "What's going on?"

"We're going to the ARA after all. That's what's going on."

Say whaaaat?

I open one eye.

He's talking about The Annual Realtor Awards. The ARA for short. It's always held on the third Friday of July every year, specifically for the elitist and most successful CEO Real Estate Realtors/ Brokers responsible for leading New York City's grandest real estate.

And my father just happens to be one of those men.

And then he does his thing: pacing up and down my bedroom in that expensive dark pinstriped Givenchy suit. "If the world thinks I'm declining an award show for Héroux Estates simply because Mirko fucking Meadows will be there, they have another thing coming."

My heart jumps a beat at the word.

Meadows.

Tate's father is going to be there… *I wonder if Tate will go.*

"Do I have to come?" I sigh, opening both eyes. "I'm kind of tired and—"

"It wasn't a fucking option, London." My father stops pacing in the middle of my bedroom, and the crow's feet around his eyes dig into his skin at the glare he shoots me. "Get! Up! This year we need to stand united as a family. Are we united if you're still here in bed?"

I gulp down. "No."

"Exactly," he spits.

It's the first time he's ever wanted me to come to the ARA (for reputation's sake), but... *I really don't want to go.* Not only do I want to write another journal entry to Tate, but Mother Nature called two days ago, and with the tempest of cramps stabbing my lower stomach and upper thighs like it's hell on earth, I just want to stay in this bed.

"For fuck's sake, London! GET UP, BITCH!"

Bitch.

Before I know it, I'm slipping from my silk bedsheets.

Oh no.

I'm pretty sure my wrist is about to snap from the rough grip my father has around it as he drags me out of bed with a violent tug. I don't have enough time to brace for a landing before he shoves me to the floor.

"Dad, stop," I say, tears pooling in my eyes at how he tightly takes hold of my ponytail and, without mercy, pulls me to my feet with it. "Dad, please stop. You're hurting me."

All he does is laugh. Laugh in my face. And I wish I could just run away.

I thought the blisters on my hands from gymnastics were bad. Those formed as a result of my coach punishing one gymnast for being late by making the rest of us work on the bars with no grips. But this throbbing ache in my wrist that feels as if it's on fire is worse.

He lets go of my ponytail... *God, my head hurts.*

Roughly gripping my jaw, my father slams me against my bedroom wall, so I have nowhere to go. The fiery anger in his soulless navy eyes makes me dizzy.

"When I tell you to do something, never *ever* challenge me by not doing that," he growls, slamming his fist against the wall inches from my head at such a velocity, some strands of hair blow over my face.

A chill rushes up my spine, and I begin to shiver despite the warm summer breeze.

"Look at me when I'm talking to you!"

I do.

My father scoffs, and his grip tightens on my jaw until I whimper. "If you embarrass my legacy at these awards tonight, you have another thing coming, understood?"

I nod as the first hot tear slips down my cheek.

"You don't talk. You don't make eye contact. You don't do anything I don't ask you," he hisses and takes a step closer, so I'm boxed in. "*Verstehst du?* Do you understand?"

Again, I nod, feeling that knot of emotion at the back of my throat begin to sting.

"SPEAK, LONDON! FUCKING SPEAK!" My father growls. "You are not some mute, even though perhaps the world would be better if you were."

The words reach out and rip out my heart.

Until I'm bleeding out.

Cold.

I gasp, and before I know it, my next words are out in a whisper, "What is your problem with me?"

My father pauses, cocks his head to the side, and instantly, I know it was a mistake. A big mistake with how shallow his breaths have become.

My father is an intimidating man. A tall, elegant, *violent*, and intimidating man.

Our extended stare down scares me, and I can taste metal in my mouth with how hard I'm biting down on my lip. He continues looking down at me, and if looks could kill... *gosh.* I'd be dead.

Just like all those times he's threatened my mother with killing me.

My father's cold chuckle is replaced with a devilish smirk. "What did you just say to me?"

"Dad..."

"What did you just fucking say to me?"

I just stare.

And stare.

And stare.

Until I hear heels slapping against the marble floor outside my bedroom, and… there she is.

My mom.

Wearing the most perfect little white dress, her lavish blonde hair is up in a swirl bun. Those flawless velvet red lips are no doubt a show to tell the world that Mrs. Héroux is still at the top of her empire. With her king right by her side.

God, the whole thing makes me sick.

Chanel N°5 floods my bedroom as my mother steps in.

Piercing her lips at me, she flickers her heavily mascara-coated lashes to the back of her husband's head. "Sterling, darling, our driver is on standby. I don't want to keep him waiting and—"

Sterling holds his hand up, waving a finger in the air to signal her to stop. All without ever glancing at her once. Like she's a trained animal. "Wait, wait, wait. Hennings can wait a whole century, see if I care. Do you know what our daughter just told me? Do you know what she just said?"

My father is still staring at me with a clenched jaw.

Mom scoffs. "What?"

"She just asked me what my problem was with her."

They glance at each other, pause, and then simultaneously begin laughing.

Laughing.

Coldly laughing.

Like I'm the biggest joke in the world.

It's then that he strides toward her, and I finally feel some type of breath refueling my lungs. But it doesn't last long because the second he presses his lips on my mother's, he blindly grasps the vase of flowers I have on my tallboy, turns, and recklessly throws it at me.

A startled scream escapes me at the piercing sound of shattering glass as the flower vase misses me by inches, slamming just above my head, the shattered pieces flying across the room and raining down on me like snow.

The water's coldness splashes down on me, soaking all my hair and pajama top. And despite the coldness, warmth is all I feel. Just warmth.

It's as if the broken petals baptize my skin, and it isn't until I look down that I notice all the little cuts on my arms from the velocity of the broken glass; thorn scratches, ones that ooze blood and others with little pieces of glass stabbing into my skin.

Oh. My. God.

The glass!

"You want to know my fucking problem? You want to know MY FUCKING PROBLEM?" my father shouts so loud, my ears begin ringing. "I'll tell you what my fucking problem is, London."

I run toward the bed as he speeds to me, but he's too fast and grips my hair once again to pull me back against the wall.

His lipstick-stained mouth meets my ear in a chilling whisper, "You're a disgrace. A *disgrace*, London. That's my problem with you. That's your mother's problem with you. That's *every*body's problem with you."

No matter how badly I don't want to cry in front of him, my vision blurs into a million tiny bubbles. The ache in my throat finally bursts, and I chain my mouth shut to hide the sobs.

You're a disgrace.

The cuts sting, but it's nothing compared to my heart and how much it hurts.

"And I won't take that a daughter of mine is so dismissive to her own reputation. You're getting older, so you know what that means? It means the media will begin noticing you. You're nothing but a worthless bitch now, but you just wait until those articles come out, labeling you as *Sterling Héroux's daughter*. That's right, *sweetheart*, you'll never simply be *London*. You'll always be your father's *daughter*. Understood?"

A millisecond after the first sob escapes is when the first sting to my cheek happens.

I try to fight it. Fight his grip as I slam my fists against his chest and try to shove him away, but he's too strong. He's too tall. And worse—he doesn't even stumble once.

"And another thing you should know, us Hérouxes don't shed a tear. I see you crying again, and I'll hit you so hard, you'll wish you were never born."

"Because that's what was going to happen, London," my mom spits. "We were never even going to have you, so listen to your father."

Panting, I move my head to the left and just look at her. *Help. Help me, Mom.*

She glares back and raises a brow before walking straight. Out. The. Door.

My mom leaves me with the monster.

The monster she married.

The one who's supposed to be my *Vati*—my *father*.

But he isn't. Not in the slightest. I'm convinced Sterling Héroux could never be.

He's just a rich boy who grew up to be an even richer man. But richness doesn't equal love.

My father steps back and observes all the scratches and cuts, lingers his gaze on the bruises on my upper outer thigh where he kicked me a week ago that's now a blotchy yellow, and then a little higher to the scar between my thumb and pointer finger created by yours truly.

In this moment of silence—other than my wildly beating heart that I can hear all over—my father looks at me, and his expression becomes motionless.

But if I thought there was an ounce or even a speckle of regret or acknowledgment in him, I was wrong. Luckily, I knew there wasn't from the start.

Because he doesn't apologize.

He doesn't heal my wounds.

He doesn't promise this is the last time.

He simply slaps my cheek again, and while my head is still spinning, he sets into devil mode.

He hits me.

Over and over again until I can barely breathe.

He doesn't go for the face because the Annual Realtor Awards are too important to him for questions; he goes lower where nobody can see. My stomach. My ribcage. My back. He hurts me until he's satisfied, and then more while I scream out with tears streaming down my cheeks. Screaming out and praying for anybody to come save me.

But there's nobody in this luxurious Manhattan penthouse who can do that.

Nobody.

It's just my father, my mother, and me.

With every hit, I scream a little louder and claw at his hand until all that's left in my throat is a coarse struggle. The pain throbbing across my body only intensifies when I tumble to the floor. My father takes my ponytail in his grip and drags me across the marble with it and into my en suite while I beg him to stop.

But he doesn't.

Of course he doesn't.

Letting go of my hair in the en suite, he stares down at me, and I curl up into a fetal position. After a moment, I press my head against the marble, where a chunk of my hair has been ripped out, and he laughs. Repeatedly. As if this is some sick game to him. As if I'm not his daughter. As if this isn't real life.

"Get fucking dressed. We don't have all night. If you're not ready in precisely twelve minutes..." His eyes narrow to small slits, and he scoffs. "You don't even want to know, London."

Then he pats down his blazer's lapels, turns his back on me, and walks out of the en suite like nothing has happened.

He's sideways to me.

Everything is sideways as those leather shoes walk away, every violent thump echoing into my ear and throughout my body.

He reaches my bedroom, but I can't see him when he yells, "And clean this shit up!"

More thumps, and then my bedroom door slams shut.

That's when I want the sobs to come back. When I want to drown in the waves of my tears. But it never comes. I don't have it in me to cry. I'm too exhausted, and my body is weak.

My eyes are burning from all the tears I've cried already. Those from not only tonight, but from weeks ago, months ago, years ago.

I always used to think women who found themselves in abusive relationships could leave at any time, but now as I lie broken and bruised on my en suite floor, I know it's much more than that.

Women can't just leave.

They don't fall in love with the abuser. They first fall in love with the *man*.

I didn't learn to love my abuser. I first learned to naturally love my *father*.

Nobody falls in love with the abuser first.

The abuse comes later.

And when it does, it's terrifying.

But women can't just leave.

They can't because they'd be judged and shamed for not being strong enough to leave earlier.

Because it's not only the physical but also the psychological. The emotional. The fear.

Because if they dared try to leave, they'd end up at the bottom of the Hudson.

Because sometimes there simply is no way out... like my father and me.

Except sometimes there is.

And if I shut my eyes hard enough, I can see it. My escape.

It isn't Tate.

It isn't the moon.

It's myself, four years from now, leaving Manhattan for good and restarting my life.

If I ever get the chance to.

Aside from the nail scratches on his right hand, there are no traces of the man Sterling Héroux was a mere thirty minutes ago. As I stare up at my father while camera flashes light up the red carpet like flashes of thunderstorms, part of me wishes I could tell everybody the truth.

The truth about him.

The truth about our family.

But as my mother's and father's grins widen at the camera, and he pulls me closer to his side, we play happy family.

I smile for the cameras. Every single last one of them.

I smile and smile until my cheeks ache.

Until my heart continues to break.

Until it hurts to breathe.

We're at the red carpet entry, pretending our lives are perfect just before we step into the Annual Realtor Awards. That's the thing about my family... false happiness is our specialty.

The Hérouxes never have a dull moment.

They are perfect.

Sterling Héroux is perfect.

If those claims were true, I wouldn't have had to wear my white and pink plaid Chanel *long-sleeved* tweed dress during this extremely humid summer night. After my father slammed my bedroom door shut, I managed to get all the glass out of my hair and skin. I then had the world's shortest shower and self-medicated the cuts on my arms with antiseptic cream and bandages.

I also cleaned up the broken flower glass, wiped the water, and threw away the fresh pink roses with shaking hands. But now I'm here. Here to represent my father's legacy with a golden smile. And I must be okay with it.

As my father laughs at something an interviewer says behind the dividing fence—where all the other press and photographers are—a loud voice booms from the left of us, and all the air leaves my body.

Oh.

No.

Not tonight.

"Well, well, well, look who decided to show." Mirko Meadows coldly chuckles. One hand clasps his wife's and the other his step-daughter's as he approaches us with his eyes straight on my father.

Rivals at play. That's what they are.

And then… everything… just… *stops* for me.

The flashing cameras.

The bright lights.

The talking.

It.

All.

Stops.

And I'm pretty sure my heart is two seconds away from exploding out of my chest when somebody steps out from behind Mirko, and those piercing Atlantic blue eyes become all I see.

I drown in them, in his eyes, just like I do every single time I want a little dose of death.

Tate.

Tate Meadows is here.

He's here staring right back at me.

And I know it's a cliché, but he really *does* take my breath away.

Chapter
FIVE

London

PAST.
A few seconds later.
London and Tate are fourteen.

All the emotions from earlier swirl up in a little ball of crushed paper and are replaced with the best feeling ever—being *seen*. Because that's exactly how Tate makes me feel right now.

He looks gorgeous in those expensive black slacks and custom-tailored blazer. He's wearing a crisp white dress shirt that hugs his torso, and the first two buttons are undone, exposing some of his naturally lightly tanned olive skin.

There's also a flash of the start of a thin gold chain that disappears beneath his shirt. He's sans tie with the sleekest Italian leather dress shoes I've ever seen.

Every time I see him, he's turning more and more into a man. His face is even more defined with that jawline so strong. I can't stop staring at his Cupid's bow and kissable full lips like Marlon Brando's. At the soft cleft in his chin and piercing blue eyes; a real-life James Dean, Paul Newman, and Kirk Douglas poured into one.

He's taller.

So much taller.

And his dark caramel brown hair, *gah*, it's so sexily tousled and somehow seems darker.

It's the first time I'm seeing him in a suit, and instantly, I hope it's not the last.

If I blinked, I would have missed the slow, sexy smile he flashes when his eyes meet mine. A smile that says everything within seconds; *I've got you.* But just as it appeared, it drops.

He comes to a halt by his younger stepsister, Maddie, who rolls her eyes when she sees me and then continues typing away on her phone. But I don't care about her. Or Mirko Meadows. Or Sandra Meadows. All I care about is *him.*

I make a mental note to jot this very moment down in my journal tonight. I can already imagine it will be something like this…

Tate,

You looked as daring as the darkest of storms tonight. I just wanted to kiss you. Want to kiss you. I wonder if you'd let me. If you'd taste as sweet as ripe peaches, just like I imagine…

Come and kiss me,
London

I've never been kissed before. Or had a boyfriend. Or anything else. I guess I've just never believed in teenage angst or love before tonight. Teenage years should be for school, friends, and figuring out who the heck you want to be. But as I stare deeper into those Atlantic blues, a part of me wants to break all the good girl rules.

I'm so sick of being the perfect daughter. There's a part of me that belongs to Tate Meadows, and it craves for me to reckon with like a storm.

My father clenches his jaw at the arrogant smirk on Tate's father's face.

This is going to be trouble.

Slipping his hands in his slack pockets, my father arches a dramatic brow at him and grits, "Is there something I can help you with?"

"Oh, okay, I get it." Mirko practically laughs. "The cameras are on, so you've got to put your good guy face on. Gotcha." His gaze softens when he looks at my mom. "Long time no see, *Mrs. Héroux.*"

"Go to hell, Mirko," she grits through her teeth while flashing a grin and a wave at the cameras.

"I don't need to go there. I think you're already there with this husband of yours."

"Oh? One that loves and supports his family, you mean?" my father taunts, tightening his grip around my mom's waist. "Tell him, my darling Ramona, tell him how it feels to have a husband like me."

"Cloud nine."

I almost roll my eyes into the back of my brain.

Cloud nine? Yeah, *right.*

"Seriously, Ramona? *Cloud nine?*" Tate's father scoffs. "You mean having *an imbecile* as a husband? I mean, yeah, maybe the sex is good, but have you seriously been concentrating on the developments he's representing? My company can eat yours alive with our eyes closed."

My father jumps in. "Oh, I don't know about that. Who's getting closer to collaborating exclusively with LéVont on Park Avenue? That's right, Héroux Real Estate is."

"If Park Avenue was Manhattan's only asset, we'd all live there."

I flicker my gaze to Tate, who's staring my father down like there's no tomorrow. His tight jaw is clenched, and I don't know if I hate or encourage the darkening fury fueling his eyes.

Even though our fathers are talking quietly, too low for any report or recording camera to hear, their words are vicious, just like the judgmental stare down between our mothers.

"Shove that excuse up your fucking ass, Mirko. That's how you like it, right?" My father doesn't stop the taunting as he coldly laughs to himself. Egotistically shaking his head, he presses a finger to the center of his lips. "Now, tell me, Meadows, is it the Dom Pérignon or

Château Cheval Blac that turns you into an *alcoholic beast*? Or am I mistaken and it's *both*?"

Maddie stops typing on her phone, and every single muscle holding the strings of Mirko Meadows's arrogance snaps.

His face visibly whitens, and the shocked gasp that escapes my lips has not only Mirko clenching his jaw, but Tate looking at me. And I don't like the agitated look in his eyes. At all.

But Sterling Héroux doesn't care about the line he's crossed. He could never care as that conniving smirk slowly rises up his lips. "Yeah, that's right, fucker. I bet you wouldn't want the media to know that, hmm? You've gone this far keeping rehab and your temper tantrums on the down-low. Wouldn't want any of this to surface, would you?"

Mirko steps closer and growls, "Who the fuck told you?"

"Told me *what*?"

"Don't play fucking dumb, Héroux. Who. The. Fuck. Told. You?"

"Hmmm, what's that saying people always say?" My father's smirk deepens as he pretends to think. "*Oh!* That's right. *I know a guy.*"

Mirko scoffs. "Despite being the monster you are, Sterling Héroux, I thought you would at least be capable of having an inch of respect. I guess it's not in your blood."

"What do you mean *in his blood*, Dad?" Tate scoffs. "He doesn't even have a fucking heart."

I slap a hand over my mouth to hide my soft giggle because as much as I'm supposed to be in the 'Support Héroux' team, I can't help but agree with Tate. My father doesn't have a heart. In fact, that word isn't even in his vocabulary.

Tate's comment makes the Meadowses laugh. It's a victory laugh, which leaves my mother rolling her eyes and my father fuming so hard, I'm sure thick white smoke will explode out of him any second now.

Especially after he grinds his teeth and hisses, "Tell your son to watch his fucking mouth."

Mirko fiercely wraps an arm around Tate's shoulder. "Do it yourself, Héroux."

"Tell. Your. Son. To. Watch. His. Fucking. Mouth."

"I. Said. Do. It. Yourself."

I'm pretty sure if their glares could last until hell freezes over, they would.

"Mr. Meadows and Mr. Héroux, it's a rarity seeing you both to-gether!" a reporter from behind the iron fence calls out, and all our undivided attention turns to her. She's a redheaded woman, short, and no doubt just graduated from college. "Does that mean there are collaborations emerging?"

"Over my dead body!" my father *jokingly* shouts with that Cheshire grin.

"Well, I can certainly arrange that!" Mirko adds, matching his fake grin.

And then the Meadowses and Hérouxes do that thing all rich people do to amplify status and hide our wounds—we laugh. Proudly. Loudly. Like we weren't just tearing each other apart mere seconds ago.

Appearances.

Appearances.

Appearances.

And before I even know what's happening, my father clasps both my mom's and my hand and power walks us down the red carpet and into the event hall.

A grand marble staircase leads up four floors to the huge room the awards must be set in. And when I say *huge room*, I mean a space the size of an entire Park Avenue Penthouse.

It's *gorgeous* with tall ceilings, massive crystal chandeliers every-where, and the sleekest white sheer drapes lacing the walls. Round marble tables are spread out all over the room, and the stage on the right side seems just as inviting with a large wall screen with a PowerPoint slide reading: *Welcome to the 45th Annual Realtor Awards.*

Many wealthy realtors and their families enter the room and find their allocated tables. Perfect hair. Perfect custom-tailored clothes. Perfect faces. I've been around so many of these people that I can tell the genuine from the false. And my lungs squeeze in shock at how many relator men and women with their families *genuinely* smile and hug each other.

BossBabe women who are fixing their daughters' hair with de-votion in their eyes.

Self-made men who are actually explaining the ins and outs to their sons, not shit-talking their mothers.

But I find myself staring at the fathers and daughters more. Watching their fathers simply loving them, pulling out their seats for them, and gently holding their hands… unlike my father's death grip on me. He's roughly dragging me along as he searches for our table that I swear the heels of my Louis Vuittons my mom forced me to wear are going to snap.

"For fuck's sake!" My father growls when we come to a halt by a table up at the front, near the stage.

Seven seats surround the table.

Three table places labeled *Héroux*, right next to four labeled *Meadows*.

I chew on my lower lip. *Wellllll, this is going to be a problem.*

Letting go of my hand, my father flags down one of the coordinators in a black velvet tuxedo, royal blue bowtie, and white gloves.

The man notices my father and rushes our way.

"Yes, Mr. Héroux," he says with a thick French accent and smiles. "What can I do for you?"

My father gestures toward our table. "I'm not sitting at this table with the presence of the Meadowses. I have contributed greatly to these awards and refuse to be thanked with *this*!"

"Oh, *oui, monsieur*. I understand perfectly, Mr. Héroux, but seeing as you only just notified The Annual Realtor Awards that you were attending in person tonight with your family, this was the only available table. I… How can I say, *reconnaître*—understand—that sitting with the Meadowses is not… is not… Uhhh…"

"*Ideal*," my mother impatiently snaps with those pierced Ruby Red lips of hers. "Jesus…"

The coordinator nods repeatedly with an anxious sweat working up his brow. "Yes, *ideal* is the word. *Excusez-moi, madame*. I understand sitting with the Meadowses is not ideal, however, I'm afraid there is nothing that can be done. If we move you, it will cause a ripple effect." He gestures to all the tables. "I-I should have to move them to there, and them to there. An-And those there-e to here. I would then need to mo-move you to there, and them to over there, and the o-ones over there to there, and then—"

"SO JUST FUCKING DO IT!" My father's voice booms across the room, causing heads to snap in our direction. "IN ALL THE TIME YOU WERE STUTTERING, FRENCHIE, YOU COULD HAVE JUST FUCKING DONE IT ALREADY!"

"*Monsieur*, I understand you are angry, but—"

"Do you understand that I can get YOU FIRED IN THREE SECONDS? THREE!"

I'm pretty sure the tips of my ears are burning a dark scarlet. *This is so embarrassing, oh my God. Everybody is staring at us.* I instantly want to curl up in a little ball.

Letting out a nervous laugh, my mother smooths her hand over my father's tie, his chest frantically rising and falling. There's that vein popping out of his head again. The one I wrote in my journal to Tate about.

"Darling, it's okay. We can sit with the Meadowses for one night. It doesn't mean we have to engage in any sort of conversation," she smoothly murmurs, pressing a kiss on my father's stubbled jaw before turning to the Frenchman with narrowed eyes. "Leave. I think you have done enough for tonight. If you don't ensure we are not seated with the Meadowses at future events, then I will be the one to see you fired, not my husband. Is that clear?"

The poor guy is shaking as he nods. "Yes, yes. Of course, *madame.* It is clear. *Très clair.*"

"Good. So, leave."

The poor Frenchman rushes away so fast that he collides with one of the tables, and gasps echo throughout the entire room when he trips face-first onto the floor.

Quickly rushing to his feet again, he speeds away and through a door at the end of the room. All that remains of him is a single white glove right by my father's shiny leather shoes that the Frenchman somehow lost in all the commotion.

Leather replaces the white silk when my father stomps over it before casting a glance around the room with a fake smile. "If any-body knows the name of that man, kindly let me know at some stage tonight. He was attempting to flatter my wife while my daughter and I were right there."

Everybody's eyes shift from him to me. *Gosh.* I swallow the golf-ball-sized lump stuck in my throat as their stares continue, and I wrap a hand around my petite waist because I feel so self-conscious.

The action instantly backfires, and I wince at the ache of the forming bruises.

You'll never simply be London.

You'll always be your father's daughter.

Understand?

A sharp breath escapes me. I can't even look at my parents as I slip into the *Héroux* labeled seat that's right next to a *Meadowses*, silently praying that it's Tate who'll sit in the seat to the right of me.

Slowly, everybody returns to their normal chatter, forgetting the moment that was.

My parents take their seats to the left of me, my mom opting to sit in between my father and me. They're too busy speaking in German to each other to notice the first whiff of a musky sandalwood blend that has my heart bouncing like crazy.

My fingers nervously trace the details of my dusty pink Chanel clutch on my lap. Over each leather quilted diamond-shaped section…

Breathe.

Breathe.

Breathe.

I don't know if I'm ready to be so close to Tate Meadows again. It was only six months ago that he wrapped me in his arms while we watched the New Year fireworks, but now those months feel like years ago. Because we've changed so much in these six months. Grown. And I'm not sure I can pretend to hate Tate tonight.

Hate him like my parents always need me to.

Their hate for the Meadowses is natural, and perhaps mine is too when it comes to Maddie, Mr. Meadows, and Mrs. Meadows, but when it comes to Tate… hating him is the most unnatural thing I could ever do in my life.

And I hope he feels the same way too.

Because after the night I'm having, I just want to talk to somebody. Talk to somebody real. *Feel* real.

I want to forget everything that happened tonight. All the hits. All the words. All the glass. I just want to forget and get lost in Tate instead, no matter how jittery it makes my entire body.

The seat slips away from beside me, and I get a better hit of that scent as Tate takes a seat. It's beautiful.

He's beautiful.

So fresh and mature.

Leaning my left elbow on the table, my hair slips over my shoulders as I look at Tate. And I never swear, but all my brain keeps repeating is *holy fucking shit. Is he even real?*

He's too perfect to be real. It's all I keep thinking as the rest of his family slips into their seats at our table. Just like that, my parents and his are already loudly fighting again.

Maddie's *still* on her phone.

And Tate and I... we haven't stopped gazing into one another's eyes, and I wonder if he also wishes we could escape this place and hide away at our favorite bench instead.

Nobody is concentrating on us.

Nobody at all.

And I'd like to think that's part of the reason Tate never drops his slow, sexy smirk as he reaches out his hand and spreads his fingers over my trembling ones under the table.

Electricity ripples up my entire arm and circles around my heart, embracing it tight. I just need to look at Tate once, and all the big butterflies in my stomach grow wild with need.

He dominantly flips my hand over my purse, so our fingers intertwine before squeezing my hand. *Tight.*

I squeeze back. *Longer.*

My smile grows, and the trembles lacing my fingers melt away, just like my heart.

Six months ago, Tate Meadows asked me if he could hold my hand until the New Year came. Now, he confidently grips it without asking, possession glazing his eyes. It tells me this is what he's wanted to do since he watched me walk inside my apartment that night.

"Hey there," Tate murmurs, that smirk of his merging into a smolder. His voice is so much deeper than the last time. Manlier. "Pink really looks good on you, LonLon."

"It's my favorite color."

He slowly eyes my *pink* dress, *pink* purse, and *pink* ribbon in my hair.

"Yeah, no shit." He chuckles.

I hide my laughter in a pearly white grin and my cheeks heat up. *Already.*

Gulping down, I lean forward so he can hear me whisper, "You look really good in a suit." I flicker my gaze down to his thumb, which softly caresses mine. "I didn't expect to see you so early. It feels weird seeing you in the summer... but in a really good way, you know?"

Tate glances between my eyes and smiles. "I know, LonLon. Surreal is the word."

LonLon.

Why does he keep calling me that?

Tate leans forward, and I'm pretty sure my heart beats into overdrive when his warm lips brush against my ear. "I really want to talk to you. *Alone.* There's so much I want to say. Go to the bathroom in the lobby. I'll wait five minutes, and then I'll meet you."

As much as it hurts to suck in a sharp breath because of the forming bruises, I find myself doing it naturally as I gasp at Tate's words.

He wants to sneak away. Exactly what I want too.

My heart has never raced this fast before. Never for a boy.

Chewing my bottom lip, I nod. "Okay."

Tate pulls back before anybody sees. He squeezes my hand once more before slipping it from his grip, and my heart involuntarily sinks because I instantly miss his hold. His touch. His security. *Everything.*

I turn to my mother and do my best to conceal my flustered grin. "Mom?"

She's so immersed in the argument that I need to call her twice. When she finally snaps my way, her eyes narrow. "What?"

"I'm just going to the ladies, okay?"

She shrugs and turns back to the conversation.

Okayyy.

Setting my clutch underneath my arm, I stand, and Tate subtly winks at me.

Heart, please don't fail me.

I walk out of the room, my heels slapping against the marble floors, and a grin carved on my lips that couldn't be any wider. I don't think I'll ever forget how much the heat of his touch sets me free.

I don't have to wait until winter.

Not this year.

He's here.

I come to a stop by the grand staircase.

Wait a minute.

Confused, I scratch my head and look around the mammoth grand place. *Uhmmm… Now, hang on a second.*

Damn.

Where the hell is the lobby bathroom…?

Tate

This has got to be the longest five minutes of my life. Glancing between my father and the Hérouxes, I don't even know what they're bickering about, but they haven't stopped being at each other's throats since the moment we sat down. It's as if they're incapable of being civil... *because they can't.*

Looking down at my Rolex, I decide enough time has passed for me to sneak out of this shithole without anybody noticing I'm *actually* trying to escape with London.

London.

"Mads," I whisper over to my stepsister, Maddie.

We get along most days, but she's my baby stepsister, and I'll always protect her with my life. *Even* when she glances over at me, rolls her eyes, and turns back to her phone.

"What?" she snaps, the most unamused person in this whole damn room.

"Levi wants to call me. I'm just going to head outside for a bit. If your mom or my dad ask where I am, tell them that, okay?"

"Mmhmmm."

I continue looking at her and that exaggerated purple eyeshadow, but she never gives it.

Standing up, I leave my blazer at the back of my seat and stride out of the room. With each step, my heart feels as if it's about to explode at the very thought of seeing London.

These past six months have been torturous without seeing her. I regretted that deal with her the second I watched her step inside her apartment.

Only meeting once a year?

Pfft. Who the hell did I think I was?

The freaking tin man who has no heart?

And just like that, it all slows down for me as my shiny black Italian leather shoes come to a halt at the end of the grand hallway. It's a secluded area, closed off by a dark sheer drape that's opened by a fraction. The ceiling is taller than a Manhattan penthouse, with gold detailing and polished beige marble like I'm in a gorgeous landmark in Florence or Rome.

Except what I'm looking at is more beautiful than any carved marble could ever be—*London*.

I have no idea why she's staring out at New York's dazzling skyline through these floor-to-ceiling windows instead of meeting me near the lobby bathrooms, but right now, I don't care.

All I care about are those waves of honey-blonde.

The way the shortness of her dress has me staring at those lean, long legs.

Her rosy vanilla scent flutterers through the air, fueling me like it's my gasoline.

Fuuuck, London Héroux is a gorgeous teenage dream, and she doesn't even know it.

London still has her back to me, and if she hears me step into this secluded area, she doesn't show it. She stands lonely, and all I want to do is wrap her in my arms.

So I do.

Roughly closing that drape behind me, I step forward with every reverberating breath trapped in my lungs. Closing the gap between us, the tips of my Italian leather shoes meet the edges of her silvery heels, and I snake my hands around her petite waist from behind, hugging her to my chest.

Tight.

Then *tighter*.

I'm so much taller than London that my hips graze against her lower back.

I pull her flush against me, feeding into her warmth as a soft gasp escapes her. Her entire body tenses in my grip, but when my fingers blindly lace around hers and I squeeze them as if to say *baby, it's me*, she relaxes.

Relaxes completely from my touch.

And maybe I'm sick for liking the way I affect her like this, but I wouldn't want it any other way.

I like the way my signature smirk makes an appearance when I dive my face into her neck and breathe in her scent.

Her.

Her.

It's so full of her.

London's soft hair tickles my cheek as I hug her in the solace of my arms. We stare out at Manhattan, just two tattered souls robbed of the world as we *don't* know it. The one we could have had but never will because of our blood. Blood that could have been sweet, but instead, it's sin.

"God, I missed you," I whisper in her ear, letting out a slight moan when all I get in return is rapid breathing. "Missed you so fucking much, London."

"Tate..." she murmurs, her voice the softest I've ever heard it. Exactly like honey.

"Mmhmmm?"

The room is dim, only the Manhattan skylights brightening it in small doses of light. I prefer it this way. Like it's just her, and me, and Manhattan.

London leans her head into my chest, exposing that perfectly long neck of hers. Her eyes remain shut as she says, "Can I tell you something? Honestly?"

"You know you always can."

She gulps down. "I missed you a heck of a lot, but I didn't know if you were going to miss me the same way. If you were even going to remember me, let alone remember to meet in six months' time."

That breaks my heart. It really freaking does. Not that she doubted me, but that she's so conditioned by her parents' neglect, she thinks the entire world is like that. That she probably thinks I'm like that. But I'm not.

How can I neglect the best thing that's ever happened to me?

"You thought I wasn't going to show?"

Silence.

"You really think I wasn't going to show?"

S.I.L.E.N.C.E.

Clenching my jaw, I recklessly spin London around and don't miss the breath that escapes her as I pin her against the window. Her back presses against the glass, and its coldness also seeps into my skin as I plant my hands against it near both sides of her head, boxing her in.

Those eyes snap open, and pain is all I see looming inside those baby-blues seconds before she blinks them into warmth.

My brows knit in concern.

Why did she look like she was in so much pain for a minute?

Is something hurting her that she's saying nothing about?

But I know London. I know she'll tell me the issue if she really wants to. So I brush it off.

"London," I breathe, pressing my forehead against hers. "London, did you really think I wouldn't show at the end of the year? Please, answer me. I want to know."

Slowly, she nods.

"Oh, LonLon." I sigh and brush my lips against her forehead. "I've spent every day of the past six months thinking of you. Telling myself what a mistake it was to only give us one night out of all the three hundred and sixty-five."

Smiling, sparkles shoot through her baby-blues like tiny arrows. "Really?"

"*Really*. I wouldn't say it if I didn't mean it."

"That's honestly so sweet, Tate."

"I'm not sweet. I'm just being truthful."

London nods, and her long waves bounce around the curve of her breasts in that tight pink dress. *They also look different, as decent as I'm trying to be.*

I smirk. "You were supposed to meet me by the lobby bathroom. What happened?"

Her nervous giggle makes me wish it could be just her and me all night.

I don't want to go back to those awards. I couldn't care less about them. Not after all the vodka flasks my father forced me to fill for him and slip into his blazer's inner pockets tonight before we came here.

"Yeah, wellll, about that…" She can't stop giggling. "I kind of got lost. Just a little bit."

"Ohhh, just *a little bit*?" I tease.

"Okay. Fine. More like *a lot*. I got distracted by this view of Manhattan… I love it yet hate it at the same time."

I love yet hate myself for staring at you, LonLon.

Make it stop.

Make me stop wanting to know everything about you.

Because I can't stop staring.

I stare at her while my heartbeats and breaths tangle into one big giant mess with her name on it.

London bites her lower lip, and when she does, all I want to do is kiss her. Her lips are so glossy and pink. I wonder if she'd taste like cherries or strawberries more.

My best friend, Levi, has already had his first kiss. The idiot can't stop talking about it, so I keep reminding him that it didn't really classify as a first kiss. It was a dare with some random girl at a party. There were no feelings behind it. No love. That isn't a real kiss.

I know fourteen and a half is generally young for a first kiss, but it isn't in New York City, where experimenting and rebelling against neglected affection seems to be our normality. I've been fantasizing about it. *A lot.* It's not that I haven't gotten the opportunity to have my first kiss—real or not—it's just that none of the girls at school or at parties are the one I want.

None of them are London.

And as I glance down at her now, at those plump lips that make me die inside, I wonder if she's ever been kissed. I wonder if it was a non-feeling kiss or a real one. I wonder why the mere thought of another boy kissing her slowly has jealously rushing through my veins.

My jaw involuntary grinds just thinking about it.

Nobody can kiss London Héroux.

Nofuckingbody but me.

She's mine.

"Do you know how beautiful you are, London?"

Despite her blush, she frowns like she doesn't believe it. "You wouldn't think that if you…"

"If I, *what?*"

"Nothing."

My eyebrows knit together. "No, no, what were you doing to say?"

London shakes her head fast. *Too* fast. "Nothing, I'm okay. Promise I am."

Except, I never asked her how she was… And when somebody says they're okay like that—*that* rushed—it often means they're *not okay.* Which would explain the pain in her eyes earlier.

Deciding I want to put an end to this and unravel every little thing about London, I take her hand and start walking backward.

London begins laughing as she walks with me, her pink purse

still tucked under her arm. I swiftly lead us closer and closer toward the drapes.

"Tate, I... I don't want to go back to the awards."

"We're not."

"Oh. Then where are we going?"

I shoot her a slow, sexy smolder. "You'll see, LonLon. Promise it's a place you'll like."

And when she brightly grins, and her scorching warmth rushes through my hand, I swear I want to die.

Die.

Right here.

Right now, as I run away with the girl I'm supposed to perpetually hate by my side.

Chapter

SIX

London

PAST.
Thirty Seconds Later.
London and Tate are fourteen.

Mental note: Buy a whole new journal to write down everything I'm feeling right now.

Butterflies. I'm drowning in butterflies when I stare into his deep blue eyes. Those types of butterflies roaming wild inside my stomach that have me losing my breath over and over again.

The rooftop.

He took me to the rooftop of this building, and whoa… it's breathtaking.

Escapism.

Glittery.

Lively.

Glancing around at Manhattan lit up late at night with this warm summery breeze reminds me why I love New York so much. It all comes back, despite my pledge to leave it behind when I graduate from high school.

I know it's crazy that I'm thinking this far ahead when I haven't even survived my first day as a freshman yet, but if I want to live in a world without my abusive father, escaping this city is the only way out.

No matter how deeply it'll break my heart.

Expensive porcelain pavers align the ground, but the rest of the large rooftop is filled with plants in all sorts of terracotta pots, air-conditioning vents, and a mesmerizing glass railing that surrounds the entire rooftop.

Nobody is up here but us, and there's something just so calming about it.

Turning away from the skyline with a smile, I sit down next to Tate, whose back is leaning against the glass railing.

I set my purse beside me.

He hasn't stopped watching me, and when my face lights up with a toothy grin, his own grin is indescribable. I love it so much, it makes those butterflies go crazy.

"Wow! It's incredible, Tate. How did you know I love skylines so much?"

Tate shrugs and scoots closer to me on the rooftop.

It's ironic how we're sitting, with only the moonlight lighting up our silvery vision, just like when we're at our bench.

Taking my hand in his, he sets it by his knee and traces small circles on my skin.

I like it when he does that.

I like how he loves holding my hand.

It always seems to calm the parts of me that seem so out of reach—like my heart.

"I didn't know you loved them. I guess I just assumed because you always seem so drawn to them. Like the night we met, you kept staring at those buildings beyond the lake."

I gulp down. "Yeah, skyscrapers make me feel free... It's strange, I know."

"It isn't strange." Tate smiles, cocking his head against the glass so he can see me better. "There must be a method to the madness, huh?"

I find myself laughing. "Maybe."

"No, really, I mean it. Why do they make you feel free?"

"Well, my parents own the penthouse of The Saxton. My

relationship with my parents is… let's just say, messy. I find the need to escape a lot."

"Why?"

I open and close my mouth several times, attempting to string the right words together. "I guess you could say there are times I don't want to be myself. I wish I could wake up a different version of London Héroux. Be somebody else, but I fear I'll always be the version of myself I hate."

There's so much laced in his stare, clouded emotion I've never seen before, but he doesn't say a word.

Not one.

He just pierces his lips and stares, and stares, and stares.

And as I swallow thickly, I think I prefer it this way. That he didn't reply. That he gently squeezes our interlocked hands instead. Because if he did reply, I'm not sure I would have held it together.

I continue with my story, despite the air between us growing thinner. "My window faces across the street, and I'm virtually looking into all these apartment windows. The bright city lights help me relax and fall asleep. Storms also do that—calm me. But sometimes, I just stare into all the different apartment windows and imagine myself being those people instead."

Tate smirks. "So you stalk your neighbors?"

"Oh my God, no." I giggle and shake my head. "I just really like people-watching."

"Observing."

"Yeah, exactly… Besides, the people in Manhattan should learn to close their blinds."

"Do you have binoculars and everything?"

"Oh my God, you're so annoying, stop!" I laugh and playfully shove his chest. "No, I don't."

Raking a hand through his sleek hair, Tate boyishly chuckles. "Sure, sure. As if you don't."

"You think you know me so well."

"I do."

The air crackles between us, and I focus my gaze on the bright, full moon.

Longest bathroom trip in the world? I think so.

"Do you think our parents will start to notice we're gone if—"

"What's the craziest thing you've seen?"

I shut my eyes and begin to think. "There's been a lot, actually. A doctor lives in the apartment opposite mine. He always wears scrubs. He had this girlfriend for like forever, and seeing them always made me happy. A year ago, they had what I assumed was a family dinner, and he got down on one knee. I bet the ring was gorgeous; you know, him being a doctor and all. Anywayyy, three weeks ago, she left with a suitcase, but they kissed before she got in the taxi, so I thought she was going on a work trip or something..."

"Oh no..."

"Oh *yes*."

"It wasn't a vacation?"

"Nope, it seemed it was her bachelorette weekend. I kept staring at the apartment all night. It was pitch-black. At three-thirty, the light of their entry flickered on, and the doctor stumbled inside the apartment with some redhead. They made out so hard, they fell on the floor and then... you know, *did it*, right there on the Italian marble."

"You know you can just say *they fucked,* right?"

My eyes widen because I didn't expect him to say that.

"I..." Heat rushes up my cheeks, and I lick my dry lips. "I... I prefer what I said."

"Of course you do."

What's that supposed to mean?

"You're such trouble. You know that, right?"

"I do." He winks, all confident-like.

"Anywayyy, I didn't see the redhead leave his apartment until Sunday afternoon. His fiancée came back that same night. The next day, when he was at work, she walked into their bedroom and started jumping up and down as she laid a wedding dress on the bed. I felt so sick watching her. Like literally felt so bad for her. They got married last week. I know because they came back home in this Ferrari, and... she looked so gorgeous. Last night, she wasn't home. He had that redhead over, and my God, it was a full R-rated movie."

"Shit, poor wifey."

"Yeah, it's pretty bad she doesn't know a thing. I just want to give her a hug, you know... Her husband didn't just cheat on her, he made a whole hurrah out of it. But it wasn't just that redhead. There was somebody else too..."

"As in a threesome?"

I look down at my hands, and my mouth gets all dry. "Yeah, I guess so."

"Fuck, that's hot. Did you watch?"

I'm pretty sure my cheeks are the color of beets when I snap my eyes to him. "That's beside the point."

Tate smirks while stretching out his long legs. "Another girl joined in, right?"

"Nope. Another guy. Two guys and one girl in total."

Tate's jaw drops, and his hand pauses over mine. "Shit, I would have totally thought another girl… So, you *did* watch?"

Crickets.

Crickets are all I hear as I not so subtly bring my knees to my chest and slip my hand away from him to wrap around my thighs.

"Well, uhhh…" Feeling his smirk deepen, I not so innocently smile. "For like two seconds, and then I continued with my homework."

Which is half the truth. I watched on for a solid minute before hiding under the covers, hyperventilating yet curious.

"Why do you find it hard to fall asleep?"

I shrug. "I don't really know. I just do. I'm an overthinker."

"Ah, so you're like me. Overthink every bad thing that could happen until it hurts to breathe."

I look at Tate, like *really* look at Tate, and there isn't a glimmer of the smirk from before. It's just pure, raw emotion. Interest in his eyes.

He's not joking anymore; he's stripping down the walls and letting me in. And his reference of it *hurts to breathe*… I feel it crash all over my body.

It hurts to breathe for me too.

Especially because of my father.

I'm trying my best not to show any glimmer of agony to Tate, but my bruises and covered-up cuts haven't stopped aching all night. Haven't stopped throbbing. Even a soft brush movement over them makes me see stars.

Like when Tate pressed me up against the floor-to-ceiling windows earlier.

It hurt me so much, but it wasn't his fault. And I certainly wasn't going to tell him the reasons why.

I thought I did a good job at hiding the pain, but there was a look in Tate's eyes when I accidentally let out a grimace that told me he noticed it. Because that's the thing about Tate Meadows. He *notices* all the little particularities and makes all the little things matter. *Like right now* as he looks at me so brazenly like it's hurting him to breathe.

Musky sandalwood ripples all over my skin when Tate lazily reaches out in the silvery moonlight and cups my cheek. The way the moonlight casts its shadow highlights all his beauty.

Those cheekbones.

That Cupid's bow.

His gold chain that shines like crazy.

And it's here, as his hard thigh brushes against mine, and he rubs small circles over my skin, where I feel most alive.

He glances between my eyes so melancholic; he looks so sad, and suddenly, Manhattan drowns to complete silence.

It's just him.

It's just us and our warm breaths.

I can't even feel my heart when he whispers, "There shouldn't be any thoughts keeping you up at night, baby. What are you trying to escape, LonLon? Yourself? The world? Your parents?"

I'm quiet because I'm so taken aback by his words.

Nobody has ever called me *baby* before. Nobody has ever cared enough to acknowledge my pain. Perhaps it's because I don't want anybody to save me but myself. Perhaps it's because I like that Tate Meadows has his own customized nickname for me.

I don't know how long passes before his touch slips from my face, and instead, a possessive hand rests just above my right knee. I can hear my every heartbeat at the base of my throat.

Sparks ignite beneath Tate's palm as he slowly inches it up my thigh.

Oh...

Just when he reaches the hem of my Chanel dress and his fingers smooth over my big purplish bruise there, I reach down and grip his fingers so he can't caress no more.

Oh.

My.

God.

My lungs are burning, and I can't even look him in the eyes with the way my heart folds up and dies inside.

It all hits me.

Tate Meadows isn't trying to feel me up. He's reaching for the bruises.

The ones my...

I thought this dress would have been safe for tonight, considering it hides all the glass cuts on my arms.

I was wrong.

Because as I glance down now, I realize just how much it's risen up to expose my upper thighs even more and how much of the bruises— from when my father kicked me the other day—it now shows.

Tate breaks out of my grip, his jaw tight when he attempts to reach for the busies again, but I shove his hand away.

"Tate, don't. Please."

He slips his hand up again, and I scoot back.

This time he listens and pulls back without me needing to say the word. But the nerves circling the pit of my stomach tell me I don't need to say them. *The bruises say it all.*

"*These.* Are *these* what you're trying to escape?" Tate grits, but I know the aggression isn't for me. "God, London. Are you trying to escape from being physi—"

"I just had a really bad fall on the balance beams last week."

Tate keeps on staring, so I continue, "I'm a gymnast. My coach trains all of us like crazy. I was trying an advanced move on the beams and almost had it, but landing didn't exactly go to plan, hence the bruises."

"Is that right?"

"Yeah."

"Yeah?"

I gulp down. "Yes."

He's fuming, and I know he doesn't believe my lie, but I'm grateful he lets it slide.

Tate looks at my face, the bruises, and then back at my face. He whispers a quick, "Okay," and we don't talk about it again.

But there's tension in the air.

Thick, explosive tension that didn't exist the other two times we met.

Tension brought on by age, growth, and sentiments.

One originated from the fact that perhaps those monsters your parents warn you about hiding under your bed don't actually scare you at all. Perhaps they crawl out from under your bed at night to protect you and are there to embrace your lonely heart instead.

Tate makes me so nervous that I don't really know what to say next.

All I do know is that my heart is slowly picking up, aching from the flashbacks of my father earlier. And although I feel something is holding Tate back, as if he wants to ask me something but is restricting himself, I ignore it because right now, I allow myself to be a little selfish.

Selfish because I crave his presence more.

Standing up, I stretch my legs and look around the skyscrapers to calm me.

Nothing works.

"You're stressin'. Come here, LonLon," Tate says, reaching out for my hand. "Come."

Swallowing thickly, I take his hand, and all of a sudden, he's tugging me toward him.

"Oh no! *Tateee!*"

Not expecting the yank, I let out a petrified scream, tumbling down. I don't know if I trip over myself or if my ankle spasms, but I'm falling.

Fudge. Fudge. Fudge.

My heart jolts, beyond the glass railing all I see.

Oh God.

Life flashes before my eyes.

This is it.

This is how I die!

It's as if Tate is the real-life Superman, the way his secure hands grip my hips and steady my fall, saving me from almost plummeting to my death. The crash isn't as brutal when I topple onto him, straddling his waist to break my fall.

Geez!

I shut my eyes and want to slam my head against the railing for being so clumsy. *You go, girl, embarrassing yourself in front of Tate Meadows.*

But when his warm chuckle echoes through my chest and I smile into his neck, I know he would never judge me.

Slowly looking up at Tate through my thick lashes, my cheeks heat from just how close we are. His hot breath hits my lips, and I swear if there was a gust of wind, it would brush our lips together.

Somehow, yet again, he's found another way to hold me in the solace of his arms, tracing over my tweed bouclé-covered hips with his thumbs.

"Is falling on somebody when they gently tug your hand your specialty?" Tate smolders, and *damn him* for looking so good in a suit while doing so.

I jokingly glare at him until laughter breaks the space between us. And that's when I notice where my hands are… right by his crotch.

Like *literally* on his crotch.

All the color drains from my face.

Gasping, I pull my hands away. "Oh my God, I'm sorry! I didn't mean to… I just… when I fell, I must've… Why am I so awkward?"

"You're not awkward, London. It's okay."

"No, like I'm literally the most awkward person in the world! I never know what to say, and when I do, I trip and land on your… *ahhh*, I'm so pathetic."

"You're not pathetic, LonLon."

"Yes, I am, I'm… I don't know. I'm so weird!"

That slow, sexy smirk comes back and drowns me in him. "God. You're so damn cute when you're flustered, you know that?"

"Nooo!" I groan and slap my hands over my face so he can't see me. "I'm not cute, I'm—"

"Beautiful," Tate breathes, emotion laced in his voice. "You're right, *cute* could never be enough. You're *so fucking beautiful*, London Héroux, and when you blush like that, I just want to kiss you breathlessly."

I don't mean for my gasp to be so loud.

Beautiful. Kiss you. Breathlessly.

Oh my…

"Let me see how you blush for me," he sexily whispers, and I'm so enticed, I can't do anything else but show him.

I'm bare to him.

Completely bare as I slip my hands away from my face, and he studies me. My eyes. My nose. The soft freckles on my cheeks that resurface whenever it's the season to get sun-kissed.

I'm so grateful the silvery moonlight probably covers the deep scarlet tinge on my cheeks, but it's also possible he can still see a glimpse of redness and how it's all for him.

I'm pretty sure Tate can hear my vigorous heartbeats; that's how close we are.

"You're beautiful." He smiles, an antidote to all my wounds. "So beautiful, it's unreal."

There goes that pang in my chest.

Never letting our gaze slip, he rushes his thumb up to my lips and parts them at the center. "You're so pretty when you blush for me like this."

My tongue brushes over his soft skin, and I swear to God his eyes darken when he smooths over the gloss.

"Tell me, LonLon." He sucks in a sharp breath and continues to study me. "Have you ever been kissed?"

My mind goes numb with the way he's caressing my glossy lips like that.

Have you ever been kissed?

Does he want the truth? Or does he want the non-loser version?

Has *he* ever kissed anybody before?

I bet he has. He's way too gorgeous for other girls not to notice him. If he doesn't have a girlfriend already, he'll sure have one by the end of summer. Boys like Tate Meadows become the popular jocks at high school, and when they do, nobody can stop their pantie-dropping smirks, beastly athletic ways, and controlled cockiness.

I gulp down. "I, uh…"

Tate grinds his jaw in anticipation.

"I've never had a boyfriend before."

"That's not what I asked."

A breath escapes my throat. "I've never been kissed before. I'm… I'm kind of saving all my firsts for the right person. *The* special person. Because to me, it's important, especially my first kiss, you know?"

"Mmhmmm." Tate smirks. "Do you fantasize about it?"

"Sometimes."

Okayyy, more like *a lot.*

Like the times I practice kissing the back of my hand and pretend it's him. Or when I French kiss it. *Weird?* Weird. *See, Tate, I warned you I was weird like that.*

Wanting to change conversations before I embarrass myself beyond return, I say, "I feel the universe always listens to me. I really needed you tonight."

He frowns. "Why do you say that? Did something happen?"

Yes. Everything happened.

"No, nothing like that. I just really wanted to see you."

Knitting his brows, Tate cocks his head to the side as if there's more to the story. "There's this look in your eyes when I know you're not okay. I saw it tonight on that carpet, I saw it moments ago when you told me the beams created those bruises, and I'm seeing it right now."

"There's nothing to worry about."

"Don't believe you." His gaze flickers to the bruises by my upper thighs, and I hate we're back here. "London, I—"

"I really don't want to talk about it tonight. Please, can we not talk about it?"

"Only if you promise you're okay."

I weakly smile at him because even though I'm not, I hope to be one day.

"I'm okay."

I'm scared that if I look into Tate's eyes for too long, he'll see straight through me, which is why I go a little daring to distract him instead.

Wrapping my arms around his neck, I lean into his chest and shut my eyes. The solace of his embrace while I'm here straddling his waist comforts me more than any other type of medicine ever could.

The world doesn't seem as cruel as it did earlier this evening now that Tate is all I breathe. He hugs me back. We've done a lot of that tonight—hugging. I think it'll become our thing.

My ample breasts press into his chest, and I blush into his neck when he lets out a curse word. I've caught him staring at my boobs a few times tonight but have pretended to ignore it.

We embrace while Manhattan grows wild underneath us. I don't care what my parents will say when I return to the table. All I care about is him.

A Meadows, a Héroux, and the moonlight.

"We have about two minutes until our parents notice… if they haven't already. Tell me everything I've missed these past six months, LonLon."

I brush my hair back, cautious to hide the clump of hair my dad pulled out. I expose my ear, and the way Tate's eyes sparkle with delight makes me so happy.

His lips brush over my earlobe, and his hot peppermint breath has the best kind of chill rushing down my spine.

It only deepens when he kisses the edge of my ear, right by my butterfly diamond earring. "You held your promise. The earrings! I told you they'd look so good on you."

"Thank you. Butterflies are my favorites."

"Why?"

"I think I like how free they are."

Tate's lips slowly trail down my jaw before he pulls back and smiles. "Tell me more."

"There's not too much else to know, really. My life is pretty much consumed with gymnastics. I began when I was two."

"Wow, that's impressive. You want to go pro or something?"

"That's the dream, but the future isn't too clear for me. It's never really been."

"Don't stress, there's always time. I mean, I don't fucking know what I want to do either."

I run the pad of my finger over the beginning of his thin gold necklace. "I see the profanities have upgraded."

Tate laughs. "Yeah, reached full capacity. I can thank my father for that."

"You two seem… close."

"Close?" He shakes his head. "It's all for the cameras, London. We're so distant. Entering that house with them, it's like stepping into—"

"War."

He nods, tracing small circles on my lower back. "Exactly."

Sighing, I glance past Tate and into Manhattan. "It's the same with my parents. I wish I were eighteen. I just want to leave." I dive my face into his neck again, my nose grazing his warm skin, secretly loving how familiar I've become to his touch. "I…"

"Tell me, London."

"I just want to run away to the moon with you," I whisper. "I really do."

Silence fills the air.

I can't see his face now, but I hope he's smiling.

"I'll take you to the moon one day, LonLon. I'll take you wherever you like."

Aww.

He kisses the side of my head, and his lips linger. "I want to know everything about you. Every little thing."

Tate glances down at me, and I can't resist reaching up and tracing over his smile lines.

They're beautiful, just like him, and only extend as our grins deepen.

"What are you saying, Tate?"

"I'm saying I want to be your secret, London Héroux. And I want you to be mine."

"Your... your secret?"

"Yes. I want to sneak out and see you, no matter the month. I can't wait another six months."

I look back and forth between his eyes, and suddenly, everything seems all right. "So then don't."

Our stare lasts a lifetime until his grin deepens as he reaches over to my purse. "I won't."

Sitting back up, I watch Tate pop open my purse and pull out my phone. He hands it to me, and I unlock it before he begins tapping and typing away. "Don't worry, I'm not hacking you."

"What are you doing?" I laugh, glancing at my phone upside down in his grip.

"Putting my number in, LonLon. How else are you gonna call me?"

Pretty sure those butterflies just exploded.

I smirk. "Who says I'm going to call you?"

Tate gives me a playful wink, and there goes my heart again with its double backflip. "Fine, don't call me, loser. I'll just text myself, so I have your number and call you instead."

"What if I told you I'm not the type of girl who gives my number to boys?"

My smirk melts into a grin when he lifts my chin up to meet his eyes instead of my phone.

"Then I'd say I ain't just a boy, LonLon." That slow, sexy smirk of his returns. "I'm your ticket to the moon."

I melt—*melt*—as I watch Tate create a new contact. He types in his number, but his thumbs hesitate at the 'first name' section.

"Do your parents check your phone?"

I shake my head.

Within seconds, he types in *Tate Meadows*, takes a selfie of himself, and hits save.

He saved his number in my phone.

After texting himself the middle finger emoji, which has me snickering, a boyish half-smirk crawls up his lips, and he slips my phone back inside my purse. "Call me whenever you want to hide away from the world, and I'll do the same, LonLon."

With a grin burning my cheeks, I collect my purse and stand up.

There's nothing else I can say to Tate. Nothing else I can say without us staying up on this rooftop for a lifetime. Because right now, that sounds like the perfect dream. Being wrapped in Tate Meadows forever.

Giving Tate one more look, I turn on my heels and begin walking toward the rooftop exit door until I hear him call back.

"London?"

I glance over my shoulder, my hair blowing in the sultry breeze. "Yeah?"

"You won't have trouble falling asleep tonight. I'll be there on the other side of the line, making you feel all right."

I grin.

More than I have in six months.

And just like that, all my heartstrings tangle together in Tate Meadows-sized knots.

Chapter
SEVEN

London

PAST.
A couple hours later…
London and Tate are fourteen.

Entry Nine. In purgatory with you…

Tate,

Last night, you looked as daring as the darkest of storms. I just wanted to kiss you. Want to kiss you. I wonder if you'd let me. If you'd taste as sweet as ripe peaches, just like I imagine…
See? I knew the thoughts I had when I first saw you on the awards' red carpet

would be the first I write down in my journal the night after. You're too important to forget, Tate Meadows, and I know there's a part of me that hates myself for caring so much. Caring about you, but I do, and I don't know what else to do.

I have three highlights of last night. The first was being on the rooftop with you. The second was when I finally got home. The third is what happened after that... You.

I don't think I'll ever forget the smug look you not so subtly gave me when neither my father nor yours won the Best Realtor of NYC award. It was the most prestigious award of the night. We both knew it. Everybody in the room knew it, and yet a tall blonde-haired woman with a pink power suit won it instead. She kind of made me think it's what I'd look like when I grow up.

Don't you think it's ironic how after that award was presented to her, both of our fathers didn't say a word? They just remained there with tense jaws and scary eyes. I kind of thought my father would have walked out of the building or told my mother and me that we were leaving, but he didn't. He just sat there in his seat until the final award was called. I wonder if he stayed because your father stayed. Do you think that was why?

The ride home was dead silent, Tate. No, seriously, it was. I could hear the arms of our driver's wristwatch tick away—that's how silent it was. As bad as it is to say, I'm kind of glad my father didn't win. I know he would have held it against me. Told me that I'd never reach his level. That the Hérouxes always win against the Meadowses. But tonight, that didn't happen.

The Hérouxes lost.

The Meadowses lost.

But you and I, Tate, I think we won tonight.

My father took out an antique glass vase the second the private elevator opened to our penthouse. The antique vase upon the entry table that my grandmother sent all the way from Germany. It was gorgeous, with swirling streaks of yellow, tangerine, and white. But one punch from my father had it tumbling and shattering into a million pieces all over our marble floor.

He didn't even pause. Crunching glass

echoed throughout my body as my father stepped over the glass. He just simply strode down the hall to his bedroom and slammed the door shut. It was his way of saying good night.

I think I stood frozen in that spot for a good minute. It brought too much back. A crazy type of déjà vu of not even a full twelve hours ago. Back when something else happened, Tate. Something worse.

My mother tightly gripped my wrist just as I was about to walk away. She stared down at me with viper eyes and hissed, "If you ever disappear for that long at another one of these awards, I won't be making a cover-up for you again. You'll have your father to deal with."

All I could think of was why she made up a cover story for me to begin with.

Do you get it? Because I don't.

My mom hates me. Why did she want to help me? To make everything go smoothly? Maybe.

I was panicking so much with visions of you invading my mind that I told my mother the reason I disappeared was because the bathroom line was long, and I felt sick once I was in there. I told her I wanted to wait in the cubical until my nausea eased down.

I don't know if she believed me, but she let me go. I ran to my bedroom so fast, I swear my heels almost snapped. Heels I flung across my room the moment I locked my door. I hate stilettos, Tate. I hate them with a passion, but my mother gives me no option but to wear them.

After I licked off my ChapStick, changed into my favorite pink silk pajamas, and dove into my bed, I hugged Mr. Bunny extra tight. I have my reasons for why after everything that happened today. Reasons that relate to my father smashing that antique glass vase. Reasons I don't feel comfortable enough telling you right now... no matter how desperately I wish I could just tell you the truth.

And then you texted, and it officially became the best night of my life.

Tate: I'm in bed and staring at the moon... I hope you are too.

I couldn't have been faster to glance outside my floor-to-ceiling windows and above all the penthouses in view. There

I was at a quarter to midnight, goofily smiling at the moon.

I typed back with a grin. In fact, I don't think that grin slipped off my face all night. You made me smile so hard, I can still feel the ache in my cheeks now, and it's the night after.

You make me happy, Tate. I hope you know that.

I texted you back, telling you that I was staring at the moon too, and it reminded me of you. You replied instantly, saying it reminded you of us. I questioned that 'us,' and you said now that our souls have collided, there would never not be an 'us.' No matter what that 'us' may be.

That had my heart swelling so big. And then it turned into an air balloon when your name flashed across my screen with that perfect selfie you took with that perfect suit and perfect eyes.

I got so nervous at the very thought of speaking to you again.

My heart jumped at the sound of your raspy, sexy voice, and I sank into my pillow, still trying to process how this happened so fast. How you just took my phone out of my purse, inputted your number, and called. The dominance in that move... it means you care too, yeah? (I hope you do)

You actually called, Tate. You actually kept your promise to make sure I fell asleep okay.

Because that's exactly what you did.

You eased my pain without even knowing the root of that ache. You didn't pry. Didn't ask questions I was still too raw to answer. Didn't talk about the bruises. Didn't try to 'fix me.' And I appreciated that because all I wanted was to talk to you. Freely. Without any pressure.

The call was... different. I've never spoken to a teenage boy on the phone before, so I guess you were my first, Tate Meadows. And you know how much of a deal that is for me.

There were moments we laughed (softly, or else my parents would have heard). Moments where you asked me so much, and moments of complete silence, but it was the most peaceful and comfortable silence ever. I stared at the moon the entire time we spoke. You're right—it does remind me of us.

There was a point where you asked me

what I loved the most, and I told you more about myself than I did anybody else. I kind of answered with a lot. And sometimes when I'm excited, I speak really fast, just like you said you do too. But I think I spoke so fast that I don't really know if you understood or remembered everything I said, so I'll make a list here of the top three things you should never forget about me.

(Yes, I am well aware that *the* Tate Meadows will never read these entries, but writing really helps me relax and forget about the world, so I'm still going to do it. Okay? Okayyy)

The official top three list of what you, Tate Meadows, should never forget about me, London Héroux:

My loves. I love the beach. The sun. Golden Age of Hollywood films. Anything bright and lively because summer is my favorite season. My therapy is gymnastics, dance, strawberries, music, and anything pink. I think I could listen to Lana Del Ray, Pink Floyd, and Nirvana forever. I like all their normal vinyls and limited-edition ones, too, because I prefer to listen to songs on my vintage record player. They just seem much more natural and crisper like that. There's so much more depth, and you can hear that soft crackling, and gahhh, it's so beautiful. Somebody could steal my heart with records, I'm telling you, Tate.

I don't have many friends, and those I do have are just dance and gymnastic friends, so instead, I drown myself in literature. I love books. All types of books. Fiction. True crime. Poetry. Romance. But lately, I've really been loving poetry. Any of the classics, but my favorites are Edgar Allan Poe, Wolfgang von Goethe, and Plath. Before this year ends, I really want to get a job at this cool vintage bookshop I always pass by. I don't know what it is about books, but words just make me come alive. And feeling alive is all I ever want.

Despite my crazily strict diet because of gymnastics, I love candy. Any kind. Especially the little pink heart-shaped ones. I call them strawberry fields, and I always find a way to sneak at least one or two in my gym bag before practice. I also like baking sugar-coated heart-shaped cookies. They're so good. Maybe one day I can bake some for you... if you like.

So, there you have it, Tate—the flashcard to my life. (Unless you already remembered all those things I told you last night, in which case, this list I just made you would reaaaaaally be awkward)

I learned some things about you on the call last night too. That you work at this cool art deco movie theater on the Upper West Side that late at night shows classic foreign films. That you get along with your stepsister, Maddie, half of the time. But whenever I asked more, like dive-into-your-life kind of questions, you always brushed them off by asking me more...

Why?

Why don't you want to talk about yourself?

Did something happen? Is something currently happening that's making you all closed up?

Then we figured out we're going to different private high schools in Manhattan when this summer ends. I didn't know how to feel about that. I still don't. I'm going to St. Marie's. You're going to Glorsin St. Claire's. I wish we were going to the same, but they're both prestigious high schools with the elite of elites and pressed suits for uniforms.

Gosh, I hate that word—elite.

I told you that, and you just laughed. "LonLon, we're going to be the only ones at St. Marie's and Glorsin St. Claire's who wish we weren't in it."

I laughed back because you're right. I'm so scared of everything high school will bring, especially at the thought of you not being at mine. It's almost like our parents orchestrated it.

In a way... I don't know, I think I feel relieved about it but also anxious. Anxious because you won't be there to calm me, and I won't be there to bear witness to all the girls wanting to be yours. A funny feeling settles in my stomach at the very thought of that.

I once read this article that stated high school could be one's destroyer. The toxicity. The mean girls. The illegal drugs, sex, and alcohol. It's daunting, you know, especially for somebody like me. I just hope I learn to swim through it and not drown trying.

That's exactly what I was trying to explain to you last night, but I failed miserably to get all my words out. But I think, in your own way, you understood my fear. And it wasn't until I woke up this morning and saw our call still going on almost seven hours that I realized I must have fallen asleep on you. But you didn't hang up all night. You let the call run. Almost as though if I had a nightmare and needed you, you would have been there for me—just like you promised.

I haven't stopped thinking about you all day. I had gymnastics from 8 a.m. to 6 p.m. today. Coach only allowed us a two-week break at the start of summer, but now we're training right through. It's the only way to advance if we want to excel in competitions and advance levels. So, although I may be tired, with aches, thinking about you is worth it.

Because every time I see you, all those bruises on my thighs make me realize what I want from life—respect. The same respect you give me. Because, Tate Meadows, you take all the angry, the broken, the empty, and the lonely out of me. And you replace it with you. Just you.

You make me feel like I'm in purgatory, aiding the devil's heat with angel wings on me.

Can you...

Just, please...

Please promise me you won't ever forget all of the things we said last night.

Can the moon always be ours?

London

Chapter
EIGHT

Tate

PAST.
Three Months Later.
London and Tate are fourteen.

"So, what do ya say, Wolves? Are we gonna eat these starvin' little Lions alive, or are we gonna eat THESE STARVIN' LITTLE LIONS ALIVEEE?" Coach roars, grinning as our football team erupts in cheers and shouts.

Coach can't stop grinning and patting us on the backs as our team assembles by the end of the tunnel, which leads to St. Marie's High School football field.

This isn't our first away game of the season, but every single game has to be better than the last. It's the only way to survive in this sport and not get eaten alive. Just like Coach said.

He's already proved himself to be a champion in the two months since freshman year began. He's fresh out of London. And although all of us guys tease the heck out of him for being our *football* coach instead of *soccer*, he's a really good coach.

I'm not just the captain and star quarterback of Glorsin St. Claire's Wolves, I'm also the most competitive guy out here. Competition is laced in my veins, and in a world where you either win or you lose, my father has always pushed me to be stronger.

Push harder.

Be better.

I hate him for it. I really freaking do. But during times like these, where that heated adrenaline rushes across my body after pre-game warm-ups, I need his words. Even when they taunt me and manipulate my trust.

To win is to advance.

To come second is to be the winner's runner-up.

Our Wolves football team's chant breaks me out of my thoughts, and I join in beside my best friend, Levi, as we all bounce on the balls of our feet and clap vigorously through the chant.

Once it's over, there are even more cheers and a few words of encouragement from both the coach and me before we're all fist-bumping. It's only then when we all finally face toward the exit of the tunnel and watch on that the upbeat atmosphere of the game to come grows wild.

There's this fire in the pit of my stomach as I look out at the football field, bleachers, and tall fluorescent flood lights. It's just before dusk, and the usual cloudy New York sky is being held hostage by the darkened purple, burnt orange blend. It's like a piece of Van Gogh or Monet's artworks. Like the Dali one my father slammed his fist through three months ago.

Now that's a story and a half.

An incredibly sad one.

There's another tunnel directly across from us where the yellow and white football uniform of The Lions is obvious.

Some of them make way for their Lionesses' cheerleaders to jog out through the tunnel and onto the football field, but some are just straight-up assholes and make them go around them.

Levi, my best friend, smirks over at me as I smooth down my black and emerald-green football uniform. "Ready to rock and roll, dude?"

I grin back. "Ready as I'll ever be, bro."

We've been best friends since forever and do everything together, including smashing our rivals' dreams of victory. Because tonight the St. Marie's Lions are going dooown.

"Wolves! Let's place our backs against the walls so these lovely ladies can pass, all right? Thanks, guys," Coach calls out from behind, but I completely miss it, too zoned in on the field and focusing on going over game strategy in my mind.

"Meadows!"

Why is Coach calling me?

"Meadows! Back against the wall!"

Everything becomes a fog as four girls in short cheerleading uniforms rush out from beside me and onto the football field. *Wait, what? Girls?*

What are they doing in this tunnel?

My brows knit together. *Huhhh?*

"MEADOWS! HAVE YA LOST YA EARS?"

What the... *hell?*

Confused, I turn around, and somebody slams into my chest with so much force, they go tumbling down before I can even comprehend what is happening. My football helmet follows.

Honey-blonde.

Honey-blonde is all I see as I reach out and grip her forearms, pulling her up before she can hit the ground.

Frenzied blue eyes stare back at me and widen.

I'm pretty sure I'm choking on my breath right now.

London.

London Héroux is right in front of me, and there's nothing I can do but softly smile.

It's been three months. Three months since I saw her last. Three months since I called her the night of The Annual Realtor Awards, and then the next night, when I told her it was probably best if we didn't talk until New Year. Like our original plan.

Why?

Because I'm an idiot.

An idiot who can't resist her and would probably get both of us in trouble if I didn't control myself with this rule.

I knew it would kill me, and I was right because it did.

It *is* killing me.

But seeing her right now in the flesh makes all the ache go away.

Even though my grip loosens on her forearms, my thumbs brush against her soft skin, giving way to the sparks crawling up my skin. And as a warm yet surprised smile works up London's lips, I wonder if she, too, feels the same as me.

Those eyes. That bergamot rose and vanilla scent. The rosy, plump lips.

She's different but the same.

Older, if that makes sense.

My eyes skim over her face, assessing for any injuries. "You okay?"

"Yeah, I'm all right. Those girls and I came down the wrong tunnel. The rest of our cheer team is already out there. Sorry, I... I didn't mean to slam into you."

I don't know why, but her reply has me smirking. "Didn't think you did."

London softly giggles, all flustered.

Gosh, I love hearing her laugh.

My hands slip away from her touch, and she glides her hands over her slicked-back hair before tightening her high ponytail.

I catch myself staring at that pink ribbon threaded around her ponytail holder for a second too long. It's so pink, so silky, and so perfectly *her.*

The moment is cut short when one of the cheerleaders on the field calls out her name, and London scrambles past me.

She's out of the tunnel in record speed, apologizing to the girl and rushing over to the larger group of cheerleaders, but not before giving me one last glance. Her stare extends, and it has me clenching my jaw because while I knew she went to St. Marie's High School, it didn't register in my mind until now.

I know it came up in conversation months ago, but I hate that I was so caught off guard by it. *By her.*

Just as Levi makes his way back to my side, she looks away.

Ouch.

I watch on as another cheerleader throws London two yellow pom-poms, and they organize themselves.

Within moments, the announcer welcomes them to cheer, and they take their sweet time walking to the field; some cheerleaders even backflipping their way there.

"Shit," Levi whispers. "Wasn't that Héroux's daughter?"

I cross my arms over my chest. "Yeah, think so."

"She's hot."

My clenched jaw tenses. "She's all right."

"You don't think she's hot?"

Yes, man, I know she's hot. I just don't want you to know I think so too.

Don't want you to know I've seen her three times before tonight.

Or that I'm seeing her again in two months.

"I never said that. I just think she's—"

"Yo!" Levi peeks his head out toward the bleachers. "Think her father is up there? You know your fathers will get into a full-on brawl if they're both here, right?"

"Well aware, asshole." I laugh. "I don't think he'll be here. Sterling Héroux doesn't exactly strike me as a football kind of guy."

"Rightttt…" Levi nods and turns back to me, all smug. "Probably poker or some shit."

We both jump as Coach clears his throat from behind us. "Okay, so now that mother's group is ending, can ya both concentrate on the game we came here to conquer instead?"

"Yes, Coach," we say in unison.

Coach backs away, and Levi and I share a look. Loud pop music has my head snapping toward the football field, and after their chant, the cheerleaders begin doing their thing.

It's impressive.

Synchronized.

But I can't keep my eyes off London.

With every single cheer, spin, and jump, she's all I see. She's incredible. Easily the most talented… *and beautiful.*

She's smiling. Grinning. Beaming. But I can see straight through it. The smile never meets her eyes. Something isn't right. She's faking the happiness written on her face. Faking it with a well-executed cheer routine.

It makes me feel a kind of way because all I can think back to was that night three months ago and those bruises on her thigh. The ones she wanted me to ignore.

Is everything okay, London?

Do you promise?

Let. Me. Help.

The routine ends with two cheerleaders being held up high by their team. London is one of them and jumps up into the splits with the beat of the music before landing gracefully on the field with her feet.

Watching her perfect each move makes me so proud she's living her dream.

As the field erupts with cheers for them and both the chants of the Wolves and the Lions, I can't help but clap the loudest for her.

As if it's some strange type of telepathy, London's gaze meets mine and pauses.

My heart jolts, and we share a smile, a real one, and it reaches the eyes this time.

It feels as if a cloud masks over me when she turns away and rushes to the Lions' section bleachers with her cheer team. Like I'm not going to concentrate on anything else but her during the entire game. Distraction is deadly, especially when maintaining a reputation.

The Lions are called out to the field first, and even more cheers boom across the field.

"They'll be screamin' just as loud for us, you'll see. Let's eat 'em alive, Wolves!" Coach roars, and I hear some of the guys behind me begin to jump on the spot to build momentum.

Knowing us Wolves will be called next, I blindly reach down to collect my football helmet, and when I do, something else brushes against my fingers.

I glance down, and all I can say is, *thank God* for the roaring crowd because it masks the gasp that unexpectedly escapes my throat.

A strawberries and cream ChapStick.

Strawberries and cream.

Flipping it over, my eyes roam over the **LH** marked on the top.

Marking ChapSticks for the 0.001% of ChapStick stealers in the world? Hmmm, I see.

Smirking, I quickly fist it in my grip before any of the other boys notice. *Okay*, I'll just give it to her when I pass her. No biggie. I'll make the action so small even Levi or Coach won't notice.

Problem solved.

God, you're such a desperate jerk, Meadows. You just want to talk to her again, don't you?

We're called out, and like Coach promised, the crowd goes just as wild for us. It's deafening. And a smug part of me wants to say they're screaming even louder.

As we run out toward the field, I make note to stay on the outer left of our team.

London isn't looking my way; instead, her eyes move back and forth slowly across the crowd.

Who is she looking for?

Are her parents actually here supporting her?

Wellll, I better make this even faster than I anticipated. Don't want her getting in trouble for talking to me if they're here.

Slowing beside her, my fingers brush over her arm as the rest of my team bolts past me.

"Hey, LonLon…"

London's eyes widen when I subtly hand her the ChapStick. "Oh my gosh, thanks."

"It's okay. You must have dropped it when you slammed into me like a damn freight train."

She gives me a playful look. "Now *that's* a little dramatic."

"Oh, is it?" I tease, flashing her a slow, sexy smirk. "'Cause that's what it felt like."

London's cheeks heat up as she gestures beyond me. "You have a team that needs you."

"Wanna meet me at Fausto's after the game?"

"You mean the diner down the road?"

"Yeah, that's the one. Fausto's."

She chews her bottom lip, a habit I've noticed whenever she's nervous.

"Tate, I…" Her voice softens so only I can hear as a few cheerleaders step closer to us. "I really would like to, but I won't be allowed. My parents don't even want me to cheer. I need to be home straight after this game ends."

"Why? Are they here?"

"No, they're not here, but I… I'm sorry, I can't."

"Ten minutes, that's all I need."

Sadness pools in her eyes. "They'd kill me, Tate. I'm sorry. I really am."

Letting out a sigh, I nod as if I get it. Because I do. That doesn't mean I'm not a little disappointed, not in her but in our situation.

I mean, what are the chances of us meeting like this? Two months early.

"It's all right, I get it." I nod slowly. "I've gotta head to my team now, so I guess I'll see ya."

Turning around, I start jogging to the Wolves when her voice pulls me back.

I glance over my shoulder at London, who has that Chapstick clasped in her hands so tight, it's as if it's her safety net.

A wide, warm smile spreads across her plump lips. "I'll see you in two months, yeah?"

My heart clenches.

Two months.

I wink at her just to see that smile deepen. "Two months it is, strawberries and cream."

"Two months."

"Oh, and, London?"

Time slows as her ponytail blows softly in the chilly New York wind. "Yeah?"

"It was really, *really* good to see you."

And then, with a knot growing in my stomach, I'm gone.

  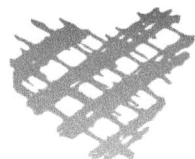

Chapter
NINE

London

PAST.
Some Hours Later.
London and Tate are fourteen.

TATE: You looked really good tonight; I wish you said yes to Fausto's.

LONDON: You know I really wanted to go, but my parents...

TATE: I know, I know, our parents would have killed us both. :(

LONDON: And thank you, by the way, I'm blushing into my pillow... *embarrassed monkey emoji with hands covering face*

TATE: God, what wouldn't I do to see that blush in real life... *heart-eyes emoji* But it's true. You took me by surprise tonight. I didn't think you'd be at the high school football game. You never told me you cheered, but I guess it would make sense, seeing you're a gymnast.

LONDON: Yeah, I only got into it last year. I somehow finally convinced my parents that I can handle it in between school, dance, and gym. It's a lot now that I'm in ninth grade, but I love it. My body has never ached this much, but it's all worth it. Butttt let's talk about you, star quarterback! Let's be honest, you rocked tonight. It's why you won. Is it wrong that I was rooting for you more than I was my own football team?

TATE: There's nothing wrong with that. I mean, have you seen me? *Winking emoji and wolf emoji*

TATE: I'm joking, I'm joking, haha!

LONDON: Oh my god, you're such a fool, Tate Meadows. Fool. And yes, I'm grinning.

TATE: You know you like me being a fool.

LONDON: Is it bad that I really really do?

TATE: Nothing is bad if it sets you free, LonLon, you know that, yeah?

LONDON: Mmmm, are you saying you're good for me, Mr. Meadows?

TATE: Are you saying I'm not, Miss. Héroux?

LONDON: Are you flirting with me?

TATE: Are you?

LONDON: Oh my gosh, stopppp.

TATE: Why? You blushing hard for me again, or did you actually never stop?

LONDON: You're so full of yourself.

TATE: Ladies and gents, London Héroux has claws. How do you put your strawberries and cream ChapStick on with them claws, LonLon?

LONDON: Is your sole purpose on this earth to embarrass me?

TATE: Basically.

LONDON: Typical.

TATE: Question for you...

LONDON: Mmhmmm?

TATE: Does that strawberries and cream ChapStick really taste like strawberries with cream?

LONDON: If it didn't, it would be false advertising.

TATE: So it actually does?

LONDON: Yeah, well, I mean, you're not really supposed to taste it, but I do. Like, I don't eat it because that would be gross... and weird, but if I lick my lips, I can taste it.

TATE: So if somebody were to kiss you, they'd be able to taste it on their tongue?

LONDON: I, uh, I, umm, I think so...

TATE: You think, or you know?

LONDON: Well, umm, as I told you once, I've never kissed anybody before to know if it's true, so uh, right now, I just have to say; I think so, yeah.

TATE: So, if I were to kiss you, London, would I be able to taste it on my tongue long after?

My phone slips from my grip and onto my pillow. It's 3:00 a.m., and although I know I should be sleeping, I'm up, talking to my crush. *Yes, my crush.* Because that's what Tate Meadows is to me.

My heart is palpitating in my chest as I reread his text for the fifth time. If I thought my skin couldn't get any hotter because of Tate, I was dead wrong.

I don't know how he does it, but something about him awakens all my deepest desires and curiosity alike.

Giddy.

Giddy is the perfect word for how Tate makes me feel as I pick up my phone and stare down at the message.

Biting my lip softly, I readjust myself on my bed, where I'm lying on my stomach and being held up by my forearms.

Does Tate Meadows want to kiss me?

LONDON: Yes, you'd taste the strawberries and cream a little, I guess. But, uh, I mean, you'd taste strawberries anyway. I really like those kinds of candy, remember?

My heart doesn't stop racing as he responds instantly.

TATE: Of course, how could I forget? You should make me try one sometime.

I grin stupidly into the night, my heartstrings tightening.

LONDON: Question for you...

TATE: Hit me.

LONDON: Have you ever dreamed of your own type of wonderland? I don't mean in a kiddy type of way. I mean 'wonderland' as in a world you wish to forget all your problems and escape in.

TATE: Yes, but you go first.

LONDON: Have I ever dreamed of wonderland?

TATE: Yeah.

LONDON: Yes, I have. Get ready for a long response...

TATE: All good. I've got popcorn... I'm kidding. *Laughing emoji* Type away. I'll be here waiting, LonLon.

LONDON: Okay, so yes, I have dreamed of wonderland. If I shut my eyes hard enough and long enough, I can imagine a world where everything is okay. Candy floss trees. Streets made of bubblegum. And hearts made from red hard-boiled candy. The heart-shaped ones that come in those fancy wrappers you can never quite take off perfectly without some of the paper sticking on the candy. But it's okay. It's okay because that type of candy is my favorite. I like the way it tastes like strawberry fields on my tongue. But mostly, I love how it makes me feel. Like some single taste of the sugar rush makes me want to run away into my own wonderland. What does your wonderland look like? Is it made of candy like mine? Do you wish you could disappear into it whenever you think of it and never come back? I hope it does, makes you disappear, that is, so I'm not alone in that.

It takes Tate six minutes and thirty-two seconds to reply. I know because I've been nervously counting each second.

Six minutes and thirty-two seconds filled with those three little dots that mean he's typing, appearing and disappearing like some sort of messed-up magic act.

I can't stop thinking that maybe I said too much.

That I got too deep at the end of the text.

I don't talk to guys, and I don't know if Tate's one of those guys to really talk deep. I fear I've scared him off by being too intense, and that's part of the reason I hold my breath for most of those last thirty-two seconds before his reply finally comes.

And apparently, Tate *is* a deep kind of person... *exactly like me.* He talks about those deep, deep truths. Those that tear at the soul and then at the heart's broken pieces. Those that other fourteen-year-olds don't understand or relate to, but Tate does.

He isn't afraid... of me.

And it makes me think that maybe, just maybe, he's also a broken mess behind a pained fake smile.

TATE: LonLon, I've dreamed of a wonderland too. It's just that mine isn't exactly like yours. But firstly, I've never tried that candy before. Do you have some? Bring me one when we meet on New Year's Eve, yeah? I wanna know what your kind of escape means. My wonderland... it's water. Depressing, I know, but water always makes me feel like home. When I was five, my parents left me unsupervised in their grand lap pool during a party, and apparently, I was drowning before my mom realized what was happening and jumped in. I guess my brush with death brings on a fascination with what death would feel like. Is it cold? Warm? I once watched this show when I couldn't sleep that said it's like this great white light rushing to you, so then why do I imagine death so dark? What does it smell like? Feel like? But most of all, does it taste like strawberry fields? Because maybe it can taste exactly like that if I'm drowning in these oceans with your favorite candy on my tongue.

Oh whoa...

His words touch me in ways nothing else ever has before.

LONDON: Oh my, I'm so sorry, Tate. That must have been so traumatic for you, especially at that age. But... Do you really want to know what death tastes like?

TATE: Yes. Whenever I look at you, I do. Because I think death, like all else in this world, also has its beauty in a cruel and twisted way.

LONDON: Why? Aren't you scared of it? I am.

TATE: Why, you ask? Because whenever I look at you, I forget how to breathe, and isn't that the point of death, to feel complete and utter numbness? It is, LonLon. It's exactly that. I'm not scared, and you shouldn't be, either. It's just another part of life.

His outlook on life lodges an ache at the back of my throat. It's as if this is a different Tate.

A real Tate.

The raw, vulnerable, emotional Tate.

The one he shields up and disguises in smoldering smirks, being Glorsin St. Claire's star student and jock, and his life for thrill.

But right now, tonight, I see beyond it.

I see a glimpse of the guy he is when the cracks begin to show.

And I want more of this real side of him.

> **LONDON: But I already feel numb. I feel numb every second of every day except when I see you. I don't want to be numb forever. I want to be free.**

> **TATE: Free like a butterfly, huh?**

> **LONDON: Exactly.**

> **TATE: Then let life set you free, but I believe only death can do that to me.**

> **LONDON: Don't you feel free?**

> **TATE: No, I feel trapped, and I think only you can understand that.**

> **LONDON: Is it your parents that make you feel that way, or life?**

> **TATE: In a strange way, both.**

> **LONDON: Do you want to talk about it? You always want to know a lot about me, but I feel you keep a lot to yourself, like your deep, dark thoughts.**

> **TATE: Don't really wanna talk about it, but I appreciate you asking.**

My thumb halts for a few seconds before I hit send.

> **LONDON: I want to ask you something, but you don't have to answer if you really don't want to, okay?**

> **TATE: Okay...**

> **LONDON: Is it true you never see your real mom anymore?**

His response comes minutes later when I've already typed up a text saying to disregard it.

> **TATE: Where did you hear that from? The tabloids?**

> **LONDON: My father was ranting on about it one night to my mother. Normal Meadows gossiping and backstabbing, you know. But I just wanted to know...**

> **TATE: It's not that I never see her, it's just best if I don't see her.**
>
> **LONDON: Am I pressing too much if I ask why?**
>
> **TATE: Not pressing too much, but I just don't feel like talking about it right now.**
>
> **LONDON: I completely understand. I'm sorry.**
>
> **TATE: It's okay. I'm gonna try to sleep. Good night. Sweet dreams, strawberry fields.**

Damn.

Panic sets in because I feel like I overstepped and that's the only reason he wants to end this conversation so abruptly. I didn't mean to set him off.

Sighing, I sink my head into my pillow with bittersweet thoughts clouding my mind.

Ugh!

Did I just stuff it all up?

> **LONDON: Maybe I shouldn't have asked you about your mom...**
>
> **TATE: Nah, it's all right, but I don't think we should talk about her again.**
>
> **LONDON: I respect that. Thanks for sharing your truths. Night, night! x**

That knot in my throat tightens, and I hate how numb I feel when '*delivered*' at the bottom of my text message never changes to '*read.*'

I stare and stare, but Tate never sees the text.

And when I close my eyes and finally fall asleep, I dream of Tate. Of myself.

Of him and me—*together.*

And in the dream, we're drowning in a strawberry-colored ocean that's as deep as the Atlantic and as tragic as both our tangled, broken souls.

The dream is on replay.

Over, and over, and over.

Until it forges into a nightmare because in every single version, we don't survive the fateful waves dragging us down—into death.

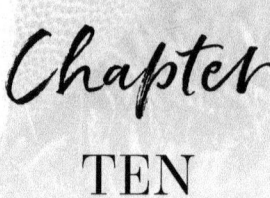

Chapter

TEN

Tate

PAST.
Two Weeks Later.
London and Tate are fourteen.

*S*o much for freaking resisting her.

Tapping send, I slip my phone into my math textbook as Mr. Fay writes on the whiteboard.

> **TATE: I know it isn't New Year's Eve… but can you meet me at our bench on Saturday night? Say 7:30 p.m.? I really miss you and want to see you, LonLon.**

Her response lights up my screen moments later.

> **London: Hi Tate, I really miss you too. Okay. See you then. xo**

I grin like a damn fool in math class.

LonLon wants to see me too.

LEVI: Where the hell are you, man? You're literally missing everything. Sasha just flashed everybody her tits! So yes, just in case you're wondering, it does suck to be you right now, asshole.

Smirking, I roll my eyes at my asshole best friend's text. Levi Prescott, the most closed-up guy one could ever meet, king of not-giving-a-damn, and my brother from another mother all rolled into one.

TATE: I'll be there in thirty. I'm just meeting somebody I want to bring.

'*Delivered*' switches to '*Read*' in zero-point-five seconds.

And then those three little balls begin their juggling act.

LEVI: Meeting somebody? *Depressing Mona Lisa Emoji x2Bro, you could have told me before I rocked up at this party alone like a fucking loner. Who are you meeting? Where are you? I'll meet you there. Meet-up could be a set-up, you know...

And then a second text...

LEVI: You're not buying some illegal shit, are you? Because I'm telling you, everybody around is sketchy. You'll give him the cash, and ka-BAM, son, you'll be dead, sinking to the bottom of the Hudson, and I'll still be here wondering where the hell you are, Meadows.

So okayyyyy, did I also mention Levi Prescott is a product of dark humor?

No?

Well, I just did, so note that down, ladies and gents.

TATE: Why the fuck are you like this?

LEVI: God's plan, bro, God's plan.

Shaking my head, I can't help my deepening smirk as I glance over my shoulder and scan the path behind me of Central Park. It's two minutes until seven-thirty, and I'm sitting on our bench, but London still hasn't shown.

In our late-night call the night of The Annual Realtor Awards, she did mention that her parents have her on this ridiculous 7:00 p.m. bedtime… Maybe she's still trying to sneak out?

Maybe.

Turning back to my phone, I begin typing away just when Levi's name pops up on my screen. The idiot is calling me.

Loud music booms through the phone before my best friend's voice shouts over the music, "So, who's the sketchy guy you're meeting?"

Dear God, help me.

Smiling, I rake a hand through my tousled hair. "It's not a guy… it's a girl. But she isn't sketchy."

There's a slight pause.

"Wait, did you just say a girl?"

"Yeah…" I clear my throat, well aware that I haven't told Levi anything about London yet.

It's not that I don't trust him. It's that he'll tease me. Probably warn me against anything to do with a Héroux, given my family's rivalry with them, which is why I haven't told him.

I've told him nothing about our first-time meeting here years ago when we were kids.

Nothing about the second time. Where I held her close and kissed her tears until midnight.

Nothing about months ago when I saw her at The Annual Realtor Awards, how I called her later and fell asleep to the sound of her soft snores on the other line.

I feel guilty not telling Levi. I really do. He's my best friend, and I know I should, but I guess in thirty minutes, he'll know anyway.

Levi's voice breaks me out of my fog. "Do I know her?"

"You know of her."

"So I know her," he huffs.

"No, you idiot, listen." I sigh. "I said you know *of* her, not that you know her."

The lively background music becomes our only backdrop before his laugh cuts through the line. "Bro, are you freaking crazy? Knowing *of* somebody and *knowing* somebody is the same thing."

"How are they the same damn things when one specifies having physically spent time with them before?"

"Shit, why do you have to look so deep into it, Mr.

My-Blood-Type-Is-O-For-Oxford? I know her. That's all that matters. So tell me who she is."

"How many beers have you had?"

I fail to add *illegally*.

"One."

Silence falls, and then…

"Okay, *two*. About to literally drown myself in a third one if you don't tell me."

"Can't. You'll see when I get there, bro."

Before Levi can say anything else, I hang up and smile, slipping my iPhone into my back pocket. I'm wearing classic light blue jeans, white Converses, and a faded charcoal Rolling Stones band-tee I can't get enough of. It's basic attire. Basic. So why did it take me a solid forty minutes to choose?

Because of her, my mind taunts me.

You want everything to be perfect for her.

Speaking of London… I cast a glance over my shoulder, flickering my eyes around the path that leads to this bench, but there's nobody in sight that matches her descriptions. Just joggers, moms with strollers, and a little far back, a camera crew that must be shooting a sunset scene for some TV show.

No honey-blonde.

What if she doesn't show?

What if she thinks my idea of going to a party together to kill her fear is completely insane?

As an orange-blue sky casts over Manhattan, I actually find it strange to be in Central Park during the day. I mean, yeah, it's my normal running route, but being here this early, waiting for London… it seems odd.

A good odd.

We've never met this early in the day before, and the burgundy-colored metal bench feels lonely without her.

Where is she?

Almost automatically, my phone buzzes in my grip.

> **LONDON: Hey, it's me. I'm like two secs away.**
>
> **TATE: Hey there. I don't see you…**
>
> **LONDON: I can roll fast… :P**

Wait, what? *Roll fast?* Who says that?

Perplexed, I cup the back of my neck and look around. Still nothing.

She's not here.

TATE: Did you just say, 'roll fast'? You can't be two secs away if I can't see you yet.

LONDON: Just stop being annoying and look toward your left instead.

I laugh and slip my phone away.

London, London, London, you're going to be the death of me one day...

Standing up, I round the bench and lean against it. Only after I cross my arms over my broad chest do I look over to my left, just like she requested.

And the waiting game begins...

Except, I don't wait long. Not even a blink. Because the second I see the first glance of her and a continuous smooth swoosh glides across the ground, a match ignites me.

London Héroux is the fire that keeps on burning. The fire that burns away all my scars and dark flaws I keep down inside.

With her, I can simply be myself, the Tate without all the mommy and daddy issues attached. Those I don't dare talk to anybody about. Those that crawl into my skin and seep until guilt finds fear, and together, they headlock all my trauma until it hurts to simply breathe.

It also hurts to breathe when I'm with London, but with her, it's the good type of breathless. The kind that reminds me that I'm alive. Still kicking.

Like watching her right now.

My jaw drops open. *Holy...*

Wine-red short sundress with small white polka dots. Frilly white-trimmed lace socks. Strawberry patterned '70s style roller skates.

Yes. Roller skates.

My girl is rolling toward me happily on roller skates. I seriously wasn't expecting that.

Wait. Did I just say, 'my girl'?

Hell yeah, I did. 'Cause it's true. She's mine, even if she doesn't know it yet.

She'll always be a part of me.

My almost fifteen-year-old mind is trying to comprehend why this angel in red is all I seem to think about. Why I keep on restlessly tossing and turning at night because I want to find a way for London to tell me the truth about those bruises. I know it's not gymnastics.

It can't be with that doomed look in her eyes.

Somebody's hurting her.

Somebody close, and it hurts not knowing who. It hurts not being able to do a single thing to help but be the blinded bystander.

It's why I can't help but smile as London nears me on her roller skates. She seems so happy today. So free. Her soft blonde waves blow in the wild, creating a magical slow-motion moment and those baby blues warm.

She's giggling, laughing, holding out her hands to me as she slows, and I clasp them, helping her stop, when all I really want to do is kiss her into heaven.

"Holy shit!" I slowly scan her skates. "Roller skates? Wow, is there anything you can't do?"

She sets her cross-body duffle by our feet. "There's plenty I can't do."

"Oh yeah? Name one."

Grinning, London chews on her lower lip for the longest time. "Well, I can't play the ukulele…"

I fail miserably at a straight face. "It's literally the easiest instrument to play, LonLon."

"Beats me."

I laugh as our hands slip away, slowly like detaching two magnets. "You know, blondie, this isn't The Amazing Race. I'm not a pit stop. I mean, do I look like Phil Keoghan to you? You're allowed to be a little late without showing off your talent."

"You really know how to ruin a moment, don't you?"

I smirk. "Didn't know we were having a moment…"

I like teasing her. I also like her getting all flustered like she is now, her hair a little messy from the warm fall breeze. Her cheeks are coated with a tinge of red—dark like her dress.

London does her classic playful eye roll, and now that she's close, I realize the rhubarb hue on her cheeks is permanent—actual blush. She has makeup on today. The full set. I've only ever seen her skin bare; I mean, even at the awards, I'm pretty sure all she had on was pink gloss, but this evening it's different.

And trust me, I'm obliged to notice.

I have a stepsister who I swear stores half of her makeup in my bathroom because all of hers is full.

London's all dolled up. All for me. Sparkly light pink eyeshadow. Glossy red lipstick. Onyx mascara so perfectly placed.

Yes, she's beautiful.

Yes, she looks like every teenage boy's dream.

But she doesn't need all this. I think she's so stunning naturally, without all this shit.

London.

My natural beauty.

My hands snake around her silk-covered hips so instinctively. Automatically. And I know I shouldn't notice, dear God, I know I shouldn't, but the fabric of her dress is so thin that I can feel the outline of her underwear underneath. How the sides are thin and ripple as if it's made of lace.

Fuck.

Between *that* and her ample breasts, which press against my chest, her cleavage becoming more and more exposed with every frantic inhale and exhale, a heat rushes up my spine.

If it were up to me, I'd forget about the plans I have for us and hold her like this forever. But it's so hard to read her. So hard to know if she feels the same way, and it kills me.

"Hey, angel," I murmur, my voice extra raspy because suddenly, I forget how to breathe.

As I've said before, I get that a lot around London. Breathless.

London grins back girlishly, her pearly whites so straight and shiny in the setting sun. "Hi."

"Roller skates, LonLon? Do you know how freaking cool that is?"

"I think you're giving me too much credit."

"I don't. I think it's credit well due."

"You're going to give me a big head."

"Humble and honest is all I think when I think of you," I say. "Egomaniac isn't you. You should celebrate your wins and be proud of yourself more. It isn't selfish to love yourself, Lon."

"Okay." She playfully punches my arm. "Well then, thank you very much. Honestly."

I nod. "My pleasure."

It doesn't take long for me to ask London to do a little roller skating technique. It's right when a group of three women with strollers turns into our path that she gets all embarrassed and tells me she can't, but when I relay that information to the three moms, their eyes light up. They come to a standstill and encourage her to show them the technique.

I encourage her more, and her nerves begin to melt away.

She tells me she needs music for rhythm, so I scroll through my phone to the latest Lana Del Ray album and play a random song. After London told me she loves her music, I downloaded her album to try and understand London better. You can tell a lot about somebody from their playlist.

I get the song playing.

London smiles at the moms and finally agrees.

But I love it the most when she shoots me a stink eye as if to say, "Don't worry, Tate Meadows, I *will* kill you later." I love it more when I mischievously smirk back—*So kill me then.*

And then she starts the routine. It can't be more than forty seconds, but it's the most astonishing forty seconds of my life.

London is moving gracefully in the depths of Central Park like a ballerina on skates. She doesn't miss a single beat, moving across the ground with the swift rolling of those strawberry roller skates. It's as if she was born for it. Born to be a star.

London does some angelic spins, C-shaped twirls to full 360 circles, and rolling jumps.

Confident. Relaxed. Stoic.

That's who London is when she doesn't let the demons crawl in.

I get mesmerized watching her. Mesmerized by how her eyes remain shut until the final show-stopping finish. That's when she comes to a halt, a few feet away from me, and the bashful smile returns. It's almost as if she's ashamed for doing as well as she did. Timid.

"Wow! That was astonishing, lovely!" One of the moms gasps, and they all begin clapping.

But nobody is as loud as me with my claps, whistles, and full-blown grin.

A mom with a Yankees cap turns to me with a tender smile. "You must be so happy for your girlfriend. All she needed was a little nudge from you and look at her go!"

Girlfriend.

"Yeah, she's a natural." I grin.

And then they leave, walking straight down the path.

London comes around to my side, and I wrap an arm around her shoulder. Pulling her close, I murmur, "I'm so proud of you, LonLon. *See?* You did it and didn't even have to kill me in exchange."

"You… you liked it?"

"Mmhmmm, you looked so graceful."

"Well, my heart feels like it's about to beat out of my chest, so I don't know about graceful."

London gasps when I press a hand to her chest, right over her warm cleavage that makes me feel a type of way. I feel the beats of her wildly beating heart. "I think you'll survive, angel."

When those baby-blues flicker up at me and all London does is grin, I reach down toward her small duffle and push the strap over my shoulder.

You're graceful, baby.

That's when she breaks out of her trance, scrambles to her skates, and quickly says, "Oh, I probably should take these off. The skates are detachable from the shoes and—"

"Relax." I smirk with a chuckle, loving that she stress-talks at a million miles per hour. "I ain't going to start running off with your duffle."

Frowning, London looks down. "I'm sorry. I do that sometimes. Talk fast when I get nervous, like you do too."

"There's nothing to be nervous about. Besides, you're the one who literally rolled into this park with skates on. You can't have bursts of confidence and then be a good girl."

She looks at me through her thick onyx lashes, and that lip bite rushes heat down.

"What if I want to, though?" she purrs as if it's a different London. One with a look in her eyes that I can only describe as the desire to break out of her good girl armor and rebel instead.

"See what I mean?" My smirk deepens. "Stop messing with my mind, Héroux. There's no need to be nervous with me."

I visibly see her gulp down. "I know, but you just make me nervous."

"What type of nervous?"

"A good nervous but still..."

I fall to my knees and reach for her skates. "Well, what can I do to break that nervousness for you?"

"What are you doing?"

"What does it look like I'm doing? Taking off your skates."

"Oh, okay..."

London places her hands on my shoulders to steady herself, her touch electrifying me instantly.

I'm convinced she feels it, too, by the way she pulls her hand back at first. But I cover my palm over her knuckles and press her hand into my muscle, forcing her hand to stay there.

I don't dare look up. I simply concentrate on detaching the damn plate and wheels from her stylish sneakers.

"What can I do to break this nervousness of yours?" I ask again.

It isn't until I manage to detach the rollers and place them beside me that she replies, "You can... you can tell me why you didn't correct that lady when she assumed I was your girlfriend."

Girlfriend.

I don't know how one simple word can squeeze the cords surrounding my heart, but it does.

Still on my knees with my hands wrapped around her slender ankles, I glance up at her. London's staring down at me hesitantly, and it takes a minute to register how close I am to her body. To her. So close that her bergamot rose and vanilla scent comes back in waves.

I hate how much I like her.

How much I want her.

I've never felt this way before.

And just like that, as darkness begins to blanket the evening sky, a bolt of thunder rumbles from the heavens and seeps inside my chest.

Heavy, bittersweet rain showers down on us, licking our skin and lacing the air with its fresh, earthy scent.

I clear my throat. "What did you want me to say, LonLon?"

"I don't know..." She shrugs. "The truth."

"But is that *really* what you wanted?"

"I... I don't know what I want."

I don't know what I want.

I scoff. *Scoff.* Because I know that's a straight-up lie, and she should know it too.

London slips her hand from my shoulder, and I tug it right back. This time when I cage her hand against my broad shoulder blade, I don't slip my fingers away. I trap her there. To me.

My jaw clenches twice as I stare up at her. "I don't believe you, London."

Her painted plump lips part to nothingness.

"I think you know exactly what you want, but you're just afraid to say it."

"Tate," she warns as rain continues to lick our skin, heavier now as the sky darkens to evening madness.

But neither of us seems to care, and our clothes become wetter by the second.

My nostrils flare. "Tell me it isn't the truth! Tell me I've got it wrong!"

London's only defense is a thick swallow, and all the confusion sprawled on her face is replaced with a glare. Eyes narrowed. Nose scrunched up. Tensed jaw. That's her.

I'm figuring you out, London Héroux, and you don't like it...

"Hmm yeah, that's exactly right, London. I don't have it wrong." I slowly stand to my feet, making sure my nose softly grazes up the center of her body as I do, caressing her skin through the silk. When I'm finally towering over her with my ever-growing cocky smirk, I cup her chin and ignore the gasp she makes when I whisper, "You say you're nervous, so why come here so confidently with roller skates? Huh? Why let me hold you? Why wear this dress when you know I'll go insane?"

Her mouth falls open. "Because I... because I thought you'd like it."

"I do like it. I like everything about it, and that's the freaking problem, London," I growl, walking us backward until I have her ass pressed against the metal bench.

Our bench.

I look between her hazy eyes, disgusted that I like the fury that rumbles within them. "Can't you see that? Can't you see I shouldn't like it as much as I do?"

"I don't get it, Tate. Why are you angry all of a sudden?"

"Why are *you* angry?"

"I'M NOT!" she spits. "I'm confused! There's a difference! You went from happy to the devil in your eyes in like two seconds! Why are you acting like this?"

"Because I don't like it when people lie to me!" I roar, my blood bursting as I kick the side of the bench. The metal fucking kills like a motherfucker.

Gasping, London's eyes widen to complete shock.

"Lie to you? What, I..." Her voice softens over the rain. "I didn't lie."

"You did, the moment you said you didn't know what you wanted."

"Because I don't."

Narrowing my gaze, my smirk deepens. "Liar."

London has no defense.

None at all as she swooshes my hand away from her jaw.

I don't miss the way her fists clench up by her sides. How her mouth pierces shut in anger.

I know I'm an asshole for making her feel this way, but I can't do this without clear intentions set. I can't keep on meeting her at Central Park if she doesn't know what the hell she wants. I need to know.

"What are we, London? *Friends*?" I grit, almost offended, the word laced in venom. "In your eyes, are we honestly that, huh? Are we *friends*? 'Cause I can't be just friends with you."

"Our parents—"

"Don't need to find out."

"But the paparazzi—"

"Won't find us."

"You're unbelievable!" She fumes, pushing off the bench and stepping away to create some distance before turning toward me.

"*You*." She points. "Why are *you* even asking me if you seem to have it all figured out? Huh? After all, you're the one who organized this very meet-up!"

"Because I still don't know how you feel about me, Lon—"

"Oh my God! Isn't it *obvious*?" London screams, waving her hands around her face, all flustered. Her hair sticks to her cheeks as the heavens violently pour down on us. "Why are you making us go around in circles, Tate? Do you think I'd sneak out of my apartment complex for just *anyone*? You don't know how tangled my heart is inside. How confused I am because I have never done this before. I don't do these things, okay? I don't. Do you think I'd be here, Tate, for anybody else but you?"

Fuck.

I hang my head low and suck in a breath. "No."

"Then what does that tell you?"

Air crackles between us, and when I lift my gaze to her, guilt lodges in my throat.

"I. Like. You. Tate. *A lot*. I like you, Tate Meadows, and I need you more than I've ever needed anybody in my life. You don't even know the half of it, Tate, of everything that's going on... but whenever I'm with you, everything just fades. All my anxiety, the stress, it just all fades. It fades because of you." London breathes, her voice cracking on the final words as she looks at me as if her entire life is falling apart. "So, is that what you wanted me to say? Huh?"

All my anger just melts away, like she's the sweetest of cough drops.

The recovery from all my self-inflicted madness.

The perfect calm to my storm.

She likes me.

A. Freaking. Lot.

"London, I didn't mean to—"

"Is that what you *want*, Tate?" Her voice is louder now. *Fiercer.* "For me to look like a complete nerdy fool for having a crush on you when you're forbidden to me? While you go off to a different high school and completely forget about me? Forget about me because you'll have all those perfect preppy girls wanting to be yours? Because it's true. That's *exactly* what will happen. You'll forget about me. Just like everybody else around me continues to do."

I take a step forward, but she's shaking her head with a crumpled-up face.

Distress.

That's what she's buried under.

She doesn't even collect her duffle bag or her skates before she bolts away, her soaked dress hugging every inch of her perfect body. My heart beats rapidly to the tempo of the rain.

"London!" I run after her, coldness seeping through my Converses with every loud thump I make through the splashing puddles. "*London*! London, stop! *Please*! Please, don't go!"

"Leave me alone, Tate!" she yells, her words all merging into one as I catch up and grip her wrist, tugging her back.

London tries to fight against it, telling me to get off her, but I hold her tighter.

She's forced to do nothing else but slam into my chest as our freezing bodies collide.

I cup her cheeks so dominantly as if she'll disappear right here if I don't. In my hold, her labored breaths only intensify. It's like everything's coming out at once. The emotion. The anger. The desire. And I let it. I let her feel everything I so wickedly threw over her minutes ago.

"You don't get it, do you?" London's voice breaks, her light eyes a beautiful glassy mess. "I'm so crazy about you that I write about you in my darn journal. Every single day. I write *to you* to get my feelings out, knowing you'll never even read it. So while I come here on roller skates, wearing this dress and let you hold me because *I* like it, I also do it to impress you."

My mouth falls open, and I think I stop breathing.

Entirely.

She writes about me in her diary?

"Oh my God!" London's eyes widen, realizing what she's said, and she covers her face. "I can't believe I just told you that! You weren't supposed to know that I... that I..."

When she slips her hands away, streaks of onyx-colored mascara blotch around her eyes and rush down her cheeks. I don't know if it's the rain or if she's crying, but either way, it hurts me.

I pushed her too far because of my own selfishness.

Because I had to know she needed me.

Needs me.

Just like I need her to survive.

Rain continuously drips down her nose, landing on top of her Cupid's bow. Droplets collide and outline her lips, intensifying the gloss. And it's those same lips I can't stop staring at. Those I want to claim with my own lips, tongue, and breath. Those I want to beg mercy with.

London's baby-blues seem so dim now. So melancholic. All because of me.

She thinks I'm gonna fool her.

Forget her.

Use her.

God, to hell with her parents. To hell with everybody who's hurt her. She's scarred so deeply that she believes the entire world is out to get her, including me.

"LonLon," I whisper, aching to win her heart back. "I'm sorry. I'm so sorry I… *Fuck*." I inhale sharply. "All I wanted was to know what you truly felt about me. I get you're scared. I get this is all new to you. It is to me too. And I would never ever take advantage of that. I'm sorry I made you feel like this."

London's chin begins to tremble as I kiss away the tears on her cheeks.

"I don't ever want to be the reason you're crying. It breaks my heart, angel, it does."

"It's okay," she murmurs back after some time. "It's not your fault."

I pull away from her cheeks and look into her gloomy eyes with a frown. "It is, London."

"No, it's not. It's triggers. When you get those outbursts of anger like that, it scares me because it reminds me exactly…" She gulps down. "I don't ever want to see that rage again, Tate. You want to ask me something, you ask me, and we have a conversation. I'm not standing for anything less than that. Please promise me that?"

"I promise, LonLon, cross my heart and hope to die." I nod desperately, trying my hardest to swallow down the aching knot at the back of my throat, but it never eases. "Forgive me."

I tip her face higher and rest our foreheads together. We stay like this forever as the rain only gets harder, and I swear to God it means something when London's arm wraps around my narrowed waist and pulls me closer.

Her fingers push under my soaking shirt, unsticking the wetness with the pads of her fingers before her nails graze up and down my back.

Every soft yet sharp slice feels like I'm slipping into purgatory with her.

Only I don't know if it's heaven or hell we're heading to next.

But either way, I don't care. I don't care because I'm with her. *Her*.

"I could never forget you, London," I murmur inches from her lips, so she knows the truth. We're so close, our noses touch, and some of her wet hair blankets my eyes, but I don't mind. "And you don't need to impress me, London... You already do that. Naturally. Even when you think I don't notice."

I bring a hand up to skim over her face. "*This* makeup, it's not needed. *You* don't need it. If you like it, that's different, but you're a natural beauty without all the illusions your parents force on you. It's not you. Just be yourself. Completely yourself."

Her hot breath teases and taunts me as she traces my dimples of Venus by my lower back. The action has her nails grazing against the waistband of my jeans, and it drives me insane.

I shut my eyes with a sad smile and continue, "That's all I'll ever ask of you—to be you. That's all I want. You're jealous, but there's no need for you to be jealous, so trust me. I don't want the future prom queen, cheerleading heartbreaker, or any other girl. I just want you, London Mila Héroux. *You.*"

"I feel the same way." A slow, beautiful smile sprawls along her lips, and it's all I need. "And I forgive you, Tate. I'm sorry too. I... I just want to hide away from the world with you too."

"God, that makes me so happy." I sigh, relieved. "I meant everything I just said, LonLon."

"I know."

We stay like *this*, silently wrapped in each other, for what feels like forever. I really want to fucking kiss her, but I don't know if it's a step too far.

London's trembling in my grip from the coldness, and when I suggest we go to a café to warm up, she says we should go to her penthouse instead. Apparently, her parents are away for the weekend.

I agree, and we walk to her penthouse hand in hand with the devil taunting my every move.

Kiss her.

Kiss her, Meadows.

It's all I can think about as the private elevators open to her luxurious apartment filled with everything marble, brass, and every single feature one would see in a historic Italian masterpiece. It's exactly the type of penthouse I expected Sterling and Ramona Héroux to own.

Water from the rain drips down our bodies to the floor, and

London is quick to disappear down a hallway before reappearing with two towels.

I gaze at her as we dry off. There isn't an inch of her that isn't wet, but gratefully, I only really have my Rolling Stones T-shirt to worry about. It's soaked and sticks to my broad chest like damn glue.

Thanks, Manhattan.

Gripping the back collar of the T-shirt, I slip it off in one movement, and that's when I notice London is checking me out. I know she's trying to be subtle, but she's not. Not in the slightest. And I can't help but smirk.

When I clear my throat, I almost want to laugh at her widening eyes, like she's just been caught. *Which she has.*

"I, ummm." She smiles bashfully. "If we head to my bedroom, I can get changed and probably find you an oversized sweater that you can wear inside. I don't want you getting a… a cold, you know."

I simply nod, and with a smile, motion for her to lead the way.

She does, and *holy shit…*

Her bedroom is even pinker than I imagined.

It's so her. So girly meets the right amount of rocker blues. It's her safe space filled with sparkly pillows on her bed, a vintage record player on her tallboy, and a diamond paper crane chandelier above her queen-sized bed.

She flickers it on and lights the room in a soft, warm pink and white glow.

Vintage posters of Pink Floyd, The Rolling Stones, and Lana Del Ray align the closest wall before her tall floor-to-ceiling windows look out on Manhattan. But what I love about London's bedroom the most, aside from the fact it smells like her, is that her beloved Mr. Bunny lies on her pink pillow.

Every time I look at that teddy, I can't help but think of myself…

Of her.

Of an us.

And that makes me happy. So happy.

Kicking off my Converses, I lie back on her bed with a smolder and reach out for Mr. Bunny. "You still have him, ha?"

London stops rumbling through her wardrobe to glance over her shoulder. Her hair sticks to her cheeks, smile lines seeping into them through her grin. "It's *she.*"

I arch an amused brow. "Huh?"

"Mr. Bunny is a girl."

"Wait, wait, wait..." I chuckle. "So let me get this straight, you've got a teddy called Mr. Bunny that isn't a bunny, and *now* you tell me that *Mr.* is actually a *Mrs.* this entire time?"

Laughing, London pokes out her tongue. "Shhh, let me be."

"Never." I slowly smirk and playfully throw her Mr. Bunny. "You're so weird, blondie."

London can't stop laughing as she tosses Mr. Bunny back to me, just as another lightning bolt lights up the sky. "You're weird back, Meadows."

The teddy hits my chest and bounces off me to her frilly pink bedsheets. The whole thing fascinates me. How much she likes pink. I find myself smoothing a hand over the soft sheets, trailing my finger over the frilly lace, wondering what it would be like to spend a night here. Holding her.

I think I crave that. Being close to her, that is.

It's why I don't tease her too much when she hands me a dusty pink Care Bears oversized sweater, and I slip it on... *because I'd take anything London is willing to give to me.*

Her time.

Her heart.

Her favorite Care Bears sweater.

And when she disappears into her en suite to get changed and the door clicks locked behind her, I hit my head against her pillow and stare up at those brightly lit paper cranes.

And oh, did I mention I'm grinning like a goddamn lovesick fool? Well, I am.

That grin doesn't drop. Not even after I text Levi to say I'm not coming to the party and switch off my phone before he can call or text back.

My heart's all funny, and I don't know why, but all I know is that it has to do with London.

She's definitely my fucking crush.

I like her. *Like a lot.*

And all I want to do is stay in this bedroom with her forever.

It's her safe space, I know it is, and it doesn't make me less of a guy to admit I want to make it mine too.

Chapter

ELEVEN

Tate

PAST.
Fifty Heartbeats Later.
London and Tate are fourteen.

*H*oly guacamole, she said she wrote about me in her fucking journal! I sit up on London's bed in two-point-five seconds.

Why the hell am I only remembering this now?

That damn journal could be a landmine to all her deepest thoughts.

Roaming my eyes across her bedroom, I make an oath with myself that I'm not going to steal her journal. *Buttt*, if I do happen to find it and it's open, I'm legally allowed to have a little looksie, right?

Wrong, the angel on my shoulder taunts.

You're just looking for excuses to know more about how she really feels about you, asshole.

Forget about the journal. It's her private thoughts. Don't even mention them, okay?

I sigh. *Okay.*

I shake off that little devil disguised as an angel, and just as I lie back down, the en suite door clicks open. My heart returns to a million beats per second, but I play it cool by crossing my arms behind my head and throwing London a playful wink as she emerges.

I was wrong if I thought she couldn't get any more beautiful.

London doesn't have any makeup on anymore. She's a natural beauty, just how I like it.

Tossing her soaked dress behind her on the bathroom floor, she steps forward until her knees graze the bedsheets, brushing my feet.

I swear to God it takes a full minute for my eyes to roam up her body, wanting to absorb every single inch of her. She's wearing long-sleeved silk pink pajamas, and just by staring at her baby blue eyes like I am, I realize how much we've grown in these past years. And that where we are today—broken teenagers in high school—we're a fraction of the people we'll grow up to be. And she's the person I want to grow up beside. I hope she wants the same too.

Wrapping an arm around her petite waist, London smiles down at me. "I hope you don't mind I'm in my pajamas. I know you probably wanted to take me somewhere, but with the storm and the cold, it's probably best if—"

"If we stay right here." I grin, finishing off her words.

London nods.

Sitting up, I scoot closer to her until my feet hit the hardwood floor. I'm so tall that when my arms wrap around her hips, I'm almost level with her face while sitting up. "That's perfectly okay, LonLon. In fact, I think I prefer it better here."

"Yeah?"

"Mmhmmm."

Slowly, her hands slip through my damp hair and slick it back. I like the heat that rushes up my spine at the way her nails softly trail up and down my neck. I like it so much that I hug her tighter and smile into her chest.

"Have you ever been in a teenage girl's room before?" she murmurs.

"You forgetting I have a stepsister?"

"Ah, right, I don't know why I always forget about that. You don't talk about her much."

"Then ask me anything about her."

"Umm… How about you describe her in three words?"

I nod. "Relentless. Secretly-caring. Purple."

"Purple isn't a suitable adjective."

"It's her favorite color and basically everything she wears, so yeah, purple is a suitable adjective in my book."

"Okay." Her next question comes moments later when my thumbs begin soft circles on her hips. "Have you ever been in a teenage girl's bedroom besides your stepsister's?"

London, London, London, I know what you're alluding to...

So why don't you just say it?

A slow, sexy smirk raises my lips. "LonLon, are you trying to ask me something?"

"No." She shrugs, her eyes flickering to her window, but I see the tension crawling up her body. This isn't just a curious question for her; it means something. "Just want to know if you've been in another girl's bedroom before."

"You want me to be honest?"

"Always."

"I have. Several. I go to a few parties, you know, live by the 'status quo' and all."

Her breath hitches.

My smirk devilishly deepens.

Oh, are you jealous, baby?

Yeah, you're so goddamn jealous, LonLon. I see it all over.

"Oh, that's..." London's eyes find mine, and they're so obviously dimmed. "Cool."

I frown. "I didn't hook up with them if that's what you're not so subtly asking. I may be rebellious, but I'm legal."

Some of that dimness begins to lighten, despite concern shining through.

"Did you kiss them?"

"No."

"What were you guys doing?"

"Just hanging out with my friends, you know, like you do at a party."

London bites her lower lip. "Did... did anything else happen?"

"I don't see the relevance in these questions, London."

"I'm just asking..."

"I was in their rooms because some of my circle at St. Claire's are girls. Not all, but some. It's just natural with my stepsister and her friends always hanging around us guys, you know? Ironically, Maddie's birthday is at the end of January, so she's in the same grade as me. As us."

"Oh."

"Come here, angel," I murmur, nudging her forward until she's practically sitting in my lap.\ *Well*, straddling me with her legs around my waist.

The last time we were kind of like this was on the rooftop of the Annual Realtor Awards. But tonight, it's just us and no interruptions.

London's warmth baptizes all my sins and scars. I like how I can see the soft freckles of her cheeks clearer now, how they're like a dazzling constellation of stars exploding in the Milky Way. And as I stare into her eyes with a lazy smile, I hope she knows I would never lie to her.

That I'd always tell her the truth.

Like I have.

"But this is the first time I'm in a girl's bedroom when it means something to me. It means you trust me."

"I do," London whispers, her fingers trailing down my jaw. "I trust you more than anybody in this whole entire world. I feel like… like I could tell you anything, and you wouldn't judge me. At all."

"Good," I growl, bucking my hips forward, so she's even closer. "So don't be fucking jealous because if there's any girl I'm kissing while in their bedroom, it's you, LonLon."

I love the gasp-turned-grin that escapes London when I spin us around, pinning her back on the bed. We're still so intertwined together with her legs around my waist that when I push myself higher on the bed, she does too.

My body is pressed against hers, keeping the weight off with the way my forearms sink into the sheets beside her head. But I can feel her every heartbeat, her every hot breath caressing my lips, and the heat of her body pressing into mine.

I probably shouldn't notice her hard nipples stabbing through the silk of her shirt, but I do. I notice everything, including the way she's looking at me with so much need it's as if she may die right here if I don't touch her more. Don't hold her tighter. Don't devour her now.

"*Fuccck.* I really want to kiss you," I whisper seductively against her lips. "But I know that if I do, there's no turning back. I'll want to kiss you forever, and our parents won't allow that."

"*Please*," she purrs, rocking her hips against mine. "Please kiss me, Tate Meadows."

I can't let go of the strangled breath in my throat as our stare intensifies into something beyond words. So much need. Desire. Like we were born into a world with dead ends, no matter how badly we both want it.

I gulp down, my heart racing. "I'm sorry… I can't."

The sparkle in London's eyes doesn't let go, and it's what drives me to do what I do next.

I go to the next best thing and dip my lips to her neck, her wild moans filling the room as I blow hot warmth before I kiss her skin. They're soft kisses at first before they turn into reckless and crazed open-mouth kisses, my tongue tasting the sweet rosy vanilla on her soft neck.

Dear God, I want to suck her neck forever.

As I devour her neck, I imagine it's her mouth.

Each kiss gets filthy dirty, just like I crave.

It feels so good that I find myself smirking against her neck at the way she moans my name with every sexy nibble. It turns me on—so freaking much. I want to do everything with her.

My hips uncontrollably grind against hers when I plant a kiss on the base of her neck, bite her softly, and then suck on the spot until her fingers trail under my fucking Care Bears sweater.

Until she's panting.

Until I'm sure I've made a mark.

Until I roam my tongue over it continually.

When I finally pull back and brush a thumb over the soft red love bite, my gaze flickers to London.

She slowly looks up at me through her lashes, all dreamy, blushing so deep.

It's special, watching her grow wild beneath me so beautifully like this at a single hickey.

And then… *it must hit her.*

"Tate!" She gasps. "Oh my… did you just…?"

"Mmhmmm." I smirk down at her devilishly, possessively, and I growl, "I did because you're fucking mine, LonLon, and this New

Year's Eve, I'm going to kiss your lips instead. In two months, I'm gonna kiss you hard, London Héroux. I don't care about the risks."

Grinning, London runs a tongue over her lips, glistening them sweetly. "I'd *really* like that."

"Of course you will. So will I, LonLon. I wanna hear you say my name like that again."

"Turn us around."

"Why?"

"Because…" London, not so innocently, rushes her fingers up to brush the spot I devoured on her neck. Her gaze darkens. "Because I really want to do it to you too."

I spin us around in record speed, and her giggle fades the moment she's on top of me. London flips her damp hair to the side, giving me a perfect view of that hickey. She looks at me like a sinner on a fucking church pew.

Leaning forward, her lips slowly meet my neck, and *oh my fucking God.*

My eyes almost roll into the back of my brain. That's how good it feels as electricity rushes up my neck, intensifying at the center where she's kissing.

"Oh, baby, yes," I groan, squeezing her toned ass and involuntary pulling her closer. "Make me yours, LonLon."

Her lips are the softest things I've ever felt—like clouds. Strawberry-colored clouds I want to suck on. Her tongue grows wild, circling my sweet spot before the kisses continue. And damn, those sexy little nibbles, I swear to God, London Héroux can't be a good girl the way she knows how to drive me wild.

Heat rushes across my entire body, blurring my sanity.

London sucks on the spot on my neck, hard, just like I did.

When she pulls away smiling, she runs her tongue over my throbbing hickey. Then she does again, slower this time, teasing me until she circles her tongue up my neck, around my earlobe, and then whispers, "I feel like the luckiest girl in the world, Tate."

I trace the outline of her swollen lips with my thumb. "Because you are, babygirl."

"I wish our parents didn't hate each other."

All I do is nod.

"But I kind of like that this is our secret."

I'm in such a fog from how good that love bite felt that I'm pretty sure I'm hallucinating this gorgeous blonde on top of me. But when I reach up and kiss her forehead, and she's real, I thank God she is.

I spank her ass. "You're telling me, baby."

She giggles as she slips off me, and instantly, I miss her touch.

My gaze zones in on an item at the bottom of her open wardrobe. "You have a guitar?"

"Ummm…" London glances over her shoulder at it and sighs. "Yeah, but I'm still learning to play. No impressive skills to show off like I did with the roller skates."

"Want me to teach you?"

London's head snaps my way with a hopeful smile. "Really?"

"Yeah, anything for you. Just tell me the song, and I'll tell you if I know it."

"Let's go with my favorite song… *Wish You Were Here*' by Pink Floyd."

My jaw drops in the same second my heart pangs.

I look at her as if she is crazy. "No freaking way! That's my favorite song too! Shit. I seriously didn't take you as a Pink Floyd kind of girl, but I think the night you told me that you adored them, I liked you even more."

London runs to get her vintage white acoustic guitar, hurries back my way, and I snuggle into her from behind.

Before I take the guitar from her grip, I longingly kiss that love bite on her neck that's even redder now. The perfect shade of us.

I make sure the guitar is tuned and smile as I begin to play the opening to "*Wish You Were Here*" with its classic distant chord progression.

I play the song numerous times to have London get the idea of every single note. Every time I play the song, the warmth in her eyes deepens. It feels like hours pass with us together, me teaching her guitar, and it's the most poetically beautiful thing.

We laugh. We groan. We smile.

We get teary-eyed from the lyrics.

We simply live life.

Tonight means a lot to me because *this song* means a lot to me.

She means a lot to me.

This song got me through a lot of shit when I was growing up, and as I hand London the acoustic guitar and teach her how to play the song, it feels surreal.

She butches the song, but I'm determined to teach her properly, so I take the guitar from her and play the song another two times. The second time, I take her hand and have her press it against the wood, so she feels every vibration of the guitar's echoing strums.

"It's all about feel," I say. "Once you get it, it really isn't that hard."

London nods and pulls her hair into a high ponytail with just a few strands covering her eyes. I love the way she bites her lip and has her head down in heavy concentration as she starts the song again.

I lie down on the bed and shut my eyes as she plays, savoring her melodies.

"You're not going to watch me?"

"I'll be able to tell if you're executing it like this better. I like to savor more by ear. Close your eyes and just feel it, you know?"

"Whatever you say, captain." She laughs and continues playing.

It sounds a little better, but it feels like she's rushing the strums and then attempting to catch up with the timing by skipping some notes.

I shake my head, a perfectionist at heart. "Nope, stop. You're going too fast. I felt you look at me like you were trying to see if I was giving you any indication that you were getting it or not. Then you just hurried all the notes. Let's try that again, LonLon, yeah? I want you to get it. Remember, you're in control. Timing is everything."

London practices the song over and over and over again until it becomes a melody of perfection. When I open my eyes, she finishes the last note and just looks at me in anticipation.

Playfully slapping her knee, I grin. "LONLON, YOU FUCKING GOT IT!"

"OH MY GOD!" London squeals and embraces me tightly before scrambling back to the guitar. "Oh my God, I can't believe I got it. My fingers are literally shaking, but I want to play it again before I forget it."

We're laughing hard before she starts the song over, and this time, I can't help but softly sing the lyrics. She joins in, our voices so beautifully interlaced. Beautiful like her.

This time, I don't shut my eyes.

I keep them open and gaze right at her because I don't want to miss a second of her beauty.

London's voice is like honeyed sin. Sweet perfection. And together with my raspy gravel, I finally feel seen. Maybe that's why emotion laces my throat with every breath, and her eyes turn all glassy. Because with each instrumental part of the song, we simply stare at each other, and then just like that, we sing the lyrics synced.

> *"How I wish, how I wish you were here*
> *We're just two lost souls*
> *Swimming in a fish bowl*
> *Year after year*
>
> *Running over the same old ground*
> *What have we found?*
> *The same old fears*
> *Wish you were here."*

The depth of the meaning in the melancholic, bittersweet lyrics we're singing hits me hard. The lyrics are so us, and those that stand out the most are the ones that hurt the most.

When the song ends, it's as if it's a new awakening between us. I don't realize how blurry my vision has become until I gulp down and stare out the floor-to-ceiling windows, and all of Manhattan's glowing little lights are a kaleidoscope of circles.

"Hey, you okay, Tate?"

Continuing to look away, I nod.

But I'm not okay. I'm anything but okay with this fire burning up my lungs.

But London can't know that. I need to be strong in front of her. I can't give in to the thoughts circling my mind. Those that kill me inside. Those I mask away from everybody.

"Can I admit something, London?"

"Yeah."

"I wonder how fucked up our lives would be if our parents weren't the people they are. Yes, they're rich and earned it, I get it, but why gloat? Why buy fancy fucking whiskey that tastes like ass? Why neglect their children?"

"Because they can," she whispers into the night. "Because to them reputation is everything."

"Exactly. Do you think my parents have ever given me one embrace? Nothing. It's like they're completely void of affection."

White noise fills the pace, and then...

"You're pretty affectionate for somebody who has lacked it all this time."

I suck in a breath and finally look at her. She's frowning, and that hurts me. And yet, I admit to her something I've never dared speak out loud before. To anyone. "Because I crave it."

I hate that her eyes soften—as if she's sympathetic—because I don't want to be viewed any differently for it. I just... I just want her to see me like before. Not like some neglected fuck-up I've conditioned myself to believe every time I look in the mirror.

"You crave to be loved, Tate?"

I look down at my hands. "Noticed. Loved. Seen. All that shit."

"Ditto."

"Yeah, I've noticed. You've got that same pain in your eyes I see in myself whenever I stare myself down in the mirror."

"The pain of wanting to be a different version of yourself but not knowing how, right?"

Suddenly, that fire rushing up my lungs eases because finally, somebody else on this earth understands me. That sees me. And suddenly, I don't feel so alone.

"Right, LonLon."

London reaches out her hand, and she's all I want to escape into when she laces her fingers through mine and sadly smiles. "We're almost to the moon, Tate. Just keep believing."

I squeeze her hand tight because, for once, she's the only real thing in my life.

The only fucking thing, and I don't know whether to laugh or cry at that.

I just wish you could always be here, LonLon.

Chapter
TWELVE

London

PAST.
Two Months Later.
NYE London and Tate are turning fifteen.

"But, Mom, everybody from gymnastics is going over to Katie's for the New Year. I'll be the only one not there."

"I said you're not going, and that's final." My mom doesn't even bat her steel-blue eyes my way for a second before returning to line her perfectly big lips in the main bathroom's vanity mirror.

It's the bathroom she shares with my father, and just like the entirety of our penthouse, it's so lush and beautiful. Italian marble. Expensive brass. Frangipani essence mist floating in the air.

All this beauty, and here I am, sighing. "Mom."

"What?" she snaps.

"I wouldn't be asking if I wasn't desperate. The girls at gymnastics already think I'm a loner—"

"Let them think whatever they want, London. See if I care. Also, this is the first time I'm even hearing of you wanting to go to this Katie's tonight."

Shaking my head, I play with my hands. "I… I actually told you three weeks ago."

"Well, I've got other things on my mind. You should have advised my PA."

"I did that, too, last week, Mom."

"Well, she didn't tell me about it," my mom huffs. "So this doesn't seem like a me problem, does it?"

Typical. Her personal assistant is out to get me too.

"London, you're in gymnastics to perform, not to make friends." Setting down her lip liner, she picks up her favorite rouge red Chanel lipstick and applies it perfectly. "Besides"—she stands back, analyses her face, and returns to bronzing up her cheekbones a little more—"Victor LéVont has so kindly invited our family to his New Year's Eve celebrations. Your father is already there because he wanted to talk a little business with Victor beforehand. So, what would he think if you weren't there?"

Ah, right.

Victor LéVont.

The smug French gentleman whose high-stakes developments are taking over Manhattan. The one I've heard my father talk on the phone to with a wolfish grin, desperate to be the brokerage representing his next development's sale.

Before I can even answer, she steps away from the mirror, and all my hope deflates.

I need to figure out how to sneak out of LéVont's party tonight.

It isn't Katie's New Year's Eve party I'm so interested in sneaking off too. It's meeting Tate at Central Park for our annual meet. Lying about the entire thing was the only way to get to him, but it's backfired. I feel trapped. Trapped in the vicious cycle of the ultra-rich tonight.

At midnight, it's my fifteenth birthday, and I refuse to start it without seeing Tate Meadows.

Adoring herself in the mirror, my mother pushes her breasts together, spilling her cleavage even more in the tight deep V-neck gold sequenced minidress she has on. It's extremely short. And when I say 'extremely short,' I mean, *can't-bend-over* short. She never dresses like this for my father. Not *this* risqué anyway.

Part of me thinks back to a few years ago when I used to catch random men in the living room with my mother whenever my father was away on a work trip.

She never knew I saw the men, but I did.

They always came around midnight, so whenever she thought I was sleeping. But I couldn't sleep well back then. I still don't. I was either already wide awake at that hour, or I'd wake up to nightmares, or to *them*.

I heard their voices.

Their laughter.

And after it had happened three times and I knew it wasn't my father she was speaking to, I sneaked out of my bedroom and crept against the edge of the wall until I could peek just a little into the living room.

Every night it was a different guy, yet they were all the same.

Tall. Wealthy. Charming. Fancy European suits. Foreign accents.

I don't know if my father ever caught on, but it's as if she's changed tactics because she hasn't sneaked other men in for a while. I don't know why they came around. For business. For pleasure. For a mix of both. But I feel it deep in my core that my mother hasn't been faithful to my father.

Perhaps that's why she disregards the way he abuses me so much because she isn't even present when she's with us. Perhaps it's all pretend. She was seventeen when she had me. My father was twice that. I can understand her bid to escape, but I shouldn't be the scapegoat.

I just want to be her daughter, that's all, but all she's ever done is detest me for existing.

I know for sure one of those men she sneaked inside our penthouse was Victor LéVont. I remember because he was over more than once. The number of times I saw him is more than I can count on my hands. It was *a lot* of times. I understood that with him, it wasn't a seductive visit to manipulate him into working with Héroux Real Estates. It was simply to escape my father.

That would explain the roses Victor would bring her.

The French he would softly speak and how my mom's grin was the widest I've ever seen.

The way he would kiss her roughly, passionately, as if he just wanted to run away with her.

When it got to that stage, I would quietly rush back to my

bedroom and duck under the covers. Once I even threw up in the toilet because I didn't know what any of it meant. If my mom would leave my dad. If she would even *tell* him. If Victor would come one night when my dad was home...

But none of it happened.

None of it at all.

Because my father would come back from his work trips and wouldn't suspect a thing. But I know my mother. I know her more than she thinks. And I know the thin pearl necklace she puts on tonight when I follow her into her bedroom is much more than just a pearl necklace.

It's the one in the red velvet box Victor gave her years ago.

The one she told my father her parents sent her from the Netherlands for her birthday. Victor bought it for her one year when my father was away in Paris. The year before I met Tate. The one where Victor and my mother drank champagne, made out, and he told her he loved her. All while I frowned on the hallway floor, confused, thinking my family as I knew it was over.

But she can never know I saw it all.

It's why I don't say a word while she puts the pearl necklace on.

Why I do what she says and rush to my room to slip on my pink faux fur coat over my white sweater dress and nude mesh diamond fishnet tights. But I keep my white Dr. Martens. My mom pushes me into her Audi with our driver, Hennings, behind the wheel. Once we're off, she texts my father we'll be there soon and begins criticizing how I did nothing to my hair.

I spend the entire drive staring out at Manhattan as the 8:00 p.m. sky darkens with a sliver of the celebratory night to come. But as we pass Central Park, all I want to do is jump out of the car and run to that bench. The one filled with Tate and me and all our secrets.

But I can't, and that's what hurts the most. The fact that I have to act delighted to be attending a party my mom's illicit lover is hosting. A lover my father doesn't know a thing about.

Chaos.

Chaos is all this is.

The fine restaurant Victor LéVont is using for his New Year's Eve party is solely operating for his private function. I've heard this authentic French cuisine restaurant has a two-year backlog, but LéVont seems like the type of man who moves mountains. Just like my father.

A Frenchman greets us at the entrance of the lavish restaurant, checks us off the list, and leads us to a set of five golden elevators.

"Welcome to LéVont, Mrs. and Miss Héroux." He grins while pressing the open button of the second elevator. "I wish you both a happy New Year's Eve. Mr. LéVont is waiting for you at our penthouse restaurant floor. Thank you, and please enjoy your time here with us tonight."

"Thank you, *monsieur*." My mother flashes him that drop-dead gorgeous grin, and the second the two of us step into the elevator car and the doors close, her grin drops into a full-on glare. "Fucking sleaze, did you see the way he was eyeing me? I should have reported him to management or Victor himself."

"Victor?"

"Yes, that's what I said. Listen when I speak," she snaps, fluffing up her hair in the glassed-mirror walls. Her Cartier bangles cling together like they're in band rehearsals. "Victor has a stake in the company."

Whoa, what?

My jaw drops. "So he named the restaurant after himself?"

"No, he doesn't have that authority. He just developed this entire restaurant and part-owns the company. However, the head chef named the restaurant after Victor. Loyalty. That's what your father told me anyway."

"Wow. Is he some type of god or something?"

Sighing, my mom checks her phone before sliding it back in her clutch. "To some, I guess."

Is he to you, Mom?

I study her face to watch for any indication that she'll slip up, seeing as we're talking about the man I saw her with, but her poker face is on full blast. All I get is a completely motionless stare before it turns into a glare with an arched brow.

She looks like a supermodel.

A stunning supermodel with the one thing missing by her side…

Or so I thought.

Because as soon as the elevator opens to the restaurant and we step out, public enemy number one is the first person I see. Sure, I notice just how many people are in this room—close to five hundred, I would say, and the night hasn't even started. Yes, I notice the heavenly jazz music played by a live band. The floor-to-ceiling windows looking out on our dazzling city. The high society with their fancy clothes, champagne flutes, and superficial mingling. But Victor LéVont is all I *really* see.

And gosh, how he sees my mother.

Seconds ago, the Frenchman was smugly chuckling in a group of men, and now he's striding up to my mother and me in a confident, tall stride. His bubbling champagne flute is in hand.

A wicked grin carves up Victor's lips, his dimples deepening through his dark stubble. The navy power suit he has on feels like it was made for him, his presence awakening a strong, musky vetiver scent to float in the air.

I don't miss how the soft mood lightening has his shiny gold tie clip with a cursive **VL** engraved on it glimmering.

"Ramona." His smoldering grin extends, like the gentleman I know he *isn't*. "I'm so happy you made it. You look *magnifique*. Beautiful."

His French accent is thick but alluring. I've watched too many movies to know that foreign men can do that to you. Cause that funny feeling in the pit of your stomach because of their exoticness.

It's happening to me right now.

It's sure happening to my mother too.

A scarlet flush crawls up her cheeks when Victor presses two lingering kisses on either side of her cheeks. He then leans forward to whisper something in her ear, and she giggles.

Giggles.

I've *never* heard my mom giggle in my entire life.

Which explains why, mentally, I'm dropping my jaw. *Is this some kind of Matrix?*

Who swapped my mom out, and what happened to the real Ramona Héroux?

Or... is this the real her? The one my dad disabled?

When Victor pulls back, his piercing gray-green eyes drop to me. "Good evening. You must be…"

"Hi, I'm London." I smile softly, offering my hand like my parents have taught me.

It doesn't matter how awkward I feel extending my hand to my mom's lover—past lover. It's an expectation.

Victor's handshake is firm as if it's just another business deal.

"Victor. Victor LéVont. Pleasure to finally meet you," he introduces, and when he pulls away, he rakes a hand through his slicked-back dark wavy hair with a few silvery strands. "London, you have your mother's eyes. Anybody ever told you that before?"

Oh?

I smile awkwardly. "Uhmmm, no, actually, you're the first…"

"Well, it's true, so believe me." Victor softly chuckles, his gaze darkening the second it flickers to my mom, who is not so subtly checking him out. "Ramona, you didn't tell me you had a little twin."

"You knew I had a daughter."

See how she just stuffed up?

She said 'knew,' not 'know.' Past tense means past history—unfinished history.

"Never told me she was the spitting image of you."

"Shhh, don't you flatter me." She laughs, and the goofy grin she has on those bold red lips is genuine.

Victor may act like the perfect gentleman, but that beastly side of him has his eyes stopping on those lips for a second too long. He gulps down some of his champagne, remaining in that power stance as he keeps on staring over the flute's rim. Staring until those gorgeous eyes slowly move back to me.

And yes, he's beautiful, in every kind of older man type of way, but my mom cheated on my father with him. And as much as I despise my father, I don't know how to feel about it. Numb, really, that's all I feel. I just hate how I'm in the middle. That I know something about my mom and Victor that they don't think I do. That I'm *again* still playing pretend.

"You see how she treats me, London?" Victor teases, his stare hot. "You're my witness, okay?"

Oh, I'm a witness all right.

I really don't know how to respond, so I say the first polite thing that comes to mind. "Congratulations on developing the restaurant. It's beautiful."

Victor slowly smirks and squeezes my shoulder. "Thank you, darling, but you should also thank your father for it. Héroux and

LéVont are going to be the only powerhouses in this city. Fuck the Meadowses, right?"

My mom gasps. "Oh wow, Victor, so you've signed on H.R.E. for your new developments here?"

H.R.E. = Héroux Real Estate. You're welcome, peeps.

"As of eighteen minutes ago, yes." He nods, his smirk forming into a full-blown grin. "Also, don't worry, *mon putain d'ange parfait*, I didn't kidnap your beloved husband. He's somewhere around."

Mon putain d'ange parfait.

My breaths slow.

Oh my God. Oh. My God. Oh my God.

Internally, my jaw drops. I know exactly what Victor just said to my mom in French...

Mon putain d'ange parfait.

My fucking perfect angel.

The wide-eyed look my mom gives him tells me he shouldn't have said it. Because when her head snaps toward me and all I do is stare back, her jaw tightens, and the look she gives Victor is one of death.

He arches a brow at her, communicating something with his eyes that I'm so out of the loop of. My mom not so subtly gestures toward me with her head, and his jaw clenches twice.

Side note: I don't care about reputation's sake; I'm definitely telling Tate about this.

Tate.

My heart skips just thinking about him.

Victor turns to me, and my neck hurts from just how tall he is. "So, tell me, London, what is there I should know about you? Are you in high school? Looking to keep real estate in the family?"

"Yes, I'm in ninth grade at St. Marie's. A freshman. And right now, I'm not too sure about what I'd like to be when I'm older. Real estate... I'd like it, I guess, but I'm not certain."

"Well, okay, can I let you in on a secret?"

"Mmhmmm."

"You just said, 'Real estate... I'd like it, I guess.' London, *like*, and *I guess* won't give you the strength or drive to succeed." Even though he's still talking to me, he looks at my mom all longingly and broody as he says, "Only *desire* will do that. Isn't that right, Ramona?"

My mom gulps down and plays with her pearls.

His gift to her.

His eyes slowly drop there, then lower to her cleavage with a sharp breath. "Unless, of course…"—he pauses before continuing, his voice softer—"that desire is always looming in the background. *Interchangeable.*"

They just keep on staring at each other until the tension grows realllllly awkward. Awkward as in I'm pretty sure if nobody else were in the room, they would have made out by now.

"That's, uh, very… true." I weakly smile and rock on the balls of my feet, hoping to break the tension. "I just really want to survive high school first."

"You will." And that smolder returns as he brings the champagne flute to his lips but halts from drinking. "You're Ramona Héroux's daughter, after all, so everything is possible. Isn't that so?"

Before any of us can say a word, my father appears out of nowhere in a tux with a Cheshire grin and two champagne flutes. He hands one to my mom. He brings the other to his lips.

"Darling," my dad murmurs, kissing my mother slowly, and there's nothing more awkward than the way Victor and I both gulp down and exchange glances.

My mom doesn't seem the slightest bit happy when she pulls back and gulps down her entire champagne without ever meeting Victor's gaze.

My father pulls her close. "Did you hear the news, sweetheart?"

"Yes, indeed, I think it's time to celebrate." She nods, and they all raise their glasses to chin-chin. "To this being the greatest collaboration Manhattan has ever seen."

They clink glasses.

Victor quickly excuses himself and leaves.

My mother walks to the other side of the room.

Never once glancing my way, my father strides away and joins a group of businessmen.

And here I am, left standing in the remains of what was a business toast from hell, only none of them knew it. In this crowded room, I'm all alone—*again*—awaiting midnight like a mockingbird trapped in a LéVont-sized cage.

Chapter
THIRTEEN

London

PAST.
Three Hours Later.
NYE London and Tate are turning fifteen.

Three hours later, my soul is eating me from the inside out. It's 11:00 p.m., and I can't stay here for a second longer. I need to get out of here. *Now.* The crazy amount of people in this restaurant has made me claustrophobic. I feel dizzy. This tightness in my chest is the last thing I want leading up to my birthday at midnight… *and seeing Tate.*

I need to think of a way to escape LéVont's party.

Think.

Think.

Think.

My eyes scan the room, and *still*, I come up with nothing. My father is still talking to that group of men, but both my mother and Victor LéVont are nowhere to be seen. Brushing past the standing guests who are mingling and eating fancy food from lavish silver trays, I walk farther through the restaurant, desperate to find her before she finds me.

And then I do.

Beyond a red barrier rope to the balcony.

Secluded from the rest of the guests.

With the one and only LéVont.

My heart jolts as I step over the red barrier rope because it's not something I would usually do. I'm the girl who follows the rules. Who makes them. Not the one who breaks them. But I find myself doing just that as my Dr. Martens softly hit the ground, and I disappear out of sight from the other guests as Manhattan's cold breeze hits my face.

Victor and my mom are standing right in front of the outdoor herb garden, strategically shielding themselves from the other guests because it's the only section of the floor-to-ceiling windows that's tinted and protected by a wooden covering with fairy lights. A secret getaway.

They can't see me from where I stand. They're a good ninety feet away, and their faces aren't to me. I probably wouldn't have recognized them at first if it wasn't for that golden minidress that sparkles in the moonlight.

Victor chuckles at something my mom says, and his hands slip to her hips. It isn't long before they roam to her ass and squeeze tight. She allows it with a grin, telling him something inaudible.

I cringe because they're standing close. Like *real* close. Noses-almost-brushing close.

It feels as if someone is clenching my heart tightly, waiting until it bursts. I don't know what this means for my family. Is she going to divorce my dad? Embarrass the Héroux family? Run away with Victor to France and leave me alone with my father? The latter thought has bile rushing up to my throat because I don't think I could survive it.

I fear it.

Fear *him.*

So as much as my mother and I may not be close, I need her to stay. Stay with my father.

She shakes her head at something Victor says, but the second his hips grind against hers, she begins nodding.

What are you agreeing to, Mom?

Victor pushes her up against the herbs and loops a finger over her pearl necklace to tug her even closer.

My eyes widen in horror.

Oh no, is he going to…

That's when he lowers his head, and I can make out the smug smirk on his lips seconds before those said lips crash against my mother's. Slowly at first, before their kiss grows far more reckless, like they're crazed wolves.

And my mother allows it.

Every. Single. Second.

"Oh my gosh," I whisper, slapping a hand over my mouth to mute the gasp.

All the nerves swirling in the pit of my stomach threaten to rush up in the worst way.

I think I'm going to be sick.

It's confirmed when Victor's hands disappear under my mom's dress, and I don't know whether I want to go up to them to stop them or simply run away. Before my heart can even decide, my mind already has. I hurry back inside, almost landing flat on my face when I trip over the barrier rope if it wasn't for a hand that grips my forearms and steadies me on my feet.

"Hey, are you okay? You look like you've seen a ghost."

Dark denim and leather.

It's all I see as I flicker my gaze up to a boy who looks around the same age as me.

He has a kind smile on his face, a smile that almost seems out of place with his rough buzz cut, leather jacket filled with studs, and dark melancholic eyes.

"Hi." I smile sadly, silently thanking him for helping me with a nod. "Yeah, I'm all right, just a little…"

Melancholic Leather arches an amused brow. "Just a little…?"

Anxious.

Homesick.

Desperate.

I clear my throat. "Desperate. Desperate to leave here."

For someone I've never seen before, he seems to calm my nervous mind. That means a lot to me because I'm not one to trust just anybody. But this boy seems different from the rest of the people at this party. He isn't superficial, false, or an over-exaggerated extrovert. He seems calmer. Reserved. Desperate too, like he's craving to run away from here, just like me.

"Then why can't you just leave?"

"It's complicated. My parents... really want me to stay."

"Ahhh, gotcha, I get it." He scoffs with a sly smirk. "Fucking up-holding reputation, right?"

"Your parents are the same?"

"Worse. Although I just live with my dad."

Oh, okay. So, Melancholic Leather *does* get me.

I wrap a hand around my waist and step out of the way for a second as a couple holding hands passes us. When we're standing close again, I find myself giggling.

"What, bro?" He chuckles, his eyes boring into mine. "You laughing at how depressing our lives are?"

"No, I'm laughing because I'm calling you *Melancholic Leather* in my head since I don't know your name."

"It's Nicandro." He grins warmly, and yet there's still that hint of darkness in his presence. "Although I kind of like *Melancholic Leather* better. Do I look like some type of sicko to you?"

"Maybe..." I jokingly tease before shaking my head. "I'm kidding. I know you're a good guy."

"A good guy about to help your ass out of this place."

I gasp in bewilderment. "What? Wait, oh my gosh, really?"

"Yes, girl-with-no-name."

Right. I never did give him my name.

"Oh, I'm London."

"As in that freaking bridge that's falling down?"

I grin. "Yup. That's the one, all right."

Nicandro throws me a wink. "I'm just playing with ya. I already knew who you were. *Everybody* knows the Héroux family and their empire. But yeah, I can get you out of here."

"Really? I'll like love you forever if you're able to. How can I pay you back?"

"By telling me why you want to leave Victor LéVont's *lavish* New Year's Eve party. Note how sarcastic I was on that 'lavish.' So, yeah, why do you want to leave? And no lies. I've been programmed to see straight through them, London."

Hearing Victor's name gives me straight-up nausea.

Ick.

"You really want the truth? Okay." I sigh, flickering my gaze to my father, who's on the opposite side of the room with his back to me. I turn back to Nicandro and hold out my pinky. "You seriously have to oath that you won't say a word to anybody. Please? I know this could backfire, and I know I don't know you, but for some reason, I feel like you understand."

Nicandro's eyes playfully narrow. "Can we at least fist bump instead? I'm not really a pinky promise kind of guy."

We fist bump, and that's when I notice the set of silver and onyx rings he has on. *So cool.*

"Okay, soooo," I begin with a nervous breath. "I have this tradition with someone. We meet at Central Park every New Year's Eve. We made a pact that it's the only night we meet in the entire year. So if I don't make it to see him tonight, I've… I've lost this year."

Nicandro just keeps on staring until my anxious smile grows. "Um, Nicandro, everything okay?"

"Mhmm, I'm just wondering when you get to the part where you mention the guy's name."

"Oh, I…" Darn my face for burning up so fast. "I didn't think that was important."

"No name, no deal." He shrugs. "It's completely up to you."

I weigh up my options, and in the end, I need to take the little risk for the bigger reward.

"Fine," I agree. "But come closer. I don't want anybody to overhear."

Nicandro takes a step forward and lowers his ear to my lips. It's only then that I can smell the tobacco clinging to his leather jacket. Gulping down, I slip my hands into my coat pocket to prevent myself from playing with my fingers, a habit whenever I feel anxious.

"Tate," I whisper.

"Huh?"

"Tate," I say a little louder, a bullet of the unexpected lodged in my chest. "Tate Meadows."

Nicandro pulls back with a gasp, and I don't like the way his eyes widen so frantically. "Tate *Meadows*? You're kidding me, right? Your dads are two seconds away from killing each other!"

Crap. This is not how I wanted this to go. At all.

I do everything within me not to let that bullet go off inside me, which is why I remain composed. *Well*, at least try to act it because inside, I'm trembling, and regret sets in.

Maybe I shouldn't have told Nicandro…

Oh my gosh, I'm such a fool!

How could I have told him? A complete stranger!

"Dim the panic in your eyes, babe. I gave you my word when we fist-bumped, remember?" He squeezes my shoulder, and seeing just a glimmer of that warmth return in his gaze settles me slightly. "I ain't gonna tell anybody, even if I think this little tradition you have with Tate is volatile."

So much for acting composed, London.

"I know it can be a little hard to comprehend—"

"Just *a little*?"

"Okay, a lot, but it just… makes sense for us."

Nicandro nods as if he understands, but I don't know if he truly does.

He glances beyond me for a moment. "So, are you guys together or something?"

"Oh my gosh, no, not like that. We're just…"

Nicandro's eyes find mine as he arches a judgy brow. "Friends?"

I shrug, my heartbeat in my throat because I don't really know what we are. "I guess, yeah."

Nicandro stares at me for a full minute before he bursts out laughing. It isn't just any kind of laughter, it's almost to mock me, and I almost want to ask him what's so funny.

Ironically enough, his next words explain just that, no matter how much I hate the bitter metal taste they leave on my tongue.

"Seriously, London? Come on, you've got to be smarter than that. Can't you see he's trying to play you? Keep you as his little plaything until he has the right moves to manipulate you?"

I'm seriously taken aback, because yes, I know Tate is part of the popular crew, and he has serious confidence, but he isn't a manipulator. That isn't him. Not the one he shows me anyway.

"Nicandro, I don't think—"

He shoots me a look of pure disgust. "Look, I go to Glorsin St. Claire's and have almost every class with him. He's not the type of guy to simply have a girl as a *friend*. At every party I've ever been to, there's been different girls hanging around him and his crew. It's all a game to him. I can swear to you on that. So whatever Tate's intentions are with you, they aren't just for the damn fireworks. He'll leave you high and dry, London; that's all Tate Meadows will do. Believe me."

My heart slows.

I can't even get my thoughts together before he says, "Okay, so you ready?"

Huh?

My brows knit. "Ready for wha—"

"WHAT THE HELL, LONDON?" Nicandro growls, bawling up his fists in complete and utter rage. "How can you say that to me? HOW DARE YOU?"

I can feel the color draining from my face as the entire room quietens and heads snap my way. Gasps echo through the entire restaurant, and the jazz band's trumpet comes to an abrupt stop.

Oh.

My.

Gosh.

Everybody is looking at me. No. No. No.

I widen my eyes at Nicandro, not knowing what on earth is going on. *What is he talking about?* We just met, and weren't we just talking about Tate? What just happened that I missed?

"Nicandro, please lower your voice," I whisper, my heart racing in full panic when I see my father pushing through the guests to get to me in my peripheral vision. "Nicandro, please."

"No, I'm not going to lower my voice," he grits, taking a few steps back before pointing my way. "I will never, *ever* forgive you, London Héroux. Thanks for ruining everything!"

Nicandro storms off into the crowd just as my father takes his place with a look in his eyes that can only be described using the word venomous.

"What the hell is going on?" my father grits through his teeth.

"Nothing."

His jaw tightens. "You're lying. What did you say to him?"

My mouth opens and closes like a fish. "I, I seriously don't know what I said to—"

"You're coming with me." He hisses and roughly grips my wrist so tight, I silently yelp.

I don't even have time to actually walk, probably because he's dragging me through the guests so fast that I need to jog to not have my wrist dislocated.

As my father tugs me away toward one of the elevators, I glance over in Nicandro's direction just in time for him to look my way and throw me a wink. And just like that, every single bone in my body freezes up.

Wait...

Wait a second, did he just wink?

Wink?

Logical reasons pass my mind like crazy, and then my jaw drops because it all makes sense.

This was all Nicandro's plan.

His plan for getting me out of here.

I tell him about Tate. Nicandro makes sure I leave.

And oh, bless his soul, because that crazy plan is working... *Well, except for the fact that everybody is now staring at me all judgy as if I've grown a third eye.*

Oops.

The second the elevator car closes with my father and me inside, he explodes.

"WHAT THE FUCK WAS THAT?" he growls, slamming me up against one of the walls with clenched fists. The real Sterling Héroux comes out as he grips my jaw tight like I'm made of paper. Paper he wants to crunch and never see again. "You fucking brat! What did you do?"

The severity of what just unfolded hits me like a ton of bricks, and suddenly, it's not a celebration anymore. It isn't a tiny victory dance since I'm leaving. It's the complete opposite.

As I gulp down thickly, pressed against the elevator wall with no-where to go, everything just backfires right in my face. Sneaking out... not even seeing Tate... anything would have been better than *this*.

"Dad, I'm really sorry," I whisper truthfully, hoping this can be enough. "I honestly don't know what I said for him to react like that."

Snapping my eyes shut, I do my best not to wince when his grip roughens. I can feel the bones of his fingers violently seep into my jaw until it aches, destined to leave some marks.

He scoffs, dismissing the way my hands tremble when he pushes off me. "Pathetic."

Pathetic.

I swallow my pride, knowing he's right.

Pathetic is all I'll ever be in his eyes. And the world.

Leaning against the opposite side of the elevator, he shakes his head continuously with a scoff that says it all. That cocky smirk parts through the arrogance dripping from his fancy tailored tuxedo. "You're a fucking embarrassment, London. What am I going to say to all those guests now, huh?"

Frowning, I look down at my feet. "I'm sorry, Dad, I didn't mean for this to—"

"Look at you. Can't even complete proper sentences without crumbling. You expect me to go out there and correct *your* temper tantrum? No. No, you're going to learn to do that yourself."

My heart jolts at the unexpected bang of my father hitting the 'open' button so loudly. And when hundreds of eyes land on me, I realize that the elevator was never moving to begin with.

"Ladies and gentlemen, my daughter wants to apologize for the uproar she created." He grins at the guests, fooling every single one of them as he kisses my forehead and gently tugs me out of the elevator car. "Go on, darling, they won't bite. I promise."

I know they won't, but you might, and that's what scares me.

Can't you see it, Dad?

The rubber heels of my Dr. Martens squeak against the marble floor as I step out of the car, and that alone makes me want to shrivel up and die. Death doesn't faze me in moments like these, where I can feel the heat of all these elite goddesses and gods glaring me down.

What's even worse is that the hot stare I feel at the back of my head is worse.

And the most lethal.

Clearing my throat, I tell myself it's better to get this over and done with, which is why I stare down at my hands as they tremble.

I trace over my palm lines as I speak. "I... I'm sorry for the disturbance. I didn't mean to cause any chaos. I'd also like to apologize to Nicandro for what I did… I will learn from this, um, misstep. Have a good New Year, everybody. Thanks."

Some of the guests begin clapping, but my father slaughters those echoes. "London, dear, let's try that again. It would be great if you looked at the guests while you spoke. What have I told you about business deals, sweetheart?"

The fact that my father doesn't even speak to me on a regular basis, let alone talk business to me, must register in his head when I simply stare at him over my shoulder.

He answers his own question. "Trust is all in the eyes. You remember that, London?"

"Oh, yeah," I lie, "I do now."

"Perfect. So how about you try that again? This time, eye contact, okay?"

It's actually disturbing how sickly sweet his voice is. I've never heard it like this before, especially toward me. He has never called me *sweetheart*, or *dear* like this before tonight.

He's torturing me.

He knows he is.

He knows how much I hate public speaking and when the attention is all on me.

I despise it. So very much. I'm a cheerleader and do gymnastics because I love the sport and its escapism, not for the attention. I know it probably stems from my fear of oral presentations at school, but being exposed to high society lives like these makes it worse. One laugh in my face, and my entire career could be over before I even get started.

The monster called doubt eats up my self-worth, second by second.

I desperately need a glass of water or my favorite heart-shaped candy to cure my dry throat. My palms have turned all clammy from the stares, and I'm sweating like it's nobody's business. And yet, through all my nerves, I inhale a breath, put on my best fake smile, and repeat the words I said only moments ago.

Only this time, I never take my gaze off Manhattan's elites.

I don't spot Nicandro at all.

What happens next feels like a blur…

My speeding heart. The claps and smiles of the guests. Returning to the elevator. The doors closing to complete silence between my father and me. Me curled up on the floor with my head by my knees to ease the bile stuck in my throat. Because throwing up on my father's shiny Italian leather shoes is all I need to make this worse as we inch closer to ground level.

Blur.

Blur.

Blur.

That's all it seems to me.

The way my father tells me how pathetic I was for not getting the apology right the first time. The way all I feel is numb when he tells me I've made a fool out of him tonight. The way he screams and says, if I question his reputation in front of *his people* one more time, I'll be sorry for it.

He roughly pulls me up by my wrist, and seconds before the doors ding open takes hold of the side of my head and roughly slams it against the mirrored wall.

Stars.

Stars are all I see as I scream out in pain and quickly cup the left side of my head that's throbbing like crazy.

Owww! Oh my God, that freaking hurts!

"Get out of the damn elevator, London. I'm taking you home."

My vision blurs, but it isn't because of tears. It's my eyes. I can't see properly.

I squeeze my eyes shut, praying this is all a dream, but when I reopen them and see a scared fourteen-year-old girl staring back at me, I close my eyes again and swallow down my tears.

This isn't fair.

It isn't fair he treats me this way.

He really hurt me this time. This is so much more than a bruise. I just feel it. It's more.

Grogginess kidnaps my entire body as I press my face against the wall. *What's going on?*

"London, let's fucking go," my dad snaps, tugging on my wrist, but I find it hard to move.

"Wait a second, please, I…" A terrified noise escapes my throat. "I can't see straight."

His shoes slap against the floor, and the elevator doors slide shut.

Just when I think I'm alone and can finally breathe a little easier, my father spins me around with one hand. The other grips my throat as if to really choke me as he slams me against the wall. The throbs intensify.

That's when I realize he never left the elevator—he just stalked toward the elevator buttons to re-shut the doors.

Fire brews in his glare. "Do you want me to do that again?"

I touch the spot that throbs, and when I look at my hands, blotches of blood coat my cold fingertips.

Blood. Oh my God, blood.

Hyperventilating, my heartbeat slows to a single line as I look up at my father through my lashes, all of my fear, and whisper, "Y-You…" My voice cracks. "You hurt me, Dad."

He doesn't even glance at the blood, so unfazed by how much I'm breaking. "You're fine."

"But I—"

"I said you're fucking fine. It's a small cut. No big deal. I didn't hurt you, so suck it up."

"But I don't feel okay."

And then it feels like I'm falling into another dimension…

My father's angry eyes are the last things I remember before waking up in a bright white clinical room.

I squint, blinded by this room. It's too bright.

What is going on?

Where am I?

I squint more, trying to make out the shadows moving in front of me. It's… it's my father and a doctor. I blink away the fog, and my vision becomes a little clearer.

Doctor?

Why am I in a hospital?

I wince at the throbbing pressure on the left side of my head, and it moves the doctor's attention my way. His face blurs once more, but I feel him reach out his hand to thread through mine, and he tells me to squeeze it.

He's British.

I squeeze his hand as much as I can. Which doesn't sound strong enough according to the words he speaks to my father.

My father.

Nausea rushes up my throat at the very thought of him, and I don't know how the doctor makes it in time to hold an emesis bag by my mouth before I throw up.

As if on cue, my stomach grumbles, and that's when it dawns on me that I haven't eaten dinner. The rest of the night comes back to me in flashes…

Victor LéVont.

Wanting to escape his party to meet Tate.

Victor and my mother kissing on the balcony.

Melancholic Leather—Nicandro—helping me leave.

My father slamming my head in the elevator and how it bled before I fainted.

God.

It's all too much.

Emotion clenches my heart in waves as I throw up once again. The doctor is quick to discard the emesis bag, and then returns to my side with a soft smile. "Hello, London, my name is Dr. Duncan Harris, and I'll be taking care of you tonight. Your father has advised me of what happened. You've taken a little bit of a tumble and fainted. Is that so?"

My gaze flickers to my father standing in the corner of the hospital room without a glimmer of guilt in his eyes.

He stares back, emotionless, simply expecting me to agree. Agree with the fact that *I* was the one who fell and caused this head injury before I fainted. Not him.

Turning back to Dr. Harris, I nod slowly, knowing the consequences of going against my father.

Dr. Harris continues talking about how he suspects I have severe swelling and a concussion. How when I was brought into the hospital, I had a seizure because my body went into shock as a result of the concussion. How I may need stitches. How I'll be having a CT scan soon and will remain in this hospital room for a while for more tests and observation.

It means no Tate.

No Tate and no Central Park.

No Tate, no Central Park, and no hopeful beat in my heart.

Heartache. Complete heartache because not only is my father the reason I'm in the hospital with a head injury, but he also took away the glimmer of confidence I had left, and the one thing I look forward to the most…

Seeing Tate.

It hurts my heart so much. I wish I had convinced him that we didn't have to wait until this New Year's Eve. I should have made him kiss me that stormy night he left a love bite on my neck and taught me my favorite Pink Floyd song on my guitar. I should have spent the past two months wrapped in his blue-eyed warmth.

Because now it's too late.

Too late for anything more between us.

Because now, *this* is how I'm spending New Year's Eve this year… in a hospital bed, gazing out of the window at the moon as colorful fireworks light up the sky, signaling it's midnight.

The New Year. The *Happy* New Year.

The one without him by my side.

Happy Birthday to us.

Giant, hot tears roll down my cheeks, and I wipe them away before my father sees.

I silently pray that wherever Tate may be, he'll forgive me.

That he doesn't think I don't want to see him when it's the only thing I ever want to do.

That somehow, and in some way, we're still looking at the same big bright moon.

Our moon.

Because whenever I'm with Tate, I know I can be almost to the moon. And without him, well… the world seems like a scary place.

Which is why I can never see him again. Not after tonight. Not after the monster's mark.

Because as much as I adore him, I can't go through this again. I can't survive another hit. Another falsified cover-up. Another day in hell.

Because my parents have been lying this whole entire time.

Tate Meadows isn't the monster in this story…

My father is.

Chapter
FOURTEEN

Tate

PAST.
A Couple Hours Later.
London and Tate are fifteen.

It's 2:00 a.m., and she still hasn't shown up. This isn't like London, at all.

She wouldn't just leave me hanging like this. I refuse to think she would end the pact we made so abruptly. The one where we'd meet every year by this very park bench and spend the time leading up to the New Year talking about everything and anything.

But now that time has passed.

Time slowly crawls with a hollowness in my chest because the New Year came without her.

I've been sitting on his damn bench for five hours straight, only getting up to pace around on occasion just so my circulation doesn't result in my imminent death. Because that would be fucking tragic.

So where are you, LonLon?

Is it true you don't want to see me anymore?

I'm worried. So fucking worried something happened.

The longer time passes without her, the more I want her close.

It's one thing if she couldn't find a way to sneak out of her penthouse, but it's another if something bad happened to her. The thought alone makes me sick to my stomach.

I've texted her. Tried calling. No response.

My hands have grown clammy holding this pink velvet jewelry box for so long. So clammy, the streaks I've made over the soft fabric have become permanent. It was so perfectly planned for our meet-up this year, but now it's ruined. Everything's ruined. Because she's not here, the fireworks have come and gone, yet I'm still here waiting like a fool, just freshly turned fifteen.

A loud wail of ambulance sirens floods my mind from somewhere beyond Central Park.

Probably some idiot with third-degree burns due to illegal fireworks.

I slump back on the bench and shut my eyes, waiting, and waiting, and waiting. But her voice never comes.

London Héroux isn't coming tonight.

She doesn't want this anymore.

She doesn't want *me*.

And this fucking morbid silence hurts me more than words could because I'm lonely again. Lonely—just like I was all those years ago when I used to escape the toxic world inside my Manhattan brownstone for this park. When I was ten years old and would escape my father's violent outbursts and my stepmother's hollers with nothing but the glittery lake, the moon, and the chill of New York City.

My phone buzzes in my hands, but it means nothing when I glance down at the text and… *thump, thump, thump.*

That's my heart.

Exploding.

For all the wrong reasons.

I freeze up in complete shock. Numbness is all I feel at the words. At the sender. At the finality of it all.

LONDON: I'm sorry, but I can't do this anymore, Tate. I can't spend New Year's Eve with you. Not this year, not any other year. Not ever. This has to end. You know it does. Please don't try and change my mind. You won't. This is for the best. For both of us. I'm deleting all texts; I

suggest you do too. Goodbye, Tate Meadows, and thank you for

That's all. The text. The end.

Thank you for what *exactly, London?*

Are you thanking me for being the product of a freaking mind game? Huh?

My jaw clenches, and it hurts to breathe. Hurts because none of this feels real. I can't believe this is happening. She wants to stop? *Why?*

Is that all I was to you, LonLon, a game?

My texts asking *why* go unread.

My calls don't ring out.

Either she's blocked me or shut off her phone.

She doesn't want me.

Anger. Confusion. Foolishness. It's all I feel. But most of all, it's my crazily beating heart I'm concerned about because it's torn.

What. The. Hell.

I thought loneliness equaled silence.

I thought loneliness equaled death.

But then, one night, this blonde girl stole my spot on this very bench, and ever since then, my heart's felt a little warmer. Year by year, I've grown obsessed with the thought of seeing her again. She's all I ever dream about, her and nobody else.

And now, just like that, she's gone.

Gone and never coming back.

And that loneliness… that silence, that death, it's more potent than ever. Because as I stare out at the lake with a clenched jaw, and her birthday present tightening in my grip, all I want to do is dive into those waters and never get out.

I want its coldness to coat my skin with need.

If this is the end of London and me, if she wants no more, then I want to drown in the fateful waters while staring up at the bright full moon that will always be ours…

Tonight, loneliness equals fear because the thought of losing London Héroux makes me feel exactly that.

Because I have. Just lost her. Forever.

Why aren't you here, LonLon?

Why would you do this to me? To us?

Why, when we were almost to the moon…?

PART TWO

TO THE MOON AND BACK

present

Chapter

FIFTEEN

Tate

Almost Three Years Later...
CHRISTMAS EVE / DECEMBER.
Tate and London – both 17.

I'm addicted. I'm still addicted to London Héroux, despite how deeply I hate her after everything she did to us.

I'm not an addict, but my father's been one his whole fucking life...

Alcohol.

Rehab.

Home.

Alcohol.

Home.

Rehab.

On repeat.

He's been somewhat sober for years now, but the forbidden 'A' word is still written in his blood. The same blood pulsing through my veins, heating at the very thought of another one of his liquor-induced fuckups.

But if there's anything I've learned from my father, it's that addiction kills, and I've never believed it more than right now, as the memories of London Héroux reignite inside my mind. I feel them all over my skin, rippling over every muscle and stretching over my chest like a kanima's myth.

But most importantly, I hate myself for thinking of London three years after she ruined us.

I've never been in love before.

Never believed in love at first sight.

Don't think love even fucking exists.

But, as kids, whenever I was with that blonde angel, dopamine fueled my brain. The feeling she gave me was better than any happy little pill or vodka shot ever could.

I've woken up every day for the last three years, wondering how I would feel if I ever saw London Héroux again. Some days, I settle on detachment; others, it's bittersweet. And on those days, where the world feels like it's caving in, the most accurate description would be nostalgia.

Nostalgia.

Sweet old fucking nostalgia.

What a motherfucker it is to me.

I've been dying a slow death. No, seriously. I can't even live my life without being reminded of her everywhere.

Pink Floyd.

Roller skates.

White Doc Martins.

Pink silk scrunchies.

Fucking *strawberries*, because London always raved about those damn red heart-shaped candies that she called *Strawberry Fields*.

And yes, I've felt this way ever since she abandoned me on that Central Park bench years ago. I've also felt like I've been drowning in the Atlantic a little more every day, plunging to my death.

No matter how desperately I want to, I can't seem to forget all that makes London just that—*London.*

Fuck.

I look like a full-on sleep-deprived frat boy in the middle of the

SAT with the way I'm rocking this gray hoodie and buttoned-up jeans. Except, I'm no frat boy, and the SAT isn't for another few months. I mean yeah, everybody at school loves me, my circle rules the school, and I'm a well-known prolific jock, but I'd rather just disappear, thanks. And, no, I don't know what the hell I'm talking about.

Spraying on some Armani cologne, I step out of my moody, modern bedroom and quietly walk down the two flights of stairs. I make it to the first floor, and ever so carefully, tiptoe through my Manhattan brownstone's spacious hallway. My father, stepmom, and stepsister, Maddie, shouldn't be awake yet, but I can't take the risk of being caught sneaking out of the house this early.

I'm almost there, almost safe, and then…

Shit.

I come to a jolting stop, where the hallway opens to the kitchen, the front door in my line of sight. The silky fabric of my stepmom's robe shines in the silvery moonlight, flooding through the large kitchen window. She's in the middle of pouring herself a glass of wine when she pauses and glances over her shoulder at me.

Ah, shit.

I'm a good fifteen feet from the front door. I thought I could get out of here without detection; apparently, I was wrong in the worst way. My stepmom purses her lips at me, and I blankly glare back, pissed.

Seriously? What is she doing up at this hour?

Sabrina Meadows and I aren't exactly what one would call *close.* (Side note: same story with my dad). When she first entered our family with her daughter, Maddie, I locked myself in my room for a week. Every day Sabrina would softly knock on my door, attempting to coax me out with warm cookies and her infamous hot cocoa. I wasn't taking any of that shit, not even at nine.

Eventually, Sabrina just stopped trying. I don't need her pretending to be my mother.

I already have one.

One I can't wait to see the second I turn eighteen.

Sabrina knows that. She knows it well. She knows not to cross my fucking line.

My stepmom's features are dimmed in the minimal lighting, and yet, I can still make out her slight frown way too clearly. She married my father, Mirko Meadows, for his love, but all she's getting in return is wealth, recklessness, and copies of his rehab bills. I don't know what she sees in him, but then again, I don't know how he could possibly forget my mother like that.

I mean, it's not like she's dead.

She's *alive*.

Fucking alive and he acts as if she's gone.

I inhale a sharp breath, feeling sick to my stomach with all of the demons creeping in.

In his own way, my father is freaking killing my mother, even while she's still alive.

That's what I hate about him the most.

The fact that he's forgetting his first wife, just like he's forgotten me.

The fact that he didn't wait even a few seconds to propose to another woman before the divorce paper ink dried.

Sabrina Meadows is the reason my parents' marriage crumbled. Because she flashed her tits when she was drag racing her Audi against his Jaguar on the Golden Gate Bridge and the rest is history. And yes, that *did* actually happen. In my presence. I was nine and in his passenger seat, an innocent witness to their madness.

Talk about growing up fast.

And I don't take well to rejection, or feeling invalidated, but my father specializes in just that. Guess ever since I was a little boy, I've been collateral damage. An impending therapy bill.

"Tate? Is that you?"

I want to roll my eyes to the back of my head and die.

No, it's the big, brown freaking bear.

Yes, of course it's me, Sabrina.

"The one and only," I murmur under my breath, feeling my shoulders tense as I do my best to ignore her stare and walk past the kitchen.

I pull out my house keys from my pocket just as her dramatic voice clearing stops me. "And where do you think you're going at this hour?"

How much do you want to bet that she has her hand on her hip? Huh?

One thousand?

Five thousand?

Nine thousand? Ten? Okay, ten. Deal.

With a tense jaw, I turn on the balls of my feet, and it's actually luck that I did because I was about to walk out of this damn house with only fancy European socks on.

I glance over at my stepmom and, ohhh, *wowww*, hello, well, if it isn't *a hand on her hip.*

Pay up, dude.

Sabrina doesn't look the least bit impressed, and I squint my eyes, vampire-style, when she flicks on the chandelier light above us.

"Tate, I'm waiting for a response." She pouts, her perfectly-manicured red nails drumming on the marble kitchen island until it does my head in. "Hellooo, Tate?"

"Yeah?"

"Haven't you heard a word I said?"

I have, but that damn drumming is killing me, ma'am.

Clearing my throat, I glance around until I find my Converse by the wooden umbrella stand and slip them on. It's only after I quickly tie them up and count to five that I stride over to her, my six-foot-one frame towering over her.

I plaster on a fake-ass smile. "I need to head out, Sabrina. It's important."

Her eyes widen. "But it's almost five o'clock in the morning, on Christmas Eve! What do you think your father would say about this?"

I almost laugh in her face. *My father? Please. He doesn't even know what day it is anymore.*

"I'm going to the gym with Levi and Wesley."

"At 5 a.m.? That's a bit excessive, don't you think?"

If only you knew I was actually sneaking out to reminisce about a fucking bench in Central Park...

"Nope," I casually shrug. "5 a.m. works for all of us boys. We're going to the gym and then getting some breakfast."

I'm not surprised with how natural the lie slips off my tongue.

I've been doing this for too long.

Lying to the people I love.

To my mother, who's suffering from his cruelness.

To my grandparents in Paris when my mother got admitted.

To Levi the first night my father lashed out in one of his alcoholic-filled rages.

That night, my father created that scar I love to hate. *Love* because it reminds me of everything that I am. *Hate* because I despise everything I am.

It's why I keep my eyes level with my stepmom, never blinking or glancing away, because those are signs of a liar. The best thing to do when you want somebody to believe you through and through is to have a convincing face—serious, but not too motionless—which is exactly what I do.

My stepmother stares at me for a lifetime with guilt lodged in her doe brown eyes boring into mine, and then it all just fades away. Sabrina gulps, turns on her heels, and returns to the spot by the kitchen barstool, where she sips on her wine all alone.

Oh?

"Alright," she murmurs, staring out the window at the twinkling Manhattan stars. "Have a good gym session, Tate."

And then she downs the rest of her wine.

My brows furrow together. *Well, okaaay, that was strangely easy…*

I unlock the door and grip the handle, just in time for her to hiss, "Next time you want to lie to my fucking face, Tatum Lee Meadows, don't be wearing jeans when you use *the gym* as your excuse."

I stop breathing.

Fuuuck.

My jaw ticks as I slam the door shut behind me.

Manhattan's early morning madness greets me instantly with beeping horns and red brake lights. Its coldness kisses my neck, *just like London did once*, but it's nothing compared to my cold heart that, unfortunately, only melts for one specific blonde.

I step into my light blue vintage 1969 Ford Mustang with a clenched jaw, speeding through New York City, until I reach Central Park like a fool. Coldness seeps into my bones with every step I take to the bench that gives me air and destroys me at the same time. I still come here every night, and most early mornings, when I simply want to forget.

I'm so sick of it all.

Sick of Sabrina.

Sick of Manhattan.

Sick of this fucking life.

I feel like I'm dying, and with every day that passes, I'm getting used to the silence.

London Héroux used to revive me.

"God," I whisper under my breath, as even more memories of her flood my mind as I sit on the freezing red metal bench that overlooks the twinkling stars, dazzling lake, and lit skyline.

There's an ominous glimmer of the silvery moon, blanketing the brightening skies, and usually, it would pump oxygen into my lungs, but right now, through all my heartache, anger, and hate, I don't care about any of it.

All I care about is that it feels as though I'm suffocating.

The bright, full moon is too much of a reminder.

Because *she* is a constant in my mind...*Still*. Even after all this time.

There's so much I want to say to London.

So much I want to hear slip out of her mouth.

An explanation.

An apology.

Anything.

Just like that, numbness overtakes me, and I'm transported back to when I was fifteen on New Year's Eve, waiting for five hours on this exact bench for my *LonLon*.

Waiting all alone, wishing I could just drown in that icy, cold lake.

Wishing I could drown in this cruel world with the girl with the prettiest smile.

Wishing I could drown while staring up at the bright silver moon that was always ours...

Until it wasn't.

Chapter

SIXTEEN

London

Three days later...

There's one thing I hate more than Tate Meadows...*my parents at each other's throats.*

They're fighting...*again.* It's the fourth time in the past five days. Broken glass. Vicious screams. Tainted promises. A recipe to the cruel madness within our luxurious Manhattan penthouse.

I never asked for this.

I never asked to live life in the fast lane.

But with parents, who own a multi-million-dollar real estate company, and me, turning eighteen in four days, my choices are limited. *No matter how different it may look to others from the outside looking in.*

Sleek charcoal marble floors...Triple-high ceilings with crown molding... Lavish floor-to-ceiling windows with views of the Empire State Building to Park Avenue to wherever the heck you like...Too bad *it all isn't me.*

Expectation has laced my veins since I can remember. In fact, at times, I think it's engraved in my blood. A destiny brought on by my parents that I've always been too skittish not to uphold.

Good grades.

Good morals.

Good girl.

Keeping. Up. Appearances.

It's probably why every time I glance at myself in the mirror, I see a smidgen of the woman I once knew. A fraction of London Héroux, the only girl in New York City who wishes she could escape it.

Don't get me wrong, I'm not ungrateful or spoiled; I'm quite the opposite. Honestly, I just wish I could breathe a fraction more without feeling caged inside this Madison Avenue apartment—The Saxton.

Without the basis of my life being determined by wealth, power, and the latest gadget.

Without a prolonged, devilish desire right here on the tip of my tongue to taste rebellion.

I just want a family. A *real* family.

A family who loves me.

A family who doesn't see dollar signs in their eyes with every single thing they do. Who doesn't treat me like a walking ghost. Whose prospects for me aren't just a higher than 5.0 GPA, Cornell University, and some white-collar travesty.

But I'm beginning to realize I'll never get that kind of family…

Why?

Because my parents' shouts always get louder.

More heated.

Dad isn't happy. Not in the slightest.

Expected.

Mom is screaming at the top of her lungs.

Elegant.

It isn't about money, or business, or something as materialistic as a Rolls Royce. (*Well, not this time, at least.*) It's about Mom, about what she's been doing, about how Dad notices every time she returns from being away on a business trip, the glimmer in her baby blue eyes is never quite the same.

I've noticed it too, but I've never said anything.

I especially didn't say anything when she left early last week, while

I was scarfing down breakfast, and I noticed that the tinge of cologne chained to her signature rosy Chanel No5 didn't belong to my father.

She's been cheating on him...

I realized it many moons ago. He's only catching on now.

He's begging her to tell him who the guy is with a frantic growl in his throat. She denies everything. They go on. Again and again and again, like a record on a vicious cycle.

Please make it stop.

They probably think I'm asleep or can't hear them; after all, I am standing down the long marble hall, just outside my bedroom door. They're all the way down the other end of the hall and inside the second living room. I can barely see them through the opened gap. Just faceless voices of the night as glints of light trickle through the large floor-to-ceiling window at the end of the hall to my right.

The moon cuts shapes into my cream skin, making the silk dusty pink robe I have on a colorless kaleidoscope of nothingness.

My father comes into view at the small gap leading to the living room. Glimpses of him. *Pacing.* It's all I've ever remembered him doing in every situation...

Moments after he leaves black and blue marks all over my skin with every vicious hit, which has been becoming more and more frequent: simply because I exist.

Moments after the first cruel pang in my chest at his disappointment when I received a B+ in chemistry.

Months ago, when he found out I applied for a part-time job at that vintage bookstore uptown and he went there himself to not only terminate the application but threaten the owner. So long as I live with my parents, they forbid me to get a job. For them, I am only good at working hard to become a level-ten gymnast, something my father stripped me of recently, leaving me without any forms of escapism. They also took away my credit card after that, so I'm broke.

And that pacing continues *now* as the reputation my father built this family on crumbles at his feet over an alleged affair scandal.

It doesn't take too much to anger my father, but these days, I know I need to tread carefully. It's why I always stay here, cheek pressed against the doorframe, eager to take in anything I can hear, since they never tell me what the arguments are about.

Again, a part of their bid not to taint the Héroux name, but I see beyond that.

My heart jolts at my father's cold scoff, and a slice of him comes to light at the end of the hall. Expensive pinstripe three-piece suit that no doubt is a part of Hugo Boss' or Burberry's latest collection. Perfectly slicked back salt and pepper hair. A glass of Japanese whiskey in his grip, the liquor known to be his best friend during the elitist business deals or tainted nights like these.

Yeah, that's my father, all right.

Sterling Héroux.

German immigrant turned crazed New York millionaire.

Egotistical. Vicious businessman. Poor excuse of a damn father.

And yes, Sterling *is* his first name.

"I swear to god, you better be telling me the truth, Ramona," he snarls, blindly pointing his index finger at my mom while still gripping his whiskey. "I find out this is true, and it's the fucking end of you, understood?"

"Oh, go to hell, Sterling," my mother, who's still out of sight from where I'm standing, scoffs.

I can picture her crossing her arms over her chest and giving Dad a pointed '*go fuck yourself*' look.

See, it isn't all sunshine and roses with my parents. Money can buy you a hell of a lot, but it can't buy love. Or devotion. Or tenderness. (Or a tall shiny Christmas tree because my parents have never cared for it). And that's something that scares me beyond words.

The redness up my father's neck continues crawling. "*Go to hell?*"

"Yeah, go to fucking hell."

"Classy." He mocks her with a shake of his head, his jaw tensing as he sets the whiskey down on the gold cabriole-legged marble coffee table.

Heels slap against the floor until Mom comes into view. Her blonde locks are swept up in a clip as she stares up at the man she's loved for the past twenty years. But their expressions are both so pointed. Toxic.

"You don't believe me?" She frowns, her light gaze flickering between his eyes. The softness in her tone surprises me as she trails her perfectly-manicured fingers up his chest to his shoulders and slips off his blazer. "What can I do to prove to my darling husband that I'm his and only his…"

The blazer hits the floor in a thud.

I inhale a heavy breath.

My father remains motionless, staring down at her with complete chaos in his eyes. Chaos that begins to simmer little by little as his wife slowly undoes his vest. It's thrown recklessly out of sight. The moment she starts on his white dress shirt, I retreat back inside my bedroom, that is until he reaches out to roughly grip her right wrist, forcing her to stop.

I halt and watch on with an even heavier cloud looming over me, ready to rain down my hurt any second now.

"You think you can fuck me into believing you, huh?"

"Sterling…"

"Are you having an affair with another man?"

My breath staggers because I know the answer.

Yes.

LéVont. Victor LéVont. It has to be.

"God, no, Sterling." Her face scrunches up in pure disgust, while cupping his five o'clock shadow, as if her life depends on it. *Because it does.* "Of course not. I would never do that. There's nobody else, you've got to believe me."

Liar.

My eyes shut at the tension headache starting. It always happens this way. *God.*

How can she lie like that to him?

Doesn't she love him?

My throat dries up, watching my father recklessly grip her chin and pull her closer. They are inches apart now. So close, their noses brush together, lips parted like starved animals ready for the kill.

Their stare-off lasts what feels like a lifetime. And all of the hustle and bustle of the city that never sleeps is drowned out by my wildly beating heart. I can feel it everywhere. The pads of my fingers. Inside my ears. At the center of my throat. Pins and needles. I feel everything and nothing.

White noise fills the loving words that should be between my parents as my father finally gives my mother something.

His shoulders visibly relax as he lets out a breath and whispers against her lips, "*Versprich mir.*"

Promise me.

I'm pretty sure her eyes shut, but I can't quite tell from the skylines lighting up the living room. Her hands wrap around his neck and a soft smile traces her lips, like she's a teenager in love.

"*Ich verspreche.*"

I promise.

"*Du schwörst auf London?*"

My ears perk up hearing my name, and I don't know how to feel about it.

Do you swear on London?

"Yes. I swear on London, yes." She nods back without hesitation, lips almost brushing together. "You know I love you, Sterling. Please don't ever doubt that."

Trust my mom to curse my name without even trying. She's blatantly lying to his face, for god's sake. How can he not see it? He can't be *that* susceptible to her lies.

"If you love me…" he murmurs, his hands snaking around her waist and his fingers sinking into the fabric of her emerald pencil dress. "Then learn to fucking show it, Ramona."

Before I know it, his lips crash onto hers, and all their simmering, built-up anger transforms into pure heated passion. It's wild and senseless, rough, just like all of their toxic sharp edges.

They kiss.

They pretend it's all over.

Yet, I'm left bearing witness to the tension that'll lace the air tomorrow morning, chained by the memories of tonight. I never know what's real with them, and in exchange, my realness begins to dim, with or without their influence.

Knowing I can't take anymore, I slip inside my bedroom, without a sound, and lock my door. A new habit. For what I'm about to do—*necessary.* There's a lump at the back of my throat as I stare at my laptop positioned on a bookshelf, looking down on my queen-sized bed. *Do it.*

Don't overthink it.

Just do it.

Slipping off my robe, I watch it slide off my body, the silky material bunching up on the hardwood floors by my bare feet. My gaze flickers to the lacy emerald-colored negligee underneath, and I wonder if my recent lingerie purchase is a little too much. My tits practically spill out of it, and it's a backless, G-string style, leaving scraps of sheer and lace not covering much of my petite frame.

My hands run along my lingerie-covered hips.

This is what you want, London.

Just a few days and I can do this…I can make my own money without Mom or Dad knowing. Money that'll no doubt allow me to move out of this penthouse before high school graduation.

I crave the escape of being somebody else before I suffocate, even if it's only for several hours at a time, every few nights. This is the person I—London Héroux—want to become when the lights turn low, and loneliness takes a toll.

Need. Love. Affection. It all seems so far-fetched when I'm myself, or rather, the person my parents intend for me to be.

Summoning up the courage, I throw on a charcoal Pink Floyd faded band tee. The pads of my fingers skim over the fairy floss pink wig on my quilt cover, each piece of hair soft like a cloud, for a girl as sweet as honey and as psycho as Joker's lover.

I can be somebody else in four days.

Anybody else.

I don't know who I'm trying to convince because I know in my heart of hearts that I've already decided. Made up my mind. Ironed out all the details. Planned every single step, *all except for one…*

The lump in my throat thickens as I sink onto the bed, and my nerves bundle all together.

You can do this.

The moment I shut my eyes, my fists involuntary clench around nothing, my nails digging into my skin, but the prolonged sting gives me pleasure more than pain. Pleasure because it makes me feel alive.

Feeling alive.

It's something I almost never feel. Not since…

Gosh.

I slam my laptop shut and lie down on my bed with tears coating the back of my eyes.

Come on, London.

Next year will be your year.

"I can…" I whisper into the night, as winter's cold-snap seeps through the lace and into my bones. "I can do this."

Enticed isn't a normal cam girl site. It's exclusive and requires a heck of a lot of identity just to register to get in. *Enticed's* pledge is security and it values both performers and voyeurs, ensuring they feel comfortable, safe, and secure. It's the elite of the elite, and although I hate that word, it means something when one strips themselves down for complete strangers online.

The idea of a screen between me and *them* makes me feel protected. Giving love to my body and empowering myself…*being in control.* It's what I crave most.

My father has degraded me enough, my mother too; I just need a little freedom.

Freedom.

I crave it, just like I crave calming the jittery nerves taking over my body. Because right now, there doesn't feel like there's a heaven and hell, only a purgatory filled with illicit thoughts as a form of fucked-up therapy.

Once I'm inside the site, my stare-off with my dashboard becomes a western movie sequence. No amount of composing myself calms me down.

Breathe.

The butterflies floating around my stomach are half evil, half angelic. Some feel like their wings are little magnetic daggers stabbing me from the inside out and redefining the law of Shakespeare's sadism.

The other butterflies fuel my body with sparks, the good kind that have me anticipating what this new normal could be like for me.

Anxiety begins to set in like never before, electrifying my every breath and strangling the base of my throat like a vise. I want to push through it. *I need to for myself.*

"Four days, London," I whisper. "*Four.*"

But it all becomes a blur as the tension around my throat tightens. This feels like too much. *It's too intense.*

Maybe I can't do this.

Crap. You're such a freaking loser if you back out, London.

Before I know it, I'm shaking my head and counting to ten to ease my breathing.

Loser.

I don't understand this part of myself. Why am I so scared to take the leap when my heart is screaming for it?

Shutting my eyes, I try to ignore everything else but my heartbeat. Again, I count to ten. This time slower. Until the pitter-patters in my chest have stabilized to a normalized rhythm. One that wouldn't get me admitted into the ER.

I'm okay.

Reopening my eyes, the girl with the frazzled steel-blue eyes stares back at me in the bathroom mirror.

"I'll finally be free," I whisper to my reflection with a defeated, small smile. "I just need the new year to come, and then I'll be free."

It's a broken oath to myself. But an oath, nonetheless.

One I have to keep.

A good girl's secret.

And just like that, as I reenter my bedroom, my parents' shouts down the hall recommence. Frighteningly loud, like thunder howling at hell's door. This isn't going to end well. I can feel it. It won't be good.

Why?

Because my father didn't believe her...

Chapter
SEVENTEEN

Tate

Four days later...
NYE / DECEMBER.
Tate and London are turning 18.

"Sooo, let me get this straight." Levi chuckles, handing me back the joint. "You met *the* London Héroux on a Central Park bench almost *eight years* ago, developed a crush, and didn't motherfucking tell me anything about it until *tonight*?"

I glare at my best friend from the driver seat of my parked vintage Mustang. *Basically.*

Desperate to not get caught in the late-night craze, we're sitting so fucking low in the leather seats, my back is starting to ache. But I don't care because this stakeout is worth it.

It's New Year's Eve, minutes away from your birthday and days out from senior year recommencing, you shouldn't care, Meadows. You shouldn't care about where London is. You shouldn't care that this is the first NYE you're not on that Central Park bench—hopelessly waiting.

Fuck.

Remind me to strangle myself later, thanks.

The silvery moonshine seeps into my car, lighting up the darkened shadows of the night that some call fear; yet, I find comfort in them. And with every car that passes by, patches of red light up my best friend's wicked smirk. A smirk that hasn't fallen off his lips since I made the stupid mistake of letting him in on a secret…

A *huge* freaking secret I've kept from him for way too long to numb my insanity.

"It wasn't a fucking crush," I grumble and clench my jaw, adamant to set things straight.

"Bro, it was. You're saying that right now to protect your broody masculinity but rewind a few years and you were definitely crushing hard."

"Okay, fine. It was a crush. Whatever. I was nervous at the time."

"Nervous about what?"

"That you'd tease the shit out of me. I mean, come on, man, a guy's gotta have some secrets."

Levi's jaw drops, as if I just told him I'd been fucking his girl, but I know it's just one of his freaking dramatic acts. "Not when you have a best friend like me, asshole. You're lucky I love you, bro, or else I'd be kicking your ass to the side…I just can't believe she sent you that text and never showed!"

"Yup." I sigh, taking a long drag of the joint, its illegalness staining the air.

Staring out the windshield at London's penthouse apartment, and then lower to the entrance, I wish it would all just disappear. I wish *I* could disappear.

"Biggest fucking travesty of my life. London really fucked me over."

Manhattan's late-night traffic becomes a backdrop to the white noise crackling between us.

I feel Levi turn toward me, but I keep on staring forward. "You think you were in love?"

A long breath escapes me… *Was I?*

Was I in love with London Héroux all those years ago?

I don't know why the entire thing pisses me off so much. No, let me correct myself. I *know* why *she* pisses me off.

She abandoned me.

Rejected me.

Walked away from us when we were almost to the moon, and I will never forgive her for that. I will never forgive London Héroux for toying with my emotions, and as a result, *now*, I'm the most emotionless motherfucker out here…

Well, aside from Levi that is.

Together, we're basically a two-guy band of depression, dark humor, and late-night joint sharing. And, *oh*, fucking abandonment issues. Can't forget about that one.

"I dunno," I admit, taking another hit on the joint and embracing its effect completely.

It calms my rapidly beating heart.

Makes me numb.

Just like I crave.

"Yes, you do, Tate."

"Okay…I felt like I couldn't breathe when I was around her, but fuck, does that mean I really wanted her, or that I was just becoming straight up diabolic?"

Levi takes the joint from me and puffs it, clouds of smoke framing his face.

"Fuck if I know." He sighs, shutting his eyes as he leans his head against the passenger seat. "It could have been both. You could have been in love and subconsciously also hated yourself for it at the same time. It's kind of like being suicidal but craving just one final dose of life before you plummet to your death, you know?"

"Jesus Christ." I turn to him with a half smirk. "Do you always have to be so depressing?"

Levi literally only opens one eye to glare at me. "Blame my father, not your broski, he made me this way."

"I know he did, and as I told you before, he's a fucker for it. Both our fathers are for what they've done to us psychologically and emotionally."

Levi presses his hands together to heart-center. "Amen, and namaste, brah."

The car rumbles with our laughter. I steal the joint before he gets even more high off this shit.

"And now?" he asks.

"What do you mean?"

"Well, I'm startin' to feel a little high, but what I meant was, how do you feel about London Héroux *now*? Like what would you do if you saw her?"

"Nothing," I admit. "I've got nothing to say to her."

"Bullshit."

"It's true."

"Nahhh. Hold up, hold up, hold up. Let me get this straight, Tate." He turns around in his seat, so he can look at me properly as I smoke some more. "You're saying that if she were to waltz her way into your life right this second, like appeared from the air like it's the damn Matrix, you wouldn't do anything?"

"Correct."

"Hmmm." Smugly, Levi's gaze narrows in question and flickers to my jeans. "Does your dick feel the same way?"

Failing to keep a straight face, I burst out laughing and playfully punch his arm. "I seriously can't with you."

"What?" He chuckles. "I'm serious. Just 'cause your head says no, your dick doesn't have to."

"Why are we talking about my dick?"

"Because you're acting like one for not telling me the true."

Wait...Hold up.

I look at him funny. "Did you just say *the true* instead of *the truth*."

"Fuck off, Einstein." The chickenshit takes the joint from my lips and takes a couple more drags. "Bro, I'm telling you that if you see London, you'd be like, *Hey baby-baby, I'm sorry, forgive me, you wanna suck my c—*"

"Ayeeee!"

I slap the back of his head, and all he does is laugh like he's the real-life Joker.

"That's definitely not gonna happen, Levi. I'm not apologizing because there's nothing I should be sorry about. This entire thing is *on her.*" I growl, getting worked up at the mere thought of her. "We had an pact to meet at that bench every New Year's Eve. London told me she felt something too, and then two months later didn't show at the bench."

"Damn straight she didn't."

"London left me hanging like a damn fool and blocked my number, so I couldn't contact her. She's calculating, manipulative, and deceitful, and I won't lower myself to that. She doesn't know the shit I've been through since. I'm not the same guy I was two and a half years ago. I'm done being the nice guy, so fuck that, fuck her, and fuck everything else with it too."

Continuing to stare with a straight face, Levi dramatically blinks twice. "You done?"

I grind my jaw, simmering the fiery tension threatening to explode. "Yeah."

"Look," he sighs after a while, "as much as I love being your shrink, this is a conversation you need to have with her."

"I'm not talking to her, and that's final."

Levi frowns, and for a guy that feels no emotion, there's a hint of concern pooling in his eyes.

"Look, Tate," his voice softens. "I know these past couple years have been tough, like really damn tough, especially with what happened with your—"

I'm quick to shut it down. "Don't want to talk about it. Or *London.*"

The serious look I give him shuts him up, and as I look out the windshield, I can feel his hot stare burn through the side of my head. My gaze flickers over the empty entrance of London's apartment, and then to the free parking space directly in front of my car. It's used for pick-ups and drop-offs.

When are you coming back home, London?

"Sooo, did you guys ever make out or any of that shit?"

Ugh!

Shutting my eyes, I groan because this guy doesn't know when to stop. "I said I didn't want to talk about it, Levi."

"As your best friend I'm obligated to ignore you. Did you guys make out?"

"No."

"Ever kissed, just really chaste?"

"No."

"Kissed at all?"

I sigh, exhausted. "Nope."

"Anything else?"

"I kissed her neck, squeezed her ass, and taught her to play a Pink Floyd classic on her guitar."

"Did I just hear you say, '*Pink Floyd*'? Am I hallucinating? But did it lead to anything is my question?"

Yeahhh, I'm definitely not telling him about our love-bite craze.

"Not really..."

"Then it doesn't count."

"Jesus."

"Did you guys ever go out on a date?"

"No."

"Did you guys ever get a little touchy feely?"

What the...hell?

I snap my head to him with scrunched brows. "What the fuck was that?"

"What the fuck was *what*?"

"*Touchy feely*? We're not, like, five!"

Levi snickers coldly and rakes a hand through his jet-black hair, slicking it back. "You're so off your shit. You're getting pissed off for nothing. Sheesh, this London girl really got you good."

"Shut up. No, we didn't touch in that kind of way. Like ever."

"The hell? Then what type of fucking crush was it?"

"A serious one that made me feel like I was drowning."

"Wow, that was so beautiful and deep, bro." Levi pretends to wipe a fake tear. "Tell me more."

I roll my eyes and continue, "You don't get it. London and I could talk deep, or even not at all, and whether it be in the silence or not, she would really get me. Make me feel really seen. Being around her... it did things to me. Plus, we were more the cuddle and handholding kind of friends."

That word '*friends*' almost gets lodged in my throat, because I know how much more London and I were. I even admitted it to her. But at the end of the day, what did it do for me?

Nothing.

Just made me feel like I was drowning in the Atlantic a little more every day.

"When was the last time you '*cuddled*' my ass, *friend*?"

I shoot him a death glare. "I'm going to punch you in the balls in a minute."

Levi completely ignores me. "No, but seriously, I thought you guys would have kissed or something at least."

"I wanted to. Numerous occasions. I was going to kiss her that night of our fifteenth birthday, but she never showed."

"Damn, that's actually fucking depressing…In a way, I know you don't want to hear it, but maybe it was for the best. I mean, could you imagine if it kept going and your families found out? Brooo, you wouldn't be here talking to me about it. You'd be hundreds of miles away, like some posh Manhattan guy in some British boarding school for sure, drinking English fucking breakfast tea at two-*fhur*-ty o'clock without your stepmo-*thah* or fa-*thah*."

I arch a brow. "Now are *you* done?"

Levi darkly grins. *Grins.* And let me remind you, ladies and gents, this guy *never* grins.

I take the joint from him and hold it hostage from my best friend.

"Well aware my parents would ship me off if they knew what went down, but that doesn't mean she can just disappear out of my life like that. Who the hell does London think she is?"

"Dunno."

"All I know is I hate hearing her name out of Nicandro's mouth at school. They're like best buddies, so what."

"*Ohhhh.* So that's why we're waiting in front of London's apartment at a quarter to eleven at night? For her to come home from one of her Friday night meet-ups with Nicandro?"

"Precisely," I nod, as if it's the most normal thing. "It doesn't matter how badly I don't want to be here, I just want to find out their dynamic. Apparently, from what I overheard Nicandro say, they go out almost every Friday night. Like what is that? I don't know what she says to her parents, but she gets out."

Levi is about to respond when a beat-up black car pulls into the parking spot in front of me.

Nicandro.

It must be Nicandro's car.

Indescribable anger fuels my veins as Nicandro steps out of the driver seat with his iconic leather jacket. He rolls his shoulders back, shakes out his feet, and has that cocky grin on his face.

"Where do you think they went?" I mumble over at Levi without glancing over.

"Rock'n'roll party? Tattoo parlor for his ever-growing illegal tats? Drive-in cinema?"

Hmm.

London's not the party kind of girl, so I'm excluding that.

Tattoo parlor for him? No, why would she sit through that?

The latter would explain him stretching like it's the first time in hours, but I can't be certain.

London steps out of the passenger side, and *whoa...*

Thud.

Thud.

Thud.

My heart goes into overdrive, and I hate myself for it.

I don't expect the breath that gets caught in my throat at the sight of her silky, honey blonde hair alone. This is the first time I'm seeing her in close to three years, and holy fuck, she's so different. Older. But in all the best kinds of ways.

Those big blue eyes are still so striking, her lean legs are even longer. I hate the small smirk that raises up the corners of my mouth at her plump, glossy lips. They gleam in the moonlight, so obsessively coated.

Some things never change.

Despite her being so petite, London fits all the natural curves of her body. Her ample breasts are so large, they almost seem disproportioned to her tiny waist. And it's summer, which means she's even more sun-kissed under the soft streetlight, which glows a warm heavenly light across her body, as if she's a real-life angel...

Except she's not.

And I know that firsthand.

It doesn't matter how beautiful seventeen-year-old London Héroux is, it doesn't change anything for me.

Not my anger.

Not my grudge.

Not the way I will never fucking forgive her for walking away from us.

Nicandro says something to London over the roof of his car and she starts laughing, her smile lines deepening. A smidgen of that sweet sound ruptures through my car, into my chest, and I can't do anything but bare witness as it seeps into my tangled heartstrings.

Couldn't you have opened the door for her, you bastard?

They seem happy. Peaceful. Well acquainted with one another.

I hate it.

I hate him. I hate her. I hate everything about this.

Levi and I slip the hoods of our sweatshirts on and slide even lower in our seats, so they don't see us as we observe a little more of their interaction.

Stilettos.

London is wearing stilettos. I remember how much she told me she hated wearing them, but her mom forced her to wear them from such a young age.

I'm so lost in my brain that when I roam my eyes over her short white tennis skirt, fluffy white coat, and pink and cream pattern sweater vest, I slow by the deep plunge of her V-neck sweater. As much as I hate her right now, I'm not blind to her perfect cleavage in that tight, crop sweater vest.

It taunts me.

Ruins me.

I want to run my tongue over her soft skin, right there in between her tits.

I want to mark her there with my mouth, just like the love bite I left on her skin the last time we ever saw each other. On that stormy Manhattan night two months before we turned fifteen. Where after our guitar session, we cuddled until close to midnight, before I told her I should leave.

I don't want London Héroux; I just want to show her that she's mine, *even if she's not.*

So much time has passed. Years that didn't need to. Especially now that she's out with Nicandro so damn freely.

That could have been me.

That could have been us.

Why did you give up, LonLon?

"Fuck, she's gorgeous. You should have kissed her, Tate."

Sighing, I glance at my best friend. "Three years too late for that advice, man."

Levi meets my gaze, eyelids heavy as he studies me. "Tate?"

"Yeah?"

"Tell me honestly…Do you miss her?"

I stare and stare with my heartbeat drilling my throat before shaking my head. "No, not a little. Not even at all."

Levi parts his lips to say something, but for the second time tonight, he's interrupted with the soft rumble of Nicandro's car.

We glance up through the windshield at the same time, only to see Nicandro's car pulling away and driving through hectic New York City traffic. That's when panic begins to set in, because London isn't at the entrance of her apartment complex, which means one of two things.

1)   She slid back inside the car with Nicandro and now they're driving off into the night.

OR

2)   After she got out of the car, she went straight inside the building, and we just missed it.

I lean forward, trying to see deeper into the entrance of the apartment building through the windshield, but I don't see any blonde-hair beauties.

It's only a few minutes until the new year...

Fuccck.

"What kind of damn stakeout guys are we?" I groan, sitting up in the driver seat. "We completely missed her!"

"The hell? We literally looked away for a second, how did that happen?"

"I don't know, but do you think we should follow Nicandro? Wait... *Fuck*, where did he go? Now I've lost his car too!"

"I swear to god he was here just a second ago—"

A loud knock on the driver side window has my heart jolting.

What. The. Fuck.

I swear to God, all the color drains from my face at the baby blue eyes staring back at me. It's a wicked game the way London's glaring at me with such malice, like she isn't the person who ruined us. The person who let down the boy I was and flawed the man I am tonight.

"Shit!" Levi jumps beside me. "Either I'm real high, or this is your worst nightmare!"

The second I roll down my Mustang's window, London leans down so we're eye-level with a look of carnage brewing in her eyes.

"Tate Lee Meadows," she grits, slapping her hands on her hips. "What do *you* think you're doing *stalking me*?"

Stalking her?

Seriously?

Scoffing, I take a long drag of the joint and take pleasure in the way London's nose (cutely) scrunches up when I slowly blow out the white smoke in her direction.

"Wow, London," I sneer, already shaking my head, "We haven't seen each other in three years and *that's* the first thing you say? Really? Seems like you've lost your touch."

"Maybe I've lost my touch, but you've lost your mind! Did you seriously think I wouldn't notice you? I mean, come on, who else would have the courage to park their Mustang in the middle of Manhattan?"

Clenching my jaw twice, I stare out at the space Nicandro's car was moments ago, and it takes all of my composure not to explode.

Calm down, Meadows.

"He's not a good guy, London. I'm just trying to protect you."

"*Protect me*?" She screeches in complete outrage. "God, Tate, are you freaking serious?"

"No, are *YOU* FUCKING SERIOUS?" I growl, almost three years of pent-up anger scorching through my blood. "I waited by that bench for five hours, London, *five*!"

I slam my fist against the wheel to emphasis every staccato word.

"Five!"

Hit.

"Fucking!"

Hit.

"Hours!"

Hit.

"And you never showed! You told me this had to end between us, for me not to question it, even if it's been the only thing I have been doing since you fucked me over. That's right, *Little Miss Perfect*, you fucked up. Big time. You fucked me over good. But that doesn't mean I stopped wanting to protect you!"

London takes two steps back and narrows her gaze. I don't miss the emotion stabbing at her throat as she whispers, "Goodnight, Meadows."

Goodnight? Seriously? Is that all I deserve?

She demoted me from Tate to Meadows.

Touché.

She begins walking off, her heels slapping against the street, and I can't help my scoff.

Panting, I stick my head out the window. "Yeah, go on, *leave!* Because that's what you excel in doing, right?"

London stops dead in her tracks but doesn't dare look back.

"Go on, walk away, London! It isn't like it's anything new!"

It takes precisely four seconds before she's stalking back toward me.

"Listen here, idiot," London grits, coming so close to the car window that that familiar scent of vanilla and sweet coconut fires me up even more. "I'm not the kind of girl you can taunt and call *Little Miss Perfect* and expect me to be okay with it. I'm far from the girl on roller skates you used to know, and quite frankly, I'm not putting up with your idiocy!"

"Did you just say *idiocy*?" I chuckle darkly. "Fuck, who even talks like that?"

Levi takes the joint from me and eyes her slowly. "I sure don't."

"Well, then I feel sorry for you," she sneers.

"Don't feel sorry for me, babe, feel sorry for Tate."

The two of them have a stare off that turns deadly.

London lets out a huff and turns back to me. "Can you tell your friend to stop looking at my tits?"

"Tell him yourself." I shrug. "But quite frankly, he can look wherever he wants to look."

"It's called common courtesy."

Common courtesy.

"*Ohhh!*" I smirk devilishly with strained breaths. "Like the shit you pulled on me when you begged me to kiss you and then abandoned me two months later? Huh? *Righttt*, yeah, common courtesy can be a pain in the ass, can't it?"

All London does is stare, *and how she stares...*

"If you're open to a mature conversation, let's do it, Tate. If not, goodnight, and kindly do not let me find you here again."

Levi leans toward me. "It's a free country. He can park wherever he wants to park."

"How nice of you to bring a support team and...smoking illegal substances in front of my residence. Wow, classy. I could call the police, and this could all be over, you know?"

That's it!

I've fucking had it.

I'm so fired up that I practically kick my door open with so much force, she scurries back, inches from the traffic as cars sound their horns.

I hate how my hand automatically reaches out to pull her closer, so she's safe.

I hate how London's gaze softens for a mere second before animosity takes over.

I hate how I still feel that electric heat on the pads of my fingers because of her touch.

In fact, it's intensified since the last time.

Gritting my teeth, I let go of her wrist like its venom because, to me, it truly is.

"Go ahead and try calling the police, see if I care."

"I...Just stop. If I told you to stay away from me, it was for a good reason, Tate."

"Don't know if you've noticed, but I'm not really the guy who follows the rules."

Clenching her jaw, London's hot gaze roams my body, not-so-subtlety checking me out.

Hmmm...

Our stare deepens. A moment of silence crackles between us, laced with history.

"You..." London murmurs quietly, "you look so different."

I ignore her completely. "I said Nicandro ain't a good guy. He's using you."

London parts her lips but says nothing, which is damn torture for me because my gaze drops to those luscious lips for longer than I wanted it to. That night, when I taught her the notes of "*Wish You Were Here*," comes back to me, but then so does that pink velvet jewelry box in my hand that I never got to give her, and any glimmer of hope vanishes.

London begins walking away and I stride right behind her, towering over her as she rounds my vintage, baby blue Mustang and steps onto the sidewalk.

That's when I realize she has no intention of turning back, so I quickly circle her, until she has no other option but to stop and look up at me.

"Tell me you're not dating that piece of shit."

London swallows thickly and it feels like a lifetime passes before she whispers, "No. Not that it's any of your business, but no, I'm not dating him."

"Good."

The sadness clouding her eyes deepens in the Manhattan city lights. "I told you that I want all my firsts to be with that special person. I haven't...I haven't found that person yet."

"You're never going to find that person if you keep on running from how you truly feel."

She shuts her eyes and counts to ten out loud.

Huh?

London sucks in a final breath, and when she opens her eyes, I see just how glassy and lost they've become. I'm ashamed of how badly I want to fix her pain. And then I remember, it's on her. All on her.

"I..." Her voice softens as she slowly rakes a hand through her long hair. "I didn't run from you, Tate. You have to believe me. *Please*."

Liar.

"You broke an oath."

London looks anywhere but at me.

I shake my head, so over this. "There's nothing to explain, London, you obviously don't give a shit. That's the bottom line."

She doesn't say a word.

"You said you had a reason, so say it."

Silence.

London's eyes flicker to me and turn glassy, but not one teardrop falls. She's holding it in. She thinks she's strong if she doesn't cry, but she's only fooling herself.

"I was just the guy to practice with, huh?" I spit in utter disgust.

I've waited so long to talk to her, and now that I am, she has nothing to defend herself with. It means it's all true. I'm nothing to her. *Nothing.*

"Congratulations, you played me well, London. You and I both know I'm right. I was your fucking practice because you seem to hold down a conversation just fine with Nicandro."

"You don't know Nicandro."

"From what I see of him at school, I know him well enough. I see the way he looks at you. He's not your freaking friend, London, *believe me*. All he wants is…" I slowly caress the rim of her skirt. "To get in *here*."

London bats my hand away before I can caress her exposed midriff.

"Nicandro just wants to fuck you. Mark my words. He doesn't care about you."

I snarl at the flustered scarlet blush crawling up her cheeks because it isn't for me.

It's for *him*.

"You may want to forget everything between us existed, fine, go ahead, forget it," I hiss, stepping so close to her that she needs to crane her neck all the way back to look at me. "But I hope you don't forget how much you used to blush for me. The wa—"

"Tat—"

"The way we could just escape the world together. How you never gave me a taste of your wonderland. So go on." I inhale a sharp breath because I don't like the way sentiment toys with my confidence. "*Go on*, forget about me, London, because from this day forth, I'll forget about you too. And trust me, you'll wish I never did. Believe me. Next time I see you, you're nothing to me, London Héroux, absolutely fucking nothing."

"Tate, I—"

"Remember all those times I said I wanted more, because starting tonight, I'm going to fuck you over just like you did me." I threaten her with a devious smirk, brushing my fingers against her jaw, emitting sparks. My smirk slowly deepens. "*I promise*."

I glance between her sparkling doe eyes, my thumb reaching up to trace the rose-pink-tinged gloss on her lips that reminds me of cotton candy. I'm just about to continue my attack when fireworks sizzle and pop, screeching above us, lighting the otherwise darkened Manhattan sky in a charged kaleidoscope of vibrant colors. New Year cheers surround us, but I don't care.

We're eighteen.
We're legal.
We're…

London's glassy gaze stays on me as she parts those plump, kissable lips. I can't stop staring at them, at their softness, all while the city grows wild. It takes everything in me to ignore the vicious thumps drilling my chest, every beat conflicting me with alternating thoughts of her.

I crave you.

I hate you.

I want you.

Where were you?

Damn it, London, why do you do this to me?

"And trust me, London Héroux…" I growl, edging closer to her. "You will hate me for it more than I hate you this second."

Eyes wide, she gasps, her sharp inhale piercing my soul.

Our heated stare doesn't falter for a solid twenty seconds as I wait for something, *anything* from her, but I get nothing. *Absolutely nothing.* And that's when I truly know all our history is irrelevant. Every single part of it. Irrelevant because she's nothing to me, exactly like I told her.

"*Happy. Birthday.*" I seethe, clipped, my aching jaw ticking.

I witness those baby-blues dim, and it confirms everything…

London Héroux doesn't mean a thing to me.

Not anymore.

Our love snaps away like a frail branch on a devilishly stormy night.

Pushing away from her, my shoulders are tense as I confidently stride to the driver's side of my vintage Mustang.

This is the end.

This is the end of the world as London knows it.

I'm going to make it hell for her in every single way possible.

Just like she did to me…

Only worse.

I ignore her pleas for me to, "*stop*" and "*wait.*"

I ignore the heavy hits of nostalgia flooding my mind.

I ignore any part of me that's telling me to turn back, and fortunately, there isn't any.

The second I get in my car, I speed out of the parking spot, revving my engine through a crowded Manhattan Street, not even daring to look back at her in my rearview mirror.

I keep going.

Faster.

Harder.

No matter how deeply the sadistic side of me wants to see her standing behind on the sidewalk in pure dread, to see her crying, in agony for me, I don't look back at her.

I.

Don't.

Look.

Back.

But Levi does.

In my peripheral vision, he glances back, between our seats, out the rear window. "Shit man, are you sure this is how you want to play it?"

"Precisely," I grit, stepping all the way down on the gas. The thrill of adrenalin meeting carnage fills my lungs with the oxygen she stole from me the first day we met. "I'm addicted, Levi. I'm addicted to London Héroux, and hating her is the only way to make it all fucking stop."

For good.

Chapter
EIGHTEEN

London

Two days later…
JANUARY.

Swallowing my pride, I tap send, knowing just how deadly the butterflies fluttering across my chest are… *Still.*

> **LONDON: Hi, it's London. I know this is really random and you probably don't want to hear from me, but we really need to talk. I need to tell you something. Please.**

Almost three years ago, I betrayed Tate Meadows, my devilish teenage dream. I walked away from him when we needed each other the most. I've hated myself for it since that day. For the agony that comes along with every pitter patter caged inside my heart for him.

For the agony that must be in his.

Tate has every right to hate me, that I know, but I so desperately wish he knew the truth about that New Year's night. I wish he knew all about LéVont's party and the events that followed.

Two days ago, when I caught him staking out my apartment building with his best friend, Levi, I was so close to telling him the truth.

It was trapped in my throat—lodged deep, along with all the emotion of the last few years. But then Tate told me that he hated me. That he wanted to destroy my life, and I thought that perhaps it was better that way…

It's better for both of us if he hates me.

Tate Meadows was my first crush—my *only* crush—the boy that turned into a broody man filled with lovesick hate. He used to be (*still is*) my everything.

He was the first thing I used to think of when I woke up, and the last when I fell asleep.

My escape.

My secret.

All mine.

It didn't matter that our fathers have been feuding since forever. That we're enemies. Elite, Manhattan enemies.

Tate is the only boy I've ever sneaked into my room, the one who held me tight, taught me my favorite Pink Floyd song on the guitar, while wearing my Care Bears sweater, and the only one to give me a love bite so tenderly.

Back then, I was crazy about him. I used to write entries in my pink leather-bound journal and address them to him, even though I knew he'd never see them. I haven't written in that journal since the day I was discharged from the hospital. *That was the last time.* But every so often, I find myself digging up that journal I keep hidden away, and reading through the entries of my past.

I let nostalgia and thrill fill my veins, and then…*melancholy.*

I deserve it.

I deserve Tate's vicious words.

I deserve all of the hate he has toward me.

Now, I don't think I can ever tell Tate the reason I didn't meet him years ago on our infamous Central Park bench, with the silvery moonlight kissing every inch of it. I can't tell Tate why I sent him an unfinished text while I was in hospital, that fireworks blanketed my panoramic hospital window, worsening the severe concussion my abusive father caused. Why Tate and I could never make sense now—in the real world—no matter how badly I wish things were different.

I miss him.

We were almost to the moon.

But now something's changed. Something important. And Tate deserves to know this...

Buzz.

My breath hitches as my phone vibrates in my hand, notifying me of a text.

I glance down, my entire body freezing up when I see who it is. Tate.

Tate Meadows.

Oh. My. God.

He replied.

It's been almost three years since we last texted. He hasn't blocked my number.

> **TATE: What? What do you want? I'm at work.**

I cringe.

Okayyyy, maybe not the best introduction to all of this... But, I guess a shitty reply is better than no reply at all, right?

Wrong, London.

Ugh! *Why do I have to overthink everything?*

Chewing my lip, my thumbs hover over my screen for a solid minute before replying.

> **LONDON: Oh, I can message you later if you like?**

> **TATE: Stop.**

> **LONDON: Stop, what?**

> **TATE: Stop acting like nothing happened between us. Like nothing changed. Like two days ago didn't happen. It did. Everything changed, and it's all because of you. I'm not your friend, London, so either you tell me what the fuck you want, or I'll block your number.**

Ekkk.

So much for the *'he didn't block my number'* moment I had earlier.

> **LONDON: My father believes St. Marie's isn't prolific enough for me anymore...I'm moving to Glorsin St. Claire's when Christmas break is over for the last five months of senior year.**

Yep, that's right, peeps, I'm moving to Tate Meadows' private high school, St. Claire's.

I repeat: I'm. Going. To. *St. Claire's.*

Oh, one more time for the people in the back?

Okay. Okay. Let's do this.

Dramatic voice clearing moment

I REPEAT: I'M GOING TO FREAKING DIE!!!

My father wants to crucify me, he really does. This entire move wasn't a conversation; it wasn't even a let's-sit-down-for-dinner-because-I-have-something-to-tell-you moment. Nope, my father has never had that amount of decency (in front of me anyway).

Sterling Héroux thrives on the superficial and filthy rich. He loves money, Japanese whiskey, and oh, he also has a subscription to *arrogance* that he renews every. Single. Day.

Arrogant.

Horrific.

Cruel.

You name it, he's got it.

I can't explain how many times I've gone to bed without dinner because I couldn't stomach being at the same dinner table with him anymore (whenever he *is* home for dinner, which is rare). My father isn't the type of man one should admire; he's the man who has emotionally, physically, and psychologically abused his daughter since she was nine…

That daughter is me.

Me.

London Héroux.

And I keep on having to survive him every single day.

Nothing's changed.

If I seek help, he will kill me. *I know he will.*

I feel like I'm drowning.

Constantly.

Every hit, every scar, every tear shed mean nothing to him. It means nothing to him because it was exactly in one of those moments of rage that he took out on me last week that he gripped my throat and hissed, "*You're going to St. Claire's for the remainder of twelfth grade,*" before strangling me so hard, I thought I was going to die right there, pressed against my pink bedroom wall.

My mother stood, watching.

Just like she always does.

Taunting me further.

Tate, who I've hid this all from, used to be my escape from all the abuse. He was my safe space. My home. And then my father came along and ripped to shreds every single one of my lifelines. He is the reason I had to let Tate Meadows go. He is the reason I have no friends. He is the reason my trust issues constantly flare.

My reply to Tate instantly flickers from '*delivered*' to '*read*,' but it takes exactly eight minutes for him to text me back.

Eight.

Part of me wants to believe he needed to do something for work (side note: I wonder if he still works at that cool art deco movie theater on the Upper West Side that always shows classic foreign films late at night), but I know Tate well enough to know that isn't the case.

He is pondering what the next five months with me in his life will truly mean for him, and it hurts me to think I'll probably never know.

> **TATE: The fuck is your father trying to do? Does he know our history?**
>
> **LONDON: No.**
>
> **TATE: It's not going to work, London.**
>
> **LONDON: Glorsin St. Claire's is my only choice.**
>
> **TATE: No, I meant us, we're not going to make it going to the same school.**
>
> **LONDON: You think I don't know that?**
>
> **TATE: When did you find out?**
>
> **LONDON: A little over a month ago.**
>
> **TATE: Are you going to be all over Nicandro in my face?**
>
> **LONDON: I go to school to learn, Tate, not anything else.**
>
> **TATE: Ha! Well, that's the greatest joke I've ever heard!**

My brows knit together.

Asshole.

> **LONDON: I really mean it.**
>
> **TATE: So do I.**
>
> **LONDON: Do you really hate me that much?**
>
> **TATE: I think our last meeting can answer that question for itself. Okay, you're moving to my school, whatever, is that all? Because I really need to get back to work.**

LONDON: Oh, there's something else...

My heart doesn't stop racing as I send him a second text.

LONDON: Can we make a promise?

TATE: A promise? Are you insane? London, you fucking broke my heart with the last promise we made, remember? I wasn't lying when I said I'll make your life hell, so what do you want from me?

London, you fucking broke my heart.
My breathing becomes a strangled mess.

LONDON: For you not to make a fool out of me when I start at Glorsin St. Claire's. I know you hate me, but please, Tate, don't torment me at school. Ignore me if you have to, but I really don't want to have this bad blood in the hallways.

TATE: No promises.

I squeeze my eyes shut.
Shit.

Sighing, I sink lower in my bed, hiding under the sheets, as the silvery moonlight coats my hands, highlighting that white scar I want to forget. I slowly tap my nails on my phone case, thinking.

LONDON: Then please just ignore me. Please, Tate, it's one favor.

TATE: How can you possibly be asking me for a fucking favor after what you did to me? Huh? Are you delusional or some shit, London Héroux? You're still not sorry, are you?

If only he knew the real reasons why...

LONDON: Please, Tate, you have to understand that I did it because I had to.

TATE: Then tell me those damn reasons.

I can't.
I can't let him into my crazy life.
And so, as much as it haunts my soul, I don't respond.
Those three bubbles continuously appear and disappear, driving me crazy.

> **TATE:** All right, I'll ignore you at school, but I still fucking hate you.

> **LONDON:** Okay, that's fine.

> **TATE:** But it's going to cost you...

My fingers slow on the touchscreen...
Cost me?

> **LONDON:** Anything.

> **TATE:** It's something you stole from me.

> **LONDON:** *Stole* from you...what? Tate, I didn't steal anything from you.

> **TATE:** The night of our fifteenth birthday, on that NYE almost three years ago, I was going to kiss you...

"Oh my god," I whisper into the dead of night, hating how reckless my heart is beating.

> **LONDON:** You...You wanted to kiss me?

> **TATE:** You know I did, London. I've waited for almost three freaking years, hoping you haven't kissed another guy because I want to be your first. That foolishness has since mended into selfishness. And we may be seventeen now, but if you want me to ignore you, then I want to be your first kiss.

My bedroom echoes with my loud gasp.
Yeahhh, I'm pretty sure my ovaries just exploded.
My head is spinning, too much in a haze to tell him that I've already done that first.

> **LONDON:** I, umm...okay. When?

Oh God, I'm such an idiot! Who replies back to something like that with, '*okay, when*'?

> **TATE:** You'll know when. Don't text me again, London. I mean it.

My cheeks heat as I shut my phone, laying it on my chest. I know I shouldn't be like this, but if *this* is what hell with my rival feels like, then I want all of Lucifer's heat.
Every single flame.
Turning over onto my stomach, I foolishly grin into my silk pillow.
Tate Meadows, my enemy, wants to kiss me.
Selfishly.

Chapter
NINETEEN

Tate

The ominous, midnight sky glimmers around the brazen full moon, and suddenly, nothing feels real.

It's just darker.

Colder.

Eerier.

Life could be perfect, except it isn't.

Because London's not here.

And why would she be?

She's not here beside me on this Central Park bench.

She's not here to clasp my fingertips, to let me kiss wild.

She's not here to hear the three little words lodged in my throat…

I miss you.

Or a rendition of the other three-letter-words, weighted and plunged inside my chest.

I need you.

I hate you.

I want you.
I love you.

The buzz of the chain-link fence opening echoes throughout my chest, eating away at my nerves and everything else with it.

The security guard, a rough seven-foot monster, meets my gaze and nods beyond the fencing. "Reception will guide you beyond this point."

I shoot him a curt nod, slipping my hands into my jeans as I step through the gates.

Fuck, why am I so nervous?

I can't think of the last time anxiety fueled me like this (*well, a time that didn't include being in the proximity of London Héroux*), but I guess it's expected. I'm finally eighteen, which means one thing and one thing only for me right now...

I get to see my mom.

My real mom.

For the first time in years.

My father, Mirko Meadows, has had her chained in this exclusive psychiatric hospital for *years*, on the outskirts of Rochester, New York—five hours from the city—an outcast from society.

Years of not seeing the outside world.

Of no visitors, not even one.

Of nothing but herself.

I'll forever hate my father for it.

Hate him for not taking care of her like he promised.

Hate him for taking her away from me, for forbidding me to feel her love.

I would be a fool if I didn't admit how deeply it's hurt me, because it has. I've grown up in a home without warmth. No love. No affection. Only desolation, trauma, and coldness. I've grown so cold on the exterior, being Mirko Meadows' son, but today...*today* means a new start.

My Converse slap against the endless glossy-floored corridor, every loud thump reverberated back inside my chest, in exchange for another unsynchronized heartbeat. Black-and-white pictures in brass iron frames line the walls, some dating back to the 19th Century.

Nurses.

Nurses.

Nurses.

And their patients.

Patients like my mom.

Fuck.

I swallow the lump in my throat, finally feeling some type of relief when I reach the reception desk. Two women with vintage royal blue uniforms glance up at me from behind their computers at the exact same moment. For some reason, it shoots a shiver up my spine.

It's not me; it's this place.

The cold air is eerie and it's just white noise. White noise, coldness, and the stench of death.

"Hi," the blonde-haired receptionist grins up at me from behind the desk, flashing me her pearly whites. "What can I do for you, Mr...?"

"Mr. Meadows."

Something flashes across her eyes, something I can't quite explain.

Does she know who I am?

"Mr. Meadows." She clears her throat, but that grin is never quite the same. "How can I help?"

I motion to the visitor badge nestled on my leather jacket. "I'm here to see Elizabeth Meadows. I'm her son, and have already been cleared by security."

"One moment please."

The receptionist slaps her fake nails across the keyboard for the longest time, the constant ticking making my skin itch. But then she stops, softly bites her lip, and holds my gaze with an arched brow.

"Tatum Meadows?"

"Yes, I'm Tate Meadows."

"Hmmm, well, it seems that your name is blacklisted from her visitation list. The way it looks on my screen, there are limitations in place, which restrict you from visiting your mother."

Ah, Jesus Christ.

"Yes, I know. I already had to explain this to security upon entering." I sigh, aggressively rubbing my stubbled jaw. "My father had a court order, which restricted me from seeing my mother until the day I turned eighteen. I turned eighteen ten hours ago, so I'm lawfully able to now."

"*Ohhh!* Got it!" She clicks her tongue with a playful giggle. "Our systems usually take a few days to update, and in the interim, my manager needs to oversee the change; however, because he's away, I currently have authority to do just that. Okay, do you have ID, Mr. Meadows?"

I slide my driver's license over the desk before she can even finish the sentence.

Ms. Nail-Tapper goes back to typing away.

Sighing, I fold my biceps over my broad chest, my gaze casually drifting to the other receptionist, only to find her eyes have never left mine. The red-haired woman seems younger than the blonde, probably a trainee, still in college or something, as she fluffs up her hair and not-so-subtlety overcorrects her posture, popping out her tits.

"Hi," she murmurs, all hot and breathy.

I flash her a slow, panty-dropping smirk. "Hello there."

Her cheeks flame.

I don't look away, remaining fixated on her.

Three...

Two...

One...

Flustered, she turns away with a bashful smile, unable to hold my stare.

Mmhmmm.

My smirk only extends because that's the kind of motherfucker I am.

But I hate it. I hate it so much because throughout that entire moment we had, London Héroux sat in the forefront of my brain. Honey blonde. Honey blonde is all I see. Constantly.

God, I hate her for destroying us.

So. Fucking. Much.

Ms. Nail-Tapper finally hands me back my license, grinning. "She's on level 7, Room 505. You can take the elevator to your left; it'll take you directly to in front of her door. I'll notify the nurse currently with her that you're coming up."

"505. Okay, thank you, girls."

Ms. Nail-Tapper's eyes slowly roam to my lips. "My pleasure, Tatum."

Tatum.

I throw the redhead a subtle wink because that's the asshole I am before heading to the elevator. But once I'm on the seventh level, that's when everything begins to sink in, and I remain in the large art deco styled elevator for way longer than I should. So long the doors re-shut, and I need to brush my fingers against the button to reopen them.

Fuck.

Fuck.

Fuck.

I shut my eyes, swallowing my pride because this needs to be done.

I need to see my mother. I. Need. Her.

God, I need her more than ever.

With a sigh, I'm out the elevator, rolling the tension out of my shoulders, and just like Ms. Nail-Tapper said, I'm standing right in front of what I believe to be my mother's room.

505 is written in cursive on a cast-iron sign on top of a solid white door. The walls are also white, preventing me from clearly seeing inside. All I can see is a swaying dark shadow behind a small, frosted-glass window.

Breathe.

You can do this, Tate.

It's your mother for god's sake.

I know I can do it, it's the anticipation that's eating me alive.

My fingers brush against the cast-iron door handle, and it twists in my loose grip without me doing a single thing.

What the...

Dark, brown eyes meet mine, the second the door wedges open. A nurse in a crisp white uniform, that echoes the late '50s, stares up at me. A few strands of her hazel curls cascade out from under the vintage nurse cap she has on. I'm almost grateful she offers me a warm smile, because I'm frozen in place.

"Hi, I'm Nurse Paige, you must be Tatum."

Just as I'm about to respond, a distant yet familiar whiff of lavender taunts my soul.

Oh my...

Something moves in my peripheral vision, so I shift my gaze to the right, not expecting the air to be pierced from my lungs when I do.

There she is.

Elizabeth Meadows.

My mother.

Her piercing, baby blue eyes still have the sweetness in them I remember, but it's only an inch. Now, confusion coats them, alongside a loneliness that only intensifies the longer she stares at me. Cocking her head to the side, she narrows her brows as if she's trying to figure it out.

As if she's trying to figure *me* out.

Fuck.

And that alone is enough for me to give into the knot gripping my throat.

Nurse Paige clears her throat. "I'll leave and let you have some privacy. I'll be outside if y—"

"No." I softly shake my head, my eyes still on my mom. "Stay here. Please."

"Tatum."

Desperate, I turn to the nurse. "*Please.*"

I don't know what she sees in my face, but it's enough to have her stay. "Very well."

Emotion clouds my thoughts as I step forward, closer to my mother who's seated in the middle of a floral-patterned couch, fisting an assortment of crayons.

Every single one of the crayons are snapped in half.

Just like my heart.

While the room is fairly spacious, it's nothing close to being home. One lonely bed, one living room area, and there's a door to what I assume is a private bathroom. The dullness of the overcast skies outside kisses every inch of the room. Three windows align the black wall, all barricaded with protective iron, giving it a prison feel.

The second my Converse brush against the edge of the couch, I feel helpless. She's not even looking at me now, just fixated on the drawing pad on her lap, her breathing shallow. *Too* shallow. I feel so out of place, like I've disrupted something she doesn't want me to be a part of, but I haven't, and that's the hardest part. Fuck, *everything* about this is hard.

The fact that my father stole all her money to build his empire.

The fact that my mother isn't a fraction of the lively woman I remember.

The fact that my mother doesn't even acknowledge my presence when I sink down into the space on the couch beside her, my clammy hands rubbing over my jean-clad thighs.

"Elizabeth," Nurse Paige softly says, sitting on the other side of Mom. "You have a visitor."

My mom continues staring down at the drawing pad, a frown etched on her lips.

"Elizabeth?" the nurse repeats, this time closing her hand over my mother's, covering the wonderland of crayons. "Elizabeth, there's a visitor here for you. How about we say hello?"

My mother shakes her head.

No.

"Hi Mom," I murmur, doing my best to keep the nerves at bay. "It's me, Tatum."

Nothing.

Nurse Paige shoots me an empathetic smile. "Elizabeth isn't feeling like talking too much today, as you can see, not even art is inspiring her."

My brows knit together in concern. "Is that…normal for her?"

"It fluctuates."

A dagger slices deeper into my heart.

My mother was once a renowned artist, in love with oil painting, stunning watercolors, and the finest brushes. Now, as it seems, obnoxious colored crayons are her oasis instead.

"Is it…" I wince. "It is possible that she doesn't remember me?"

White noise crackles between us.

Nurse Paige flickers her gaze between my mom and me, and I already know the answer by the twitch in her lip.

Yes. It's possible.

Of course it's fucking possible, Tate.

Anger fuels me because, if I had it my way, I would have seen my mother during these past ten years. I would have seen her monthly, weekly, *fuck*, even daily, if that would heal the inconsolable pain rippling through me right now.

I feel so sick.

My father did this.

He did this to me. To *us*.

He ruined my only remaining blood.

"Mom, I'm here," I persist, this time louder. "*Mommy?*"

Nothing.

Fuck this.

I do what I've craved doing since the first moment I saw her here. Launching forward, I wrap my arms around her petite frame, pulling her into the solace of my touch. I bury my head in her golden locks, breathing in her calming lavender scent and letting it heal all my blues.

"I miss you," I whisper, not expecting my voice to break, for my gaze to turn glassy. "I miss you so damn much. I'm your son, I'm your son, Tatum Lee. *Tate.* Please know that I've been trying for so long to visit—"

My mother's bloodcurdling scream cuts me off as she begins shaking in my hold, fighting to get me off her, screaming for me not to touch her, that she's not who I think she is. But I can't. I can't let her go now that I've just found her. I need her. Just for a little while, I need to spend some time with her. I need her to remember me. I need her to tell me I am loved. *Fuck*, I…I…

"I'm your son!" I beg, hurt edging through. "Mom, please try to remember."

"NO!" she protests, slamming her fists against my chest, my leather jacket being stabbed by a multitude of colors all at once, hard and sharp, but I don't care. "Get away! Away!"

"Mom, *please*. Please, I'm—"

The same rosy-pink lips that used to softly sing to me part, and when they do—anarchy.

"I HAVE NO SON! *GO AWAY!*"

Boom.

A bullet launches into my heart.

Irretrievable. Unsurvivable.

Forever bleeding out.

I…

Fuck.

All the air gets knocked out of my lungs.

I'm numb. I'm numb all over, hot tears involuntarily burning down my cheeks as I gaze at the one person I thought I'd have by my side forever. The rejection hurts, just like London's did.

This is Frontotemporal Dementia at its worst.

This is broken love at its worst.

And it's killing me.

White noise fizzles between us. The fear in her melancholic blue eyes will forever haunt me, I know it will because it already is.

I slip my hands away from her warm touch. *Numb.*

The nurse walks me to the door, her tender words a blurry, distorted mess. *Numb.*

Back inside my car, I have nowhere to go, nowhere but hell. *Numb. Numb. Numb. Numb.*

It's just me and the loneliness of rejection, all twisted into one. I don't know where I go from here. Pretending to be okay is killing me, because I'm not okay. I'm so far from it.

The last pieces of my heart keep aching. Breaking.

Until I finally know how to escape the numbness.

The cause of all of this.... *Mirko Meadows.*

Chapter
TWENTY

Tate

I know *exactly* where to find him.

My father, Mirko Meadows, is the only motherfucking real estate agent, aside from Sterling Héroux, who can be found inside his Manhattan office instead of with his family on New Year's Day.

I don't play the role of the fool, I knew he'd be here, seated in his leather throne surrounded by staggering silence, floor-to-ceiling windows, and materialistic glass awards.

An assembly of open files are sprawled across his white marble desk, alongside a half-empty crystal bottle of whiskey. The expensive bottle is placed in the center of the chaos, like a damn paper weight.

Staring into the distance, my father slowly swirls the amber liquid in his highball glass.

Predictable.

My dad is a trainwreck: his red silk tie undone, hair all disheveled, his usual slicked-back curls now sticking up, as if he spent the entire night here, furiously tugging his fingers through it. There's no doubt in my mind that he, in fact, spent last night here working away like a maniac, while a kaleidoscope of explosions rocketed the Manhattan skies, one firework at a time.

Mirko's tired eyes slowly meet mine, glazed over with that all-familiar illicit glimmer.

There's no fight in him.

No deliverance.

Not when he's like *this*.

But that doesn't stop my rampage over what he did to me, because he knows *exactly* what he's doing. Even on days like these.

"*You*," I seethe, pointing to him as my Converse slap against the glossy clinical-like tiles. "How the fuck could you do this? How the fuck could you do this to her? To *me*?"

Arrogantly scoffing, my father ignores me completely as he downs his liquor.

"You did this!" My fist slams against his desk, knuckles instantly throbbing. "To. *Her*."

Fire crawls across his eyes, but it's nothing compared to the anarchy lodged deep inside my heart of hearts.

He doesn't say a word.

Not a single one.

Just silence.

Silence.

Silence.

And it only eats me up more.

Mirko Meadows knows precisely who I'm talking about. I see it in the way the muscle of his jaw clenches beneath his salt-and-pepper stubble, almost mechanically.

"And don't you dare, not for one second, play the card of a noble father and tell me you did this all for her benefit. You didn't! You did it all for you! All for *yourself*! Because that's the only thing you're ever good at, *hmm*?" I round his desk, viciously shoving files off it, so I can lean against it properly. "Isn't that right, Mirko? All you're fucking good for is self-destruction." A sly smirk crawls up my lips and I lean closer, my voice lowering, "'Cause that's what leads you to *alcoholism*, right?"

That does the trick.

Just like I knew it would.

Mirko arches a brow, sinking further back into his leather throne. "You done?"

Wise guy.

And then, he simply goes back to staring, malice in his gaze, without a single word ever escaping his pierced lips. He reaches for the crystal whiskey bottle and pours himself another three fingers.

"You're dead to me, Mirko, do you hear me?"

Nothing.

Done with his shit, I storm toward his office door when—

"Tate?"

I turn back. "What?"

"Did she remember you?"

My pulse thumps against my neck.

By the clench in my jaw, we both know the answer. *No.*

"Hmmm…" A slow, mocking smirk etches my father's lips. "Thought so."

I don't stick around for his half-drunken cackle. I run, wishing I was never born.

Chapter
TWENTY-ONE

Tate

There London Héroux is, looking like a beautiful, blonde, heart-breaking dream. I've always known fate was destined to fuck me over; I just didn't think it would fuck me over to the extent of her new locker being right opposite mine.

Constant reminders of her, that's where this will lead me.

I've ignored my enemy, London Héroux, all day, just like she begged.

During the early morning assembly, when the principal introduced the new A-grade student.

During English Literature, where she happens to be in my class. (*Side note: she sat in the front row.*)

During lunch in the neatly-pruned yard, where I side-eyed her for like two point five seconds, watching as she leaned against an oak tree, laughing with Nicandro. I may or may not have given Nicandro a death glare when we locked eyes as I passed them. *That fucker.*

So, as you can see, my track record for the past six hours has been pretty neat. I can ignore London Héroux. Of course, I can.

Okay, I fucking can't and it feels as though I'm bursting at the seams, but I'm fine.

Really, I am.

When I told London I was going to ruin her life on New Year's Eve, I wasn't lying. But now it's January, and we go to the same elite school, and I have to catch a whiff of that rosy vanilla and coconut perfume every time she's near...*like right now*.

It's the end of the school day.

Seniors are busting out the doors of the hallways.

My best friends, Levi and Wesley, are stepping out of the school doors, disappearing from sight. We always wait for each other, but I told them during lunch (while glaring Nicandro down) to leave without me because I have to speak to a teacher after school.

I don't have to speak to no teacher after school.

Remember what I said about always successfully lying to those I love the most? Yeah, well it hurts deep in my core, but if I don't want my damn world to collapse, I gotta do it.

Leaning against my locker with my arms crossed over my broad chest and left foot against the metal door as if I own this place, I glance left to right, gauging the circus unfolding in front of me.

Seniors.

The anti-social nerdy ones are bursting through the hallway, heads low, buried in books.

Jocks are flexing muscles and bragging about how we're going to win the championship, and although I should be a part of those conversations, I couldn't give a shit right this second.

The punks are sticking bubble gum to the walls, helping each other out with eyeliner and talking obnoxiously loud about some punk rock gig this weekend.

The hopeless romantics are making out in the middle of the hallway, forcing everybody to walk around them, as if they're marble statues stationed ten feet apart.

The posh, uptight, *I'm Mommy and Daddy's favorite*s, have their heads held high, avoiding everybody with their egos and parents' money literally growing out of their asses, even though I've witnessed them snort coke in the school bathrooms and take molly at our wild house parties.

But none of those seniors matter aside from one—*her*.

There she is, the blonde goddess, sorting through her locker as if she's a neat freak.

I can't take my eyes off all of those things that make London—*London.*

Pink velvet scrunchy.

Doc Martins.

White fishnet tights underneath that short black and emerald-green skirt, outlining those gorgeous legs.

I've witnessed this girl transform into a woman. A fearless woman filled with confidence, integrity, *and malice.*

From how deeply I used to adore her, I can't believe how broken she made me. Unapologetically. I hate that she just disappeared out of my life. I hate that she played me. I hate that my body still deceives me just thinking about her. That there's this heat rushing up my spine, my heart beating wildly, and butterflies exploding through me. I'm a fucking man, and yet, London Héroux gives me butterflies. The bad kind of butterflies. Even when I'm supposed to despise her existence…*but I can't.*

Not when I inhale a strangled breath.

Not when London shuts her locker and spins on her heels.

Not when those piercing baby blue eyes stare into my soul like sweet venom.

It's in that moment, with my back pressed against my metal locker, that I realize it doesn't matter what London Héroux does, I will always want her more. I'll always want to be her firsts. The one and only person to press my lips against those plump pink wonderlands. I'll always be the one to reminisce about the New Year's Eves when we were kids, and how Central Park doesn't feel the same without her. Through all of my hate, and all of my jealously, she's my lethal addiction.

London's eyes widen a fraction when all I do is stare with a clenched jaw.

There's so much I want to say to her.

So much I want to hear slip out of her mouth. An explanation. An apology. *Anything.*

Our past rushes through my mind like a freight train, starting from the first night we ever met on that stormy Manhattan bench, staring at the moon, just two lost souls trying to find their way home.

Staring at London now, as she remains frozen in her stance, lips parted, looking so damn beautiful in our St. Claire's uniform, I don't know what to do. Students continue rushing past us, but it all feels like a slow-motion scene out of a movie. Where everything is moving so fast, but time slows for us. London is the only real thing to exist.

The more bodies rush past us, the more flashes of red and emerald-green I see, the more agony laces through her expressive eyes.

The more the knot at the back of my throat intensifies.

The more I know our history was all a lie, fabricated by her.

The more I know ignoring London Héroux for the last five months of senior year isn't just a promise, it's a kiss of a death. The kind that will ruin me slowly, leaving me with her sweet venom aftertaste on my tongue.

It's that exact same venom I taste as London flickers her gaze away from me.

And just like that, she blends into the crowd, rushing out of the school doors, so quickly, I lose her in the sea of students. It's like this for the entirety of January. We roam like dancing ghosts in the night, without ever saying a word. It's just her and I—divided. It's just heated glares whenever we pass each other in the hallway, loaded in teenage angst, silence, and heartache.

Numbness takes over every time I see her, pacifying me.

Just like it always does…

Ever since she ran.

Chapter
TWENTY-TWO

London

Three months later...
APRIL.

"Babe, it's absolutely fine you're nervous about being on *Enticed*, but all you have to do is push through them. Sooo..." Heather's leaning by the lockers, the second I slam mine shut, her signature smirk on full display. "Sooo...is it finally going to happen this weekend?"

"I think so." I nervously grin.

"YES, GIRL! Tell me how you're feeling about your first time on it. I *need* to know!"

I can't help the laugh that escapes me.

Oh, here we go again.

"There's nothing to say." I shrug as if it's nothing, while I pull my English Literature books to my chest, but my new friend isn't convinced. "The nerves got to me months ago, that's all."

I haven't gotten past logging into Enticed...

That's going to change at the end of this week. It has to.

The smirk doesn't leave Heather's lips as she narrows her hazel eyes in question, and instantly, I know I'm in trouble. I know that look. The one where Heather won't be satisfied until I spill it all. And what Heather wants, Heather gets.

With long dark waves, fuchsia eyeshadow, and a personality to match her quirky yet fierce style, Heather is easily the most defiant girl in twelfth grade. Not only that, but her dreamy British accent has the ability to soothe my every issue like sweet chamomile and sugar.

We've been friends ever since I stepped into Glorsin St. Claire's three months ago, credit to Nicandro. She, alongside my guy friend, are the only ones I truly trust here. Heather and I are complete alter egos. Yin and yang. But I wouldn't know how to survive without her. I'm so lucky to call her my friend. Which is why I need to tell her all the ins and outs.

Both excitement and bittersweet winter blues are hitting me hard this morning.

"Earth to freaking London!" Heather yells, blowing out a piece of lilac gum, almost decapitating my nose with the pop. "Girl! I swear, if you aren't going to go on *Enticed*, I'll—"

"Heather," I whisper-shout, darting my eyes around the rowdy school hall as we squeeze our way through students to head outside. "If you're going to say *the* name, at least say it a little lower. The last thing I need is the entire school knowing."

My friend dramatically rolls her eyes. "Okay, okay. Mustn't tell the world that the Manhattan good girl is actually a kinky freak. Got it. Gah, you're lucky I adore you because you're such a party pooper, Miss Héroux."

Now I'm the one smirking. "Comes with the name."

"Ha! I'd like to see you say that to your father's face."

"Yeah, me too." I almost snort. "Daddy dearest would most likely disown me."

Heather throws me a look as she links our arms as we head down the large marble steps of our private high school's foyer. "As if that's the worst thing that could happen."

"You're telling me…"

We come to a halt at the bottom of the stairs, and she waits for a few students to pass before pulling me close. Her white-cropped fitted shirt brushes against mine; that's how close we're standing as she says, "Okay, spill it. How are you feeling? Nervous? Excited? Horny as fuck?"

"Heather!"

"*What*?" She laughs with a devilish grin. "It's part of the job, isn't it?"

I do a terrible job at hiding my smile as I elbow her side. "Shut up!"

"Oh, darling, you don't want this mouth to shut up. Like ever. Just call me the Kate Moss of New York City, well, the fucking brunette version at least. Anyway, stop leaving me in suspense and TELL ME!"

My heart does a double backflip just thinking about it, but then for some reason, all the nerves flutter away.

"Okay, okay, okay." I laugh softly, biting my cheek to ease my giddiness. "You want the honest truth?"

Groaning, Heather does the sign of the cross before looking up at the darkened, gray skies. "Dear Lord, give me the patience with this one..." She looks at me as if I'm crazy. "Of course, I want the honest truth, woman, I'm about to Jerry Springer your hot ass in a minute!"

Now or never, London...

"I'm actually...thrilled."

"*Thrilled*?"

"Yeah, thrilled."

Heather arches an unimpressed brow. "And I had to wait all through the first period to hear that one word?"

"Okay, girl, what do you want me to say?"

I avert my gaze to the entrance of Glorsin St. Claire's, anxious my AP English Literature teacher Miss. Thompson will spring up on us.

"Thrilled is the equivalent to '*yeah, I'm fine*' in Yorkshire, and '*yeah, I'm fine*' is pretty fucking average."

I can't help but roll my eyes. "Fine, I'll up my vocabulary, but it all depends on how it goes. No promises."

Sympathy coats Heather's eyes and she pulls me close, so it's for my ears only. She was held back a year in fourth grade, so she's already eighteen and has secretly been on *Enticed* for the past year. So she tells me.

"Everybody's first night is tough, but confidence builds. I promise. You're gorgeous, so don't let self-doubt swallow you whole. I know this is an escape for you, and trust me, it helps. *Enticed* is the safest site, and all of the voyeurs are security checked. I know the business, so trust in yourself, okay, babe?"

"Okay." Smiling, I show her my crossed fingers and we can't stop laughing as we re-enter the school.

What she can't see is that I'm also crossing my toes. That's how nervous I am.

My gaze is on Heather as we stroll down the hall, confidence in her stance. There have been so many times where I wish I could be more like her.

Assertive.

Spontaneous.

Unforgiving.

But it isn't part of my make-up, so much to my parents' disappointment.

"So, anything else that's new before I slam my head against the wall because I have chemistry in like two-point-five seconds?"

"Nope. Just little old boring me."

Heather throws me a wink. "There's nothing boring about you, cam girl buddy."

"Oh my gosh, Heather!" I grit through my teeth, my eyes probably looking like the Hulk as they widen, and I gesture around the busy hall. "People!"

"Yes, *people*, daaah" She smirks and playfully punches my arm. "See you at lunch, Miss Paranoid."

Before I can say another word, she gets lost in a sea of students and rushes down the hall to her locker.

Smiling softly, the tension in my shoulders begins to settle.

This is what I want.

I can do this.

It's time for me to prove to myself who I really am when the lights turn low and desire ripples through me. When escaping through sheer lace will feel like my very first taste of freedom. When elite men I'll never meet will watch me as the rest of the world just fades away.

That's when I'll truly start breathing again…*because I can't continue to survive without it.*

Without the very air keeping me alive.

Not anymore.

Two seconds later, I'm in AP English Literature with my books on my desk, waiting for Miss. Thompson to step in. I'm the first girl in class (*terrible*, I know…jokes), and am seated in the first row opposite the teacher's desk, just like I always do in every one of my classes.

Heather—who I only share studio art with—hates it with a passion, because it means she can't check her phone without the teacher seeing.

God, I love her to pieces.

Nicandro, on the other hand, who's my closest (and only) guy friend, and I have half of our classes together, except for AP English Literature, photography, and *football…obviously.*

Slowly, the class begins to fill with students.

Our black and emerald-green uniform continuously zooms past me as the booms of my classmates' loud voices cage me inside. Not a single person meets my gaze or quickly crumbling smile. Starting at a new school is never easy, especially senior year. They probably hate me because, in their eyes, I'm the teacher's pet. They've all made it clear. Especially by their stares in the cafeteria during lunch or every time they glare at me for getting every single question right.

A week ago, I stopped putting up my hand, but blank silence caused every single teacher to choose me to answer anyway. Being a Héroux is torture, but being the senior class nerd wrapped in silk pink bows and a single coat of mascara? *Worse.*

Miss Thompson claps her hands as she strides in, settling down the chaos of my peers' never-ending talk as they slide into seats behind me. Shouts turn to murmurs and my heart picks up at the eyes I feel burning into the back of my head.

Swallowing, I glance over my shoulder and catch two girls, in the infamous popular group's posse, staring back at me as they whisper in each other's ears, presumably about me.

Side note: Tate Meadows' crew.

Rolling my eyes, I turn back to the front of the class, where Miss Thompson is writing her name on the whiteboard in blue marker, as if she hasn't been at the school since the beginning of the semester.

"Good morning, class, and welcome to English Literature. I missed you over the weekend!"

"Oh, Miss, don't get me all sentimental now," a voice I recognize as Levi sarcastically calls out from the back, and the entire class erupts into laughter. "I won't be able to take it."

Here at Glorsin St. Claire's, I'm convinced the teachers are hired based upon the three 'C' factors…

Coldness.

Coyness.

And being calculated in their pursuit to withhold their reputation.

But Miss Thompson is the exception.

I roll my eyes at Levi's comment, pre-judging him already from the incident that happened back on New Year's Eve. You know the one, where he wouldn't stop staring at my tits during their little stake-out in front of my apartment complex with his best friend, Tate.

The teacher shakes her head and resumes writing on the board. "No need to get sentimental, Levi, I'll be sure Brontë and Hardy will be so engraved in your mind by graduation that you'll never forget this class."

"Fuck. My. Life."

The class breaks into another burst of laughter, and I can't help but sigh at my dark oak square desk.

Asshole.

"No profanities in class, Levi."

"Sorry, Miss," he snickers, and this time, I glance over at him. His gaze automatically leaves the teacher and meets mine instead, darkening before he shoots me a subtle wink.

"London!"

My head whips toward the front at Miss Thompson's shout, the frown crumbling from my lips. "Huh?"

Her eyes bore into mine with a slight sparkle as she leans against her desk with crossed arms. "Eyes up front, London."

Crap.

"Sorry, Miss Thompson."

"It's perfectly okay, I rea—" Her words come to a sudden halt as the classroom's door swings open, and the first thing I see step in are untied perfectly white sneakers…

Yves Saint Laurent sneakers.

The fanciest kind.

Oh. No.

With soft gasps from the girls behind me, my gaze slowly rakes up his body. *God, he's beautiful.* My heart thumps into overdrive the second I reach his face...*And my worst nightmare.*

Tate.

Tate Meadows.

Popular jock. Cocky star quarterback. Gorgeous player of heartstrings.

The epitome of my personal hell.

A slow, sexy smile spreads across Tate's lips as his piercing blue eyes roam across the class. They're the darkest shade of steel-blue, yet light enough to sculpt his inky black irises. The second his gaze lands on me, his stare darkens and...heats.

Oh my...

Be still, my heart.

Well, hello there, enemy.

I hate how much he still has dopamine unleashing over me.

My mouth dries and everything else dims in the room, spotlighting only him.

There's always been a bad boy edge to him, with his dark caramel brown loose waves that I want to thread my fingers through and tug...*in frustration.*

Tate Meadows has always looked like the definition of bittersweet poetry. He has heartbreaker written all over his perfectly high cheekbones, straight nose, and dusts of stubble that brush his face.

My heart jumps to my throat and I swear he can feel how hard my heart is beating when a lazy, sexy smirk carves its way up his lips. Lips that are so velvety soft that I can still feel their warmth against my skin from when he gave me my first and only love bite at fourteen.

It's scorching.

Tate Meadows isn't a *boy* anymore; he's an over six-foot-one man with a tall, lean, yet muscular physique evident under his uniform.

His black slacks fit him perfectly and I take my time roaming my gaze over how beautifully his white dress shirt stretches over his broad shoulders and wraps around his toned torso and biceps.

A couple of buttons of his shirt are undone, teasing the beginning of a gold chain hidden under the rest of his luxurious cotton.

The black and green striped tie that should be perfectly tied is undone and hangs loose down his pecs.

Code of conduct violation right there.

He holds his St. Claire blazer over his shoulder with one finger, the other shoulder laced with a thick strap, which holds an expensive glossy black leather messenger bag with the top half of Brontë's *Wuthering Heights* peeking out.

Tate Meadows is beautiful, rebellious, and...*the last person I wanted to see this morning.*

When I was younger, like real young, I remember not being able to utter their last name to question the feud between our families, without a stinging slap to the cheek from Daddy Dearest.

The Meadows name became forbidden to me.

He became forbidden.

And yet I still snuck out to see him and wrote about my boy crush in my journal.

"Sorry I'm late, Miss..." Tate's darkened gaze softens as it lands on our teacher, his cocky, Cheshire-cat smolder coming out to play. "This school is so fucking confusing on a Monday."

Miss. Thompson grins—*grins*—without ever once seeming concerned about his lack of a late pass, or the fact he swore, unlike she was moments ago with Levi. "That's perfectly okay, Tate. Please come in."

Tate lets the door shut behind him as the two idiots behind me commence their loud whispers to each other, and I catch every single word as they gush over the devil in disguise.

Wordlessly, Tate strides his way to the desk on my left, and I wish I could meet his gaze, but nervousness trickles through my veins. The giant lump in my throat has me eyeing my perfectly manicured nails instead.

My mom makes me go with her to her trusted beautician every three weeks to get the perfect French look, seeing as nail polish is prohibited within these school walls. Pretty sure she would have a midlife crisis if she saw me with chipped, unleveled nails.

Because that would be the end of the world for her...right?

Sighing, I keep my head low as Tate chooses against sitting at the back with his best friend, Levi. Instead, I'm sure his sole purpose in sitting next to me is to taunt me.

What?

What is he doing?

Tate Meadows never sits next to me, and I do mean—*never*.

I try not to make my heated cheeks obvious when Tate's desk screeches closer to mine and his bicep brushes against me as he takes a seat.

"Morning, London," he murmurs, my name is seductive ecstasy on his tongue.

I turn to Tate, a little taken aback with just *how* close he is. "Hi."

The entire class is listening in, but I don't think he realizes. Well, if he does, he doesn't even care as his gorgeous eyes bore into mine. His smolder doesn't help my palpitations as he slowly brushes a loose strand of my blonde tresses behind my ear.

Why is he talking to me?

Didn't he say he was going to ignore me, just like he has been?

Tate's fingers linger by my jaw, his touch so new and enticing, it zaps a laser through my skin, making me lose my breath.

"Hmmm." Tate flickers between my eyes with a smirk. "Anything you wanna tell me?"

My brows knit, clueless to what exactly he means, so naturally, I say the only thing that comes to mind.

"Umm..." I clear my throat. "You'll get a violation for having your tie undone."

Tate dramatically rolls his eyes and I hate how my body reacts to him. My cheeks burn, most likely rolling in shades of scarlet as scoffs echo behind me, but all Tate does is chuckle.

And gosh, that chuckle...

It's both deep and warm, everything that leads me back to his beauty.

And makes me question if he's really a psychopath because what the heck is this?

I sneak a glance at Miss Thompson, who has her back turned toward us as she scribbles something on the board.

Tate leans close and arches a playful brow. "A violation?"

"Yep," I say, popping the 'p' like I'm ready to start beatboxing in a 90's rap music video.

I cringe inside.

God, why are you so awkward, London?

Tate's knuckles brush against my cheek as he pulls his hand away.

The absence of his touch has my core tensing, as if something is missing. It has me drawing my eyes back to his.

"A *violation*?"

"Mmhmmm."

"*Really*?" he mocks. "That's all you got for me?"

The girls behind us burst out giggling, mocking me.

Seriously?

I almost roll my eyes into the back of my head.

Asshole.

Crossing my legs under my desk, I simmer the heat between
my thighs from looking at him so intensely. It's difficult to continue
looking, without wanting to drown in those dark oceans. Especially
when I know the tide will soon rise up to swallow me whole anyway.

"Yes, a violation, idiot."

Tate cocks his head to the side, taunting me as his tongue runs
along his lower lip ever so slowly. It glistens, fascinating me, as the
air surrounding me grows thick. Air tainted by his cologne's masculine musky, vanilla, and rich sandalwood blend.

It doesn't take long for ballsy challenge to cover his darkening eyes
as he leans forward and whispers in my ear, "So tie it up for me then."

"W…What?" I stagger, not sure I heard it right. "You want me
to—"

"Mmhmmm, you heard me." Another darkened chuckle escapes
him when his stubble grazes against my cheek. The heat of his lips
hovers so close to my neck that I gasp. "Tie. It. Up."

Huh?

Tate pulls away smirking, but not before his lips brush against my
jaw. He just sits there, so damn perfectly in his seat, arm slung over
the back, where his blazer hangs as if he owns the whole classroom.

Tate nods toward his tie and raises his brows in question.

Wait, he's serious?

He really wants me to tie his tie?

I reach out for his tie, my trembling fingers smoothing over its
soft, luxurious fabric. My knuckles involuntary brush against the heat
of his chest, causing me to feel each of my heartbeats pulse against
the edges of my fingertips.

Great, just great.

Concentrating, I bite my lower lip and try to ignore the control his presence has over me. *I'm such a chaotic mess.* I would never just attempt to fix a man's tie before, but with Tate…it seems almost natural.

Too natural.

Just as I'm about to create the first knot, Tate's warm hand covers mine and halts the movement with a rough squeeze.

That cocky smirk of his deepens.

"Stop." The word rolls so effortlessly off his tongue. "I was kidding."

Oh. My. God.

My blood boils.

London, you fool!

Gasping, my jaw drops in shock. "W…What? You were?"

"London, London, London…What am I going to do with you?"

Ignore me for the remainder of senior year, please and thank you?

Damn him.

I feel so gullible right now. *Shoot.*

The air between us crackles, my hands hot beneath his. "I don't know."

Has this guy like hit his head or something?

Or, is it all just an act for the class to embarrass me?

Tate pulls back and my hands slip away from his tie. His intoxicating gaze never leaves mine as he buttons up his shirt and knots his tie. Then, just as I'm convinced he's about to say something else, he turns back to the whiteboard as if nothing happened…

But it did.

The waves of his touch drowned every single inch of my reputation as a *Héroux*.

It's something I've craved for years, and now with one single taste, I need more.

My entire body freezes up, incapable of moving, speaking, anything. I think I just died right here in his icy-blue-eyed chokehold gaze.

Why?

Because I have a gut feeling about the rest of senior year…And my gut has always been right, even when I don't want it to be.

Tate Meadows is going to be my undoing.

My complete and utter undoing.

My enemy.

We have too much history.

Agony. Desire. Vulnerability.

Our past swirls in his deep blue-eyed stare and as much as I hate to admit it, it unchains the butterflies inside, letting them flutter free.

The first night we met at *that* Central Park bench, I did the most girly thing one could do… I rushed home and wrote down all about him in my new pink leather-bound journal.

What was even worse was the fact that I addressed all the entries to *him* with the hope that he'd never *ever* read them. That they would simply be our forbidden secrets. Small kisses in the form of lovesick cursive onyx ink.

Lovesick cursive ink filled with heartache.

Heartache he's been drowning in since we met eight years ago.

Years now sprawled with hate, because even in this moment…

I. Still. Melt.

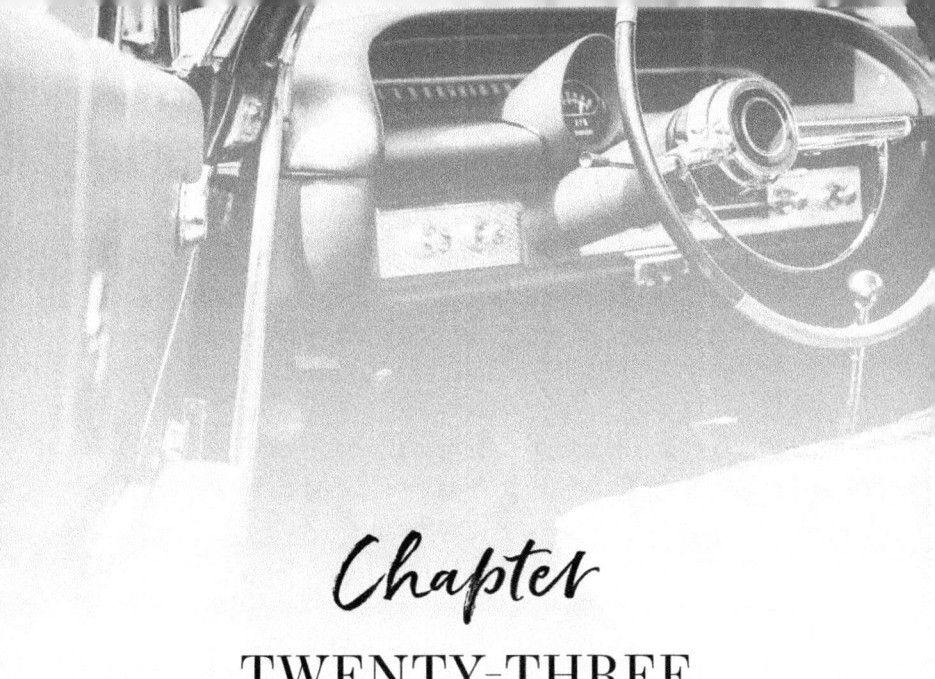

Chapter
TWENTY-THREE

Tate

All these girls at this party, and I can't take my eyes off the enemy dressed in white. *Ironic* because, despite what she wants others to believe, there is absolutely nothing angelic about London freaking Héroux.

She's the good girl, with the good grades, and the good life... *Too much good for a guy like me.*

I shouldn't want her.

Crave her.

Need her.

I shouldn't find my heated gaze lingering on those perfectly plump lips, or the way her school skirt gives me a heavenly display of her stunning long legs. Most importantly, I shouldn't want to grip her throat and recklessly kiss her whenever our shoulders brush as we walk down the hallway.

But tonight isn't about school.

She's at my house.

They're *all* at my house.

It's the party of the year…in fact, that's what we call every single party here in Manhattan. Expensive liquor, upbeat music and bad decisions that feel so good at the time is what comes to mind. Because it's exactly what's going on right now.

As *L.A Rose*'s "Heat" blasts through the built-in speakers, I bring my glass of whiskey up to brush against my lips, yet never take the sip.

My eyes flicker back to London over the brim of my glass, watching her.

Fuck. Do I look like Joe Goldberg to you?

London laughs with her friends on the daybed by my huge infinity pool, which people are swimming in.

It's fifteen minutes to midnight in the Upper East Side and dark skies make way for the mesmerizing winking stars that sparkle above. I'm grateful for the silvery moon, which shines down on the good two-hundred people partying their little hearts off at a party my dad and stepmom don't know about.

Won't know about.

It happens every time they take a business trip together. This week is Paris. They won't be back for days.

The glow of the outdoor patio heaters looms down over London, giving a warm highlight to her honey blonde hair. It's up in her signature high ponytail and light pink scrunchie. It's a typical every-day London hairstyle from school, but that's where it stops.

Her white bodycon dress seems so unlike her, as if she took it out of her best friend, Heather's closet.

It's a gorgeous low-neckline dress with a mesh top layer, ruched on both sides. Tight in all the right places, it showcases every beautiful curve of London's incredibly petite waist and hips that she usually hides in her school blouse, blazer, or an artsy-styled cropped cardigan.

She looks so different tonight.

So, so different.

I take a sip of the whiskey and a smirk burns up my lips just watching her.

A good different.

As London turns to tell her friend, Nicandro, something, my gaze instantly drops to the back of her dress. It's a backless cut-out until just above her dips of Venus, exposing her toned back and evident lack of a bra. With thin white strings creating a crisscross detailing, they tie into a bow at the bottom.

It's a dress you need help tying up at the back…*So, who helped her?* Her parents? *Don't think so.*

Her best friend, Heather? *Nope, she came with Nicandro. Heather isn't even here.*

Somebody else? A…guy? *Fuck. Me.*

And isn't she so cold?

London drips sultry girl-next-door vibes, and she doesn't even know it. I don't know when I realized her baby-blues got me feeling a kind of way, but all I do know is I don't know how to fucking make it stop.

I'm not proud of it. At all.

I hate the way Nicandro's hand slips around her waist, his light olive European skin a contrast to her jaw-dropping dress.

He leans into her with a smile, lowering his head so his ear is by her red lips. It's as if he can't hear what she's saying above the music and needs her closer to understand.

Convenient.

London's lips move, but it's inaudible from where I'm standing— right by the wet bar in my high-ceiling open-planned living room. She's all the way outside, on the wooden patio by the pool.

The shadows of charcoal, white and black furniture are a blur to me as I zone in on her, the warm in-floor lighting on the deck making the silvery stilettos she has on shimmer.

Nicandro throws his head back at whatever London says, a bright grin on his face as his laughter rumbles above all of the chatty teens and the music itself. And even though he's a friend, it kills me that he can speak to her more freely than I can.

What if he's the one who tied up the back of the dress for her?

He's the closest one to her there, after Heather, of course, and I don't give a shit that he's bisexual, that means nothing in this equation. He's a good-looking guy, all European, exotic and shit.

My eyes stay on Nicandro for a second longer and my heart plummets.

Fucker.

It totally was him.

The smirk that crawls up London's lips is breathtaking and

takes my breath away for all the wrong reasons. *I shouldn't want her. Shouldn't care about her.* I down the rest of my whiskey…*But I fucking do.*

A group of girls walk past me with fluttering eyelashes and longing gazes. One I recognize from biology waves all flirty.

I nod back, but inside, all I'm thinking is *dear god, kill me now. I don't want you.*

The second they pass, my gaze returns to London, only…*shit.* My heart stammers in my chest when I realize she isn't there anymore.

Wait, what?

Nicandro's there.

All her other friends are there.

But not the blonde goddess herself.

I scan the crowd of students dancing wildly around them, knowing she can't be too far.

Nothing.

Shit.

Tugging a hand through my tousled dark hair, I down the rest of my whiskey and slam the patterned glass on the wet bar's marble counter.

Where the hell did she go?

"You look like you've lost your fucking mind," a voice I know all too well taunts from behind me.

The slap on my shoulder confirms it.

I side-eye Levi, who's smirking like a nutter.

"Shut the fuck up," I deadpan, turning back to the section beyond those large floor-to-ceiling accordion doors. "Can't you allow me to have a breakdown in peace?"

"As your brother from another mother, I'm obliged to say no."

"Then help me look, bro."

A good two minutes passes of me stalking the whole damn patio with my wildly beating heart in my throat before Levi clears his throat from beside me.

"Question…" he shouts above the music, "sooo, what *exactly* are we looking for?"

"Jesus Christ." I pinch the bridge of my nose and glance over at him with a tense jaw. "Seriously?"

"What?" Levi's eyes widen, stunned. He raises his hands in

defense, that smirk never quite leaving his lips. "It ain't my fault, man, you didn't tell me anything! I don't know what I'm supposed to be looking at."

"*Who*, not *what*."

"Okay. Who, who, who," my best friend repeats like he's a god-damn owl.

Totally wouldn't guess he's one of the greatest jocks in senior year, alongside me of course.

"Okay. Got it. *Who* are we looking for?"

"You know..."

Levi gives me a crazed look as if I've just asked to buy out all of the joints, molly, and pills he secretly sells at parties like these.

His hazel eyes bore into mine, methodically, narrowing in their pursuit to understand what the hell I'm talking about.

"I *know*?"

"Yeah."

Levi continues staring.

"You *know her* too," I murmur close, bringing emphasis to the 'her' with arched brows.

Light-bulb moment. No?

"OHHH!" Levi shouts with a full-blown grin and half the teens inside snap their heads my way. "RIGHT!"

I wave them off, all while my best friend rolls his shoulders back all smugly.

"Ooooo," he repeats softer and jokingly brings a finger to trail up my crisp white dress shirt with a mocking smirk. "London. That's who we're looking for, hmm? *London*. The only girl you're obsessed with who doesn't want you back?"

Glaring at him, I slap his hand away.

Levi bursts out laughing. "Ooooo, the humanity!"

I swear to God, I'm two seconds from murdering the damn guy if I didn't love him so much.

Brushing down my dress shirt and pinstripe navy slacks, I finally give in and nod. "Yes. *Her*."

"Well, why didn't you say so, man?" Levi laughs, wrapping an arm around my throat like he's about to put me in a headlock. "Let's try and find her now."

"I tried, she disappeared off the face of the earth. She's not out there."

His eyes scan the crowd, and, just like that, he points toward something. "She's there. Right there in the white number next to Morales. *God*, she really is so fucking hot. Okay, we found her, now what?"

Shocked, I follow his gaze and...

There. She. Is.

"You've got to be kidding me..."

Oh, hello.

She's back...*and wait, did she really just pull out a wrapped-up burger and fries from a brown paper bag?*

My brows knit.

Did she just Postmates *McDonald's* to my damn party? She must have sneaked out from the side gate to get it.

D'fuq?

Levi sees my dropped jaw and can't stop howling in laughter. I swear to god this kid must be high.

In the absence of liquor, a raging headache forms as I come to realize if you can't beat them, join them...*right?*

"You've got a joint?"

"Plenty."

I hold out my hand and Levi rolls his eyes.

He pulls out a neatly-rolled joint from the back pocket of his slacks. I take it from him and give a soft hum as a *thank you* when he lights it for me.

One drag of this shit and I can already feel the tension easing in my shoulders. Shutting my eyes, I tip my head back.

Oh, sweet serenity.

This is exactly what I need—a de-stress.

"Fuck, this shit is good, Levi!"

"Tell me about it!"

I pull the joint to my lips and turn to him. "Think London will talk to me tonight?"

Levi's laughter eases into a soft frown. He keeps his eyes on her, cocking his head to the side as if weighing the options. "Well, you didn't exactly give her that memo when you went all Hulk on New Year's Eve and were like, *I'm gonna destroy your damn life.* Also, she won't come near you if you're in the vicinity of your stepsister, so I don't know."

"Explain."

"Well, last time I saw Maddie and London together, it wasn't good. Maddie is out for blood, you know, scared the new girl will take her crown…not that London seems like that."

I desperately take another drag, just thinking about my sister. "She hates everybody I like. I hate everybody she likes. It's what brother-ly-sisterly love is, you know."

"Thank fuck I'm an only child."

"Anyway…" I roll my eyes, "I don't have to worry about Maddie. She's on the rooftop with her set of friends and won't come down, even if the place is burning down. You know Maddie. What Maddie wants—"

"Maddie gets." Levi turns to me with a lazy grin. "*Oh*, I know, Tate, I know. She told me to fuck off the second she opened the front door to me. Still isn't over the fact I won't sell her any molly because of bro-code."

"She'll get over it, I promise."

"Again, happy I'm an only child, so I don't have to play telepathic fucking mind games."

A chuckle escapes my lips at Levi's words, and for the first time tonight, I feel a smile forming. I don't know if it's the joint, or the fact that London's in my line of sight again, but I'm content.

As the lively party kicks into full speed all around us, Levi and I lean against the wet bar's marble counter. I'm left to watch London taking turns sharing a burger with Nicandro.

What's up with my Joe Goldberg tendencies?

They're in full-blown conversation with the rest of their circle and nobody else questions a single thing as they share the fries too. When they're done, London reaches over to pull out what looks like a strawberry sundae from the brown paper M bag.

This time, she sits down on Nicandro's lap. Wesley (who's a part of my group, so what the hell is he doing there?) says something to them with a smirk and those around them laugh. Well, except for London and Nicandro, who both flip him off at the same time.

"You think they're fucking?" Levi says, ever so casually, stealing the joint from me and bringing it to his lips. "London and Nicandro."

Gasping, I'm left staring at the space the joint used to be.

Are they?

Heat runs down my spine because I've noticed the position of Nicandro's hands but thought that if I didn't openly admit it, it wouldn't be true.

London once told me her firsts are special to her. But Nicandro… is he special enough?

His hands are on her bare thighs, where her dress has ridden up, and London doesn't seem the least bit fazed. Not even as he continuously caresses her outer thighs.

Does she like being touched by him?

"I don't know. Everything about her is a mystery."

"I know, but I mean, look at his hands. That isn't on a *best-friend* level, man, that's straight up a *she's fucking-mine* level."

"They're close." I shrug. "Plus, isn't he seeing Daniel or something?"

"Nah, that ended before the end of summer. It was just a fling, I guess. I dunno."

"Thanks, TMZ."

Deadpanning me, Levi hands me back the joint. "Go. To. Hell. Rich. Kid."

"Already there." I wink and take a final drag, knowing that if I have more, I'll end up getting high at my own party.

And that's a big no.

Not with London here.

"Want to know the best way to find out if her and Nicandro are fucking?"

I nod, never taking my eyes off her. She's demolishing that strawberry sundae like there's no tomorrow.

"You steal her away from that group, find a secluded space for just the two of you, and then, you *just ask her.*"

My breath slows at Levi's words. "Wait, you mean, ask her to her face if they're fucking?"

Levi's too lost in the joint to even hide his reddening-hooded eyes. "Mmhmm, easy right?"

It takes me a moment to realize it's actually a good idea.

Just ask her?

Hmmm.

"Right." I nod slowly, a sly smirk creeping up my lips. "*Right*. God, now I know why you're my best friend. You're a fucking genius, man!"

"Yeah, yeah." He gestures a hand my way with a nod. "Just don't be rubbing up my thighs in the name of being *best friends* because of it. I prefer pussy, and I know you do too."

The smirk drops off my lips and I slap the back of his head as he leans against the counter in rumbles of laughter.

Smartass.

Within seconds, he shuts his eyes with an exaggerated yawn.

"Goodnight, Tate," he mumbles. "Tell me how it goes in the morning."

And here I am left staring at my six-foot best friend, who just fell asleep leaning against the wet bar, the joint still in his mouth.

I don't know if he's an outright chickenshit or the most intelligent guy I know.

He can be the latter for now, the poor guy.

Chuckling, I ruffle up his light hair and toss the joint out in the hidden trash. It's rough at home and weed tends to be his only escape.

Bypassing dancing bodies and couples making out like it's a real-life porno, I pass the waves of people, knowing just how much of a clean-up this place is going to be in the morning. Luxury and power can take you far, but the one thing they can't do, if you're Tate Meadows, is hire a cleaner or two to clean up this shit without them sending a scroll-length email to my parents.

And I say it from experience…

The first party I hosted a few years back with Maddie ended up with a clean-up bill in the thousands, which I gladly paid. Until our parents came home from their business trip, dripping in Dior and Saint Laurent, and confiscated my Audi for a freaking month.

Why?

Because they got confirmation of the paid bill and put two and two together, realizing what actually went down that weekend.

So now, I've learned how to outsmart them.

Sorry, not sorry.

New York's cold winter breeze hits my skin the second I step outside, the atmosphere even more wild out here as groups of people chant my name as I stride past. All I can do is give a few fist pumps and some small talk because they're not my final destination.

She is.

Nicandro's tattooed hands on London's thighs piss me off even more up close. They fuck me over because I don't want him in my house. I don't want either of them here.

Those baby-blue eyes I know too well are the first to meet mine as I come to a stop a good six feet away from the white daybed they're all sprawled out on.

London's gaze feels like milky powder-blue orbits, sending me into a breathless state of some fucked-up wonderland.

Her heart-shaped lips softly part around the small white plastic spoon, her glistening tongue darting out to glide over the creamy pink ice cream, taunting me with her heated stare. She swallows the sundae down.

Fuck, that's so hot.

I almost lose my damn mind as her tongue circles the tip of the spoon, so damn recklessly, before sucking on it, suggestively.

Jesus.

Fucking.

Christ.

My pounding heartbeat feels deadly as my cock swells in my slacks because not once in that entire show did she let go of my gaze.

I can't take my eyes off London. Everything about her. I want to suck on her lips, suck on them till all I can taste is her. Till she's bleeding a red that resembles the way my heart is tearing inside, vengeful.

I shouldn't fucking want her.

It's fucking with my head.

London probably didn't want to see me anymore purely because I'm a Meadows, and that fucking hurts. It's a permanent bruise on my soul that aches and aches the longer my fists hold my fractured heart together.

London's eyes slowly flicker away from mine and return to her group instead.

Great, just great.

Clenching my jaw, the tension in my shoulders tightens, knowing Levi's plan just backfired in my face.

Without thinking it through, my feet retreat backwards, right back to the wet bar with a passed-out Levi to my right and lost hope several feet in front of me.

I wait.

Wait, and fucking wait, for a better idea to come to mind.

It all seems so far-fetched. Completely out of touch. Until I see London slide out her phone from a pink clutch on the deck and begin typing away.

She glances behind her shoulder, past Nicandro, and she slowly scans the party while chewing her lower lip. Her thumb taps something on the screen and less than a heartbeat later, my phone vibrates in my back pocket.

Oh.

Slipping out my phone, my breaths slow as I read over who the text is from…

It's her.

LONDON: Is there something you wanted to tell me?

With my fingers freezing against the keyboard, I glance up and a curse word escapes.

She's found me.

We're playing a cat-and-mouse game.

I reply and hit send, without ever breaking our heated stare.

TATE: Meet me in my library in five. No Nicandro. No ice-cream sundaes. Just you.

Because as I said, London Héroux is no angel, and she just proved why. She loves taunting the beast inside me. Fucking up my head until I break.

And *damn,* how I'm about to break.

Right.

Freaking.

Now.

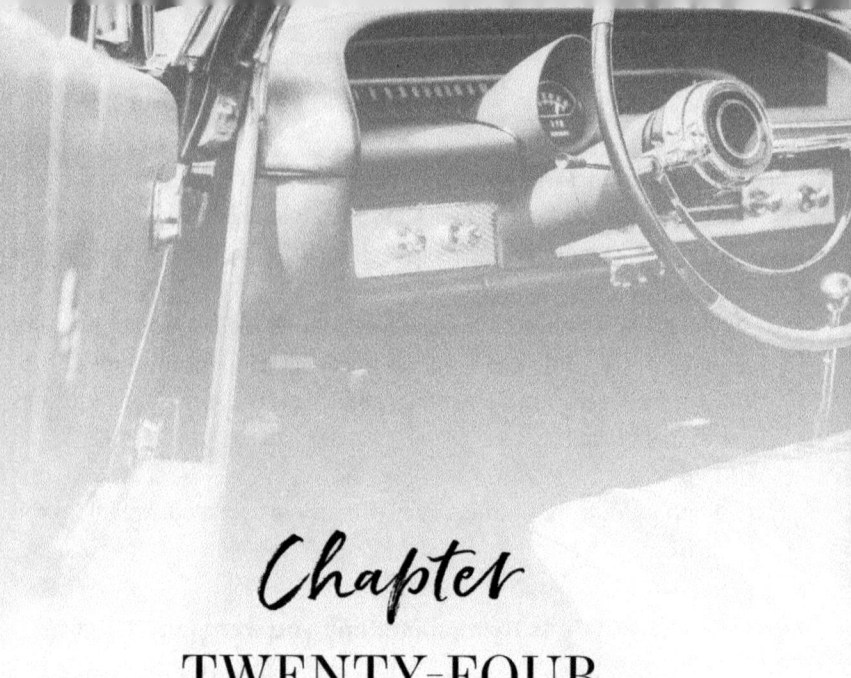

Chapter

TWENTY-FOUR

Tate

Five minutes tick away, and London is still a no-show. *Five.*

I don't get it. Don't get why I feel this way. I can sweet talk any damn woman, one too many if you ask anybody, but with *her*, it's a different story.

My heart races.

My hands get clammy.

I actually don't know what to say every time I see her, except for wanting to crucify her lack of responsibility.

That's what she does to me, makes me lose my breath, and that's never happened before.

I should have strolled up to her earlier, like the dominant guy I am, and whisked her away into this library myself. Instead, no. I made her make the move.

With my back to the door, my fingers trace the hardback spines aligning every wall of the classic oak library. *First editions.*

It's better in here.

Quieter.

No distractions with the party music drowning out to a state of nothingness, white noise trickling through the soundless walls.

London never responded to my text, but the look in her eyes said it all—*I'll be there.*

My gaze flicks to my Rolex.

It's been almost six minutes now...

Is she actually going to show?

The thoughts clouding my mind instantly fade as the library door clicks open, dousing the room with a small amount of upbeat music and endless loud chatter.

I don't need to turn around to know it's her; I just feel it.

The room returns to static white noise as the door shuts, an edge of coldness creeping inside the room because of it.

She's here.

A smirk rises on my lips and my finger halts over Austen's *Persuasion.* The ultimate story of bittersweet betrayal. *Just like her and me.*

"Tate?" London murmurs, her voice a soft sugary sound, I don't think I'll ever get sick of hearing.

I remain silent. Not giving her anything.

If she's in this library, she knows we're playing by my rules and my rules only. Because I always win.

Her heels slap against the chestnut hardwood floors, vigorous at first, before slowing to a halt right behind me.

"Tate? You said you wanted to talk..."

"You're late."

"I had to convince Nicandro not to follow me. He thinks this is sketchy."

I completely ignore the last part, his name is poison on her tongue, as I turn around to face London.

God, she's so fucking stunning.

Too bad I hate her.

"Is he your boyfriend or something?"

"*Nicandro?*" She laughs and shakes her head, but I don't miss the flush that crawls up her neck and cheeks. "We're just friends."

Just friends?

That's the biggest *cliché* I've ever heard.

Simmering my smirk, I step closer and walk around her. The

action makes London spin on her heels, her brows arched in question, and we turn so that she's the one with her back toward the bookshelf now.

Perfect.

Every step I take toward her, London takes one back until she gasps, finding herself pinned up against the bookshelf with nowhere to go.

We're merely inches apart.

Towering over her, my gaze flickers between her piercing blue eyes, wishing I could just fucking kiss all the hate out of her.

Just once.

All I want is one kiss.

"*Just friends?*" I murmur against her.

"Mmhmmm." London hums all throaty, her breath hitching. "Just friends."

My hands wrap around the wooden shelf on both sides of her head, trapping her in.

"Tell me, do you allow all of your friends to caress your thighs like that?" I sexily whisper.

London's face scrunches up in complete fury. "That is none of your business, Tate!"

"*Oh?*" I tease. "Isn't it?"

"Not at all," she snaps.

Our stare down continues until she shoves my chest, but I don't move an inch. I'm not backing down, especially when this is the first time we've had a conversation *alone* in years.

"If you have nothing else to say, I'd rather—"

"Are you fucking him?"

"*What?*" London screeches, her eyes widening in complete anarchy. Redness crawls up her cheeks like she's half embarrassed, half flustered. "Are you high? Who the hell do you think you are, asking me something like that? Where do you get the nerve? You know, what? You're *an asshole*, Tate!"

"Noted. Now answer the damn question."

"It. Is. None. Of. Your. Business." She viciously grits through her teeth in staccato.

"That's what you think. Besides, if you weren't fucking him, you would have just said so, instead of being so defensive, right?"

All London does is stare.

Okay, it may or may not be more like a glare.

But she's too beautiful to resist, even when she's pissed off at me. Even when I despise her. In fact, that turns me on even more, to the point where I can't help but brush my lips over her soft cheek, loving the way she gasps and her hot breath tickles my neck.

The further my warm lips explore her skin, the more I wilt.

I don't miss the way London's chest rises and falls against mine, or the way her heart is beating like crazy. The change in her erratic breathing is evident as her fingers almost instinctively rush up to bunch the ends of my hair, tugging me lower when I hover my lips over her neck.

I don't need to look at her to predict her deep flush; I already know it is by how warm her skin is. The way she doesn't tell me to retreat when I pepper open-mouth kisses down her neck.

My heart skips beats that it shouldn't.

I'm caving. I'm fucking caving in her closeness, her touch, her soft moans.

Dear God, she tastes like sweet strawberries and sin all wrapped in one.

Fuck, I need this.

I need more.

I need her.

In my hatred, I lose all control, erotically rolling my tongue over the place I marked my blonde devil three and a half years ago.

Sparks catch fire to my lips, sending me into a crazed trance.

London may curse my existence, but it's evident right now that it doesn't mean she can resist me.

"*Tateee*," she moans, her fingers death-gripping my waves, edging me on deeper.

My cock stirs in my slacks as my tongue grazes over each ravished kiss to her neck. I give her sensitive skin a rough nip, and that has her softly moaning my name. Over and over. Insatiably.

"*Hmmm*, thought so." I smirk darkly against her neck. "Say my name... *LonLon*."

"No."

"Don't lie to me, baby."

Out of it, London shuts her eyes in pure bliss. "*Mmhmmmm*."

Smirking, I retreat from her neck, my swollen lips roaming her left ear. "I hate you so much, London, it's why I want to leave marks on your neck again, to make you have to explain it to your parents."

This feeling is so euphoric, something so desire-filled I want to hold onto it forever. Needing more, I curl my tongue across her ear lobe, flicking it around before sucking on it slowly.

Mhmmm.

"Do you bend over for him like a good little girl and let him fuck you? Tell me. Do you let him do that?"

"Tate…" She whimpers, shaking her head softly against the bookshelf, her hair all disheveled. "I…I hate you so much right now."

"Tell me, London."

"No," she whispers in a hot daze. "No, we don't…"

"Say the word."

"We don't fuck."

My jaw tenses up.

Yeah, right.

"*Liar.*" I growl darkly against her.

Dropping a hand from the shelf, the pad of my fingers trail over the curve of her jaw, slicing down the center of her chin before lowering down her throat and neck. Goose bumps accompany my path, but her skin remains hot under my touch as my knuckles brush over her cleavage.

"I don't believe you, Héroux."

London bites her lower lip and rolls it around.

She's slipping, slipping into my world, and she can't even control it.

"You should, Tate."

Another lie.

I'm certain of it by the way the tug against my hair gets harder.

"Do you touch him?"

"Yes."

"Did you tonight before you came here?"

"Mmhmmm."

"Do you get on your knees for him?"

Swallowing hard, London blows out a jagged breath.

The air crackles between us.

"Sometimes…" she teases, and the playful-borderline-bashful smirk rising on her plump lips fucking kills me.

My cock swells just thinking about it. Thinking about her on her knees for him.

Fuuuck.

"You like sucking his cock, hmm, baby? Everybody thinks you're a fucking good girl but look at you…"

London's eyes snap open at my comment, her baby-blues darkening to the bleakest shade of the Atlantic. Her gaze flickers between my eyes and we exhale at the exact same time. "What about me?"

"You don't see it, London?" I taunt, inching my head lower so that our foreheads rest together.

The beats in my chest intensify to an unchained rhythm.

I can't breathe.

"Don't you see how fucking beautiful you are? Those eyes…*fuck.* They're like vipers."

I can't take my eyes off London's heart-shaped lips, so desperately wanting to know the sweet sin of kissing the enemy and engraving her taste on my tongue.

But I can't.

Not tonight.

No matter how deeply I'm walking the fine line of losing my self-control.

We made a promise. If I ignore her, I get to kiss her. I'm not playing that card tonight.

"You…you think I'm beautiful?" London whispers back, and for the first time tonight, her voice is stripped from the expectations. In exchange, raw emotion soothes her honeyed tone.

The same emotion I used to get from her years ago.

When she was my escape from the world.

From all the darkness.

From all the agony.

When it was just *us.*

Fuck it.

I can't do it anymore.

I need to feel her against me.

Slipping my hands to London's petite waist, I caress my thumbs over her dress, and without warning, spin her around, so she's facing the bookshelf. A loud gasp escapes London as I pin her against the bookshelf with my hips, her breasts pressing against the spines of the entire collection of Ernest Hemmingway first editions.

Her ass grinds back, unintentionally rubbing against my erection that's getting harder by the second, with just how much she fucking turns me on.

Clenching my stubbled jaw twice, I grip London's wrists and bind them together with my left hand. That's when I slam them above her head, restraining her completely.

My enemy's strawberry and vanilla scent is all I smell as I dive my face into her hair and seductively rasp, "Let's try that again, shall we? Did you get on your knees and suck his cock?"

"No."

"Have you ever wanted to?"

"Yes," she breathes out without hesitation. "A lot of times."

Jesus Christ, that's so hot.

"Do you let Nicandro fuck you?"

"No."

"*Liar.*" I growl.

Losing control, I recklessly spank her peachy ass. Hard. It has her gasping softly in pleasure. A pleasure I feed into. It's why I spank her again and again, until she's wriggling and panting, until I'm satisfied with just how crimson her ass must be under that skin-tight dress. I piston my hips into her, loving the way she softly rubs herself on me like she can't control her body either.

"I'm not going to ask again, London, did you—"

She begins nodding before I can even finish.

Yes.

They fuck.

My heart feels as if it's been torched.

I suck in a breath, my mind going crazy. "What happened to waiting on your firsts?"

"I did," London breathes, inferno-red coating her cheeks, "and it felt right with him."

It. Felt. Right.

"Do you let him touch you?"

Another soft moan escapes her lips, when I brush my lips over her shoulder, blowing out hot air before pressing a lingering kiss against it.

"Tate..."

"Answer the question, London."

"Yes."

"Are you're still honestly admitting you're *just friends* with Nicandro?"

London's cheek presses against the bookshelf as she glances over at me with a glimmer of honesty in her eyes. Softly biting her lower lip, she nods, just as my grip on her wrists tighten. "We're kind of friends…with benefits, but we're not exclusive. It's open, as long as we tell each other."

"He's bi, so that means he can fuck other men and women based on your agreement?"

Her reddened cheeks deepen. "Oh my god, Tate!"

"Well, can he?"

"Yes, he can."

"And can you too? Let other men fuck you, I mean?"

"I guess so, yeah."

I guess so. Does that mean she hasn't fucked anybody else yet?

"How long has this been going on?"

"Since last summer."

Months.

"Has anybody else touched you during that tim—"

Her blue-eyed gaze widens. "Tate!"

"*Tell. Me.*" I growl, inhaling a sharp breath spiked in lust.

London glances back and forth between my eyes. "No, just Nicandro."

Fuck.

I believe her.

I should have never listened to Levi. Now I want to know everything. Every. Single. Thing.

Anger coaxes my breaths, making me see red as I push her limits, one more time.

"Do you cum for him?"

That has her eyes widening in shock, as if the rest of our conversation was nothing compared to this question.

"You don't need to know!" London hisses in some sort of rebellion, but lust remains glazed in her stare. A havoc lust I'm sure is just as vivid in mine. "It has nothing to do with you, Tate."

"As if the rest of the questions have," I say huskily. "You're caving, baby. Admit it. You're caving, just like you do for Nicandro, hmm? I wanna know if you cum for him, London…huh?"

Smirking, I wrap her blonde ponytail around my fist and roughly tug on it, so she has no choice but to look up at me.

London's lips part to nothingness.

My smirk deepens. *Hmm…*

And then…

"Yes, always," rolls off her tongue, coated in ecstasy.

Bullshit.

London doesn't need to admit it. She's caving. Falling so fucking fast in front of me.

Jealously crawls up my veins and she isn't even mine.

The hell with Nicandro.

Breathing heavily, London's all flustered and worked up.

"*Fuuuck*, London," I sexily murmur in her ear. "Nicandro could never make you cum like I could. I'll have you drowning in heaven, baby. Remember that. In fucking heaven. *God*, do your parents know their *perfect girl* is actually a pretty, little fucking slut? It's fucked up, London, you can't have both."

One second.

Two seconds.

Three seconds.

London's jaw drops and all of the built-up sexual tension melts away as her eyes glass.

"You…you think I'm a…"

Tears brew at the edge of her eyes, destined to fall if she blinks. She keeps them in though, keeping strong, never blinking as she tugs her wrists, trying to shimmy away from me.

Oh.

My lips part to nothingness, tension fueling my body at the hurt written all over her face.

"A *slut*?" London's lips tremble at the word. "You think I'm a freaking *slut*?"

Shit.

Gulping down thickly, I shake my head. "No, that's not what I meant at all. I—"

"Oh my god, what do you mean it's *not what you meant*? Those were *your exact words, Tate*!" she grits in anger. "LET GO OF ME!"

London's body begins to tremble the second I release her. I take a few steps back, giving her space. Swallowing hard, she rubs on her wrists that tinge a soft hue of red where I held her.

Oh fuck.

I can't take my eyes off it, not knowing I was holding her that hard. I didn't mean the words that I said to her.

I really fucking didn't, and seeing how affected she's become by it makes me feel a kind of guilt I've never felt before.

"Fuck." I rake a hand through my tousled hair, hating the toxicity lacing the space between us. I can't even look at her. "I didn't mean what I said. I just think you're better than that."

"Better than what?" she snaps.

"Sleeping with a guy who can never give you what you need!"

"You can't even look me in the eye and say it, can you?"

"I…"

"You *what*? Huh? Who the hell do you think you are judging me like that? Judging me when you don't even know me!"

My eyes widen in pure carnage.

"I *know you*, London Héroux!" I growl.

"Not anymore, you don't!" she shouts, shoving my chest. "Oh, I hate you so much, Tate! I *hate* you. All you are is a *bully*. It's *my* life. *My* body. I can sleep with whoever I like, just like you can."

"I—"

"It's *Nicandro*. I trust him. I adore him. He's the only one keeping me afloat. Without him and Heather, I would be drowning in my own freaking messed-up head. So where do you get the right to question me on that? WHO THE HELL DO YOU THINK YOU ARE, TATE MEADOWS?"

London continues glaring at me, panting, her chest heaving. She's so worked up, her cheeks are the darkest shade of scarlet I've ever seen, potent with anger. Because of me.

I have no words.

None.

Because no words can console her for the things I've said. I let my jealousy take over. Jealousy I shouldn't have even had for her to begin with. But it won. *Of course it did.* This must be what addiction feels like—to crave something you know is lethal but can't resist.

"I…I just want to protect yo—" My words are cut short by the sudden stinging throb across my right cheek. I feel the slap before I hear its loud echo throughout the library.

"*PROTECT ME*?" London angrily screeches. "Look at me when I'm talking to you!"

I regret looking down the second I witness tears brimming her eyes. But they never fall.

Reaching up to cup my slapped cheek, it doesn't matter how many times I attempt to swallow the lump in my throat, it reforms. It only intensifies, tearing me apart piece by piece.

Suffocating.

It feels as if I'm suffocating, watching London break in front of me.

I've pushed her buttons.

Hit her where it hurts.

And as much as I can understand her hurt, why can't she see that she deserves so much better than non-exclusive fucks from her *friend*, Nicandro?

"Do you think it's easy? Falling for guy after guy, only to get my heart broken because all they see is one thing? And I'm not talking about Nicandro; he's a good guy. I'm talking about the rest. The other seniors. Other guys. The ones *exactly* like you. You seduce me and then call me a slut? What the hell is wrong with you?!"

"Jesus Christ, London, that's not what I meant. Nicandro…he isn't good for you."

"Oh my god, you're even more delusional than I thought!" London scrunches her nose up. "You're missing the whole point, Tate!" she roars, getting all up in my face. "You just don't get it, do you? My family is so right about the Meadows. Egotistical bullies who only think about themselves!"

Seriously?

"*Egotistical*? Really? Is that all you've got?" I scoff, shaking my head with a mocking smirk. "Where the hell do you get the audacity? You have no idea who my family really is, London, who *I* really am."

"How about *me*?" She jabs at her chest. "Do you really think you know who *I am*?"

"Never said I did."

"Then keep your opinions to your freaking self."

"You can't even swear, can you? Too pure for that shit, huh?"

London lets out a frustrated scream and storms past me, b-lining through the library for the door. The second her hand wraps around the crystal door handle, she spins around and flashes her middle finger at me.

"Fuck. You. Tate. Meadows."

"Classy," I scoff before changing my tune. "Look, seriously, I didn't think what I said would hurt you so mu—"

"Then that's even worse because it just shows how unaware you are about human decency and lack of empathy. What would beloved Mr. and Mrs. Meadows say about that? *Oh*, wait, that's right, it seems your mom is more interested in doing a disappearing act than being there for you!"

Time stops.

My heart drops and everything slows.

What the fuck?

My stomach churns at London's words. Taking three strides until we're face to face, I stare down at her, fuming with flared nostrils, while her glare feels like razors zooming through me.

"Don't you fucking dare go there, Héroux," I grit through my teeth, meaning every single word. "Talking about my mother is off limits. Do you *understand*? In the world we live in, rumors like that will kill my family, you know that. Don't you dare say that again. *Ever*."

"Or *what*? What are you going to do about it?"

Moments pass.

Grinding my teeth, the cords in my neck tighten. "Nothing."

"Exactly." Her eyes narrow until they form small slits of rage. "*Nothing*. I hate you so freaking much, Tate Meadows, don't you dare ever speak to me again. Understand, asshole?"

"Ditto, baby," I hiss.

And then, London stalks off, strutting out of the library and slamming the door shut behind her like my heart isn't bleeding out dark shades of her all over.

It's on.

It's so fucking on, Héroux.

Chapter
TWENTY-FIVE

London

I never went on *Enticed* last night after Tate's party. I couldn't. I didn't have it in me. Not after what he called me. Perhaps the word wouldn't have cut so deeply if it wasn't so loaded with such heartache and trauma for me…*but it is.*

I swear to God, Nicandro was going to murder Tate after he coaxed me to tell him what happened when I returned to him. Somehow, I managed to calm him down and get him to take me home.

My parents were still out on a business dinner when I crashed into my bed and stayed the entire night tossing and turning, pearl-sized tears cascading down my cheeks. Tate Meadow sized tears that brought an ache throughout my body I never felt before.

Numb.

I feel completely numb.

Because I could never despise somebody more than him right now.

He doesn't know how badly his words cut me. How much they hurt. Made me bleed.

I'm not the girl he perceives me to be. In fact, at times, I don't even know myself. Some call it, borderline split personality. I call it brushing the silvery line between angelic clouds and the heat of hell.

The gray zone.

The in between.

The only place I know life to truly exist.

If my life were a song, it'd be "Lithium" by Nirvana. Desire. Ache. The tenderness of lonely places…*it's the definition of me*. It's *also* the definition of the puffy sleepless blue-eyed madness I'm staring back at in Glorsin St. Claire's bathroom mirror.

It's me.

Me, myself, and I.

Me—London Héroux—with a touch of the 2 p.m. Friday craze.

This isn't like me. *At all*. I'm the girl with the perfectly painted pink nails, preppy fashion attire and silk bows strangling my high ponytail. The girl with the cherry red lips, who fantasizes about kissing men in their late thirties, but has never partaken in a game of truth or dare.

Well, a chicken to every dare.

Not a touch of liquor on my tongue, yet the darkened devil inside is all I crave. I'm the good girl who yearns for a modern-day Marlon Brando to sweep me off my feet, well, if status quo wasn't embedded in my blood from day one.

Thanks for that Mommy and Daddy Dearest. Not.

The fact that I can still smell Tate's lingering, musky cologne and the warmth of his lips roaming my skin brings a flutter to my heart I despise. He shouldn't affect me this way. Entice me. Make me fantasize and want him to heal the sins of my past.

Help. I'm stuck in the Tate Meadows' effect.

"Ohmigod!" Heather's gaze flickers to mine through the bathroom mirror as she sweeps a touch of rosy gloss on her plump lips. "How did I miss this last night?" she screeches with a dropped jaw. "He called you a fucking *slut*?"

"Mmhmmm. Apparently, I have the morals of a manwhore. We're talking about the woman who literally has only fooled around with one man in her whole life, when the average at this school is—"

"All the dicks in senior year?"

"Exactly."

It's a cliché.

I know.

A hidden scandal here in the elitist private high school on the Upper West Side. That's just the thing about our sweet Glorsin St. Claire's, we expect the unexpected with students whose only fuel is wealth, ego, and drunken lullabies mixed with head-pounding regrets. Because that's exactly what happens here.

I didn't even want to go to Tate's party last night. I knew something like this would happen and ignite more heat to the fire between him and me.

Truth be told, I'd rather get lost in a Brontë classic at home, not at a house party or a Friday night members' only party hosted by faceless dollar signs, sponsored by fake IDs, sweet-talking suits, and spontaneous thrills. But here in Manhattan, it isn't a choice; it's a requirement. And with parents like mine—who worry more about chasing money, reputation and false facades than having a family meal—it's inevitable.

"Kill me now." I sigh. "I swear Tate's sole purpose is to piss me off."

Heather rolls her eyes, almost into the back of her brain. "Jesus Christ, I want to sucker-punch him in the balls."

"I give you full permission to do whatever you like to him, please and thank you." Leaning against the tiled wall, chilly coldness seeps across my shoulders through my cotton blouse—which I always have neatly tucked into the dark emerald and black plaid uniform skirt.

Other girls, like Heather, have cut the bottoms of their blouses off and turned them into cropped-top numbers to show a little more skin and ignore the various detentions they've gotten because of it. But not me.

Oh no.

Of course not.

My mom would slaughter me if I didn't wear the perfect uniform skirt with the perfect blouse, the perfect Glorsin green and black diagonally-striped tie, the perfect black blazer with the thin emerald trim lining the edges of the collar, sleeves, and breast pocket.

And *oh*, let's not forget about Glorsin's emblem handstitched on that breast pocket like a stamp of honor. Once, at my other school, I forgot to re-pin various badges like *social justice* and *reader group leader* on my blazer after I had gotten it dry-cleaned, and my parents didn't talk to me for like two days straight because of it.

Appearances, dear.

Don't let us down for a second, dear.

Put on those badges and show everybody what you're made of, dear.

I'll tell you what I'm made of…

50% early morning caffeine from Starbucks.

25% constant schoolwork to perfection and all-nighters to maintain my predictable A+ grades.

20% Lana Del Rey's playlist.

3% the color pink.

And get ready for it…2% disappointment.

Actually, perhaps the latter is part of that 50%.

Too bad my parents don't know about how I roll the hem of my skirt up to match the rest of my posse's mid-thigh Marilyn moment. *Or* about how I shove my blazer in my locker any second it isn't required to '*showcase a professional front to other schools and set an example to the other grades.*'

A loud snap breaks me out of my trance. Heather is standing directly in front of me, her brows pinched together as she snaps her fingers in front of my face for a second time. "London? Babe?"

"Huh?" I gasp, feeling as if I've just taken my first deep breath after being underwater.

"Everything okay? You were just staring at me, and fucking zoned-out like you were on some molly or something."

"Oh," I clear my throat, apologizing with a small smile she always deems forgivable, "sorry, my mind's just…everywhere as of late."

"Because of Tate?"

"Exactly. Tate literally looked me in the eye and told me Nicandro is no good for me. Did you hear that? *No good.* He doesn't even know him! I swear to God I wanted to tell him so many things last night, I just…I just didn't know where to start."

Heather frowns and gestures to me with her gloss. "All this built-up tension inside you, it has an outlet, you know…"

I read her mind instantly. "*Enticed.* I know. I swear this has been the worst timing."

Heather smiles sympathetically and rubs her lips together. "So, what's the game plan with Mr. Tate Fucker?"

"Ignore and conquer."

"You seriously think it's going to work?"

I damn well pray it does.

A knot rises up my throat at the severity of things.

It has to.

"It did all throughout English Literature." I shrug, as if it's that simple. "I have one period to go with him, what could possibly go wrong?"

Heather arches her brows in an '*everything could go wrong*' kind of way.

God help me.

Because I know precisely how right she is.

My masterplan to ignore Tate Meadows backfires the second he slips into the seat beside me in media class. He could have chosen any seat, but no, the gorgeous villain, with brazen blue eyes, just has to take the seat right next to me.

I despise his presence. Detest his aura. Feel sick to my stomach that his lingering sandalwood scent makes me feel until it hurts.

Scattered memories of last night resurface and the words he said.

Slut. Slut. Slut.

That's all my mind can retain. No matter how many times he apologized for it last night, the word still slipped past his lips, causing a crater-sized hole in my chest.

Slut.

Anxiety suffocates my every breath.

I squeeze my grip around my water bottle, feeling Tate's hot gaze burn the side of my head.

Slut.

A four-letter word with the ability to kill.

I'm not looking at him. I can't.

I don't want to talk to him or hear anything he has to say. At all.

I'm done with him.

So done.

I'm half grateful it's the second to last period and our media teacher is letting us watch the 1950's classic, *All About Eve*. It's our film study this semester, and while I usually enjoy analyzing everything there is about the cinematography from the director's intentions, elements, to dialogue intentions, it's an impossible task with Tate's close proximity.

Our media teacher flicks off the lights and students at the back draw the shades. Before I know it, *All About Eve's* beginning film credits are rolling.

Bette Davis Eyes.

Iconic Marilyn.

Crazed eighteen-year-old staring at the projected film with the most popular preppy American jock in twelfth grade on my left, wishing I was anywhere but here.

I feel like we're some fucked-up married couple, watching this film, and one of us just filed for divorce, yet we're forced to attend our child's school performance together. Every so often, a sharp, loud sigh escapes him. It's not the black and white he's trying to break through, it's me.

It's him.

It's us.

God, I hate that word relating to everything that we are—us.

Tate has his arms crossed over his chest, his toned bicep brushing against mine with no worries in the world. Nerves that have bundled at the bottom of my stomach since his party resurface; in fact, they never left as they burn a hole all the way up to my heart.

It poisons me and I wish it would just stop. I've always had some doubt when it comes to my family's rivalry with the Meadows, but last night confirmed all my parents' claims to be true. The Meadows don't give a shit about *who* they're hurting or *how deep* they hurt people, just as long as they're *hurting* someone. Period.

"For the record," Tate murmurs, his sexy voice a low rasp I love to hate as he leans over, "I don't think you're a slut. I didn't mean the words I said last night. At all. I was just…I'm an idiot, I really fucking am."

Genuine.

He sounds so damn genuine.

God, why?

Keeping my eyes on the screen, my breaths strangle me as his stare burns deeper.

"London?"

Silence laces the space between us.

I bite the inside of my cheek and scribble down a cinematographer technique in my workbook.

Chiaroscuro elements enhance the plot set up.

Tate exhales. "Fine, ignore me. I don't give a fuck. I just wanted to tell you how I feel."

The ache in my chest expands, the one that reaches out for any sense of reality to bring me back to life.

Antidotes.

I've been living life for the past three years based on antidotes. Some love drugs and liquor, but I prefer anything pink, dance, and playing Lana Del Rey limited edition vinyl a little too loud. It's the real reason I need *Enticed*. Another outlet to escape. One where I can be myself without any night terrors.

I hate the lump that forms in my throat.

The tension.

The fact that one damn word has to bring up so many things for me.

"There is so much in my life you don't know about, Tate," I whisper hoarsely, shutting my eyes. "Stories that haven't gotten out. That never will. That *word* hurt me, so much more than you think. Nicandro makes me forget. Without him…"

"Without him, what?"

Shit.

I re-open my eyes to a blurry gaze, and it kills me I can't be strong. Especially in front of Tate. Tipping my head back, I bite the tip of my tongue and pray to God the tears roll back inside my eyes.

The lump in my throat intensifies. "Without him, I have nothing."

"Thought Heather was your friend too."

"It's not the same."

Moments pass before his silence has me turning his way. Tate's deep gaze bores into mine, and I'm holding onto every breath as his eyes flicker to my lips for a fraction of a second.

There's no smirk.

No sly smile.

No sarcasm.

Time slows between us, and it just becomes him and me. I hate the way I want to lose myself in a sea of him because of the way he's looking at me. So tenderly, with so much intrigue. Like our defenses have dropped and it's just a Meadows looking at a Héroux with no prejudices.

Just two broken shadows wanting to be set free.

"You know what I think?" Tate whispers softly, inching in closer, his scent all I breathe.

We don't get caught by our teacher talking when we should be concentrating on the film.

"What may that be?"

His heated eyes linger on me.

The air crackles between us, and then…

"I think you're afraid to be lonely."

Pang.

Right in my chest.

Beat after beat after beat.

It's as if Tate's pulled a trigger that ricochets deep into my heart of hearts. Making me see nothing but crimson-coated truth. A truth my pride is too reserved to admit, but my soul struggles to breathe through.

Lonely.

It's exactly what I am.

Who I am.

Tate's hypnotic stare doesn't do anything to subdue the pain. It's as if he knows. Knows he's tapping into those darker parts of me I've fought so long to hide from the world. It's what I despise about him most. The fact that he notices things others don't…

My flaws.

My weaknesses.

My repercussions of living a life with the little voice in my head driving me insane.

I swallow thickly. "I could say the same for you."

Are you lonely too, Tate Meadows?

Tate's gaze darkens, little clouds taking over, as his eyes move to the front of the classroom.

He's no longer a little boy; he's a man.

I don't miss the way he clenches his jaw numerous times. His nostrils flare, as if I've hit a place only flaws exist. He remains like this, staring at the movie, while the gorgeous dark whiskers of his stubble stir at his tense movement.

All until a soft chuckle rumbles up his throat, a smirk consoling the shadows of Tate's ego, as he says, "I'm not lonely, LonLon. If that's what you think…"

LonLon.

God, kill me.

"I'll believe you once you look me in the eyes and finish that sentence."

His jaw tenses as if he's physically incapable of glancing my way. It feels as though a lifetime passes before those blue-eyed wonderlands return to me for zero-point-two seconds as he mumbles, "not lonely, at all."

I arch a suspicious brow and he simultaneously arches one back with an expression that says, '*see, I just proved it,*' before glancing away.

Hmm.

Don't believe you.

You didn't convince me.

"Then say it while looking in my eyes for at least five seconds," I add. "Like you mean it."

"What's that supposed to prove?"

"*Everything.*"

Tate looks my way and a sense of calm flows through me. "I'm not…I'm…"

Clearing his throat, he curls his fists together and drops his head low.

Shoulders heavy, he gulps down and takes a deep, shaky breath as if I'm telling him to change himself. Emotion clouds his eyes; shadows of doubt as he whispers, "London, I'm not…"

"Five."

"I'm not…"

"Four."

"I'm not lone…"

"Three."

"Fuck," he curses under his breath, raking a hand through his dark, sexily-tousled hair and his eyes squeeze shut in chaos. "Don't make me do this…"

"Two and a half."

Silence.

"Tw—"

Before I can even finish, Tate's chair loudly scrapes back against the glossy floor. A whiff of his addictive cologne is all I get before I realize what's happening.

Tate storms out of his seat, his face tense as he brushes past me and all the other desks. He strides out of the classroom in such an uproar—without ever looking back—that the teacher pauses the film and begins yelling at him to come back.

But he doesn't.

He doesn't ever turn back.

All that's left is space.

Empty space.

My entire body freezes up as I'm left staring at the seat Tate was in mere moments ago. Now, only the lingering scent of his musky cologne remains, and the emptiness of a thousand lonely hearts.

And it tells me everything I need to know…

Lonely.

He's lonely too.

Just like me.

Chapter
TWENTY-SIX

London

I swear to god, these school bathrooms are my second home.

As I sweep a touch of rosy gloss on my plump lips, my gaze flickers to Maddie Meadows, who strides into the bathroom as if she owns the place. Gosh, she's the last person I want to see today.

Tate's stepsister.

She's got a stick so far up her ass to even realize her boyfriend is fucking our social studies teacher, and I literally just moved to this school less than three weeks ago. How do I know? I walked in on them last week after school, fucking right there on the teacher's desk. They didn't even notice me. Not even when I almost tripped on my untied white Doc Martens as I scrambled out. All I wanted was to ask her a question for our upcoming test, but I got a lot more than I intended.

Which leads me to Maddie Meadows.

Obnoxious prude, self-proclaimed ice queen and her iconic purple eyeshadow.

Tate wasn't lying that night years ago when he used 'purple' to describe his stepsister.

I'm not surprised at the clusterfuck eye roll Maddie gives me as she pulls out her red lipstick from her bra and swipes it over her already perfectly painted lips.

My phone vibrates in the pocket of my plaid uniform skirt and I'm quick to pull it out. Anything to avoid her hazel-eyed deadpan.

NICANDRO: Where the hell are you, Lon? You disappeared off the face of the earth and I want to get out of this place. We were going to hang out at my house, remember? Send an SOS or something.

All I can say is, thank god for free last periods.

LONDON: Girl's bathroom by my locker. Cornered by the ice queen herself…give me a second.

NICANDRO: God help us all. Try not to melt her down to complete nothingness.

Maddie dramatically clears her throat, and it forces me to look at her.

Her eyes are on me through the mirror as she sneers, "Heather abandons you for one second and you become a deer in headlights. How does it feel to be a loner, bitch?"

The fake smile rushing to my lips is ready to explode any second now.

I tuck my phone away.

Bitch?

Did she just call me 'bitch'?

Heart racing, I attempt to remember all the steps in that damn Destress Podcast I listened to last night. *How did it go, again? Breathe, set an intention…downward dog?*

Crap, I don't know.

"Uh, *hello*," Maddie snaps, spinning around to give me a twisted look. "I'm talking to you."

"Oh."

Maddie strides over to me until my back is pressed against the glossy-tiled wall, cornering me in.

Her eyes flicker between mine. "I've been watching you, *Little Miss Perfect*, do you have a thing for my brother? Because if you do, bitch, I will come for you. You don't deserve him."

My heart drops.

What?

Scoffing, I arch a brow. "Seriously. Is that a threat, Maddie?"

"I don't know, is it?" She taunts, smirking, all while snapping her vibrant lilac fake nails together. "Because I notice you stare at Tate an awful lot. So, either you want him, or you're jealous that you could never be his because all you are is pathetic, London Héroux."

My heart plummets to the ground.

All you are is pathetic, London Héroux.

Pathetic.

Maddie's hitting a nerve, and she knows it.

Heat rushes through my veins because her devilish smirk is an attorney's goldmine of proof. She's been at my throat forever, for the obvious reason. I don't know if Tate told his sister about our history, but it doesn't matter, she hates me enough regardless.

Our little stare-off lasts a thousand years, leaving me to swallow my pride as soon as it appears. Red rims of fire circle her hazel gaze, and I wonder if it's because her thick-as-heck mascara is giving her an allergic reaction or if it's the aftereffects of the coke she's probably snorting behind closed doors, thanks to Tate's best friend, Levi.

All I know is I'm making a B-line to the door and heading out of here ASAP. I promised Nicandro I'd drive him home so that we can finish up our art project together.

So, I step to the right of Maddie, but she mirrors me.

I step to the left.

She mirrors me again, locking me into the corner of the bathroom, like we're in a sitcom.

Dear God…

"Maddie, could you please move out of the way?"

She simply places a hand to her hip *and continues glaring.*

All the other girls in the bathroom are either on their phones to escape last period or gossiping about god knows what. But I'm convinced one of them is filming this entire thing.

Typical.

"Maddie," I groan, letting out a mental scream when I go to step forward, but she shoves me back against the tiled wall. "Please just move out of the way, okay?"

The girls in the bathroom behind Maddie burst out laughing, all filming us now.

"You've got something to say, huh?" I perk up my brows, waiting for her smirk to drop. "Say it."

Maddie shrugs, towering over me in those high pumps she has on. I don't know how she gets away with it. "You wouldn't know how to keep Tate even if you wanted to. My brother's probably like a new, shiny toy to you, too bad you're inexperienced and a little over the top..."

"Excuse me!"

"You heard me, London. You're eyeing the most popular guy in school, while completely forgetting my stepfather could crush yours with his thumb. I'm sure Sterling Héroux would *love* to hear that *daughter dearest* has a crush on *the* Tate Meadows," Maddie spits, crossing her arms over her chest, flashing her cleavage. "So tell me, how does it feel to be a *desperado*?"

"*Desperado*?" I almost laugh. "Please, honey, get the facts straight before you come at me."

"I'm not coming at you, you fucking bitch. Learn to *listen!*"

"Just because we're not sitting down on mint green leather seats on *Jerry Springer*, doesn't mean you're not coming after me."

Maddie brows knit up. "Jerry, who?"

Dear God, help me.

The half a dozen girls behind Maddie who are recording let out a chorus of '*oooh's*' when I take a step forward and shove the ice queen out of the way, creating distance between us. Her overkill rosy perfume is still all I breathe, but at least it isn't cutting off my oxygen supply like it was before.

"You want to act dumb? Okay, let's act dumb," I say, cocking my head to the side with a sly smirk. "If I'm so pathetic for *eyeing your brother*, which I didn't...then why did I kiss him last Saturday night at the party *he* hosted?"

Ladies and gentlemen, to get the facts straight, I'm talking straight out of my ass. Last Saturday night when Tate cornered me in his grand library, I came closer to slapping his face, not kissing him. But right now, the proof isn't in the details.

Especially not as the damn *paparazzi* step closer with shocked gasps.

Blotches of redness crawl up Maddie's neck and her reaction is everything I expected it to be. Shocked wide eyes. Pouted duck lips.

Scrunched nose. Slide across a filter and she's perfect to post a picture with the caption of what *not* to aspire to be when you're a senior in high school.

The golden-cased lipstick slips from her grip, slamming against the charcoal-tiled floor before rolling behind the vanity.

She's mortified, and within seconds, her fake nail is being pointed right in my face.

"No, he fucking didn't," Maddie snaps, scoffing to herself. "My brother didn't kiss you."

"Believe what you want to believe, but the truth is—"

"Have you even been kissed before? Fucked? I know Tate, he wouldn't kiss a virgin."

Is this girl serious?

Jaw dropped, my mouth dries up in seconds, betraying me as no words escape.

"Yeah, didn't think so." Maddie smirks all smugly. "Besides, I saw some ditsy redhead stumble out of his room on Sunday morning. So, even if he did kiss you…" A wicked smirk rises as she murmurs, "Clearly, you didn't *satisfy* him."

Blood boils my veins.

Ouch.

Before I know it, the words are out. "Oh, so just like you're not satisfying your boyfriend, hmm? Is that why I caught him plowing his cock into somebody else?"

Paparazzi goes wild with squeals that quickly turn into unsynchronized screeches when, out of nowhere, Maddie grips my school tie and slams me against the tiled wall once more. This time she doesn't stop at that, and I feel the sting before I even hear the erratic slap to my cheek.

My vision blurs, and my first reaction is to shove her blazer-covered shoulders back. Wrong move, apparently, because it turns into a full-blown cat fight. Shouts and screams escape us both as we tug and pull at each other. The damn psycho grips my high ponytail and begins roughly tugging me down, my head feeling like it's going to explode with the amount of tension with each pull.

It's triggering.

So fucking triggering.

Because all it does is remind me of my father's attacks.

Jesus Christ. *This girl wants to kill me.*

My nails claw into her wrist, desperate for her to let go before she ends up with a chunk of my hair as some type of trophy.

"What the hell did you say, bitch?" Maddie screams, tugging my hair harder.

Tears glaze my eyes. "I meant what I said!"

"I'm going to fucking kill you! He would *never* do that to me!" Maddie screams, going for my tie with her other hand, and in the midst of the commotion, she aggressively pulls at my blouse.

The buttons go flying high, slapping against every single object in the room. My heart falls to my stomach as I attempt to get her to let go of my hair to no avail. Maddie doesn't play fair. She played dirty all her life and it's obvious by the way she practically rips my blouse to shreds with those devil nails of hers.

I can't stop screaming for her to get off me, her nails digging into my skin, destined to leave marks. My overspilled cleavage and lacy white bra are on full display as the girls step closer with their phones, filming every single second of Maddie Meadows overpowering my every move.

My fingers dig into her wrist again, but it does nothing to her, so instead, I decide two can play the game and grip a bunch of her perfectly curled brunette locks and pull.

Nice-girl-London definitely left the building.

I blink away my blurry eyes, letting the tears roll down my cheeks and hating that I can't be stronger than this. We're like screaming cats on the brink of utter destruction as her grip on my ponytail has me tugging on hers even harder, until profanities are the only thing she's saying.

I hear the bathroom door slam open, but it all becomes a blur.

"What the hell is wrong with you?" I squeal, when Maddie manages to rip open the front of my bra. I quickly let go of her with a gasp and cover my tits before this video goes viral and I get expelled. "Oh my God, Maddie! You asshole!"

Her taunting laugh is all I hear as my life flashes before my eyes. I swear to God, I'm convinced I'm going to die from humiliation right here in the girl's bathroom, *and I haven't even graduated yet!*

Oh. My. God.

What a way to go. I haven't even lived yet.

It's over.

It's all over.

"The fuck is going on in here?" Nicandro's raspy shout is my sweet serenity, and within seconds, big warm arms wrap around my waist from behind. One of his hands reaches and crumbles Maddie's grip, his knuckles tensing around her until she groans, and she finally lets go of my hair.

Oh, thank God.

Stumbling back into Nicandro's chest, pants escape me as he tugs me closer to him. His musky cologne puts my body at ease, his big hands rushing up to help me fully cover my tits.

This is so embarrassing.

I catch a glimpse of him in the bathroom mirror and the clenching of his perfectly stubbled jaw has the other girls scrambling out of the bathroom, one by one, except for the Ice Queen herself. She's catching her breath, not even looking like she was in a cat fight less than four seconds ago.

Unlike me...

My silky blonde ponytail is now a bird's nest, the ends all frizzed up and fluffy. Mascara-stained tears stream down my cheeks like I'm rocking the glam punk look of the '80s, and there are vicious red blotches all over me.

My bra is long gone, slipped halfway down my taut waist, straps broken, and underwire snapped. Then, there's my blouse hanging on by a damn thread, all the sides and shoulders torn up.

Christ.

Who the hell is this girl? Hulk?

Nicandro's devilish chocolate brown eyes meet mine in the mirror, a sympathetic smirk curving its way up his lips as he lowers them to my ear and murmurs, "What happened to not melting the ice queen, hmm?"

Smartass.

Before I can reply, (*or really, kick him in the ass*) Nicandro's head cranes toward Maddie and the disgust crawling up his face is something else. He's pissed—so pissed. And he didn't even see the full altercation.

"Touch London again and I will personally drag your ass to the principal's office. I don't give a fuck who you are, Ice Queen."

"What did you just call me?" Maddie spits, eyes wide in challenge.

But I know my Nicandro. He isn't intimidated. At six-foot-three, he's the definition of trouble. Gorgeously-carved high cheekbones, lean yet muscular, tattooed arms that have gotten him close to being him expelled. We've been friends ever since he saved my ass at Victor LéVont's New Year's Eve party three years ago. Then, six months ago, things between us got…*interesting.*

"Oh, didn't hear me? Huh?" Nicandro taunts, arching a brow. "Come closer, Mads, I'll tell you."

"My brother will beat your ass for saying this shit!"

"*Ohhh,* is the baby getting defensive?" he mocks.

Giving us a dirty look, Maddie runs her fingers through her hair and brushes away some blonde hairs from her blazer before passing us with a tense jaw. *RIP to some of my hair.*

Her hazel-eyed orbits stare right into mine.

"*You,*" Maddie grits, grinding her perfect teeth together, "I'm not finished with *you.*"

Perhaps it's the fact that Nicandro's here, or I'm just sick of her bullshit, but I slip my hands from underneath Nicandro's, feeling my nipples pebble hard under his touch, and do my best to ignore it as I curl up my fists Like I'm part of Sugar Ray Robinson's crew. "Try me."

"Don't even think about it," Nicandro says from behind me when she takes a step toward me.

Maddie lets out a strangled huff, her nose and lips screwing up in evident frustration.

My eye catches the shiny tube of lipstick under the vanity. "Oh, don't forget your lipstick."

Without even turning back, Maddie flips me off, and I return the favor before she rolls her eyes and storms out of the bathroom.

That's when my heart finally settles down to a normal speed, and for the first time in minutes, I feel like I can breathe again. It's only him and me now. *Nobody else.* Just me and the guy who just saved me from my misery.

Moments pass before Nicandro softly whispers, "Wanna talk about it?"

"Not really."

Nicandro holds me tighter in the solace of his arms, resting his chin on my head. "You okay though, Lonny?"

I meet his warm gaze in the mirror.

"Yeah, I'll be okay. I'm just a little shaken, that's all." I smile softly. "Thank you for coming in. I swear I was going to die."

"You've got to learn to get some fight in you, girl."

My heart sinks because there's so much he doesn't know. So much I've kept hidden to save myself. So much my father has done to me that I need to lie about, so I can keep on breathing.

"If you don't get yourself in those situations, you don't need self-defense."

Nicandro smirks, his dimples carving into his cheeks. "And how's that going for you, Miss Héroux?"

Leaning my head further into his chest, I shake my head with a naughty grin. "Not too well."

"Hmmm, I bet it hasn't." Nicandro chuckles lazily. His eyes flicker to his hands covering my tits and he molds them softly. "Well, fuck, *hello*. You're fuckin' perfect, London, like always."

"Shut up! Stop squeezing my boobs, Nic!" I laugh, until realization crosses my mind and that laugh turns into a full-blown groan. "Oh my god! The *video*! The girls were filming! Holy shit, my life is so over if this video gets out. My parents will *kill me*. The school will crucify me."

Nicandro rolls his eyes, that's how carefree and easy-going my friend is. "They won't."

"They will!" I gasp, my eyes widen the size of planets as I turn around in his hold, not caring my hard nipples are brushing over his gray sports hoodie, which perfectly stretches over his broad shoulders. "They're going to make an example out of me, Nicandro! I'll never get the respect I've been working my ass off for. My tits are going to be all over the school!"

"Okay, first off, relax—"

"No, no I can't relax." I cringe, just thinking about the dirty looks students will give me down the hallways.

I can just see it now...

Oh my god, did you see that weak bitch?

She couldn't fight to save her life, how pathetic!

But did you see London Héroux's tits in that cat fight?

A shiver runs down my spine.

Tate pops up in my mind...He's going to see it too.

AHHHHHHHHHHHHHHH!

"London, girl, calm down."

"But…but, but…"

"*But…but, but.*" Nicandro mocks with a wink and a kiss to my forehead when I go to shove him. "Calm down, Lon. Nothing's gonna happen, this happens all the time. I promise. Okay?"

I trust him.

I trust him with my freaking life.

If only he knew that he's the only one keeping me sane…

Warmth rippling through me, a smile traces my lips as his hold tightens. "Okay, idiot."

There's nothing more that screams Nicandro than illegal joints, end-less leather, and Nirvana's "Smells Like Teen Spirit" blasting through the Bose speaker recklessly sprawled on his queen-sized bed.

Just like right now.

It's just like any other of those school nights, where I find a way to sneak away into his bedroom to ease the pain that is the world. With Nicandro, everything seems a little clearer. And although I'm never the one smoking the joint, I taste the toxic remedy on his tongue whenever he kisses me.

The post-orgasmic bliss of our friends-with-benefits agreement spreads warmth across my body, bringing chills to my arms, and I find myself wrapping my arms around my waist for some form of kinetic energy.

The chills aren't there because of the orgasm.

The chills are there because I'm bloody freezing!

Last week, the heating in Nicandro's industrial brownstone stopped working. Although it's not ideal during Manhattan's freezing winters, his father is barely around to notice, let alone to call some-body to repair it, and Nicandro…well, he seems too cold-blooded to give a crap.

It's true.

I'll never understand why he's moving around with just a pair of low-rise jeans on, while I not only have my entire school uniform on—sans blazer—but also the gray hoodie he previously had on.

I fight through the coldness. Through it all. Because none of it really matters. All that matters is the smile that crawls up my lips at the sight of Nicandro. He's in the middle of his bedroom, his toes sinking into the plush Persian rug above the dark oak hardwood floors as he rocks his body to the music like the crazy friend I love and adore.

Oh, Nicandro.

My gorgeous, gorgeous, gorgeous, edgy Mexican knight in shining armor—Nicandro.

My best friend and one of the sexiest bad boys at Glorsin St. Claire thrives on hot sex with both men and women (sometimes at the same time) whenever we're not playing *friends with-benefits*. Stunning underage tattoos, rough buzzcut, and the tendency to always save my ass.

Like last night with Tate.

Tate.

Ugh!

I watch in glee as he pistons his hips and nods his head to the beat of the classic beat, all while hanging up yet another black macrame piece on his exposed brick wall. It's so ironically him, alongside the guitar hung up on the adjacent side of his room and the familiar burning sage incense flooding my breath.

"So, what you're telling me is…" Nicandro glances over at me and smiles, "Tate just walked out of fucking English class as if it were nothing? All because you accused him of being lonely after he accused you?"

"Yup," I say, popping the 'p.' "Seems like he can give it, but he can't take it."

"Obviously not. It's like he's never been challenged like that, you know. Like he's so used to speaking his mind that when you challenged him and hinted at *his* weakness, he couldn't take it…" He pauses for a moment and turns back to hammering the wall piece. "Do you really think that asshole is lonely?"

I sigh.

Yes.

"I think the fact that he walked out of class gave me the answer in itself," I admit. "In some way, whatever it may be, he is lonely. I mean, you should have seen his eyes…it was as if I flicked a switch inside him and he didn't like it. At all."

Nicandro winks at me. "Hmm, you've got a habit of doing that, ha? Flipping switches?"

"Oh my god, Nicandro! Shut up!" I laugh and completely deflect the conversation when I nod toward the macrame. "It looks so good there!"

"Yeah?"

"Yeah, it's like it's always been there!" I grin, bringing my knees up to my chest on his bed.

Nicandro steps away from the wall to analyze the macrame.

Grinning slowly, he sets the hammer down on his tallboy and strides my way.

Man on a mission, I see.

The moment he reaches me, his cold right-hand cups my jaw and tilts my head up to meet his darkening gaze.

"Mmmm." He lowers his head so our lips brush. "*You* look good, London. More than a fuckin' piece of Macrame ever could."

My cheeks heat, a soft chuckle rumbling up Nicandro's throat when he spears his fingers through the hair at the back of my head. We're so close. So close I swear he's going to kiss me.

But he doesn't.

My forehead brushes against his and we simply stay like this, in a complete state of calmness as my heartbeats soften.

Nothing matters.

Not the world around us.

Just my heart, and his, and his room, which reeks of teenage angst and rebellion.

I find myself shutting my eyes, that smile tracing my lips never falling as I give in to the thoughts in my head. Those I know I need to tell him before I go back home tonight.

"I'm thinking tonight is the official night I finally go on *Enticed*."

Nicandro sucks in a breath, his grip on my jaw loosening but never falling. "Yeah?"

"Yeah," I murmur back. "I mean, I know I keep on pushing it back, but I really think if I don't start tonight, I never will."

Seconds pass.

Minutes.

It feels like an entire lifetime before Nicandro backs away from me, without ever meeting my gaze. He just simply shrugs and turns his back to me, returning to the macrame wall art.

My heart plummets. "Nic…?"

He simply nods.

"You don't seem too keen on me doing this."

My friend picks up his joint from where he left it on the tallboy, lights it up, and takes a deep whiff. Murky dark eyes I can't quite read land on mine. "I'm just cautious, that's all."

"I know, but there's no need to be. *Enticed* is the securest platform for me. I'll be fine, Nic. I promise." I try to offer him a warm smile, but all I get in return is a ticking jaw.

His gaze flickers from me to outside his window.

I try another approach.

"Nicandro, I know when we talked about it last time, you were clear it doesn't matter, but I just want to know if it bothers you?"

"It…doesn't." He shrugs, grinding his jaw before taking another drag of the joint. "But, even if it did, you do whatever you want, it's not like I'm your boyfriend or anything. I mean we aren't even together, Lon, so my opinion doesn't matter."

"I know we're not," I breathe, sweetness lacing my tongue with each word. I cross my legs and slip my hands underneath my thighs for warmth. "But our relationship is unique. I know it's just based upon pleasure, but I want your thoughts to matter, yeah?"

I don't expect Nicandro to turn my way because of that, or for him to come close, until he's at that spot again, cupping my cheeks, the joint still in his right hand. This time, he dips his head even lower than before, so when our foreheads brush, the warmth of his parted mouth tickles my lips.

He glances down at me intensely and every piece of me wants to unravel the chaos twirling in his deep dark eyes.

"If you think *Enticed* is what you want," he begins in a whisper. "Then it's what you do."

I look between his eyes for the longest time. "Really?"

"Mmhmmm, no matter how jealous I'll get."

That has me smiling.

"There's no need to be jealous." I slowly glide my hands down his bare chest, circling the pad of my pointer fingers over his pierced left nipple that hardens under my touch. The grunt that escapes him has me seductively biting my lower lip and glancing up to his heated stare. "There's no need to be jealous, Nicandro, because you know you're the only one who gets to touch me."

He shoots me a slow, sexy smirk "*Good.*"

Nicandro's stare darkens, and before I know it, his lips crash on mine. Wild hunger rumbles through me as he kisses me deep, like it's the first time. His touch tightens around my jaw when I wrap my arms around his neck, pulling him closer until we tumble back on his queen-sized bed.

His body pins me down and the breathless kiss ignites. He turns reckless, moaning against my lips when his tongue rushes over the center of them, asking for permission. My fingers glide up his scalp, my heart wild against his as our tongues collide.

That all-familiar sweet toxic taste consumes me.

Drags me under.

Jesus Christ.

Everything about Nicandro screams possessiveness. Jealously. *Need. So much need.*

My tongue brushes over my swollen lower lip when he pulls away, a darkness clouding his eyes that I've never seen before.

"That's right, London, nobody can touch you but me." Nicandro growls against me and pecks my lips once more. "And it's gotta stay like that because I don't want anything to change."

As he gets off me and helps me sit up, the air inside my lungs doesn't feel as trapped anymore. I concentrate on Nicandro. On the fact that he broke the rules, 'cause, for the first time, he kissed me while we weren't being intimate.

Just like that, his eyes widen a fraction, as if he just realized he fucked up.

Big time.

But I don't say anything, and he acts cool, so it's eventually forgotten.

Well, at least not discussed.

Soon enough, Nicandro seeks comfort in his joint and returns to the other side of his bedroom. With so many thoughts clouding my mind—*Enticed. Tate. That kiss*—I focus on my pearl bracelet, twirling it around until I feel a pair of eyes burning laser-deep into the side of my brain.

I look at up at Nicandro simply staring at me.

"What?" I laugh, so confused as to why he's acting like this.

So different.

"Nothing." He shrugs, again, becoming a teenage mystery when that slow, sexy smirk of his returns. "Just lookin' at cha, baby."

My breath scatters.

Baby?

Why did...

Why did Nicandro just call me, '*baby*'?

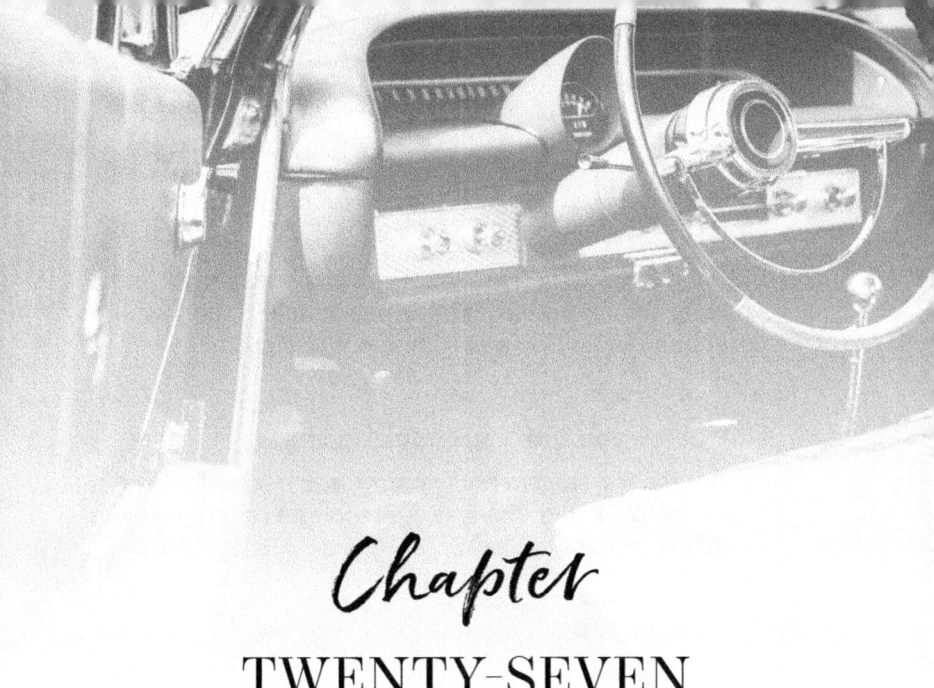

Chapter
TWENTY-SEVEN

Tate

Silence. Silence. Silence. It's all I ever hear in this house, and I fucking hate it. Its coldness seeping into my veins, rendering me incapable of even thinking straight, without the need to put on some 90's punk rock to ease the tension of an empty home.

With my father and stepmom in Paris for some *work conference* and my stepsister, Maddie, god knows where, it's just me, myself, and fucking I.

My phone buzzes in my hand as midnight strikes, and I'm left lying on top of the charcoal sheets of my bed with a single pair of gray basketball shorts on and nothing else. *Yes, nothing else.* I'm commando because I don't give a fuck. *And no, don't you judge me. It's comfortable, baby.*

After tossing and turning all night, with the homework I haven't done in the back of my mind, as well as London's statement in media class at the forefront of my mind, I'm glad I finally have a distraction.

Levi.

My phone's so bright, it creates a glow around me as I read his text.

LEVI: Thought your father was in Paris…

My brows knit at my best friend's text. *That's odd.*

TATE: He is, why?

LEVI: I swear to fucking god I saw him stepping into the restaurant I'm serving at. He looked me in the eye and stepped out like he was hiding something.

I find myself freezing up. *What?*

TATE: Are you sure you're not tripping?

LEVI: Ha. Ha. No, I'm not tripping, you motherfucker. I'd lose my job if I did. Anyway, just thought I should let you know, man, just in case.

I think for a minute.

I can outsmart my father if he was.

Toggling my phone's caller ID off so that I'll show up as an unknown number, I call him. My father's smart, so if he were cheating, he wouldn't risk having her number come up on his phone, he'd tell her to set it as an unknown number or some shit like that.

The phone dials twice, and then…

"Baby doll," my father's voice murmurs through the phone, and it's actually so awkward to hear. "Where are you, Lolita? I was getting worried you didn't get my text. I changed the location meet up. I forgot my son's friend works at where we were going. I miss you so fucking much."

Lolita?

Who the hell is that?

I can't help how far my jaw drops.

Slapping a hand over my mouth, everything I've ever believed to be true disappears before my very eyes. I hang up before I fuck up and say something I regret, and I'm simply left staring at my phone, where my father's contact profile remains.

What the fuck?

The invisible cord holding me together begins to vanish, snapping when I need it most as my mind clouds with questions. Questions I know I'll never get the answers to. *He's not in Paris?*

Why did my stepmom lie when she called me literally three hours ago?

I don't get it. I really don't. All I do get is that the pang in my chest has never stung this hard. It's lies. All lies. My entire life is a lie. Why would he hurt her like that? Hurt *me* like that?

I wish there was somebody I could talk to about this shit. Somebody to ease the pain as I rise from my bed, tell Alexa to stop my music, punch my bedroom wall with a grunt and head downstairs to the wet bar.

I don't give a fuck my fist is pounding and that there will be some clear bruising tomorrow morning, all I want is a fucking soul.

One.

One fucking soul to talk to.

Levi's at work and the rest of my friends…well, truth be told, it isn't even that solid.

I don't fucking know why London enters my mind, but she does. She's there like a permanent scar digging deeper and deeper inside my brain. Everything about her pisses me off. Especially now, as I reach the downstairs' wet bar, the silvery moon taunting me as it scatters through the sheer drapes. I pull out a generous bottle of Henley gin and pop off the cork lid.

I'm not fucking lonely.

Never have been.

Never will be.

Then why do you feel it, chickenshit?

Why do you feel like the entire world is caving in?

Ignoring that little man at the back of brain that always seems to drive me to complete insanity, I storm back inside my bedroom with a clenched jaw and a heavy heart. *Why would he cheat?*

Will the divorce be the biggest scandal of their lives?

Or will they do it Manhattan Elite style and live with it?

Thirty minutes later, I've downed more Henley than I should. It doesn't take that long. Not with the fucked-up way I'm feeling. It's a product of how I was made—a fuck-up.

Grabbing my laptop from my nightstand, I dive into the freezing bedsheets and lean against my headboard. The dull throbs in my head are nothing compared to the earth-crater size hole burning up my soul. My whole life has been a fucking lie. All of it. All my father cares about is him-fucking-self. If he didn't, I wouldn't be the only one in this huge mansion of a brownstone.

What the hell is the purpose of owning a place like this, if you don't even live in it?

With heavy eyes, I take a sip of straight gin and power up my laptop. I smirk at myself at the first thing I type up…*my usual thirty minutes to 1:00 a.m. searches.*

Why doesss London Héroux ha8t me so pucking nuch?

My smirk deepens.

God, I'm so fucking drunk.

I lift my finger into the air and smash it down on the 'enter' button.

No results.

"Fuckers," I scoff and try something else with the bottle in my left hand.

Sterling fking Hérouxxx

I burst out laughing into the darkness when he comes up. Taking a swig from the bottle, the illicit liquor baptizes my tongue yet again, drowning all my sorrows.

JUST IN: Sterling Héroux signs a multi-million deal which will secure his expansion to Dubai, challenging Mirko Meadows' Dubai announcement mere weeks ago.

Can't think of any original ideas, can you, Héroux?

I read yet another.

Meadows and Héroux to bid head-to-head in luxury iconic Manhattan development set to reach billions. What their past year rivalry predicts.

It predicts a shitshow. Even I can tell you that, Architectural Digest my ass.

I read on until it's all freaking bullshit and I just click to the next article.

Shutting my eyes, a groan escapes my lips as I search up the only person that can take away all the pain, just seeing her face restores me in the lonely hours.

Lonely.

Fuck, what am I doing all alone in my room, getting drunk on a Tuesday night?

Maybe she was right…

I am lonely.

Lonely just like London said.

Not only on the exterior, but the interior too.

Fuck.

My cold, cold heart burns for the only woman I hate, yet she's all I crave.

Londonnnnn

Not the city, you bastards. Someone get these double-decker buses off my screen.

I add her last name to the end of my search as the lit-up keyboard begins to blur into one. Shit. I wait a second for Google to load and then. *Holy. Good God, she's hot.*

Those baby-blue eyes I get lost in stare back at me as I stare at her picture on Google at some fancy-ass event and all the information I guiltily know by heart underneath it. I don't know why I care about her so much, but I just do, and that scares me more than the not knowing.

She shouldn't affect me, especially after I stormed out of the media room and decided I was done with senior year for the day.

Maybe if I list all the things I hate about her it'll make me not give a shit anymore?

"Ah, what the hell." I shrug and take yet another sip of Henley. "I'll still like her…"

Okay. Let's do this shit.

*Reasons why I, Tate Lee Meadows, should *DO* hate London Mila Héroux:*

1) **Her family are assholes = rivals = hell on earth.**
2) **We share the same birthday. New Year's Eve. That annoys me…*sometimes*.**
3) **She's…too much of an A+ grade student.** *Yeah, as if that's a defect, chickenshit.*
4) **Her lips are the perfect shade of pink and are so plump that I just want to kiss her wild and make her forget why she hates me so much with my hard cock.**

Wait.

Wait a second...

I rake a hand through my dark tousled hair, knowing that I just got sidetracked. "Let's try that again."

5) **She hates me.** *I mean, I wouldn't be creating this list if she didn't.*

6) **She doesn't trust me and has preconceived ideas about me.** *Talk about being judgy, sheesh.*

7) **I can't ever read her thoughts and she's a mysterious beautiful thing.** *The latter is kinda hot though...*

8) **My parents would disown me if I admitted that there was a small percentage of me that wished I could win over her heart, piece by piece.** *Okay, big percentage. Go big or go home, Meadows. Who cares if they disown you?*

9) **She has an open relationship with her best friend, Nicandro.** *And she likes sucking cock...Fuckkk. Why did I ask her that? Now I just imagine her on her knees, my hand fisting her hair back as those eyes, not so innocently, look up at me as I fill her mouth with my thick c—*

Great, just great. Now my fucking cock is stirring beneath my basketball shorts, getting harder by the second because of how turned on I am. Not even half of those reasons are valid enough for why I should hate her so much. *I'm such a damn mess.*

Forgetting the list from my mind, I take one last look at her picture and lift the bottle to my lips just as I click out of it. My gaze flickers to the time on my laptop: 1a.m, and I can't help but chuckle at myself...

Tired, drunk, and turned-on. You couldn't even make this shit up.

Lust-filled breaths flood my lungs. I click on Google, and without even thinking it through in my drunken state, I type up the one word I know will ease all the tension in my body, including both the emotional and sexual. A place that'll make me feel numb, just like I deserve.

I should hate Levi for introducing me to *Enticed*: an exclusive cam girl site for the elite of the elite. I can't remember the last time I was on, and honestly, it's my deep dark secret.

It's not something I'm proud of, but sometimes in the early hour blues, I just need somebody. Somebody to detoxify my body. To make me forget. To take the pain away—moan by moan.

Seeing as this platform is secure as heck and everybody has to go through rounds of verification, it's why one can't use their real name for security purposes. For privacy purposes, one can't view any cam girls from the same state, but of course, Levi found a way to rig the high-tech system, allowing us to have access to *Enticed* limitless without any strings attached, so to speak.

Scrolling through all the live cam rooms available, nothing really catches my eyes. That's the thing about this, one needs to be particular about what exactly it is they want to see.

Well, not if they're just a horny motherfucker.

Just as I'm about to gulp down some more Henley, everything stops in me as my eyes lock with one particular cam girl. It feels like all the air has been sucked out of my chest, the longer I stare into her light blue gaze.

"I must be fucking dreaming this," I mumble, inching closer to the screen, like it's the most logical explanation for the reason I'm seeing...

Oh.

My.

Fucking.

God.

My jaw drops, the damn Henley bottle almost slips out of my grip at the shock rushing through my body. There she is, my blonde goddess, staring back at me through the screen.

London Mila Héroux.

Invader of my mind.

Bittersweet enemy.

Risqué good girl.

And apparent *Enticed* cam girl?

What the hell?

I'm quick to click on her picture, and within seconds, London invades my screen in real time, and oh. My. Word. *Jesus fucking Christ, this woman is going to kill me. She really is.*

Sitting on the edge of her king-sized bed, London's only wearing sexy emerald lace panties and a bra, which spills her ample cleavage. The embroidered fabric is so sheer, I can see the outline of her darkened nipples beneath it, both pink and hard as they stab through the material.

I get lost in it all.

Her confidence.

Her smile.

Her.

And instantly, I know I'm in trouble. Big fucking trouble. Because I can't look away.

God, I'm so fucked.

My hard cock throbs, suffering against the constraints of my basketball shorts as I wrap both fists around the bottle of Henley, restraining myself from going *there*. No matter how hard it gets to breathe or think straight with London so fucking pretty on my screen like that, I'm *not going there*.

I can't.

Especially when I'm already a horny mess.

Clenching my jaw, I do my best to restrain myself, no matter how desperately I want to roll my hips and jack off to her.

It doesn't faze me that she's wearing a short lilac wig; I'd recognize those beautiful plump lips and piercing baby blue eyes I love to hate anywhere. I'll always know those eyes that feel as if she's staring right into my soul, but right now, she can't. She's only seeing herself and the comments, and the number of token pennies going up on the left-side of the screen—each level unlocking something different.

Her token amount is quite high, even for an elite company like *Enticed*, which means three things:

1) She's been live camming for a while tonight.
2) Unless she stays on for longer, I've missed a lot.
3) There's a fuck load of people watching her.

The lighting surrounding her is dim, giving it all almost an intimate feel while still being bright enough to see her. *All of her.* Calm. Confident. Giving praise to her body.

Fuck.

I swallow the lump in my throat at the natural beauty she is when a bright smile breaks on her lips and she gives the camera a flirty wave.

"Hi, HenleyKing17, how are you?" London beams, startling heat rushing up my chest at the mention of *my* username.

And yes, Henley after the alcohol I'm drinking.

Couldn't think of anything better.

Sue me.

I find myself boyishly smiling at the screen, her grin so wide. It's the happiest I've seen her in three years. She isn't the miserable girl in media class from earlier today, or the girl who slapped me, she's Rose Heartache Mila.

It's her apparent camgirl name, I only just notice underneath the screen.

Comments light up the screen, so I type up my reply and hit send.

> **HenleyKing17: I know I should say 'I'm fine,' but I'm really not. It's a fuck the society norm kind of night.**

London's lips move in sweet rhythm as she reads the comment out loud, a glint appearing in her smile when she says, "I'm with you, Henley. Can I call you *Henley*? Society is my nightmare." Her smile softens. "What's going on? Why are you feeling that kind of way?"

You, I want to say.

You, London.

But right now, she isn't that Héroux girl I've been conditioned to despise for the past eighteen years. I'm not the enemy in her eyes; in fact, she doesn't even know it's me.

She's simply *Rose Heartache Mila.*

I'm simply *HenleyKing17.*

And nothing can hurt us.

Not like this.

> **HenleyKing17: Well, I feel like I've been living a lie. Everything I do doesn't feel good enough. These past few days have been...I don't know...I just don't feel like myself, I guess.**

Thank God for autocorrect for not making me look like an illiterate ass.

> **HenleyKing17: And oh, of course you can call me Henley. Whatever you like.**

Resting her hands beneath her thighs, London leans toward the screen and her brows knit softly, while she scans through my comment.

Just as she's about to respond, a comment from some asshole pops up.

> **Gioassg30: Didn't realize we were in a therapy group, asshole. Get off.**

"Fuck you, Gio*assg30*," I mutter under my breath, drunkenly showing the comment my finger.

London's eyes widen a fraction at the comment. "While this may not be a therapy group, it's a safe space. If you don't support that, you can leave."

> **Gioassg30: Don't be like that, baby.**

> **HenleyKing17: She's not your baby. Maybe you should be the one to fuck off.**

> **Gioassg30: Oh yeah? How long have you known her for? One second, huh?**

I take another swig of the gin and chuckle at the sick fuck. "Try the past eighteen years…"

Being the guy that I am, I copy the comment I sent a few moments ago, paste it and hit send, just waiting for this idiot's tantrum.

> **HenleyKing17: Well, I feel like I've been living a lie. Everything I do doesn't feel good enough. These past few days have been…I don't know…I just don't feel like myself, I guess.**

I love the fact that London completely ignores Gioassg30's *threatening* comments toward me, and instead, a soft frown traces her lips.

"I'm sorry you feel that way, Henley. One step at a time, yeah? Give yourself credit in the times you need it the most. Just because you don't feel good enough, doesn't mean you have to diminish the person that you truly are. I know I should take my own advice, but yeah…"

Her words spark a fire inside me…*Just because you don't feel good enough doesn't mean you have to diminish the person that you truly are.*

It's so true.

But what gets me the most is her admission to needing to *take her own advice*. It leaves me pondering what's going on inside that head of hers.

Why is she camming?

Why does she go from cold to hot so fast?

And what is London Héroux truly hiding from?

Her demons? *What demons could she possibly have?* She's perfect in every way, unlike my flawed soul.

Conversation continues between her and the Voyeurs' comments, and I can't help the smile that traces my lips every time she softly giggles. Men tip her more and more tokens as she gives advice to them, something so unique and refreshing about being on *Enticed*.

Usually, it's all about fake tits, excessive moans, and exaggerated dildos, but with London, it feels so much different.

Nothing is fake.

It's all real.

Raw.

Her words have purpose—pure honesty, and it isn't all about sexualizing everything, it's simply just *her*. The *her* she never lets me see, but I so desperately crave to unravel.

Deciding enough is enough, I attempt to set the Henley bottle on my nightstand, but it tips and rolls over. Loudly crashing glass has me grimacing and then I burst out in laughter.

Ah, fuck my life.

I turn back to my laptop screen to soft erotic music playing in her background. It's so low I can barely hear it, but it's there, and part of me wonders if it's this low because her parents are home.

The thought alone has me slowly gliding my hand down my abs and cupping my hard cock through my shorts, knowing that her good girl act is wearing off and coming undone right now.

"I love this song," London whispers all breathy, her hips softly grinding against the silk bedsheets. They roll in such a rhythmic pattern, each rock spreading her thighs more and more apart, giving everybody a show of those drenched panties. "Oh God, I'm so wet…"

The comments go wild, but I don't concentrate on them, I concentrate on *her* instead. On her seductively biting her lower lip and quickly rearranging herself, so she's on her knees on the mattress, thighs spread even wider, as if she's straddling a guy, fucking him reverse-cowgirl style.

Pumping her hips as if she's gliding on a cock, she begins bouncing, those tits shaking like pure heaven. It intensifies. A hum escapes her throat all while staring into the lens of the camera, and I can't help but stroke myself hard over the cotton, imagining it's her doing it all instead.

What are you hiding, angel?

Does Nicandro know about this?

My thick cock hasn't stopped throbbing, jolting in my friction-laced grip, wanting more.

Fuck. Fuck. Fuck.

My hips rock to match hers, heat crawling up my spine, and I just know this isn't going to end well. I watch her little show, groaning when she reaches enough tokens to take off her bra.

It's all a sexy fuckin' strip tease.

The song continues in the background while London's cheeks redden, the second she slips off her bra, letting the lace drop off camera, her gorgeous perky breasts spill out and bounce with her every hip roll and grind.

Her tits.

Dear God, her tits.

They're so naturally ample and beautiful. Her nipples are the darkest shade of pink, pebbled hard, and I wanna glide my cock between them.

My strokes get faster at the sight of them.

Abs tensing, precum crazily leaks from my aching cock and I feel it erotically slip from my crown all the way down my shaft, gliding with my shorts at every rub. *Oh, fuck, yeahhh.* A soft moan escapes my lips when London squeezes her tits with a smolder, playing with them, because for sure, there's a fucking patch of my arousal on my shorts and I haven't even started yet.

The comments pick up, going so fast, I only catch a small few.

Brad8: God, you're gorgeous, Rose Heartache Mila. This can't be your first night.

First night?

AndersonRock69: Want to suck those fucking tits.

Fucker.

Gioassg30: Therapy's over and…Christ.

Wish she blocked you…

My free hand frantically darts along the keyboard before hitting send with one too many ellipses…Oops drunk me.

HenleyKing17: You're so freaking beautiful when you smile. You should do it more often, Mila………

"Thanks Henley." London grins. *Grins.* A scarlet blush crawls up her cheeks and she winks, her beauty ruining me completely. "I'll keep that in mind just for you. I promise."

I smirk. *Is she flirting with me?*

Get over yourself, Meadows.

This is her job.

"I'm never coming back from this." Shutting my eyes, I lean my head against the headboard, my crazed breaths erratic and needy. It takes every fucking nerve in my body to stop touching myself and remember who the girl on the screen is.

She's the enemy.

I can't do this.

But it all amounts to nothing, the second a soft buzz has me opening my eyes to London lying down sideways across the bed, her legs spread and a curved pink vibrator in her hand. All my self-control melts away seeing her like this; her thighs strategically hiding her pussy as she evidently slips her panties to the side and turns back to the camera with a darkened gaze.

Switching off the vibrator, she tips her head against the mattress and her eyes never leave mine as she dips it into her mouth—*deep*—like she's deep-throating it.

I instantly wish it were my dick she were taking so eagerly instead.

Oh fuck.

I can't do it anymore. I need this.

I need a release from all the built-up tension inside.

I tug at my waistband and slip my shorts down to my ankles. My aching cock slaps against my abs at the exact same moment, the vibrator dints the base of her throat. Her gaze becomes glassy, but she doesn't gag once, as she glistens the toy with her mouth before slipping it back out.

Just like a good girl.

The vibrator glisters under the light as its soft hum returns. London rushes her hands down her body, and she gasps before full-on moaning out in pleasure when she slips it inside her in a desperate, uncontrolled rhythm. "Oh, *God.*"

Her thighs continue to shield her sex, but the erotic wet sounds her pussy makes with the vibrator's every grind in and out of her tells me everything I need to know. *She's so wet.*

Precum continues to spill from my cock, pooling at the center of my abs, and I use it as lube to wrap around my scorching rock-hard dick. A hiss escapes me at just how roughly I'm stroking my shaft, jerking off at an intensity beyond everything I've ever believed to exist.

Fuck.

Spreading my pre-cum around my length, I almost roll my eyes back at the pleasure it brings, knowing we're both fucking ourselves at the exact. Same. Time.

With every sound of her moans, the buzzing of the vibrator, and her taunting wetness, I jack off faster, while rubbing the prominent vein of my cock with my thumb. Desire builds and arousal is all I see, an elation only watching London brings on, edging me further.

I recklessly stroke myself, squeezing tighter as I get to my head, slightly twisting my grip so roughly at the crown that I moan out London's name because this feels like too much.

It's ecstasy.

Something beyond anything I've ever felt before.

The complete and utter numb pleasure that comes with chasing an orgasm.

"London," I growl, my cheeks heating at just how fast I'm fucking myself, "what are you doing to me?"

Perspiration coats my toned abs, which flex the closer I get to heaven because of her.

The more forbidden this feels, the more chaotic my grip becomes.

I involuntarily slip lower off the headboard, my head hitting my pillow, and I pivot my ass off the mattress, grinding erratically as I watch her with heavy lids. *Oh. My. God.*

London goes from biting down on her left fist to mute the moans to letting her fingers weave through her lilac wig, tugging softly at it as if she needs something to clench with just how hard she's fucking herself.

Glimpses of honey blonde peek through.

Slowly, I devilishly smirk.

Oh, hello there, Héroux.

London deviously stares right at the camera with every strangled gasp. I love how she bites her lower lip as if it'll be any better, but all it does is make me wish I was right there with her, sucking on it hard.

Every last bit of my control is gone, and I don't think I've ever jerked myself so intently before, like I'm on the verge of blacking out. *So fucking close...*Pumping hard into my hand, my eyelids grow heavier with my every growl as I watch her entire body begin to quiver.

She's close.

So close.

And I want to come with her. At the exact same second.

Fuccck.

My heart is ready to jump out of my chest with how crazy it's beating.

I'm not going to survive this.

That vibrator slips in and out of her like she doesn't want to survive this either, grinding so vigorously.

She's on the edge of being completely sated, I can see it all through her sex-filled eyes and her quickened pants that match mine. There isn't an inch of her that isn't involved in craving this orgasm, and my longing body is on fire just watching her.

I want to kiss every inch of her flustered skin.

I want to cure her every ache with my hand around her throat, devouring her.

I want to curl my tongue around her nipples and erotically bite them as I ease the throbbing between her thighs with my thick...

"I wish you were here..." London whispers to the screen, breaking my train of thought. "Wish you were here doing this to me instead." The vibrations turn more intense, ricocheting through my chest at her every gasp. "Oh my god, I'm going to come... *Ohhh!*"

London's left-hand slips from her hair to dive between her thighs, her clit, the most probable avenue. She continuously circles her wrist, rubbing herself hard and fast, as reckless as my own desperate strokes.

As reckless as my heart.

As reckless as my fucked-up mind.

If this is how it feels without her pussy in view, imagine with it.

Kill me.

It'll kill me.

I cup my balls with my left hand, the liquor on my tongue making me want this even more as I caress their fullness. I imagine her doing this to me instead. Her destroying me. Squeezing them softly has a loud groan escaping my lips that I'm sure all of Manhattan hears.

I keep going. Faster and faster, matching, if not intensifying, the erratic movements of the vibrator slipping out of her. I can't stop wildly palming my crown, even more pleasure flooding me. We roll our heads back on the mattress at the exact same time, desire filling my cock's every throb as I feel it pulse madly in my hand, edging to the limit of my restraint.

I can't breathe.

I can't breathe anything but her.

All I can feel, see, and hear is her and the lingering scent of her sweet vanilla and strawberry scent.

London convulses on her bed, her left hand rushing up to slap over her mouth, and without ever losing my gaze, she comes undone with a muted scream, orgasming like a fucking goddess, so intense her eyes roll back.

My pumps increase to a speed I never knew existed. Hot air burns my lungs at the sight of her thighs shaking as she cums, squirting all over the bedsheets, gushing continuously everywhere, while still grinding on her toy, and…

Fucking hell.

I can't hold on any longer.

My abs clench tight, heat coursing through my entire body and settling in my cock as my orgasm explodes, frantically rippling through me. *Fuccck.* Hot, thick cum uncontrollably shoots all over me, hitting my torso, abs, and hand with every moan rumbling up my throat.

London…Look what you did to me.

Her name continuously escapes my lips in half-anger, half-desire filled grunts the harder I stroke myself, my release endlessly rushing out of my throbbing dick, hitting as far as my stubbled chin and inches from my lips when I massage my balls with every upward thrust.

Only when London slants on her bed, her tits rapidly rising and falling as she comes down from her high, does my orgasm settle. My cock can't stop throbbing, euphoria lasting.

London slips out her vibrator and it's coated in her cum, a sweet wonderland fucking up my mind when she brings it to her mouth and teasingly licks it all off, tasting herself.

Kinky.

She's so fucking kinky.

I want to kiss her with her orgasm lavished on her tongue.

I have no idea how I'm going to survive seeing her tomorrow at school.

Panting, I try to push that thought aside, at least for the meantime, and allow the sight of London so spent on her bed to be my only thought.

She adjusts her panties, and when she spins around, she's all covered. Between my drunken smirk and her orgasmic grin, I say this is the most intense orgasm of my life.

I'm still trying to catch my breath, her pants telling me she's doing the same as she stares deep into the screen like she's trying to reach out for a soul to ease the havoc in her eyes.

I'll take your havoc, baby.

I'll cure you.

Just let me.

It all feels like a daze. A euphoric dream. Everything I need as tension releases my body, numbness taking over, and I sink into my mattress in a complete post-orgasmic bliss.

I feel nothing.

Absolutely nothing.

And I love it—love that she makes me feel like this.

Until the guilt sets in, and suddenly, it's as if my entire world is caving in. Coldness tinges my body as a gust of wind gushes inside my darkened bedroom from my opened New York windows.

I stare at the softly moving sheer drapes, Manhattan's lit-up skyline peeking through, suddenly feeling everything and nothing. My heart aches at the emotion etching through the forming lump at the back of my throat at the realization that I just got off to my enemy.

The one girl I should never have.

The one who hates me with a fucking passion.

"Shit." I rake a hand through my hair, tugging hard at the ends. Realization seeps through all the lust and drunkenness. "I'm so screwed. What the fuck is wrong with me?"

If London ever finds out I watched her on *Enticed*, she will kill me.

Which is why she can never know.

Ever.

The knot at the back of my throat doesn't ease, no matter how hard I swallow. I hate it. Hate the word that writes itself in permanent marker all over my body as London stands up from her bed.

The word remains, all while she whispers *goodnight* and *sweet dreams* with a soft smile. Her inner thighs, that I've seen Nicandro caress one too many times, shine with her orgasm as she steps close to the camera, and after blowing a kiss, the screen turns black.

End of chat stares back at me.

Those words remain in my mind all while I do the unthinkable and pull up the private direct messages between us and begin typing away everything that I feel without ever once indicting that *HenlyKing17* is actually her nemesis: Tate freaking Meadows.

Me.

HenleyKing17: How the fuck am I supposed to forget about you now?

The second I hit send, my jaw clenches in fury at the thought that this is all too good to be true. This escape…it *can't* be an escape for me. This is *London*. The preppy A-Grade student who comes undone for elite men during the early hours of the morning.

God, fuck…

I shouldn't have ever had all that Henley.

Slamming my laptop shut, I drown into a blurry world of reality, hating how much I liked talking to her anonymously, without the fear of judgment, and how this can never happen again. *It can't.* Not as breaths strangle my throat. Because that one word fueling my mind taunts me. A word I can never erase…

No matter how deeply I try to ignore London.

No matter how many hours I spend sipping illegal liquor all alone.

No matter how badly I'm supposed to forget the only woman who saves me.

The word—*regret*—is all I feel.

All I believe to be true.

All that I really am in this world… *A regret.*

To everybody

My family. Myself. *Her.*

Except when I'm *HenlyKing17* and she's *Rose Heartache Mila*—the blue-eyed angel that was staring back at me—because that's when I truly feel alive.

In heaven.

Her heaven.

Because heaven isn't as beautiful as her. *It could never be.*

Which is why I need to forget about her tomorrow.

The rest of senior year.

Forever.

No matter how deep my lonely heart craves her touch in ways I'll never admit out loud.

Chapter

TWENTY-EIGHT

Tate

I wake up with a pounding headache, dreading the day to come. It isn't so much due to having to go to school, it's London Héroux. I'm not prepared to see her after my impulses fucked me over last night.

How the fuck am I supposed to ignore the girl I secretly jacked off to?

A girl who was once so fucking special to me?

I can't, but it's my only choice.

In order to move forward in my life, I need to do what I do best—thanks to my father's tight grip on the Manhattan high rollers—ignore and fucking conquer.

The vicious red glow of my alarm clock taunts me, its numbers consciously flashing, softly lighting up my huge, modern bedroom.

5:18 a.m.

"Nooo," I groan, slamming my head against the pillow. "Shit, that can't be the time."

I've literally been up since 1 a.m., failing to do one of the most mundane tasks—sleep. School starts in just over three hours. I'm meeting my friends, Levi and Wesley, at the gym at 6 a.m. for hardcore training. The assholes need me to keep them accountable because they keep slacking.

My phone vibrates on my nightstand, just as I'm about to turn over.

SASHA: Morning, babe. Are you up? xx

A slow, sexy smirk carves my lips.

Sasha. Sasha. Sasha.

Why are you texting me at just after five in the morning?

Sasha Jones, everybody. Emerald eyes. Red, bouncy curls. My *crush* freshman year—when unbeknownst to her, the truth is a certain honey blonde girl was my one and only crush since the moment I learned the definition of the word, no matter how madly I may hate London now.

Stop. Thinking. About. Her.

Distract yourself.

Last year, at one of Levi's full-on parties, Sasha and I made out for twenty minutes straight before hooking up. By hooking up, I mean my tongue between her thighs and then my cock grazing the back of her throat, but not sex. Yeah, that's right, I'm a virgin.

Maybe it's crazy, really fucking crazy, but I don't take the silent pledge I once made with London Héroux lightly.

We were going to be each other's firsts.

With everything.

And even though the world burnt to ashes around us, I don't want anybody else but her. It's fucked up, I know, and I'm sure some of our firsts have flown out the fucking window, but there's still some I get all fucking sentimental about, even if it hasn't happened…*yet.*

God, I fucking hate myself.

I need to forget about London. *Right now.*

I need to forget about her with an early morning distraction and an earth-shattering orgasm.

TATE: Yeah, I don't just wake up looking like a dream, why?

SASHA: I woke up really horny and really want to show you a good morning, Tate. Come over. I know you want to. It's still really early and my parents are on a double shift.

Firefighters. Sasha's an only child and her parents are almost always at the fire station, saving lives like the tag team they are. It means Sasha's alone more often. Which means we see each other more often. Which means my tongue is inside her more often. *Yeah, you read that right.*

I said what I said.

Don't be shy now.

Anyway, it just always fascinates me how sometimes life falls into place so effortlessly, and other times, it's all a fucking shitshow.

Sasha sends another text.

SASHA: I won't tell anybody. I promise.

And again...

A risqué photo of her tits fills up my screen, Sasha cupping one of them, her neon orange fake nails too fucking bright for how early it is. Her nipples salute me, but...

I don't feel a single thing.

I mean, yeah, heat rushes to my cock, but it isn't the same sensation I felt when I saw London last night (or, should I say, earlier this morning). London takes my breath away, and I hate her more for it, but Sasha...I don't feel that way with her. But...I guess it's a good thing, right?

No commitment.

No feelings.

No guilt.

I stare at the picture of her tits, but all I see smeared across them is: *This is your way to forget all about London, you asshole.*

TATE: Be there in fifteen, gorgeous.

SASHA: I'll be waiting. xo

Sighing, I roll out of bed and head into my ensuite. I catch my eyes in the vanity mirror after washing my face, totally not ready for today. My Atlantic blue eyes are dimmer than usual and are rimmed with a soft redness from my restless tossing and turning all night.

Great. Just great.

I'm well aware I reek of tobacco and weed from the cigarette I had in the middle of the night when the anxiety rippling through my blood felt like too much. I'm quick to take a hot, steamy shower, and while I come out with water rippling down my naked body and smelling like a sandalwood dream, the shower did nothing to wash away all the pain I'm feeling.

I don't think London understands the gravity of how badly she hurt me.

After getting ready for another day of senior year with our iconic black and emerald-green uniform, I sling my pre-packed backpack over one shoulder, and tuck my blazer over my arm.

I know, I know.

Don't all say it at once.

Uniform.

Blazer.

Tie.

Private school perks, yeah?

You wish you were me, baby...Not.

I manage to sneak out of my Manhattan brownstone without any detection, but the second I reach the front porch, I lock eyes with my father, who's stumbling up the stairs, a drunken mess.

Ah, fuck.

I think my hangover just got fucking worse.

Those familiar murky hazel eyes stare back at me, glazed with a self-imposed struggle I know too well. Mirko Meadows—my father— was once rocking the New York City A-game, elite style, and while he *still* is, cracks are beginning to show on the surface.

His dark hair is a mess. Red lipstick stains, so obviously not my stepmother's, are smeared all over his face. And his clothes, which are the same as yesterdays, reek of both booze and sex.

What Levi saw last night was correct.

My father is definitely cheating.

This is my father, ladies and gents, a recovering addict who isn't necessarily *recovering.*

There are a few scabs on his face, six-inch white scars from all the brawls he's been in over the years. The hospital visits. My father doesn't get violent when he's drunk, he gets violent when he's lonely. When he's tired. When he's depressed. When he's high. When he's *alive.*

Basically, I'm a product of a fuck-up, and my gravest fear is that it's blood deep.

I don't want to wake up one day and be like my father. I don't want his life. He's always chased money, boats, and hoes. If it wasn't for his one percent of brain cells still left, I wouldn't just have one stepmom right now, I'd have six or seven ex-stepmoms.

When I was a little kid, I used to admire my father, then he hit my defenseless mother one night on my eighth birthday when he thought I was asleep, and I've wanted to kill him ever since.

He wasn't even there for my birthday.

He didn't even *know* it was my fucking birthday because he was too high with ecstasy and heroin in his system, too fucked up with the rush of straight liquor to remember anything about his little boy or his wife.

Not much has changed since, and yet, everything's changed.

Dad's gotten worse.

I've gotten older.

Mom isn't here.

"How was *Paris*?" I spit.

He doesn't meet my eyes.

"You gonna just stand there or you gonna help your old man, hmm?" my father slurs, gripping onto the railing for dear life when an invisible devil shoves him back. "TATE!"

I hate how I reach out to grip his wrist to stabilize him.

I hate how I feel his Rolex and all those damn Cartier cuff bracelets.

I hate how I make sure he's okay instead of just kicking him down the stairs.

I grew up in a home without affection. Without love. Mirko Meadows is the reason why.

"You all good?"

He nods softly, clutching at his head. "Shit. Is the whole world spinning or is it just me?"

Heat rises up my neck, manifesting as angst because we've been here before. "Just you."

"What's that supposed to mean?"

My jaw ticks. "It means what it means, *Mirko.*"

Yeah, I stopped calling him 'dad' or 'father' out loud, the day he left my mom with stitches.

My father clears his throat, his drunken eyes meeting mine and narrowing in a glare. He continues staring as if he has power over me. Like he didn't just waste his money on some hooker. Like he isn't on a bender. Like he isn't about to throw up in approximately ten seconds.

"Now, listen here, Tate," he grits, drunkenly jabbing a finger into my chest, "if you speak to me like that again, I'll—"

"Save it," I grit, shoving him out of the way to jog down the stairs.

When I reach the last step, my entire body freezes up at the words he mumbles.

"You're just like your mother…"

It's as if cold water has been poured over me, extra in this deep winter breeze.

Is he serious?

Grinding my jaw, I snap my head over my shoulder and meet his glare with one of my own. There aren't enough words to explain how much I hate my father. Everybody thinks he's this fancy businessman who made it to the top with hard work. Well, let me tell you something, he's a cheat.

A huge fucking cheat.

Because half of the money he prides himself on, half of the money he began his business with twenty years ago, half of the money he spent on getting laid tonight, it doesn't belong to him.

He fucking stole it.

I know it.

I know because he stole it from my mother.

"Listen here, asshole," I growl, ascending the stairs like a madman.

My nostrils flare, revolted as I bunch up his damp unbuttoned dress shirt, bawling my fists until his drunken breath is all I smell. I stare him down, until I'm sure my eyes are devilish vipers.

"If you ever, *ever*, mention my mother again," I hiss in a low chill, "I will *kill you* myself."

Mirko stares until a cocky smirk works up his lips. "You think you're so tough, don't you?"

I shove him, and he stubbles back so hard that he almost falls off the edge of the detailed cast iron railing. "TATE! TATUM LEE MEADOWS!"

I don't fucking care.

All I do is drop my voice, sounding even more threatening, "Don't fuck with me or Mom, or you'll be sorry."

And in all my fury, I slam my shoulder into him and once inside my Mustang, speed off.

A fucking throbbing hangover and English Lit, while I'm still trying to process everything that happened last night, isn't exactly what I want walking into school. *It's self-imposed torture.*

I strut down the hectic locker-lined hallway with that familiar tension in my shoulders. Students glance over with smiles and fist pumps. I bypass them all, without even glancing their way for more than a second. Instead, I keep my focus up and straight ahead with a clenched jaw, towering over everybody on the way to class.

I'm so fucking done with everything.

I like to think the burning stares I feel all around me are more to do with my unusual bid to ignore them, rather than the fact I decided to come to school with a gray hoodie instead of my blazer. A *violation*, I know, but I don't give a fuck.

I don't care that I have my hood over my head, hiding the loose waves of my dark caramel brown hair that I've tugged one too many times this morning. It's the least of my problems.

Mirko Meadows spiraling…

London being on *Enticed*…

My mom being trapped…

Now, those *are my problems.*

It's all so fucked up and I hate it.

I hate how much I want London.

I haven't felt like Tate Meadows in a long while.

I spent every second of the Christmas break wondering what the blonde goddess was doing. I'm losing pieces of myself. My—life-of-the-party, gives-no-shit, just-focus-on-football—self.

I'm not telling a soul about what happened last night, including Levi. I want to strip it from my mind, strip it bare, and the less I think about it, the more I want it to simply fade from my mind.

As if that's going to freaking work, Meadows.

I probably look like shit, that's what they must be staring at. Being sleep-deprived while intoxicated is bound to do that to an eighteen-year-old hallucinating guy, whose entire life is falling apart. I mean, *yeah*, Sasha's blowjob did help, but it was only momentary therapy.

When I make it to my locker, Levi's already there. His is beside mine. There's a whole crowd by him. *Our group.* The IT girls, the jocks, our whole fucking popular crew.

I nod and smile, slinging my arm over Sasha's shoulder, pretending I'm amused with the conversation I just entered when I'm not even concentrating.

Facades. All fucking facades.

Get. Me. Out. Of. Here.

Nod. Grin. Chuckle.

Nod. Grin. Chuckle.

Nod. Grin. Chuckle.

"Hey there." Sasha's grins up at me, her nails slowly rushing up my chest and curling around the drawstrings of my hoodie. "Thank you for this morning."

"No," I murmur with a smirk, tugging her closer to me, her rose mist almost blacking me out with how intense it is. "Thank *you.*"

A soft laugh escapes Sasha.

Her eyes sparkle in glee, all while Levi continues talking to our other close friend, Wesley.

"What are you doing tonight?" Sasha purrs.

There's something so familiar about her.

We've spent one too many whiskey-infused nights rolling around the sheets, and smoking joints we shouldn't at hours we shouldn't be after our *non-hook-up*-hook-ups. But when she looks at me, like *really* looks at me with her emerald eyes boring into mine, lighting up, I feel...nothing.

Nothing like I do with...

I hate myself for flickering my gaze across the hall at the glimpse of honey blonde in my peripheral vision.

There she is.

London.

Pressed up against her locker with Nicandro kissing her into heaven.

His hands snake her ass, squeezing it tight, their kiss deepening with tongues going wild.

I know I should look away.

I know it shouldn't get to me.

I am the one who told London I was going to ruin her life and then decided avoidance was best, but I can't help the fury rushing through my veins. The jealously. The guilt. The desire.

I watched her on Enticed last night.

Fuck.

Forgetting everything about this blonde goddess is impossible because as she breaks the kiss with a soft laugh, her cheeks are the same tinge of red they were last night. It takes me back. Back to when I was moaning her name. Back to when she was coming undone with her vibrator.

I don't know why, but as students pass, they glance over at London, some even glare.

The hell…?

Have I missed something?

Why are they looking at her like that?

I turn back to Sasha, devilishly grinning down at her when she tugs the drawstrings of my hoodie lower, causing me to lower my head. "Sorry, what did you say, baby?"

She bats her fake spider-leg lashes. "Oh, it's okay, I asked what you're doing tonight?"

Distraction.

Sasha could be the perfect distraction to all this mess.

Leaning forward, my forehead brushes against hers, and I can't help the soft chuckle that rumbles up my throat at her soft moan.

"You," I whisper seductively against her lips, all the while my gaze flickers to the side at London. "I'll be fucking doing *you*, Sasha, if you want me to."

"You know I do."

"Mmhmmm."

Sasha's breath thickens as her nails rush up under my hoodie to the back of my neck. The touch should do something to me, leave a scorching permanent mark, but it doesn't. Her nails slowly slide through my tousled hair. I ignore her. I ignore the fuck out of all the dirty things she whispers in my ear, not letting the words sink in because I'm concentrating on what's happening on the other side of the hall instead.

Nicandro whispers something in London's ear that makes her blush. He then kisses her cheek and walks away. It leaves her flustered, a giddy smile on her lips as she watches him leave.

London looks happy.

So fucking happy.

He makes her happy.

Until her eyes dart around the hallway and land on mine, almost on instinct.

My entire body freezes up while London's smile drops to pure nothingness. Air feels trapped, tight in my chest for every second her heated stare lasers through me. London's brows knit up in…*I don't know*. All I do know is that I remain here with a clenched jaw, my mind fizzling away while the chaotic sound of students muttering before class drowns into a sea of silence.

It's just her and me.

Her and *me* across the high school corridor.

Her and me as my hoodie slips and Sasha begins kissing my neck, her teeth nipping at my warm skin and tongue slowly sucking on me, destined to leave marks.

What would London do if she knew I watched?

London Héroux looks at me like it's the first time somebody has ever acknowledged her existence. *She's beautiful.* And there's a glint in her eyes, scorching fire riddled with our past.

I hate myself for staring.

I shouldn't want her.

When I told London I was going to ruin her life, I wasn't lying.

Knowing she's watching, a cocky smirk crawls up my lips, my hands tightening around Sasha's waist while she mauls my neck with love bites, and I let her. I let her because I'm a selfish bastard that loves the fire that pools in London's gaze.

London witnesses every single one of Sasha's kisses. She watches on as I squeeze Sasha's ass and grind my stretchin' erection into her, my dick growing even harder at the voyeurism.

I take fucking pleasure in it.

Take pleasure that London's getting a taste of karma.

My heart can't stop racing. Wildly. Zapping and palpitating.

I chuckle darkly, my eyes never leaving London's as I brush my lips against Sasha's, seconds from colliding. "You keep doing that and I'm going to kiss you."

"That's what I want, Meadows."

Without overthinking it, I cup Sasha's face and recklessly crash my warm lips on hers.

I give it my all, kissing her ruthlessly. Unapologetically. Downright dirty as our tongues dance together without a fucking care in the world.

I devour Sasha, a fucked-up side of me turned on by the fact I can feel London's hot gaze staring into the side of my head. It only has me kissing her harder. Deeper. Without reservation.

Knowing she's truly not over me like she pledges, I make it a whole fucking show for her. I roam my hands across Sasha's body, smirk through the filthy French kiss as our tongues brutally swirl together and slip my fingers through her auburn hair while the kiss extends.

I kiss Sasha Jones as if it's my last kiss, all while keeping my darkened gaze on London, letting her in on the performance.

I don't care that I don't feel a fucking connection from the kiss.

I don't care that Sasha is probably reading into this more than I am.

I don't care that it'll be London I'll be thinking of when Sasha sucks my dick tonight.

All I care about are those baby-blue viper-eyes staring right back at me as I give London Héroux a taste of her own fucking medicine.

My smirk can't stop deepening during the kiss at the sight of her jaw grinding together.

Oh, two can play the game, baby girl.

And if you want to play it with Nicandro, I'll play it with Sasha.

Let's see who wins, LonLon, let's fucking see.

"My god, that was… *Whoa!*," Sasha pants against my lips, breaking the kiss for a gasp of air. "You kiss like a fucking dream, Tate." She steals another peck. "And you taste like gin…"

If only you knew…

"Do I?"

"Yeah, I tasted it earlier this morning too, but just thought…" Sasha looks between my glazed eyes with softly furrowed brows. "Oh my God, are you hungover?"

I kiss her hard to shut her the hell up, knowing if I don't, I'll slip up and do something stupid like call her *London* because that's how fucked up my head is right now. All I can think about is the blonde-haired goddess as I kiss Sasha again, relentlessly. My breath hardens and cock stirs against my boxer briefs from the very thought of my enemy witnessing every single second.

And just like that, London takes her books out of her locker, the slamming metal echoing around my heart when she slams it shut.

London's blue-eyed gaze never leaves me once as she walks away toward our AP English Literature class, giving me all the confirmation I need as my make-out session ceases.

It's going to be hard to forget her.

"What the fuck do you mean there's a viral video of London Héroux going around?"

Levi looks at me as if I'm insane, shaking his head in disbelief beside me in English Lit class. "What the fuck do *you* mean? You haven't seen it?"

What the hell?

My brows knit together in confusion. "I haven't seen *what?*"

"London and Maddie. They had a full-on cat fight in the girl's bathroom yesterday, you didn't know about it?"

My jaw hits the floor.

"*No!*" I screech, the word coming out much more high-pitched than I would have liked.

"Where the fuck have you been?"

Jacking off to her. That's where I've fucking been.

"I don't know, I think the whole thing with my father is making me feel off."

"I swear to god it was him I saw last night."

"I believe you, it was him." I nod. "I put my phone on no caller ID and called his number last night after your text…"

"And?"

"I think he's cheating. *Also*, he came home this morning and, fuck, it was so obvious."

Levi's eyes widen. "Well, shit. What are you going to do about it? Confront him?"

"And let him take my Mustang from me? Don't think so. There's ways of finding out without asking, Prescott, watch and learn."

Levi shakes his head with a smile. "You're something else, bro. Anyway, look at this…"

He pulls out his phone and slips an Air Pod in each of our ears, all while our teacher has her head down correcting papers. The video begins with my stepsister, Maddie, mocking London in the girl's bathroom, before a fight breaks out and she goes for those honey blonde waves I know so well.

There's a certain point where London retaliates and starts fighting back against my stepsister. But Maddie wouldn't be her true Maddie self if she didn't take it next-level. Their screaming, virtually killing each other, and that's when Maddie rips London's blouse and then goes for her bra, and *Jesus Christ*. All the air is sucked out of my body at London's pear-shaped tits with the rosiest hardened nipples. The same ones I came to last night.

As much as I hate London for what she did to me, watching this video makes me feel sick to my stomach. My heart shatters into a million tiny pieces, but I can't let emotion win. I've survived my entire life this far playing with my head, and I can't get past the fact that London lied and told my sister that she kissed me.

The video ends and I'm left staring, looking at my own darkened reflection, realizing just how hard my breathing has become.

Wait.

Wait a second.

That's why they were all *staring.*

"I didn't fucking kiss her," I whisper.

Levi nods. "*Exactly*. She's saying shit just to not look like the bad guy."

Chucking him back his Air Pod, I subtly pull out my phone from my blazer pocket and slip it on top of my copy of *Wuthering Heights*. (Side note: I definitely didn't get the memo to read this shit over spring break.)

Losing every breath I take, I play it cool, not letting it get to me. I pull up my contacts and tap on Maddie's. But a knock takes me out of my thoughts. It's another teacher who approaches Miss Thompson. By the look on his face, it looks serious. Miss Thompson excuses herself and vows for us to be on our best behavior for five minutes, before disappearing out the door.

I return to my phone, sending my stepsister a text.

TATE: What the hell? Why did you go after London like that?

Maddie's reply is instant. I left our house early this morning, so I didn't even see her.

MADDIE: Thanks for caring now.

TATE: What do you mean?

MADDIE: I'm not even at school and you haven't even noticed, asshole.

Shit.

She's not at school?

I rub a hand over my stubbled jaw and reply back, my gaze flickering to London, who sits alone in the front row, writing down in her notebook like the perfect A-grade student she is.

A good girl.

My gaze narrows.

What the hell did you do, Héroux?

What did you just start?

TATE: Mads, I'm sorry, I had a crazy morning and left before seeing you...What's going on?

No response.

Fuck.

"Aye, London!" I call out, causing a few heads to snap in my direction, but I don't give a shit.

I'm a witness to the way tension laces across London's entire body, beginning at her shoulders and all the way down her spine. It doesn't matter that she has her back to me, I can tell.

"The fuck you doing dude?" Levi whispers over to me.

Smirking, I brush him off. "Watch and learn, bro, watch and fucking learn."

Ever so slowly, London glances over her shoulder, her perfectly-curved eyebrows softly knitting together.

"Yes?" she murmurs, her voice such a honeyed sin, it sends shockwaves through me.

I hate it.

I hate her.

I hate what she did to us.

And now London has hurt Maddie. She's lied about me kissing her. I'm not letting this go. I said I would bring London Héroux hell, and guess what, I'm fuckin' starting right now.

"You want to spread rumors that I kissed you, you better learn to come to *me* with it, not my *sister*." I growl, the entire room falling so silent, a pin could drop and we wouldn't hear it. "Not unless you want to start a problem, Héroux."

Students gasp, while others not so subtly pull out their phones, recording.

I hate this society. I really freaking do.

But a villainous heat is roaring across my body too damn fast to care about them.

London's pink plump lips, those that used to always be coated in strawberries and cream gloss, part to a soft gasp. There's fear in her eyes, I see it the moment my stare turns into a full-on glare. Her baby blue eyes glaze over in apprehension, but it's quickly washed over with something else...*defiance.*

"I wasn't trying anything," London almost whispers. "I was...just saying the truth."

My eyes almost bulge out of my sockets. *Is she serious?*

Does she seriously want to lie to the entire school saying that I kissed her?

Fuck no.

I'm not nice guy Tate Meadows, not like I used to be.

I'm the rebellion.

The fucking antichrist.

I'm Tate Meadows, the bad boy of Glorsin St. Claire's.

Coldly chuckling, my chair scrapes against the glossy floor as I stand and stalk over to her, not giving a shit she's left staring up at my six-foot-one stance while she's still sitting.

"*Saying the truth?*" I spit, roughness in my tone. "You were *saying the damn truth?*"

"Yeah. I'm just trying to be truthful."

"A psycho bitch is what you are," I growl.

Eyes widening, London doesn't expect it. "Are you going to stop with the name-calling?"

"Only when you fucking stop with the lies." I kick the edge of her table, it screeches against the floor, startling her as I go on my hell-bent rage. "You want to act like such a good girl saying that I kissed you, but guess what, London?" I crouch down, inches from her lips and wolfishly whisper all cockily, "I wouldn't even fucking kiss you if you were the last woman alive. How does that feel, hmm?"

Gasps flood the classroom, but none come from London, who's

trying so hard not to cry. I can see it in the way those light blues gloss over, how her cheeks are the softest tinge of pink and she can't stop biting her lower lip.

If London Héroux thought that I wasn't going to bite, well, she's wrong. I'm a starving wolf, and I'll do whatever the hell it takes to get her off Maddie's back, even if that means getting a taste of her hypnotizing sweetness, like last night.

I almost love the wickedness in her stare, jaw gritted and doe eyes all dark and angry.

"Oh, okay, asshole," she fights back, finding her courage again. "Because that's *totally* why you pleaded that I owed you a kiss in exchange for ignoring me for the rest of senior year, right?"

Wellll…Yeah.

I did say that a while ago.

London still owes me that kiss, but I ain't admitting it here.

"Keep dreaming, princess, we made no deal. If we had, I'd be ignoring you, and I'm not. You're a *liar*."

"That doesn't concern me."

"*Doesn't concern you?*" I practically laugh in her face. "I swear to fucking god, Héroux, you touch my sister again, it'll be war. That's a fucking promise."

"You know what?" London slams the *Wuthering Heights* book on the desk, its echo ricocheting through my chest. "I'm so sick of *you* thinking you can bully *me*! I'm not afraid of *you*!"

She shoots up off her chair, so much shorter than me, jabbing a finger in my chest.

"I don't care what you do or how you perceive me, I don't need *anybody*, understand that, Tate? *NOBODY!*" London screams, pent-up anger at its finest, her eyes the shiniest I've ever seen. The saddest too. Like I'm *el diablo*. "I don't need *you*! Or *Maddie*! Or anybody else in *this whole fucking school!*"

Coldly smirking, I step closer to London until that familiar rosy vanilla and strawberry scent consumes me.

Lowering my head so that our noses are almost brushing, I flicker my eyes back and forth between hers in pure disgust. Only when my jaw clenches about fifty times, do I find the strength to deepen my smirk while her warm breath continuously tickles my skin, ruining me.

"How about *Nicandro*?" I taunt in a low whisper. "*Hmmm*? Do you need him? I've heard you like to suck his cock, but you don't want a relationship because you want to keep your grades. I mean, who the fuck says that?" I chuckle, loving her deepening rage. "Yeah. That's right. I bet you need him, babygirl. Need *him* to survive senior year."

London bawls her fists, just as the first pearly tear glides down her cheek, baptizing it slowly.

"You're so pathetic, London," Sasha, whose also in this classroom, mocks from somewhere behind us. "You think you can get a tattooed guy to take care of you? He doesn't care."

"He does," my blonde angel snaps.

"No," I click my tongue, "she's right. Nicandro doesn't care. He's only using you, it's so fucking obvious. He would never want anything to do with you, if you guys weren't foolin' around. Trust me."

More tears fall, and yet, she remains defiant, standing tall, confident. Her candy glossed lips tremble and even though the hurt written over her face is obvious, she doesn't move.

"He'll never want you. Who do you even think you are, London Héroux?" I scoff. "It's like you're trying to be a million people at once. Innocent, but like getting on your knees. Goes to parties, but never drinks. A descendent of the Héroux, and yet you can't stop staring at *me*. You must really hate your parents for all the shit you're doing behind their backs, huh? Ain't that right?"

"Tate, stop," London warns, emotion clouding her words, cracking her voice. "*Please*."

Air sizzles between us.

"She sounds like a desperado," Sasha fake-yawns in the distance.

"Let's get the narrative straight, shall we?" I turn around and point at all of the phones filming us. "Last Saturday night, at my house party, London Héroux tried to kiss *me*, and I rejected *her*. *That's* why she's talking shit, because she's hurt that I made her storm out of my house."

The entire class bursts out laughing, belittling London. And me? Well, I just keep on staring into those baby blues, lost in the people we once were and what we've become...

A fragment of our parents.

I'm sure what she's feeling isn't an inch of what my fifteen-year-old self felt sitting on that Central Park bench, all alone, three years ago. She lied to me. Deceived me. Just like *Mirko*.

London Héroux ruined me.

This is me ruining her back.

"*I* tried to kiss *you*?" London gasps in complete shock. "Are you *serious*?"

"Isn't Nicandro's cock enough? What did you want from me? A throuple?" I shake my head, flashing her that infamous Tate Meadows half-smirk. "Sorry, angel, but I've got something going with Sasha, and I'm not ending that to lower myself to somebody like *you*."

London looks at me as if her entire world is falling apart, and just like that, she races out of the classroom. The taunts for London get louder. My heart pangs, and that's when I realize...

Fuck.

"London!" I call out, chasing her out through the locker-lined corridors. "*London!*"

London isn't far, but the second she glances over her shoulder and notices me, she begins bolting, her Doc Martins slapping against the glossy high school floors. Without thinking, I sprint after her, determined not to give up until my lungs are burning.

"Stop! Get the hell away from me, Tate!"

She's sobbing.

Sobbing.

"London, wait!"

I catch up to her just as we turn a corner and I jump in front of her, forcing her into a frantic halt. With tears blurring her eyes and onyx-colored mascara streaking down her flustered cheeks, London holds out her hands, begging for me to stop. All the color is drained from her face, her sobs hysterical, all while her chest heaves so fast I'm scared she may collapse right here.

And that's when I see it...

My entire world stops.

All my anger, pain, and animosity simmers at the faded white scars lining her wrists, alongside other darker ones.

Fresher ones.

Cuts.

It takes a second for my body to freeze up, two for it to numb completely. *No.*

Breathing becomes too much. I know exactly what *they* mean. *No. No. No.*

London has been trying to...

Oh. My. God.

My jaw drops.

Everything just stops.

Everything changes for me. *Every. Single. Thing.*

I thought I hated London Héroux, but as our eyes lock and the depth of the reddening in hers toys with my mind, I'm not so sure. Whatever is rolling through her mind is more than just us simply fighting. There's more. There's more she's hiding. My heart...*fuck*, it breaks.

Oh. No.

Oh. Fucking. No.

"No, no, no," I whisper, surprising myself when my voice cracks. I can't stop shaking my head. Can't stop wishing I could reach out and hold her. Can't stop hurting. "Please, baby, no."

"Tate, please leave me alone!"

"I...I *can't*." I panic, instinctively threading my fingers through hers. "London, I..."

"Stop." She cries, her icy cold touch instantly slips away from mine. "Let go of me!"

"But—"

"Tate—"

"I'm so sorry," I whisper, my heart aching, breaking in two. "Forgive me, *LonLon*."

LonLon.

I just called her, *LonLon.*

Our history trickles between us.

Every single inch of hope leaves me.

There's nothing else I want but...but *us.*

London's sobs intensify, and it kills me. Only the lingering trace of her nostalgic perfume remains with me when she runs, alongside this aching dagger in the middle of my bleeding heart.

A bang rings out as my back slams against the locker-lined walls.

FUCK!

With my head in my hands, I slide down the locker, feeling nothing.

Fuck. Fuck. Fuck.

What...

What the hell did I just do?

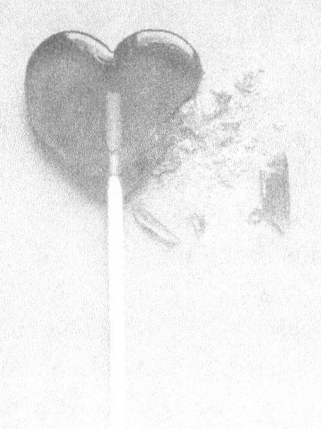

Chapter
TWENTY-NINE

London

Being locked up in a cubical for the entirety of the period wasn't exactly how I expected my day to go, but I have no choice. *I'm not going back out there.*

After the triggering fight with Maddie yesterday, the last thing I wanted was to show up to school today and deal with people's stares. It's bad enough I'm the new girl, now I'm the psycho new girl and the entire school has seen my tits, including Tate Meadows.

In another world, it would mortify me, but my pain runs much deeper than that right now.

Tate.

I can't believe how badly he belittled me. How he treated me back there in English Literature. I know I hurt him, but I have a reasonable explanation.

I hate him.

I hate him so freaking much.

Wiping the tears from my eyes is no use. They continue to flow like endless rivers, every single tear brought on by *him.*

I haven't been breathing right for thirty minutes straight. It's too much. All too much. There's this tightness in my chest, and the more I sit on the marble bathroom floor, my back against the frosted-glass divider, the more I wish I could just self-destruct.

Nothing makes me feel better.

All I feel is pain, pain, pain.

Everywhere.

Digging my nails deeper through my stockings, I puncture the sheer fabric, the deep reddening marks on my thighs reminding me I'm at school. I need to find an alternative to relieve Tate's torment, to make me numb, and I do just that, digging my nails in further until it stings, and then more.

Squeezing my eyes shut, I let the pain subside, before that numbness takes over.

You're nothing.

You're nothing.

You're nothing.

A psycho bitch is what you are.

I'm not lowering myself to something like you.

I wouldn't even fucking kiss you if you were the last woman alive.

I can't stop staring at the cubical walls.

I can't stop rocking back and forth, bile rushing up my throat.

I can't stop sobbing, feeling so hollow inside, it's as if I'm a balloon waiting to burst.

My body isn't a wonderland, it's a flawed route. Scars. Cuts. Faded black and blue bruises.

Tate's words resurface so much, but it's my fault. My fault I can't hold it together.

Useless is what I am.

It's all I'll ever be.

Tate Meadows was once my everything, my crush, the boy with the brazen blue eyes giving me his raincoat and making sure I was alright. We have so much history, spanning so many years, from Mr. Bunny, to stolen teenage daydream glances, to Pink Floyd's "*Wish You Were Here.*"

Tate Meadows was once my everything, now, he's my worst nightmare laced in nostalgia.

My father, Sterling Héroux, was right. I'll always just be Sterling Heroux's daughter.

I'll always be Tate Meadow's archenemy.

I'll always be *that* sad girl.

I'll never be ME.

Ever.

Not in this city. It's breaking my heart in a million pieces.

My lonely heart beats slower, and when I shut my eyes, I wish I could just disappear.

I wish I could go back three years and tell Tate the truth about *that* night.

I wish I could simply hold my breath and not feel anymore.

It's all I want.

I don't want to *feel.*

I don't want to *breathe.*

I, London Héroux, don't want to be *alive* anymore.

Chapter

THIRTY

London

The two videos featuring yours truly traveled faster than the speed of light. If I thought this day couldn't get any worse, I was damn wrong. Why? Because I'm currently having a date with the principal in his office. Yep. *The principal* of Glorsin St. Claire's, just about the sternest, cruelest, privileged man to ever exist.

I, never in my life, have been called to the principal's office.

I pride myself in being a good girl, with good grades, a good heart, just like my parents aspire me to be, but ever since Tate Meadows became a permanent fixture in my everyday life when I moved schools, everything changed.

Truthfully, I've never felt this alone. This little. This hurt.

I don't care if Tate hates me for breaking some stupid promise when we were kids. I will never forgive him for the way he's treating me. Okay, maybe I shouldn't have panicked with Maddie and said Tate kissed me when he didn't, but I'm not taking his shit. *Or his stepsister's.*

Principal Barrett hasn't stopped meticulously rubbing his cleanly-shaven jaw, sitting in his black leather buttoned chair, behind his dark oak desk. The pattered drapes are open, revealing a magnificent skyline view of Manhattan through his Victorian Gothic glass-stained windows.

My white Doc Martins sink into the expensive blue and gold Persian rug as I sit further back in the chair adjacent to the principal. *This is not good.*

This is not good.

This is not good.

Chills run down my spine at the coldness his office embodies. The Victorian gothic theme is represented throughout the room, with cast iron statues of horses literally everywhere. I even spotted a carved taxidermy ram skull hanging on the wall with tribal writing when I got called in.

Principal Barrett's office has got nothing on my old principal's one.

The room is laced with a spicy, woodsy scent. It feels lived in. Worked. A bookcase aligns one wall, an artwork of devils with angel wings that I'm certain date back a few centuries on the other, right beside his framed certificates, degrees, and masters. Oh, there's also a few medals, *and* a hand-drawn portrait of a little black bird with a thick teal streak down its beak.

My brows knit at the portrait.

Okay...

"London, London, London," Principal Barrett finally speaks, the roughness in his stoic voice shaking me to the core. "London Héroux."

Yep, sadly that's me all right.

Sitting up straighter, I offer him a small smile because I feel awkward doing anything else.

"Your father is Sterling Héroux, correct?"

Ummm...

"Yes, Mr. Barrett."

"Your father is in high stake real estate, some say he may even be the greatest, correct?"

"Hardly," Tate scoffs, slumped in his seat right beside me.

When we were called to the office, I felt Tate's stare burn into the side of my head, but I didn't dare give him the satisfaction of meeting his gaze. I already feel embarrassed and sick to my stomach because he saw my scars, my cuts, my only relief to my endless trauma.

"That's subjective, Mr. Barrett."

Arching a brow, an arrogant half-smirk works up his lips. "*Oh.*

So, you don't appreciate your father's hard work and determination? Well, both of your parents, I should say."

"Of course, I do," I lie through the skin of my teeth.

"Then I could imagine their disgust seeing their daughter, the London Héroux, involved in a needless fight. Fights, should I say. First with Miss Meadows, and then, with Mr. Meadows." My principal spits, his glare darkening as he adjusts his glasses on the bridge of his nose. "This behavior is catty, improper, and most of all, Miss Héroux, *unacceptable.*"

My jaw hangs open, shock rippling straight through me because I'm beginning to think through all of the fog. All of the anguish. All of the dried-up tears coated over my cheeks.

Does he think these two fights began because of me?

"With all due respect, Mr. Barrett, I—"

"I didn't ask for your opinion."

Tate groans, thrusting his face into his hands in my peripheral vision. "Fuck this for a joke."

Raising his chin high with that prestigious glare, Principal Barrett snaps his head toward Tate. "Neither did I ask for *yours*, Mr. Meadows. I highly suggest you revise your language and that you sit in your chair like a decent mundane human before you are given a warning."

Sighing, Tate sits up properly, and they share an intense stare.

Principal Barrett pushes up from his chair with so much force, it brushes against the glass-stained windows. His shiny oxfords slap against the dark oak hardwood floors, pacing, before he emerges from behind his desk with a look that could kill.

"As you can see, Miss Héroux and Mr. Meadows, it does not take a rocket scientist to deduce something has happened between the two of you. A misunderstanding, perhaps, but to me, it sounds like it's much more." He leans against the edge of his desk, arms confidently crossed over his navy double-breasted suit. "It's interrupting other students, affecting their education."

Tate leans forward in his seat, extending his hand. "But, Mr. Barrett, I—"

"NO," he grits. "St. Claire's is a prestigious high school with an exclusive selection. I can easily replace the both of you with two more deserving and eager students, is that understood?"

I nod, my sweaty palms destined to swallow me in a pit of angst.

Crossing my legs, I wince at the stinging pain covering my thighs through my stockings, but I push through. *I did it to myself.*

I don't know if Tate's presence and lingering sandalwood cologne makes my stomach swirl, or if it's all the butterflies coming alive— *still.* The butterflies trapped in an endless cycle, covered in a sinful dark death.

All I know is that my parents are going to kill me when they find out about this.

"Now," Principal Barrett continues, glancing between us. "Will one of you two advise me of the core issue, or will I have to phone your parents, not that I won't anyway. Using profound language, violence, and hindering your studies isn't something I take lightly."

Silence laces the room.

Complete.

Silence.

"SPEAK!" Principal Barrett threatens, shaking me cold. "ONE OF YOU SPEAK!"

My trembling hands rush beneath my thighs, just as Tate clears his throat. I can't even look at him, that's how badly the pendulum in my chest swings.

"Well…" Tate begins, and it's crazy just how raspy and deep his voice is. I've known him since we were ten. Now, eight years later, he's grown into a man. A viciously wild man with a tinge of both sin and heaven in his piercing blue-eyed gaze. "Despite our fathers being in a competitive New York real estate game, London and I have known each other since we were kids."

"Is that when the rivalry commenced?"

"No, quite the opposite. Miss Héroux and I were immensely close."

Principal Barrett flickers his beady eyes my way. "So, what happened?"

"A whole hell of a lot," Tate continues, "I—"

"I am looking at Miss Héroux and therefore, my question is intended for Miss Héroux."

Once again, silence slaughters the room.

This thick tension rolls around me, toxifying my air. My lifeline. *It's now or never, London.*

I swallow loudly. "Three years ago, I let him down."

"*And?*"

"Now Tate Meadows is crucifying me for it."

I expect Tate to react, to retaliate in the best way he knows how, instead, when I summon the courage to look at him, I freeze up at his Atlantic blue stare, and how it electrifies me for all of the wrong reasons. This is a boy who's grown into a reckless, bad boy jock. We've fallen into hate.

Tate says nothing.

Not a single word.

And I don't know why that makes me hurt more.

"This is a serious scandal," Principal Barrett continues, but his words become secondary to the way Tate's looking at me.

There's no hatred rippled in his eyes anymore, no malice, just wolfish desire.

Longing.

Regret.

And then he blinks, and Tate Meadows returns back to the devil I know. Clenching his jaw, he stares at our principal for the rest of our talk, never looking my way. Not ever. Not even *once.*

"You can both rest assured that Miss Meadows will be having this exact conversation too. The videos will be reviewed with my team and a unanimous decision will be made at a board meeting. This is a serious investigation for serious actions, is that understood?"

"Yes."

"Yep."

"The board has three days to decide. You both have an immediate three-day suspension until a decision is made. I hope you will both reflect upon your decisions and understand the gravity of your actions."

The second we leave, I take the opposite corridor to reenter the tunneled bridge that connects the school to the teacher and principal's wing. Leaning against the exposed brick wall, I press my eyes shut, telling myself that it's okay. *I'll* be okay. But all my breaths tangle into one big mess because I know it won't.

My father is going to crucify me when he gets the call from Principal Barrett.

I can't do it.

I can't take another hit.

I want this all to stop. Right. Now.

"London," Tate's soft murmur is inches away. Waiting.

My heart jolts, my breaths coming to a tragic halt because of him.

"Don't," I plead in a bare whisper, keeping my eyes shut. I shake my head, feeling my hair sprawling all over the brick wall. "Please don't even think about speaking to me now, Tate."

His name is venom on my tongue.

Carnage.

I feel Tate linger for a few more seconds, and then, just like that, the slap of his shoes becomes softer and softer, until they remain alive solely in my mind, fading thumps, like my heart.

When I open my eyes to a blurry vision, all the strength to keep it together pools up in the center of my throat and creates an agonizing throb. I watch on from a far distance as Tate, who becomes smaller and smaller, is almost at the other side of the tunneled bridge. I watch on as he walks with his head low, his black and emerald-green St. Claire's uniform fitting him like armor, like it was made for him. I watch on as the only boy who gave me butterflies walks away.

Three days.

I'm suspended for three days because of Tate Meadows.

Fear sets in because I know my parents will kill me, my father, possibly quite literally.

And all of a sudden, everything makes sense…

My father moved me here to bring me hell.

That's when I slide down the wall, my head in my hands, praying the devil just takes me.

Any devil. Any one at all. Just not my gorgeously blue-eyed devil, Tatum Lee Meadows.

When did the faded pink wallpaper in my bedroom begin peeling?

Shrugging, I lean my back against the foot on my bed, my ass planted on my bedroom floor. It's crazy the things you notice when you feel like your soul is being ripped out from the inside out.

I don't know how long I've been in my bedroom since meeting with Principal Barrett after school, listening to Pink Floyd on my record player, staring at my wall, lying to Nicandro in texts by saying I'm okay, even though I'm not. My three-day suspension hasn't even started, and yet, I know the full-blown effects of it. I have no idea how my father will react, other than with his fists.

To be clear, my story shouldn't be one people disregard because it makes them uncomfortable. I know it does, fuck, what do you think it does to me? But this is my life.

My truth.

It's worth saying.

And while I don't know if I'm worth living, or dying, my story... it's raw. It's bittersweet.

And in its own way, it's a rendition of the most tragic poetry I've ever read, just like Plath's.

When I was a little girl, I never knew he could be so cold. When I was six, I used to admire him. For the way he owned a successful business. For the way he loved my mother. For the way he adored me. But then I grew a little older, nine-years-old to be exact, and everything changed.

I remember the first time my father hit me. It's crazy, that thing, how you always remember your first time. It was a stormy Manhattan night, and I had just woken up from a nightmare. It would have been around two or three in the morning, I didn't know because I didn't have an alarm clock at the time, but it just felt like that hour, you know. I dreamed that a bad guy broke into our penthouse and killed my mommy and daddy, right in front of me.

I woke up screaming.

Hysterically crying.

In need of love.

Real life and fiction were so blurred at that age. I didn't know what to think. I remember it all so vividly, how lightning bolts lit up the sky, and thunder rumbled all of heaven and hell. I wanted to rush out of my bedroom in my favorite pink fluffy slippers, but with every bit of thunder, my screams heightened, and I sunk beneath my bed covers, sobbing if Mommy and Daddy were okay.

That's when I heard my bedroom door creak open.

Heavy footsteps.

A happiness trailed over my heart and wrapped around it in a perfect bow because Mommy and Daddy were coming. They were real. They were going to save me from the monsters.

All of them.

And then my father ripped the sheets off my body, gripped my jaw, and with his other hand, slapped me hard, right across my mouth.

It stopped the wailing.

The screams.

And left me with a bloodied lip for seven days straight.

Ever since that night, whenever I had a nightmare, I wished it were true. I wished bad guys came into my house. Killed my parents. Set me free.

It's been a reoccurring dream, a figment of my own fascination fixed with my own subconscious.

My father didn't rush to me to settle my tears. To embrace me in the solace of his arms. To tell me everything was going to be alright. He hit me—purposely.

I wish it was only the slap, but it was much more.

He suspended dance for a month.

He told me I was a weak little girl for crying.

He squeezed my jaw until I was certain it would pop.

I was nine years old.

Nine when I learned my father was my destroyer.

And now, nine years later, he's still the epitome of my hell.

It's evident. So fucking evident in the way those Oxfords I know too well slap against the marble outside my bedroom, and before I can move, my door slams open, hitting my wall like it always does. Bouncing twice. My father's done it so many times that now there's a permanent dent in the wall, a reminder of his abuse, not that I need reminding.

Something like this stays with you forever.

Creates scars.

Just like the ones I carve into my soul.

And here Sterling Héroux is in all his glory, pin-striped designer suit, salt and pepper stubbled jaw, and perfectly slicked back hair. Like always. A beast in gentleman's clothing. His soulless black eyes scan my room, angrily, and the second they meet mine, his fists already tense.

The way he slams my door shut makes the entire wall ricochet, but it does worse damage to my heart.

Principal Barrett called Sterling Héroux.

My father grinds his jaw together as he stomps past me, to my record player, and all I want to do is trip him. The second I reach for my phone, he picks it up and slams it against the wall, shattering it to pieces, alongside my only chance of help. But he doesn't stop there. Pink Floyd's "*Another Brick In The Wall*" comes to a screeching halt when he grips the record player and slams it to the ground. Over, and over, and over again. Until his hair's a tousled mess. Until scattered pieces of what were once special surround my bedroom, shards of my heart bleeding out.

I don't scream out.

Don't reach out to salvage my prized possession.

Don't try to recover from the numbness rippling my skin.

Instead, I watch on with blurry eyes, half alive and half dead.

Any other day, this tension would crawl over my body, rendering me incapable of speaking. It doesn't matter how many times my father hits me, every single one creates shock waves.

Usually, I would try to run.

Usually, I would try to make him stop.

Usually, I would try to save myself from his torment.

But today, there isn't a piece of me that wants to stay. Stay on earth. I'm sick, and I'm tired. And I'm over it. Maybe if he hits me hard enough, I won't suffer anymore.

I won't have these problems.

I won't struggle to breathe.

I won't be broken inside.

I would just...*fade.*

"Suspended for three days...You want to get kissed by Tate Meadows, huh?" My father growls, lifting up my entire body with a single grip on my throat. "DO YOU FUCKING LOVE TATE MEADOWS?"

I continue staring into the eyes of the man I'm supposed to call my father.

The cords in my neck tighten when my father's grip intensifies, air sucked out of my lungs when he violently throws me on my bed as if I'm some puppet.

I'll never forget the fire swirling in his gaze when his hand returns to my throat, strangling me harder, a snarl in his voice when he scarily whispers, "You're not fighting back today, huh?"

Tears pool, but I don't dare blink.

I'm done.

Exhausted.

Defenseless.

Kill me, Dad. Come on. Fucking do it. Kill me.

"You think you're smart, London, hmm? You *want* Tate Meadows to save you and take you away from here? I. Won't. Let. You. Is this why you're going after him? His stepsister?"

"I—"

"*DEN MUND HALTEN!*" He growls, his grip intensifying so fiercely, my lips part for air. "SHUT UP! BECAUSE I DON'T FUCKING CARE!"

That's when I feel my body closing in, like I'm choking on air. I slap a hand over his wrist, eyes widening in fear.

"I'll...I'll call the police," I whisper so hoarsely, compressed by his hand. *I will.*

"I'd like to see you try." My father chuckles in my face. "Pathetic little fucking girl."

Tightening his hand around my throat so forcefully that the world begins spinning. Panic heats my spine, and just when I think it's all over, and I'm gasping for air, he lets go.

I can breathe again.

"If you fall in love with my enemy's son, if you fall in love with Tate Meadows, I will break every bone in your body, understand? I will kill you, *liebste tochter.*"

Daughter dearest.

"And nobody will ever find you, you know why?" My father studies me slowly in disgust, his jaw ticking before lowering his lips to my ear in a chilling whisper, "Because nobody will even notice you're missing, *sweetheart.*"

I shut my eyes, sinking into my bedsheets with a rapidly beating heart, just in time for my father to storm out of my bedroom, not before I hear a soft click.

The lock.

"Oh no," I whisper under my breath, knowing exactly what this means.

He just locked my bedroom door, trapping me in.

He hasn't done that since the day I was discharged from hospital three years ago, the night I lost Tate Meadows. The night that changed it all. The night Sterling Héroux changed the locks so that there were two locks on either side, with the one outside being the master. Locking me in.

Instead of taking care of me, my parents locked me in here like a caged animal for days.

Until the stitches on my head were due to get taken out.

Until I recovered from the concussion he caused me.

Until I cried my heart out for losing Tate Meadows.

And now it's happening all over again...

In my mind, life has stopped for me.

All of the thrill.

The courage.

The hope.

It's all gone.

All that's left is a shell of the person London Héroux is as I flicker my eyes open, staring up at my pink diamond paper crane chandelier with a vicious ache.

With hot tears streaming down my cheeks, I mentally reopen my pink leather journal. The one I used to write everything about my boy crush in. The one I haven't written in since Tate made me feel like the luckiest girl in the world, until my father destroyed us without even knowing.

And in all my brokenness, I write Tate another secret entry in my head with my eyes trained on the ceiling.

Entry Ten: I think I'm dying...

Tate,

I wish I could describe just how deeply I truly hate you.
How deeply my hate will never be enough not to love you.

How sorry I am for breaking us, all because I was trying to protect evil.

I'm not protecting that evil anymore. I can't. Which is why I need to do what I'm going to do soon. Maybe one day, in heaven, you can kiss me in heartache. Until then, I will always hate to love you.

I always have, ever since the night we first met.

When you told me the moon was ours.

Forgive me,
London

Chapter
THIRTY-ONE

Tate

I haven't spoken to Maddie in the last three days; I haven't seen my father in the past two. I don't know where the hell he is, but when my stepmom, Sabrina, heard the news of our suspension, she shipped herself and Maddie off to a 'therapy' vacation in *Florida*.

I've sent Maddie a few texts just to check in, but she either doesn't reply or tells me to go fuck myself, so I guess she's feeling pretty good. You know, her old self.

The three days have passed, and it's the weekend. I won't know until Monday from Principal Barrett what happens now. If I'll be suspended further, or worse, expelled.

I haven't seen London in three days, since she told me not to talk to her and I walked away, and quite honestly, I've…fuck, *I've missed her*.

I've spent my three days of suspension and an entire weekend playing guitar with a loose string inside my heart. None of the riffs feel right. The lyrics don't flow. I don't get a kick out of the vibrations of pressing my hand against the wood. Nothing makes sense without London.

I never meant to make her hurt.

How the fuck can I hurt something so special to me?

That shouldn't have been my approach at all. I should have sided with London. Should have forgiven her for every single thing that happened three years ago. I should have defended her.

Instead…*I just finished breaking us.*

I hate myself for pushing her so far.

I hate myself for not hating her enough, for hating her too much.

I'm just so confused.

So battered and bruised.

So numb, I can barely recognize myself.

It's been five days since I last went on *Enticed* and saw London there for the first time. I haven't been on since. It's taken everything within me, but if I need to do this, I need to do it right.

Nothing can distract me from her, not even when I'm playing guitar, at work, or at the gym with Levi and Wesley, which have always been my destress methods to slip into a bliss of complete nothingness and escape my world, *until now.*

London's so perfectly wrapped in my story. The glimpse I got of who she really is five days ago isn't enough. I want more. *Need more.* But I can't.

She never replied to the direct message I sent her earlier this week via *Enticed.*

HenleyKing17: How the fuck am I supposed to forget about you now?

All that stares back at me in our chat is…

Rose Heartache Mila hasn't logged on in five days.

That has me worried.

LonLon, are you okay?

Fuck. When did I start calling her *LonLon?*

Part of me wonders if she ever will come back online. If the reasons to why she confuses me so much will come to light. She wants to make love to her body in the lonely hours of the night to strangers, but she doesn't want a conversation with them outside of her cam lives?

I don't get it. I really don't.

This girl is going to ruin me.

Not that she hasn't already.

It's day six, and she's logged onto *Enticed*.

In fact, our chat tells me London Héroux (*Rose Heartache Mila*) is **online.**

I wait with fated breath for my damn message to flicker from **delivered** to **read**, but…

It never does.

I'm not getting expelled, and neither is Maddie or my blonde angel.

It's Monday, and our fate is sealed, before my phone vibrates. *Enticed.*

It's Monday, and neither my stepsister nor my childhood crush is talking to me.

It's Monday, and I can tell just by staring into *her* baby blue eyes something isn't right.

Chapter
THIRTY-TWO

Tate

Rose Heartache Mila replied.

A week after I first sent her the direct message on *Enticed*, London *actually fucking replied.*

Worst part is she's sitting three rows ahead of me in class.

We have a substitute teacher today, the kind that threw us this classic line: *If you're all quiet and do the work your teacher sent you, we'll have no issues. I'll be up at the front doing my own corrections. And yes, you may listen to music, as long as I'm not hearing Bon Jovi blasting through your AirPods. Then I'll get pissed and write a note back to your teacher stating you were all bastards.*

Okay, maybe he didn't include the last part, but you get my drift.

Flicking my eyes to the substitute teacher, I make sure he's not doing one of those sneaky glances around the room before glancing back down at my phone I have sitting in the middle of *Wuthering Heights*, on silent.

I have my left elbow folded on the table, subtly shielding my phone away from Levi on my left, who hasn't stopped banging his head to his not-so-quiet-music. I'm left in peace to read the new message I received this morning in the *Enticed* direct-messaging app.

Rose Heartache Mila: You don't need to forget about me... Sorry I haven't been on or gotten back to you sooner, life has been a little crazy, but I'll be on tonight. ;)

Life has been a little crazy.
What does that mean exactly?
Why does that freaking hurt so much?

HenleyKing17: There's no reason to apologize, Rose, so long as you're okay.

A lifetime passes before those three little dots appear.

I look up through my thick inky black lashes, witnessing the exact moment London crosses her legs and tucks her phone deeper into her pencil case as she types away.

Since when did the good girl use her phone in school?
I smirk wickedly. *Since me.*

Rose Heartache Mila: I'm okay, I miss you watching me.

HenleyKing17: It was only one night...

Rose Heartache Mila: One night was enough.

Tell me about it, baby.

HenleyKing17: What are you doing right now?

Rose Heartache Mila: I'm in college. Am I allowed to say that?

College.
A lopsided smirk crawls up the corners of my lips.

HenleyKing17: You just did. ;)

Rose Heartache Mila: Oh my god, shut up! Haha!

HenleyKing17: I'll make you shut up, baby.

Rose Heartache Mila: Oh yeah?

HenleyKing17: Mmhmmm. I'll make you shut up in ways that'll feel real good.

Rose Heartache Mila: I have a question...

HenleyKing17: Hit me.

Rose Heartache Mila: How many other women have you watched since me?

HenleyKing17: Do you want the honest truth?

Rose Heartache Mila: Of course.

HenleyKing17: None. The last person I watched was you.

Bubbles appear and disappear like crazy.

I hold my breath as London readjusts herself in her seat.

This is so fucking wrong, but I can't stop.

Rose Heartache Mila: Why only me?

HenleyKing17: You feel like the only real thing.

Rose Heartache Mila: Oh my gosh. I'm blushing, just so you know.

HenleyKing17: I love it when you blush.

I wish I could see London's face right now, how much it must be tinging deep scarlet for me. But all I can see from where I'm seated is endless blonde and those pink clips holding her hair together.

Rose Heartache Mila: Come on tonight and I'll blush just for you.

I smirk.

A second message comes instantly.

Rose Heartache Mila: Oh my god...was that too cringe?

Smirking, I chuckle softly. *Why the hell am I the one blushing now?*

Fuck, I don't blush.

What am I, ten?

HenleyKing17: A little...

Rose Heartache Mila: Crap, I hate that. I'm sorry.

HenleyKing17: I was only teasing. It's not cringe. Why are you apologizing? It was sexy. You know I'll be there tonight. Wear red for me. It'll look stunning on you, Rose.

Wait.

What did I just say?

Fuck my lack of self-control!

Rose Heartache Mila: Red lingerie it is.

HenleyKing17: Mmhmmm, heaven. I have a meeting starting in five and won't be online until tonight. I'll be thinking of you until then. Even when I shouldn't. You're the most beautiful woman I've ever seen, you know that, right?

Rose Heartache Mila: Stop making me smile.

HenleyKing17: Make me.

Rose Heartache Mila: I wish. xx

HenleyKing17: Me too, Rose. Me too.

Deciding this conversation needs to be over, I log out and shut my phone with a heavy heart.

Why?

Because it seems like I'm about to break my one-week streak tonight.

My smirk darkens as London goes back to Heathcliff...

And I can't fucking wait.

Rose Heartache Mila wore red... *Just like I requested her to.*

She isn't in her bedroom, the wall behind the bed is filled with detailed macrame.

Watching London feels like sin, but *fuck*, how good it is. I love the way her face lights up whenever I comment anything. The way soft moans escape her lips whenever she fucks herself, and I whisper her name back through the distance of the screen as I stroke myself to her sounds.

She seductively fingers herself into heaven in the low light, her pussy always strategically angled away from the screen. Hearing the sucks of her drenched wetness only makes me harder. I wish I could beg for mercy between her thighs. I wish I could mold those beautiful round breasts of hers and wrap my tongue around her hard nipples, sucking into forever.

The way we come at the exact same time...

The reasons why I need to act so innocently the next day...

The fact that I can't think about anything else but her and only her...it's a sin.

Sin.

She has no idea it's me.

But it's not an addiction.

I can stop.

Mmhmmm.

I can stop anytime I like.
I can.
I promise.
I can survive a night without her.
Just watch.

Shit. I feel like I'm Heathcliff.
Emotionally trapped?
Check.
Broody bastard?
Check.
Undeniably jealous (of Nicandro Morales not Edgar Linton)?
Check. Check. Check.
Hmmm…
I lean back in my chair, knowing this hellhole some call senior year is killing me slowly. What kills me more is the fact that London never showed up to school today, which for anybody else is normal, but with her, it's a rarity.

She's never skipped a day of high school before. *Ever.* And trust me, I've noticed, even though I hate to admit it. And between forbidding myself from *Enticed*, and not getting a dose of my blonde goddess today, I'm a mess.

A complete fucked-up mess.

Maybe I am the antihero in this story after all…

I drop my edition of *Wuthering Heights* on my school desk and let it slam shut.

Nahhh.

"Love is pain, bro." Levi waves his book at me with that boyish smirk of his. "Love. Is. Pain."

Fuck. Why is this shit classified as a romance?

It's just straight-up tragic, and then some.

Just like my lack of self-control.

Okay. It's an addiction.

I know, I know.

I said I had control, turns out, I don't.

I can't spend a night without her on the other side of the screen—watching her.

London.

I love the teasing.

I love the way she flirts and pleasures herself.

But what I love most is the honesty in her chats. The deep conversations. The rawness.

It's almost therapeutic watching her in a way. A form of fucked-up sex therapy that always seems to ease my mind better than a cigarette or joint ever could.

Like right now...

I can't stop staring at London across the cafeteria, watching as she talks with Nicandro and Heather. She throws her head back in laughter at something Heather says and the tinge of red in her cheeks reminds me of the shade of lingerie she had on last night.

Some fucker stole her away for a private show after a performance I needed about a century to recover from.

As Levi stalks back to my table, my gaze flickers to my phone. I'm mindlessly scrolling, looking at things that don't matter. And when I flick my gaze back to Levi, I slow for a second at *her*, my breath stopping when those baby-blue eyes catch mine and it's instantaneous.

The way that I can instantly smell her jasmine and coconut blend.

The way the rapid pitter-patters in my chest skips a beat at her intense stare.

The guilt which eats up my pride, rendering me incapable of giving her that smug smirk the Tate Meadows from mere months ago would.

Before he got lost in a game of Russian-roulette with his fucking sanity.

So now instead, a soft, sad smile rises up my lips, but London, she just frowns.

Frowns.

And all the hope of my late-night sin fades away, even though she doesn't know it's me on the other side of the screen.

Doubt slips back, leaving me with a question that carries the entire world's weight in it...

Where do broken hearts go from here?

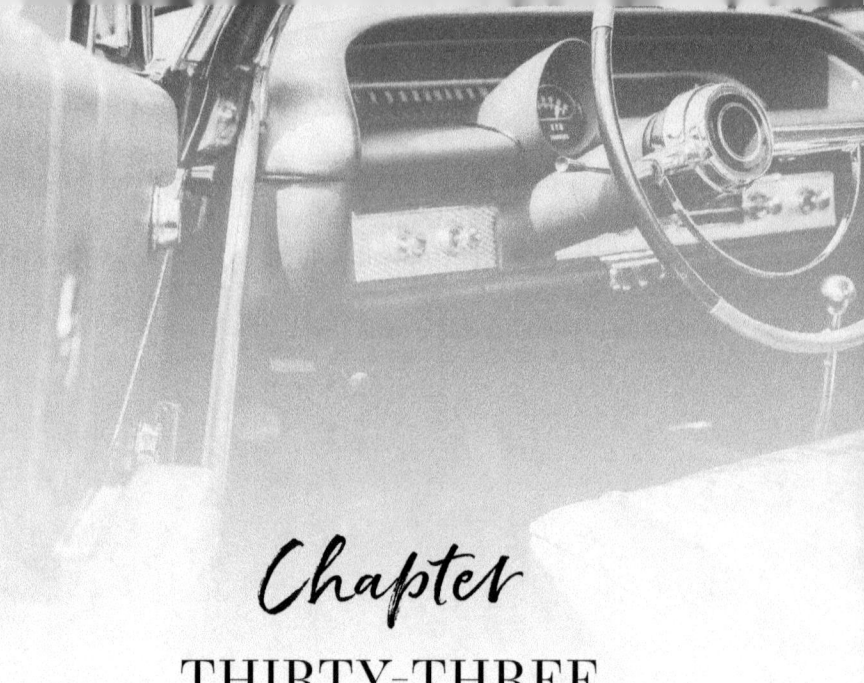

Chapter
THIRTY-THREE

Tate

One month later...
MAY.

*T*hey go to hell...
    That's where broken hearts freaking go.

Because that's what it feels like as I walk out of lacrosse practice on Thursday afternoon.

My phone buzzes in my back pocket on my walk to my car in the school's parking lot.

> **Rose Heartache Mila: Are you in a meeting?**

During our previous conversations during the past week, I mentioned I was in the entrepreneur business in Seattle, but that was all I was willing to tell her. Lying doesn't come easy. Especially when I know it can backfire in my face at any minute.

Slipping into my Mustang, one of the only cars left in the lot, I slide into the driver's seat but remain parked.

> **HenleyKing17: Just came out, why?**

Rose Heartache Mila: I'm not doing so great and really wanted to talk to you.

My brows knit together at her message. *Not doing so great.*

Wait. What's wrong?

Did something happen?

She seemed okay in English Literature today, but then again, that could just be a disguise. Just another thing London Héroux is hiding.

HenleyKing17: Tell me what's going on, I'm right here. Not going anywhere, okay?

HenleyKing17: Rose?

HenleyKing17: Rose, I've got you, okay? You have me worried. Take your time. You have all the time in the world to tell me.

Rose Heartache Mila: I don't know what's wrong with me. I feel so...I don't know. I feel like I don't know who I am anymore. You're the only one I really trust to tell all this to.

Concern fills me as another message appears.

Rose Heartache Mila: Is it wrong that you and late nights on Enticed feel like my only escapes from the world? Is it?

HenleyKing17: It depends if there should be more people for you. You don't give off much, but you seem like a pretty kindhearted person. No one else is your escape?

Rose Heartache Mila: I have a really close college friend and also a guy friend I'm really close to, but...It's complicated.

Heather and Nicandro.

HenleyKing17: Complicated how?

Rose Heartache Mila: You may judge me...

HenleyKing17: I could never. Go on.

Rose Heartache Mila: My guy friend and I are intimate. We have been for a little while. Not sex, but everything else. We have an open no-strings-attached kind of relationship. He's cool with me being on Enticed. He understands the reasons. But ever since I started camming, my guy friend looks at me like...I don't know, different. Like he wants more.

Wait, did she just say...*Not sex?* I swear to God when I confronted

London in my library that night, she told me that Nicandro fucks her. Am I losing it?

Maybe.

> **HenleyKing17: And you don't want that? Don't want a relationship with him?**
>
> **Rose Heartache Mila: My feelings are purely platonic, but I don't want to hurt him. He means a lot to me, Henley. So much.**
>
> **HenleyKing17: Then honesty is the best policy in this case. Just be truthful, yeah? Even if you hurt him, you hurt him with the truth and wear your heart on your sleeve.**
>
> **Rose Heartache Mila: You know something?**
>
> **HenleyKing17: Mmhmmm?**
>
> **Rose Heartache Mila: You're so right. I'm sorry. I just feel like I'm constantly stressing.**
>
> **HenleyKing17: Don't apologize, Rose.**
>
> **Rose Heartache Mila: You can call me Mila instead, if you like.**

I smile like a chickenshit, alone in my vintage Mustang.

Mila is her real middle name...

> **HenleyKing17: Mila... Can I ask you a personal question? And you don't have to answer if you don't want to.**
>
> **Rose Heartache Mila: Hit me.**

Dear God.

> **HenleyKing17: If you have a man to satisfy your needs, then why Enticed? I'm just trying to understand it, you know? Not judging or anything, just curious, Mila.**
>
> **Rose Heartache Mila: Fair point. Enticed gives me something being with men doesn't...Control. Escape.**

My brows knit up. *Escape?*

What does she mean by that?

What is she running from? Who? Herself? No...it can't be.

London Héroux is too perfect for that. Too put-together.

> **HenleyKing17: Why do you say that? What are you trying to escape from?**
>
> **Rose Heartache Mila: I, uh, let's just say I haven't had**

the best experiences with men. A screen between makes me feel safer. I'm learning to love myself better.

Her response boils my heated blood at the thought that something bad is happening to her. That's what it feels like reading between the lines.

If only I could understand what it was and find a way to make her feel better. As Henley.

I never could as Tate.

I could never get this close to her *again*.

I could never win her trust over *again*.

She'll never need Tate Meadows, as for needing Henley King...

Maybe.

Regret.

Elation.

Confusion.

I feel it all while staring at my keyboard, pondering the perfect response. With anger rushing up my spine for her tormenter, my jaw tenses, and thumbs slap across my screen.

HenleyKing17: Who the fuck hurt you, Mila?

I wait and wait and wait with a heavy heart. Wait for London to respond, or for those three little gray dots to appear. *Anything.* But all I get is a measly *read* notification beneath my text.

I hate the throbs at the back of my throat intensifying the ache I know shouldn't be there.

But it is.

Fuck how it is.

And it doesn't let me go.

Not as I drive myself home.

Not as London doesn't show on *Enticed* for the first time in days.

Not as I stay up all night constantly checking the chat, praying she'll come on.

Because she never replies.

And that scares me to death, more than if she had replied could ever scare me, because it's evident she's hurting about something.

Someone.

London is hurting so deep that maybe Henley is her only way out.

And perhaps...perhaps now I just fucking ruined everything.

Just like I always do.

Chapter
THIRTY-FOUR

London

"What the hell, London?" Nicandro scoffs, snatching my phone out of my hands a millisecond after I exit out of *Enticed*'s chat room. "Are you seriously talking to one of those freaks?"

My eyes widen.

What?

I'm so hyperaware of just how hard my heart is thumping that I swear Nicandro can feel my throbbing pulse when he hands me back my phone. There's heat crawling all over me, licking up my spine and across my lungs, and I don't know how to stop it.

For the second time in my life, I feel like somebody can understand me.

Somebody who cares, who wants to know me for me.

And I haven't even seen his face…

Henley.

HenleyKing17.

I swallow. "He's not a freak."

Nicandro's stormy stare doesn't leave mine once as he leans against the headboard of his bed, eyeing me slowly, like he's trying to figure me out.

For the first time ever, the heartstrings in my chest tug for all the wrong reasons. I've never felt that with Nicandro. I've never felt an inch of intimidation, or as if he's trying to make a mockery out of me. But right now, as I sit at the edge of his bed with my knees to my chest, there's something in his eyes I don't like. It's blanketed with malice, almost jealousy.

So intense I look away.

"*Not a freak*?" his voice taunts, letting out a snort when all he gets from me is silence. "Seriously?"

"Seriously," I grit, my jaw tightening the longer I keep my eyes pinned on the onyx-colored macrame piece on his bedroom wall. "They're not like what you think they are, just trust me."

Nicandro shakes his head in my peripheral vision.

"Sure, whatever. Call them whatever the fuck you want, London. You know what I meant…" The air crackles between us as he pauses, before adding, "What I *mean*."

The final word has me snapping my attention back to Nicandro, only to find that his burning gaze never left mine.

There it is again.

That look.

It's exactly what I was chatting with Henley about. The fact that I feel like something has shifted on Nicandro's end. I don't get why he's acting like this and it's pissing me off. It's so unlike him.

The blood rippling across my veins is nothing compared to the agonizing stress I've felt both at home and at school with all of the shit going down with Maddie and Tate. I thought Nicandro was my safe haven, that he would be the last person treating me this way. I guess I was wrong.

I stand my ground, arching a brow in genuine confusion, while musing soft retaliation. "What even is your problem with them? Like, why is it even bothering you that much?"

"It's not." Nicandro shrugs, but his shoulders never lose their stiffness.

They remain tense, strained by his ears, and as much as he's trying to hide it, I start to see the cracks beneath the surface coming undone. He's not the tough-as-nails guy he presents himself to be, not now. Insecurity is written all across his face, and it's so obvious by the tightness in his jaw and in the way his fists clench up, the whiteness crawling up his knuckles, one second at a time.

This conversation is affecting him, more than he would like.

Lying.

He's lying to me.

I clear my throat. "Well, obviously, it is."

"Ah, fuck it, whatever," Nicandro brushes it off, rising from the bed, only to pace his bedroom. "I'm literally done with this conversation. I don't even care. Don't want to talk about it."

Is he serious?

"Well, I do!" I grit, my voice a little louder than I intended, but at this point, I don't care. "I'm doing this for *me*, not you, *me*. I swear to god, Nicandro, ever since I started on *Enticed*, you've been different."

Well, ladies and gents, that speaks to him…

Nicandro freezes in front of me, all tall and scary, like I've speared a dagger in his heart.

"*Me?*" He chuckles mockingly, stabbing a finger to his chest. "*I'm* different? Jesus Christ, London, you don't see it, do you?"

Gaping, my heart falters.

What the hell is he talking about?

My voice is barely a whisper. "See *what?*"

"EXACTLY!" Nicandro spits, harshness in his voice, and then, he explodes. "*That* is my whole point! You think everything is fucking perfect. You start *Enticed* and it's your remedy, but it's not. Those guys, the ones who watch you, who message you, do you think they really care? Do you *seriously* think they care about you? Huh? News-fucking-flash, they don't, London! They. Don't. They just want to see your perky tits because they're sick of their wives. And that Henley guy, well, he seems like a complete asshole too. He's playing it all sweet and innocent, and you think that just because he hasn't asked to see you fuck yourself, that he's a good guy. Well, guess what, if you think he won't ask, you're just as fucking delusional as he is!"

Nicandro takes a few breaths, easing the jerking cords in his neck.

"I *care*," he breathes, fury coating his face. "I *care* about *you*, London. But no, we can't fuck because you have some love-sick crush on a man you won't ever meet. It's pathetic, London. *You're* pathetic. The only reason you're not seeing it is because you're too deep into it."

Silence.

Silence.

Silence.

Silence.

It's all that exists between us now, and it's agonizing.

Everything inside me breaks because Nicandro is the last person I thought would ever treat me like this. His words slaughter my every last hope.

The tempest swirling in the pit of my stomach is unlike anything I've ever experienced before. All I want to do is run and hide from the world. But instead, all I do is pretend.

I pretend I'm okay.

I pretend Nicandro's word don't cut me as deep as they do.

I pretend my vision isn't blurry from all of the built-up anarchy and spitefulness.

"Is that what you seriously think of me?" I whisper, my jaw ticking. "That I'm *pathetic*?"

All Nicandro does is stare, the disgust written all over his face.

It takes all of me not to storm off and leave, but I'm not finished yet. I've lost my will to live, to breathe, to simply be, but I haven't lost my self-respect. Not yet.

I glare up at him. "Wow, I really thought you were different…"

"I *am* different!" Nicandro pleads, his voice the softest it's ever been as something I can't quite describe flickers across his eyes. As if he's trying to tame the tempest already swirling inside me. He falls to his knees in front of me, taking my hands in his, like it's supposed to mean something.

It doesn't mean a single thing.

"London, please, look at me" he whispers, cradling my trembling hands so tight, it's almost as if he's losing sight of his strength. He squeezes them until it hurts. "London," he repeats. Softer.

I don't want to.

I really fucking don't.

But the second my glassy eyes meet his, like a magnet, I can't look away.

Gone is the Nicandro Morales I thought I knew. Tenderness coats him now, one I've never seen before, and I don't know what it means. I don't know what *any* of this means. And it scares me.

"*Fuck*. Can't you see it, Lon?" Nicandro brushes his forehead against mine, shutting his eyes. His hot breath tickles my plump lips. "Can't you see that I want you? That I…I *like you*."

What. The. Hell?

Everything stops. *Everything.*

Nicandro's words jar me.

He…likes me?

He wants me.

"Nicandro…"

"Can't you see how crazy I am about you?"

I don't respond. I can't. The throbbing ache at the back of my throat capsizes me.

He watches me slowly, flickering back and forth between my eyes.

The muscles in his jaw tense, protruding through. "Course not."

"Nicandro—"

"Please," he croaks, his voice a desperate mess now. "Tell me something. Anything."

God.

I close my eyes, inhaling a sharp breath. "I wish things were different. I wish I felt the same way. But we were both clear when we made this deal. No catching feelings."

I can feel Nicandro's glare piercing through me, but I don't dare open mine. Not yet.

I can't do this.

I love Nicandro. I love him as a friend, as a lover, but it's all I see him as. And after the words he's expressed to me right now, I'm not so sure I want anything to do with him.

"You don't mean that." he growls, far too close to me. "You don't mean a fucking word."

The London Héroux of three years ago was too scared to stand up for herself. To stand up to the sins of my father and anybody else that cut me deep. But right here, right now, I hold onto strength for it's my last resort. After all, there's nothing to lose when you've got nothing left.

"I've never meant anything more in my life," I pause, my voice unwavering. "I *promise*."

He doesn't like that.

Not one bit.

"You don't need *Enticed*. You don't need random men watching you. All you need is me, can't that be enough for you?" He moves my hand over his rigid cock, forcing me to feel his hardness beneath his white boxer briefs. "Can't *this* be enough?"

I can't stop shaking my head. "*This* isn't all I'm good for, Nicandro."

"Then stop acting like it is," he growls.

Excuse me?

My heart plummets. "It's an escape!"

"To what?"

I gulp. "I don't feel comfortable telling you."

"Why not? What's the big fucking secret, London? Huh?"

His stare mocks me, mostly because the answer is at the tip of my tongue. I'm so close to letting it out, to telling Nicandro the truth because, maybe, just maybe, it'll mean he'll leave me alone.

But I can't.

I'm too scared.

I just want to run from this world.

Nicandro lets go of my hands, only for his fingers to frantically skim up my thighs, rushing over my fishnet stockings so fast, he leaves skid marks. Everything's happening in fast motion when his fingers force their way up even higher, between my inner thighs, skimming the lace of my panties.

"What the hell?" I gasp, snapping my eyes open as I brush his hand away. "Stop! Just stop!"

He doesn't.

He doesn't listen.

He doesn't give a damn.

"London, please." His lips stamp their assault across my neck in unwanted rough kisses, but he doesn't budge, no matter how hard I shove his broad shoulders back. "Please just let me fuck you better. Then you'll understand how much I want you. Then you'll understand everything."

"Nic, please stop. I'm not ready to…I don't want this."

"Come on." He's back at my panties, fingering the delicate material. "Let me fuck you."

I vigorously shove him back, again and again and again, tears streaming down my cheeks, but nothing works.

"Get the fuck off me, Nicandro!"

"London, *please.*"

"Stop! I don't—"

"PLEASE! Just let me—*AHHHH! FUCK! YOU BITCH!*"

One second Nicandro is attacking me, the next, he's rolling on the floor and clutching his dick. I'm sure his profanities are only a slight indication of how hard I kneed him in self-defense.

"You act like a slut and then you don't want me to fuck you," Nicandro spits through the vulgar curses. "You're a fucking delusional bitch. What the fuck? What the fuck is wrong with you?"

Storming up from the bed, my heart is in my throat as I race to his bedroom door, the last thread keeping me breathing, snapping before my very eyes.

It's over. It's all over for me.

I'm not going to make it to tomorrow.

"For the record," I seethe, my fingers fisting Nicandro's oak bedroom door so hard blotches of whiteness baptize my skin. "Henley would never say this to me."

And then, I bolt out of Nicandro's room.

Out of his brownstone.

Out of his life.

Running.

Running.

Running.

I run till my lungs can't take no more.

Till the cords in my neck snap from the sobs.

Till I find that infamous Central Park bench and flirt with the lake, the waters of my death.

For some strange reason, flashbacks of Tate and me flood my mind. Flashbacks of him. Flashbacks of the moon. Flashbacks of us. And all it does it make my sobs intensify.

I miss Tate.

I miss Tate so much.

But it's better for all of us this way.

Before darkness, I want one final taste of life. Just one.

Slipping out my phone from my Glorsin St. Claire's blazer pocket, I don't even know how I manage to see my chat with **HenleyKing17** through the tears as I attack the keyboard, my thumbs not stopping until I'm tired, aching, my knees hitting the ground, kissing the blades of grass.

> **ROSE HEARTACHE MILA: A lot of people have hurt me, but nobody more than myself. I've kept going in a vicious cycle without ever realizing that I can stop. I can stop at any time I like. Life is dependent on how you live it, *or not*, because that's an option too. To not live it. Nothing's made sense since the moments before I turned 15.**

> **ROSE HEARTACHE MILA: You see, Henley, I was in love with this boy. His name was Tate, and he was my entire world, and then I fucked it up. He thought I gave up on us, but I didn't. He's hated me ever since. I've been holding onto a secret for so long that it's infested its way inside me, numbing everything I once loved. It's venom, a toxin, and I can't get it out. I'm going away for a while. For a long while. So this is the last message I'll ever send you.**

> **ROSE HEARTACHE MILA: I can't be on Enticed. Nothing... nothing feels like it's worth it anymore. I just wish you were here. Maybe you could make it better. Maybe you would make it worse, I don't know. All I do know is that it's crazy because I don't even know what you look like, and yet, I just want you to hold me into another life. So, thank you, Henley, for being here for me. You don't know how badly I need it. x**

It startles me, how quickly Henley replies.

And what *he replies.*

> **HENLEYKING17: There are so many things I want to say, but I don't know where to begin. Whatever you're thinking of doing, please don't do it.**

> **ROSE HEARTACHE MILA: Give me one good reason.**

> **HENLEYKING17: I need you, Mila.**

My heart pangs.

Whoa.

I remain frozen, sinking in the grass, blotchy mascara-filled tears blanketing my phone screen. His words blindside me, but in a good way, because I didn't think he'd feel the same way too.

> **ROSE HEARTACHE MILA: I need you too.**

> **HENLEYKING17: Do you want to talk about what happened?**

ROSE HEARTACHE MILA: Not really, I want to talk about you.

HENLEYKING17: Me?

ROSE HEARTACHE MILA: You.

HENLEYKING17: What about me?

ROSE HEARTACHE MILA: Tell me what you look like. Whenever I think of you, it's all blurry. I want to know the truth, Henley. Please.

HENLEYKING17: Light hair, dark eyes.

ROSE HEARTACHE MILA: That seems pretty brief.

HENLEYKING17: I'm a brief kinda guy.

ROSE HEARTACHE MILA: I just want to hear your voice.

HENLEYKING17: It's not permitted, remember?

ROSE HEARTACHE MILA: It is if you give me your phone number and we take this off Enticed, besides, I'm not even going to be on Enticed anymore.

I wasn't lying about that. It's true. Even without Nicandro's influence, I came to that conclusion a few weeks ago, the night after my father told me he was going to kill me. As much as I liked the escapism that came with *Enticed*, I can't keep hiding my bruises with concealer and foundation.

I can't keep staying quiet in my room.

I can't keep this up.

It's too risky, and I know if I don't stop now, it'll all blow up in my face.

I've made good money off *Enticed* in the time I was on it. Good enough money that will allow me to move out of my parents' apartment the second I finish college. *Well, if I don't end it all tonight.*

HENLEYKING17: I can't, Mila. It's not safe.

ROSE HEARTACHE MILA: Why? Are you…Are you married?

HENLEYKING17: No, God, no. I'm not seeing anybody.

ROSE HEARTACHE MILA: Then what's the harm? And I know this may sound crazy, but you said you need me… so why haven't you ever made any sexual advances toward me?

HENLEYKING17: Because I see more than that. I want

to kiss your tears away and hold you all night. I want to wrap you in the solace of my arms and tell you everything will be alright. I want to be anything you want me to.

ROSE HEARTACHE MILA: Do you think I'm a slut?

HENLEYKING17: No. No, never.

ROSE HEARTACHE MILA: Then what do you think of me?

HENLEYKING17: I think you're simply surviving, baby, just like me.

ROSE HEARTACHE MILA: I don't want to just survive. I want to live. I want to feel alive again. Shit, I don't know what is wrong with me...

HENLEYKING17: Then live for me, angel. Pretend I'm right there holding you, kissing you goodnight. Nothing else matters but you, always remember that, Mila. And when you don't feel like enough, I'm here.

I trace my finger over my screen, caressing where his name lights up my phone with a warmth in my chest I haven't felt in a very long time.

Through the pain, a sad smile traces my lips.

He cares.

Somebody in this world cares.

And suddenly, I don't feel so alone.

ROSE HEARTACHE MILA: Who are you, HenleyKing17?

HENLEYKING17: The place lonely hearts go.

ROSE HEARTACHE MILA: No, not hearts. You're where my lonely heart goes.

And then, I shut my phone and throw it into the grass, my stomach aching. Nerves and butterflies combine into one, trapped by the only two things I crave the most.

Death and him.

Henley.

Perhaps the biggest travesty here is that I can't have them both, because it's impossible to simultaneously have both.

Not in this lifetime.

Not ever.

Chapter
THIRTY-FIVE

Tate

I freaked out all night, contemplating whether or not I should just come clean and tell London that her savior, Henley, is actually her rivaled enemy, Tate Meadows.

The first text she sent last night, as Mila, scared the fuck out of me, because it didn't sound like she was just done with *Enticed*, it sounded like she was done with the world, and that hurts me more than anything.

Maybe I'm doing this all wrong.

What if by giving London space, I'm destroying her more?

What if she needs Tate, so much more than she does Henley, and she doesn't even know it?

The questions have been circling my mind all day, not letting me go for a second.

It's even worse now, during lunch, as my group and I are laid out in the school yard in a circle. They're talking about some party I couldn't care less about.

Sasha's by my side, her head nestled in my lap, auburn curls all sprawled out. Every so often, she glances up at me and smiles, but I don't have it in me today to read into it like she wants me to.

The second Levi saw me this morning, he already knew I was in a mood. So, like a best friend should, he hasn't given me any shit for my antisocial behavior today.

And it's that exact antisocial behavior which has had my gaze wandering off from my so-called friends to a section farther out in the yard...

Silky honey blonde waves floating in the breezy wind have my heartstrings tugging in my chest.

London.

It's *London.*

She's in the middle of a conversation, one that seems pretty heated with the way that her hands are moving around and her head is shaking relentlessly, with no one else but the Nicandro Morales.

My fucking demise.

There he is, across from her, towering over her like he's got some power over her. Power that he doesn't.

Beside him, a lilac-haired girl that I don't think I've barely had a conversation with before. I think her name is Heather, and she's British, I'm pretty sure, but that's literally all I know.

The more time passes, the louder they become, drawing attention with angry shouts, but the words are all blurred from where I'm sitting. Still, it doesn't seem pretty.

Nicandro is going off at London, scoffing and rolling his eyes, occasionally nestling his hands by his hips, but it's only to compress his clenching fists. They're whitening, just like the winter snow cascading down mountain tops in the Alpines and Mont Blanc.

Heather matches Nicandro's energy, shouting and waving her hands around, all while London is cornered against the stump of an oak tree, flickering her gaze between them. Her usually creamy cheeks are flustered in a deep shade of crimson, but it isn't a blush, it's...irritation.

It's anxiety.

It's fear.

It's trickling in her blue-eyed gaze, even though she hasn't noticed me.

Her hands are crossed over her chest, her nails stabbing the side of her Glorsin St. Claire's blazer, as if it's her only means of survival. But there's a conflict of interest in all this, because her head is tilted up high, her stance tall, and she doesn't once, not for one second, let her glare on Nicandro falter.

Shit.

Shit, what happened?

What the hell is going on?

The pang in my chest only deepens the longer London remains there.

I'm proud of her for defending herself, but the need to bolt up and rush to her aid is overpowering. But London isn't like that. She's a strong girl. I know she is. Underneath her girly shyness, secret seductiveness, and yes, under the straight-up smartass personality, she's tough.

She's strong.

She's fierce.

She knows how to hold her own.

I don't need to silence her. I *don't want to* silence.

Literally five seconds later, my thoughts become reality as London begins to bite back. Her mouth moves so vigorously fast, sharp, and concise, and it's obvious her words emit daggers by the hurt edging Nicandro's eyes.

London lays it on him, again and again, until she's gasping for air. Her heartstrings carve out against her neck with every sharp inhale.

Her cheeks are redder now, fiercer, but there's this hell-bent look in her eyes that screams not to fuck with her.

It has a slow smirk crawling up my lips because…*that's my girl.*

That's. My. Fucking. Girl.

This is what I know London Héroux to be—the fighter—not the girl in the texts last night.

The one that was so close to ending everything.

The one close to plummeting into death.

The one I wanted to save.

But as I said, London Héroux doesn't need saving. She just needs somebody to hold her in the solace of their arms. And her current solace—Nicandro—*well*, it seems like it's breaking right in front of my eyes.

"What are you looking at?"

Sasha's question makes me glance down at her, startled. For a moment, I thought I was alone.

I subtly nod toward the commotion.

Sasha turns to the side, lifting her head a bit, so she can see what I'm gesturing to.

And there's that thing that I do. I don't look at London; I look at Sasha. I watched the malice crawl up her face, a hint of jealousy leering across her eyes.

Sasha scoffs, returning my gaze with a wicked smirk. "Seems like the freaks are giving themselves a beating."

My jaw ticks.

Seriously?

"They're not freaks," I grit.

Well, at least not London.

Mocking laughter escapes Sasha. She cups my stubbled jaw, caressing it slowly, like it's supposed to do something to me or awaken a piece of me, but no.

No.

I don't feel awake with Sasha.

I don't feel any passion with Sasha.

In fact, I don't feel a fucking thing. Not with her.

"Tate, Tate, Tate…" she purrs. "Eyes. On. Me."

Clenching my jaw, twice, I can't help the anger spiraling through me. I roughly pull her hand away from me and stand, watching her practically plummet to the ground. "We're over, Sasha."

A shocked gasp escapes her. "*What?*"

Levi glances over, in the middle of conversation, his eyes wide when he sees what just happened. "Dude, you okay?"

"Yeah," I snap, contrary to my tense shoulders, flared nostrils, and the death glare I'm shooting down at Sasha as she glances up at me, disgusted.

"There's just something I've gotta do," I add.

I don't wait for approval because, quite frankly, I don't fucking need it.

All the hatred, desolation, and hurt fades as I approach London's side, my presence evidently pacifying the argument instantly.

I can feel Nicandro's hot glare burning into the side of my head, but I don't dare give him any sort of acknowledgement.

No.

My eyes are pinned on the most beautiful concoction of icy baby blue to ever exist.

London stares up at me, her doe eyes slightly wide. Her hot, plump lips part, cotton-candy colored, and part of me is certain she'd taste just like that.

I'm mesmerized by her, just like I always am, that part of me that never was able to truly forget her is grateful. So. Fucking. Grateful. Because London Héroux is a beautiful toxin, so illicit and yet, *tempting*. She's a venom that weaves into my soul and is permanently etched there.

There's so many words I could say. So many. But only two escape my throat in a rough, hot rasp.

"You okay?"

Jesus Christ, Tate. Did you seriously just ask her if she's okay? All the fucking words in the Oxford dictionary and these two are the ones you come up with? You idiot!

Strangely enough, they seem to be enough for London, whose eyes warm, not completely expecting it. Because, yeah, that's right, ladies and gents, I'm Tate Meadows to her.

Tatum Lee fucking Meadows.

Not Henley.

I'm Tate.

"Yeah, I'm fine. I can handle it," she huffs, a flush crawling up her cheeks, that's anything but the anger riddling through her.

I know it's because of me.

And for some strange, fucked-up reason, that selfish guy inside is grateful. Thankful. Screaming hella-fuckin'-luiah because I do *this* to her. I destroy her. Just like she destroys me.

"I know you can hold your own," I confess with a soft nod. "Just want you to know that I'm here, if you need anything, yeah?"

"I…" London's words fade to nothingness, and instead, that enthralling gaze holds mine, trapping me in a world of her.

Fuck.

I think I've been looking for her since I heard my very first fairy tale.

Now I know that my hate for her was just a figment of my imagination. Just a vindictive streak. Because right *now*, right *here*, for *her*,

I fucking swear I would ruin myself a million times over. A million times, if it meant her looking at me like she is right now.

Like I'm the only person that's hearing her, that's accepting her, that's seeing her.

"I, umm…" she clears her throat, a weak smile stretching her lips. "Thanks, Tate, I—"

"What the fuck you tryin'a do, Meadows?" Nicandro growls, cutting her off.

It has my gaze instantly darting to his, the muscles in my jaw tightening as I cock my head to the side, taunting him. "I suggest you keep your damn voice down when you speak to her, motherfucker. I'm here because I can be."

"It doesn't *involve* you," he spits, his eyes darkening. "Hey! Did you hear me? This. Does. Not. Involve. You."

"Don't care. I'm not leaving." I glance back to London, my arms crossing in front of my chest, and my expression softens. "What happened?"

She hesitantly shrugs. "It's nothing, I just don't want to be around him, but he won't listen to me. They both won't listen to me. They won't leave me alone."

"Because our conversation isn't over yet!" Nicandro snaps, and I have to scoff when Heather adds, "Yeah, it definitely isn't," in that fancy British accent.

"I'm done!" London shrieks beside me. "I literally have nothing else to say to you, Nicandro, it's done. I'm done."

"Seriously, London? One little fuck-up and you're *done*? Are you seriously that pathetic?"

"I swear to God if you call me that one more time—"

"You'll what?" he grits.

"She'll fucking kick your ass," I seethe, roughly shoving his chest back when he dares to inch forward, toward her. "As London said, the conversation is done. It was over when she said it was." I gesture behind him, to the open field of our schoolyard. "So, *walk*."

Nicandro's all in my face, a few inches shorter than me, and yet, he's still trying to size me up like it's supposed to intimidate me, but it doesn't.

I've got more balls than that.

"Seriously, Meadows? Who the hell do you think you are?"

I can't help my infamous smirk. "Your worst freaking nightmare, and if you don't step away from her, I'll introduce you to another thing. One. A police report titled harassment."

"Oh, please," Heather dramatically rolls her eyes. "London doesn't even want you here."

"She does, or else she'd be telling me to leave. Don't get it twisted, London's got teeth and will bite when she wants to. I'm well aware of it. But since you want to gang up on her like fucking coyotes, I'm here to tell you that London ain't no lone wolf. She's got me, for however long she wants me around, understand?"

Slowly grinding his jaw, Nicandro's gaze flickers behind me to London. He stares and stares and stares, until the only thing that remains is a fuming shell of the once intimidating guy he perceives himself to be.

"Don't come to me when he breaks your heart, Héroux," he spits.

London's fierce voice feeds the oxygen in my lungs. Her arm emits sparks where it brushes against mine as she steps forward, so that we're side by side, defiant.

"Tate won't break my heart because apparently *I don't have one*." And then, the most girlish smirk takes over those soft wonderland lips. "*Remember?*"

With one final stare off between him and me, Nicandro walks backward, shaking his head, before storming off with his friend, Heather.

He doesn't look back, yet I continue glaring, shooting daggers into his spine until they're out of sight, disappearing behind one of the school buildings.

London immediately breathes out a relieved sigh, physically relaxing as she rakes a hand through her gorgeous, blonde waves. Then, she slowly glances up at me as if I'm the moon and she is mesmerized by everything she saw.

Ohhh.

Dear God.

Her lingering smirk diffuses to a bashful smile.

"Who are you, Tate Meadows?" she breathes.

I swear I suffocate on air because she asked me that exact same question last night, as Henley, only she doesn't know it.

Shit.

Starstruck by her, I remain frozen, only acknowledging she's walking away from me when it's too late.

"Hey, wait up!" I call behind her, my Converse digging into the soft blades of grass as I catch up to her. Sprinting ahead, I spin around and jog backward to pierce her gaze.

"Hey, where you going? Don't you wanna talk?

"*Talk*?" London arches a brow, perplexed. "Why would I want to talk?"

"I don't know." I nonchalantly shrug, even though my heart is burning inside, bleeding. "I thought maybe you wanted to talk about what happened there?"

"There's nothing to talk about. Thank you for defending me, truthfully. You didn't need to, but it's over now with them and I'm happy for that."

She's happy.

She's happy *it's over*.

I quicken my jog backward when her pace accelerates. "Where you going now?"

"To the library, probably, or home. I have a free period after lunch, so no point staying."

I panic. "Want me to walk you there?"

"No, I'm fine."

Now it's my turn to raise my eyebrows. I almost scoff. "You're not *fine*, London. You just had this huge blow up with your so-called friends."

That has London rolling her eyes in that girly way. It takes me back to eight years ago, to our infamous Central Park bench. "He's not my friend anymore. Neither is she. I don't think they ever were. I truly think we were just acquaintances this entire time."

"So, what happened? Did he…" I inhale a sharp breath. "Hurt you?"

She doesn't give me anything.

"I said I don't want to talk about it!"

"I know, London, but…"

She comes to a screeching halt, digging the heels of her white Doc Martens into the grass. "*What*? What is wrong with you today, Tate? You're supposed to hate me, *remember*? Defending and then attempting to comfort somebody doesn't exactly equal vindictiveness."

"*Ooo*, vindication? Big word, blondie."

London groans. "Just shut the hell up, smartass."

Ha.

I can't fight my cocky smolder. "Maybe I don't want to be vindictive anymore. Maybe I…don't want us to be like *this* anymore."

Confusion slowly fades from London's face, and in its place, her jaw drops slightly, looking at me in complete and utter shock.

Her beautiful, long onyx-colored lashes blink a few times in a row before she shakes her head, and just like that, she's back to the London she always is whenever she wants to protect herself.

"I'm fine, Tate, I swear to God, I'm *fine*. Plus, there's people looking, okay, and I, err, I don't want to cause a scene. I just want to go home."

"I don't freaking care who's looking."

"Well…yeah, you should." She eyes something beyond me. "Your group is staring at me, and I don't want to be the point of humiliation. Besides, I'm pretty sure your plaything hates me."

Huh?

I look at London all funny. "My *plaything*?"

"Yeah, *Sasha*."

"She's not my plaything."

London gives me a *bullshit* look. "I see the way you look at her, the way you touch her, the way you let her do whatever the hell she wants to do to you. *You* like her. She likes *you*." A weak smile forces its way on her lips, but I can see straight through her strong facade and the pain pulling in her eyes. Pain directed at me, unconsciously. "You make a great couple, you really do."

Jesus fucking Christ.

Raking a hand through my hair, I tug at the wavy ends, frustrated that this has taken a full three-sixty.

My heartbeat unsteadies.

Thump-Thump.

Thump-Thump.

Thump-Thumpppp.

Warm sunshine dances across my face, electrifying my tightened muscles.

"We're not together, London, I don't like her." I step forward, my fingers softly grazing hers, clasping them so gently it makes her gasp. "*Fuck*. London, this…this isn't even about her, it's about you." I feel the crease forming between my eyes. "This is about you. About if you're okay. This has nothing to do with Sasha."

I'm not lying.

I've never liked Sasha. She's just been a distraction, and she knows it. Even if she let go of that possibility months ago and thinks we're more.

London swallows thickly. "You don't need to defend what you have, Tate. I get it."

"There's nothing to *get*, London! I don't fucking want her. Any part of her!" I shriek. "If she meant something to me, London, I'd still be with her right now. I wouldn't be here with my hands around yours, asking if you're okay. I'm speaking from the heart because I felt bad."

"So this is about empathy?" she spits, all pointed. "Is that why you came up to me? 'Cause you feel *sorry* for me?"

"No. *God, no.*"

Craving her closer, I softly rest my forehead against hers, not caring who's watching.

"Let me walk you to your locker," I breathe against her lips. "*Please.* I want to talk. Just let me. Don't think about it, just. *Let. Me.*"

London flutters her eyes shut, my words evidently toying with her mind. *Please.*

Please.

Please.

I don't know what changes, but suddenly, she's nodding, our noses sensually caressing each other.

"Okay," she finally murmurs.

The tightness in my shoulders surrenders.

Thank God.

She wants to talk and that's everything I've ever wanted—to talk with London Héroux—freely. To shift closer to the moon we once vowed we'd one day escape to, *together.*

"So, I got you something…"

London's eyes widen as she leans against her metal locker, hands fidgeting behind her back. "You got me something?"

"Yeah," I smirk, my gaze locked on hers as I blindly open my adjacent locker and pull out the wrapped gift.

To be honest, I've had this gift for London for a long time now. I was in a melancholic-infested rage when I bought it, too consumed by my own needs to worry that we were rivals in our very own way.

But I wanted London to have it.

I *want* London to have it.

Which is why I gently extend my hand, handing her the fuchsia-pink wrapped gift.

London doesn't take it straight away, hesitantly staring at it with quivered brows.

The entire thing makes me chuckle.

She finally takes it from my grip and returns to leaning her back against her locker.

The laughter and obnoxiously loud conversations of our peers echo through the high windows, just above the locker lined walls, but it instantly drowns out because London Héroux is my one and only focus. These school lockers are an oasis for deep talks and a little breathing time during the crazy lunchtimes outside.

"You wrapped this yourself?" she asks.

Ahhh, fuck.

"Yeah, sorry, I didn't know you were supposed to *figure out how to wrap the fucking gift* before you *actually wrapped it.* YouTube did me dirty."

London grins.

She grins.

"You're such an idiot, Tate."

"I know." My smirk deepens. "I know."

Holy hell, London Héroux is grinning—*at me*—for the first time in forever, and I think I'm floating into heaven, tripping right over Lucifer and into her angelic arms.

Dear God, take me now…

It feels like forever as London meticulously peels the Scotch tape. I full-on murdered the thing with tape, like it would turn into Hulk and rip itself apart.

After a century, London gives up. The echoing rip, as she claws the wrapping paper open, jolts my heart.

I hold my breath.

The gift unveils itself.

London looks down at it, and I swear witnessing her face transform from bewilderment to pure awe, a sparkle coming alive in her eyes, means everything to me.

"WHOA!" London gasps, gawking at the limited-edition vinyl.

It's Pink Floyd.

Dark Side of the Moon.

So perfectly London and me.

"Oh my gosh, Tate! Where did you find this? This is…" She takes it all in. "*Wow!* This is so fucking epic!"

"Did you just swear?"

"Shut up! Shut up and tell me where you got it!"

"An indie record shop. I saw it and thought of you, so I…Well, I…" I casually shrug. "I bought it for you."

London's blue eyes find mine, sunlight glimmering across their pooling glassiness.

A deep, pink hue burns her cheeks. "You got this *for me?*"

"Yeah, it just made sense. I wanted you to have it."

"Whoa," she breathes, bashfully, staring at me till a numbness consumes. I'm clouded by her and her sunflower gaze, those vintage rock and roll eyes that send me to pure euphoria. "You didn't have to."

Air crackles between us.

Emotion is lodged in my throat, flooded with our history. It spirals between us. I know she feels it too. *She has to.*

"I wanted to, London," I swallow thickly. "I needed to."

God, I craved it.

My body is in turmoil, suddenly tight against my private school uniform, but I push through and gesture toward the vintage limited-edition vinyl.

"The crazy thing is, the guy working at the store told me that the actual vinyl is pink, like candy-floss pink. It's such a coincidence because that's your favorite color, right? It was practically made for you, LonLon."

Her eyes widen a fraction, and it isn't until I step forward that I realize why.

I just called her LonLon.

LonLon.

Just like I used to.

And damn, how good it feels...

London takes a step forward, swarming me with her sugary coconut and rose scent.

She cradles the Pink Floyd vinyl to her chest like it's the most important thing. Like it's the only thing left. Like it is her new solace, embedded in her soul.

There's so much irony within that twelve-inch disc...

Pink Floyd's "Wish You Were Here" was the song we dueted that night I taught her how to play it on guitar while we were sprawled on her pink-colored bedsheets, years ago.

Then, the other irony is... *Dark Side of the Moon.* It's the name of Pink Floyd's most iconic album, and strangely enough, the moon is also the place I promised London we'd go to escape as kids.

London must know the irony too, it's so obvious.

"Why are you being so nice to me?" she whispers, the evident crack in her voice breaking me.

"I just," I hesitate, then say, "because I...don't think I can do this without you."

"Do *what?*"

"Life."

Again, there's that sparkle in her eyes. It breaks the ice.

"London, I don't wanna fight with you. I don't want this tension. It's been going on for too long. I just want to extend an olive branch. Call a truce."

"Why?"

"Because I don't like it when people treat you like shit. I don't like the way they were treating you back there."

"How about when you treated me like shit?"

Sighing, I close my eyes.

I know exactly what she's talking about.

The day I humiliated her in front of the entire class and accused her of lying. When I said that if she had a problem, she should come to me, not stepsister Maddie. When she ran and I chased after her, recklessly, my lungs burning, only to see the scars edged across her wrists and the way that it made me feel like dying.

Right now, remembering them makes me feel like dying.

"I know," I mumble under my breath, ashamed of my actions. "I know I treated you horribly. I wish I could take it back. I wish we could hit rewind, because I'm so sorry. Truly, I am. It's been reactive behavior. I reacted to you when you were never the issue at all. It's me and my abandonment issues. It's me and my fucked-up mind. It's me and my longing desire to crave something so desperately, even when I don't deserve it. I just...don't understand why you never showed up at the park bench that night."

"We could have had this conversation months ago, Tate, but instead, you dismissed me without giving me a chance to explain."

I flutter my eyes open, her gaze too intense, so I look down at my hands, helplessly playing with them as nerves skid across my skin.

"It hurt me, London. You hurt me so much not being there," I whisper. "All my life I've been rejected. From my father. From my mother. From everything. I thought I had you. I thought you got me. I thought you were *it* for me. So when you left, a part of me broke and hardened with it."

Empathy flashes across her face. "I never meant to reject you. Those weren't my intentions."

"Then what were they?"

London glances up, attempting to hold the tears back that redden her eyes, not letting them slip. "It was out of my control."

My eyes dance over her facial expressions, the most beautiful thing I've ever laid eyes on. I take it all in; her apprehensive expression, heaving breaths, the way she softly bites her lower lip.

"Why?" I breathe out. "Why was it out of your control?"

"My father did something and I..."

"You *what*?

"I couldn't make it."

"What did he do?"

London stares, heartache rippling everywhere as she fingers the edges of the vinyl record case, threading over the glossy artwork cover of that iconic white prism with a ray of light transforming into a kaleidoscope of rainbows.

"My father...He..."

Fuck.

I'm such an emotional mess, needing this conversation to survive. It's why I take a step forward, this time gently pinning her against her locker.

My hands rush up, kissing the cold metal above her head. And

as I glance down at her, not in intimidation, but in pure intrigue…
as well as apprehension, fear, and desire. I want to know what's got
those gorgeous baby-blues ticking.

London still has the vinyl clutched to her chest as she gazes up
at me. Her blonde hair sprawls against the locker, all disheveled, im-
itating beautifully sprawled ink.

I can feel her every breath, it's hot, tickling my lips the more I
crane my neck lower so we're at eye level. Slowly, I take the vinyl from
her grip and prop it on top of the locker, out of reach.

"What did he do, LonLon?" I say, my voice the softest it's ever
been. "What did he do to you? I swear to God, I'll kill him if he hurt
you. I will."

The pained look in her eyes kills me, reminding me once again
I'm obsessed.

In the end, London avoids the question.

Completely.

"You think I would have voluntarily walked away from you, Tate?
You are the best thing that's ever happened to me." She throws out a
shaky breath, desperately scanning my face. "You are *the best thing*
that's *happening* to me. I was in love with you, Tate. I haven't felt that
way with anybody but you. Butterflies. You give me so many butterflies, to the point where it just hurts to breathe. This vinyl, the fact that
you're right here, looking at me, you don't know how much I need
it." Her voice continues to break. "You don't know how much I *need
you*. I didn't mean to…just…*Please*, don't hate me."

I swallow hard at the thought she thinks that my soul mission
here is still to hurt her.

"I thought I hated you, LonLon, but turns out, it was just my
caged heart telling me it doesn't matter where I run, or how fast I do
it, I always come back to you." My hand slips off the locker to cup her
jaw, my thumb caressing over her glossy lips as her head falls into
me. "Don't you see I come back to you, London? *Every. Single. Time.*"

"You mean you forgive me?"

"Yeah," I manage to choke out through the throbbing at the back
of my throat. "Yeah, I said I'd be with you to the moon and back,
remember?

"Always."

"So drown the heartache from your eyes, baby girl, and I'll revive you instead."

London wets her plump, glossy lips. "How?"

"*How?*" I rasp back.

"Mmhmmm. How?"

With every fiber of my being, I give in to the past eight years filled with angst, tragedy, and heartache.

I give in to the way that she's looking at me, pleading for me to cure all her aches.

I give in to the way I ignore everything telling me to step away, because I can't.

I can't anymore.

I can't continue being Henley.

I can't resist how perfect we'd be together.

London Héroux is the cure to all my dark nightmares, which is why an eruption of euphoria takes over me as I murmur, "Like *this*."

And then, my aching lips crush down on hers. Hard. Rough. Passionate. *Selfishly devouring her.*

Her soft lips are so sickly sweet, it taunts me in the best way, in the only way I crave.

I kiss her like I mean it.

I kiss her like she deserves.

I kiss her hungrily, like without it I'll die, because I know in my heart of hearts, that that's exactly what would happen. I would bleed into an everlasting death if I wasn't here right now, kissing London Héroux recklessly with our hands roaming each other's skin. Exploring.

God, this feels so good.

She feels so good.

A desperation takes over me, one so strong it has heat crawling up my spine, egging her on as my body rocks into hers. I love the way she whimpers, grinding against me so adamantly.

Oh yeahhh.

London moans through the kiss, making my cock harden by the second.

I let her ruin me.

She lets me ruin her.

We get crazy ruining each other.

My wildly beating heart is in stitches as the kiss turns aggressive, destined to leave our lips bruised.

I viciously grab a fistful of her honey blonde waves and yank them hard, pulling her hair till her head tilts back. The action makes her gasp against me, having me smirking against her parted lips.

Like a horny beast, I take advantage of it, kissing her deeper, and I literally feel her melt in my arms, the moment my tongue finds hers, ravishing her in a dance, only she and I know exist.

A satisfied moan escapes her.

Fuck.

Fuck.

Fuccck.

London's long nails glide up my neck, caressing over my stubbled jaw before roaming higher. The way she tangles her fingers in my hair and tugs the ends in ecstasy has me growling.

More moans tangle her throat, vibrating through the kiss.

Yes, baby.

Moan for me.

Moan. For. Me.

My baby girl tastes fucking amazing, like strawberries and cream, her tongue greedily devouring mine back, keeping up with my fast-paced swirls and relentlessly erotic French-kiss.

Like she could do this forever with me.

Like this won't be our last kiss in heartache.

Like this, right here, is her death and her revival.

And mine too.

Chapter
THIRTY-SIX

London

My bruised lips are still scorching, inked in him, when we pull apart at the deafening ring of the school bell, signaling the end of lunch.

Oh.

My.

God.

Ohmygod. Ohmygod. Ohmygod.

Tate's eyes darken as I slowly wet my lips, feeling just how swollen they've become because of the kiss.

His alluring, musky vanilla cologne floods my lungs, making me feel alive for the first time in a long time. The darkness that spiked my mind only this morning is gone, replaced with him.

Wow.

The electricity sparking my body is intense. I've never felt like this before. Nicandro never has never made me feel like this, and *HenleyKing17*, whoever he may be, has only done this to me in words.

Tate's done both.

The butterflies at the pit of my stomach continue to erupt when

Tate Meadows kisses me again, this time slower, softly pecking my lips before pulling away at the loud stomps of students beginning to flood the hallway.

I'm breathing so hard, catching my breath after the kiss, that I'm almost dizzy.

Still pressed against the cold locker, I glance around, my cheeks hot as I come to terms with the fact we're not alone anymore. We were in our own little world, simply floating.

"You kiss like a dream," I whisper through my pants, sexily biting my lower lip.

Tate's Atlantic blue eyes drop there, just like I hoped. His lips are all glossy because of me, coated in my favorite strawberry and cream delight.

"Wanna get out of here?" he pants.

"You have a free period too?"

Tate softly shakes his head. "No."

"No?"

"No, but I do now."

Huh?

"What's that supposed to mean?" I arch my brow at my gorgeously reckless crush.

That hot, smirk crawls across his mischievous lips. "That I'm not fucking done with you."

Oh?

His direct words have my heart doing a double back flip, all while my hot pussy throbs.

"Well, my parents aren't home right now…"

"Are they at work?"

"No."

Tate raises a suspicious eyebrow. "No?"

"No. They're in LA. Potential client stuff."

Longing ruptures through those heavenly baby-blues. "So that means…"

"There's nobody in my apartment right now," I finish off.

"When will they be back?"

"Not until Monday."

It's Friday, which means… *An entire weekend to myself.*

Tate's arrogant smirk deepens. "London Héroux, are you inviting me to your place?"

The roughness of his voice has me rubbing my thighs together, temporarily smothering the persistent throbbing of my aching pussy.

My panties are drenched, and after that breathtaking kiss, all I want is for Tate Meadows to cure my need.

It's why I give into my rebel heart, not caring who's watching as I take his hand and slowly guide it under my school skirt, up my fishnet-covered inner thighs.

"You tell me, Meadows…"

My heart skips with every caress, shooting heat up with each touch as sparks fizzle in the form of goose bumps.

Biting my lip, I rebelliously part my thighs, gawking up at him through my thick lashes. Tate understands exactly what I want, taking over. His gaze is heavy, coated in a darkness I now understand to be lust, as his fingers confidently brush over my panties, the fishnet an added layer.

"*Fuck me, London.*" He groans, hunger swirling over his irises when he feels my pulsing wetness. It's so intense, he closes his eyes, his voice raspier, "You're dripping, all because of me."

My hands drape around his neck, pulling him closer. "*Mmhmmm.*"

"Use your words, babygirl."

"I'm all wet because of you," I breathe out, all flustered.

My breath hitches at the way Tate slowly brushes his thumb over my covered clit, taunting me with his touch. He's teasing me, doing it on purpose, circling my clit so leisurely.

Even though he's edging me, the relentless rhythm makes my lips part with an uncontainable moan.

Yes.

Yes.

"Yes! Keep doing that, Tate!"

Purposely, he does the opposite and pulls back, wickedly reclaiming his control.

I instantly feel the absence of his touch.

Ugh! Screw you, Tate Meadows!

"Tate…*Please.*"

"Not here." Tate growls, all sexually-frustrated, possessively taking my hand. "Let's go."

"Go where?"

He smirks devilishly. "Your. Place. *Now*."

Tate Meadows slams me up against my bedroom wall, his open mouth kisses intoxicating against my neck as he frantically undoes the pearly buttons of my school blouse.

Oh God… *This is really happening.*

My chest rises and falls, trapped in a butterfly effect I never want to escape.

The entire ride to my apartment in his vintage Mustang was filled with silence, a comfortable lust-filled silence. We couldn't take our eyes off each other, his hand intertwined in mine, on top of my lap, as he sped through the grid-locked Manhattan streets. He's skipping class to be with me.

Tate Meadows has my heart racing, over and over again.

He saved me.

He's *saving me* today.

Last night, I was so close to ending it all, now the solace of his touch revives all my blues. I don't want to be in a world without him. It would be too cruel.

Tate's gorgeous eyes find mine, and it's as if I'm staring into a galaxy of us. A galaxy of what could be if I just escaped the stinging in my heart.

"Stop thinking, baby," he says in that darkly delicious voice, slowing down to tenderly cup my face and caress my cheekbones. "You nervous?"

"No, never. Not with you."

"Then what is it, LonLon?"

"I just want to run away with you, that's all."

Desire drips from his eyes. "Heaven."

"Heaven?"

"Mmhmmm. I'll fuck you into heaven, babygirl, we'll run away there. You want that?"

My pussy is aching, desperate to be touched by him as our hips continue rocking over our Glorsin St. Claire's uniform.

Heaven.

Heaven with him.

I smile, brushing my lips over his. "More than you know."

Tate shoots me a beautiful grin that carves his dimples, sinking into his sexy stubble.

He wastes no time making me melt, attacking my bruised lips with a breathtaking kiss filled with him. My legs tighten around his waist, my hot skin scorching at the way the pads of his fingers brush against my cleavage as he continues to quickly unbutton my school blouse.

The soft thump of the smooth material hitting my bedroom floor has my heart skipping as I kiss him deeper, showing him just how desperately I need him.

Manhattan's coldness kisses my bare skin, deepening as Tate's hands wander over my bare stomach, grazing the waistband of my skirt, and then a little higher, teasing the edge of my bra.

God, his lips feel so good.

Tate tastes like peppermint, like sugar and spice and everything nice.

His fingers slip beneath my thighs, holding me up against the wall, then higher, squeezing my peachy ass. I can't help but tug his black and green striped tie when he spanks me.

My pebbled nipples scrape along the crisp material of his dress shirt. My bra is a sheer cream, embroidered with cute light pink roses. The same bra his eyes lock on when the kiss ends.

Tate can see *everything.* My hard, rosy-pink nipples, my creamy tits, the scattered small beauty spots across my chest, like an erotic dot-to-dot constellation in the Milky Way.

This is one of the bras I wore on *Enticed…*

Tate doesn't know I was on Enticed.

My heart pounds frantically against my chest, my tits recklessly rising and falling in anticipation as Tate glances back up at me, lust in his eyes.

"Jesus, London, do you wear these bras underneath your school uniform every day?"

Softly biting my lip, I nod.

"*Fuck.*" He sucks in a breath. "You're bad, LonLon. Such a fuck-ing bad girl."

Moaning, I grind my hips against his dark slacks, feeling his hardening cock pulse against my throbbing pussy.

"I'm a good girl," I whisper, my fingers gliding up his broad chest, feeling the hard muscles beneath before fingering the first button. "But I can be a bad girl for you."

Tate doesn't need to hear it twice before kissing me again in a frenzy. He sets me down on the floor and we go crazy, undoing each other's clothes and mauling each other's lips until we're left panting in the middle of my bedroom, practically naked.

His dark, wavy hair is all disheveled because of me, sexily sticking up while other strands fall over his eyes, demanding more. The thin gold chain wrapped around his neck intrigues me.

My lust-filled eyes roam across his body, taking in his beautiful olive skin and masculine six-foot-one physique. Muscles carve his body, carving around his toned biceps, narrow waist, and then lower, extenuating his perfectly-carved quads and perfectly-taut abs.

The grooves and dips of his abdominal muscles, alongside his vaunted V-line and short, dark hair that runs from his navel and disappears into his boxer briefs has me drooling.

He's not a boy, he's a *man*.

A gorgeous man with a broken soul, the warmest heart, and apparently, without an inch of body fat.

And then, *God…*

It's torture, the way the thick outline of his cock bulges against his black Armani boxer briefs. Desire continues dripping in his piercing blue-eyed gaze as he rakes his gaze down my body, inch by inch, checking me out now instead.

Gosh.

Tate does it for so long, hungrily eyeing my sheer bra, black fishnets, and panty-covered sex. My panties are white with lacy edges that has him groaning.

He smooths a finger over the frills, strumming the diamonds of my fishnet stockings as he does, his smirk deepening.

Giggling, I self-consciously wrap a hand around my waist. I thought laughter would flood his lungs too, but for some strange reason, Tate's smirk falls, and all that's left is a pointed frown.

All of a sudden, he seems…*different.*

Chained in a melancholy that wasn't there seconds before.

Swirling in an endless pit of doom, here, right in front of me.

But… Why?

My brows knit together. "What happened? What's going on?"

"Turn around," Tate commands, his tone all serious. "I want to see…"

"Huh?"

"London, turn around."

"What? Why?"

Before I have a chance to process what's going on, Tate grips my hips and spins me around, so urgently, my hands slap against my floor-to-ceiling mirror, halting me in place.

My fingertips sink into the coldness of the glass.

Tate towers behind me, that sandalwood scent driving me crazy.

Our eyes lock in the mirror.

"Baby, what happened?" he whispers, clenching his jaw. He wraps me up in a backward embrace, the solace of his touch around my waist. "You think I wouldn't notice?"

"Notice what?"

The air shifts between us, lust fizzling out in exchange for something more.

"Tate." I hold my breath, fearing the worst. "What's going on? You're scaring me."

His fingers gently trace down my spine, causing shivers, but when he stops by the center of it and roams two inches to the left, my entire body freezes up.

No.

God, no.

My chest is all foreign and tight, a pain rippling over me that isn't only because the patch of skin Tate's stroking throbs. It's because through all of the euphoric pleasure Tate was giving me, I had forgotten about *it.*

I let Tate consume me so intensely, numbing myself to the parts of me I detest most.

The parts of me forever claimed by him, forever scared in blue blotches and marks.

I…

I wasn't ready to tell him yet.

Courage flees me when his sad blue eyes meet mine again in

the mirror. A knot at the back of my throat forms, chaining me to a fleeting heartbeat.

I know he's seen *them*.

The bruises along my spine caused by my dad.

The whitened scars of years of spiraling violence.

Tate Meadows sees *me*. The real *me*. For the *very first time*.

And he doesn't run away from them, he leans toward them, still gently caressing my bruises before falling on his knees. Without me saying a word, he kisses them, like I'm still beautiful with them. Like I'm valid, like I deserve to breathe, like I deserve life.

Like I'm *his*.

Tate's.

The ache in my chest explodes, blurring my vision and numbing my mind. I know just how desperately his hot lips work to erase my hurt, how they linger over my wounds, petitioning to heal them.

"Who did this to you, LonLon?"

The throbs choke my throat, incapable of saying a word.

Here I am, staring in the mirror, barely recognizing myself. My cheeks are still flustered from our moment of passion, my lips swollen, and neck marked with amber-colored love bites. My hair's a hot mess, and I look like a chaotic reckoning with only fishnets, panties, and a bra seriously too small for me.

On the surface, I'm moving on from the torments of my father, but inside, my mind is a scary place, riddled with dark shadows and emptiness.

And that's my point. I'm not sure what aspect of London Héroux I don't recognize.

I don't know if it's the happiness, or if it's the sadness.

Or if it's both.

All I know, is that when Tate stands to his full height again and turns me around so we're face-to-face, the pain in his eyes tells me that he gets it.

He gets me.

He understands the happiness, the sadness, the craziness.

He understands the lonely parts inside me, the kisses in heartache.

He understands my zest for life and also my fascination with death.

He understands how I crave to be free, uninhibitedly, yet I don't know how to be.

He understands that I'm caged in this apartment, that he's my solace, my salvation.

He understands me.

Me.

More than I do myself.

And while that should scare me, it thrills me, as Tate wraps me in his arms and carries me to the bed. He lays us down, his hands automatically slipping around my waist, never letting go of me as my vision continues to glass over. Kaleidoscopes of those Atlantic blues form whenever I forget to blink.

Because that's what happens sometimes.

I forget to blink.

I forget to breathe.

I forget to eat and smile and simply be.

"Was it Nicandro?" he murmurs, inches away, his voice just as pained as my bubbling heart.

I shake my head against my bedsheets.

"Then who, babygirl?"

I gulp down, scrunching up my face as a wave of unrest zaps my chest. I try to rub it out, but it's useless. The only thing that makes it better is when Tate does it. When he smooths his hand over my heart, against my sheer bra, feeling my every frantic heartbeat.

That's when the pain softly subsides.

"Is it…" His eyes dim, searching mine. "Your father, Sterling?"

Bingo.

I forget how to breathe, just like I always do.

I'm paralyzed. So paralyzed I can't speak or move.

"LonLon?" Tate says a little louder, the fear of losing me evident. "Does he hit you?"

Tears blur my eyes, overflowing when the sensation to blink overwhelms me.

"Is your father abusive? Fuck, London. It's all beginning to make sense."

Tate's hands desperately spear across my jaw, cupping my cheeks, just as my hot tears baptize them, streaking down my face, sideways.

He kisses my tears away, and then resorts to kissing my wrists, finding my fading white lines and those not so faded, making love to them too.

"I feel so numb," I whisper through the tears, piercing my lips when it all gets too much.

"I know, LonLon, I know, but I'm right here. I'm right *here*." A crumbled, lopsided smile curves his lips. He's trying to be strong, for me, but he's breaking too, I see it in the way his blue-eyes glimmer in the afternoon sunlight, glassing over like I've never seen before. "I'll help you."

"You'll help me?"

"Mmhmmm, I'll do anything for you, as long as you tell me the truth."

The truth.

Tate is right.

I can't carry this weight alone anymore.

I'm sick of hiding, of concealing, of kissing the doors of death.

With all my strength, I fight my demons for the man with the heart-shaped lips. The one, who, when we were kids, gave me a raincoat, so I didn't shiver. The one I'll forever adore.

For me.

I fight my monsters for me.

For I deserve more than darkness.

"I'm a victim," I sniffle. "My father's been physically abusing me since I was nine."

Pearl-sized tears slowly glide down Tate's cheeks, and they speak more to me than anything else.

He feels my hurt.

"Oh my God," he breathes, a broken mess, embracing me tighter. "My darling girl, I'm so sorry."

"It's not your fault." My lips tremble. "That New Year's Eve, he concussed me."

"I'll kill him, London. I'm going to kill him for doing this to you."

All my fears rattle inside my chest, making it impossible to breathe without thinking of him.

My father.

Sterling Héroux.

Of all his inflicted abuse.

I hate him. I hate him so much for everything he's done to me.

For taking away my happiness, for burying my truth, and now, for being my vulnerability.

I don't want him to be my vulnerability. I don't want to be *vulnerable*.

I want to be strong, and free, and happy.

It's exactly what I tell Tate with a croaky voice, and he listens. He listens to me, all while the muscles in his stubbled jaw tighten and flex, as if he could kill Sterling Héroux right now.

The cries deepen to sobs, so loud Tate gently buries my head in his warm chest.

I wrap my legs around him, holding him tight, wishing we could die and be reborn into another life, right here, together.

His heart is racing, palpations that scream unrest, and yet, he shows me no fear. He's strong for me, despite his cold tears, which glide against my ear to the junction of my neck.

"Nobody's going to hurt you. Not anymore," Tate whispers against my hair, softly rocking me in his arms, an antidote to all the crazy. "You're not just a victim, you're a *survivor*. An armor of beauty. I'm so sorry I wasn't there, but now I am. It's you and me, baby. It's a forever thing."

Forever.

I like the sound of that.

With Tate Meadows, I feel so safe.

He came into my life by a twist of fate, and our souls have tangled with each other's ever since.

"When we graduate next month, we'll run, LonLon. Run anywhere you like. Somewhere nobody knows our names. Restart life and be happy, together. Just know I'll go anywhere with you."

"Anywhere?"

"*Anywhere*," Tate promises with a pained smile. "Because I'm in love with you. I always have been, in fact, I've never stopped. Baby, I've loved you since we were ten years old."

Despite my hardening sobs, I grab his face with both hands, desperate to feel him again. The kiss is slow and tender, everything that the others weren't, but everything I need right now.

Tate makes love to my mouth, deepening our kiss, his tongue stroking mine in kindness.

My heart clenches. Over and over. I savor him and his taste, whimpering, giving him my all.

We pull away panting messes, and somehow, through it all, I manage to smile.

"I love you so much, Tate."

"I love you more," he breathes. "I love everything you are and everything you are not."

His soft lips find my forehead, lingering there for a lifetime.

"I've loved you for eight years, LonLon, and I'll love you for eight million more."

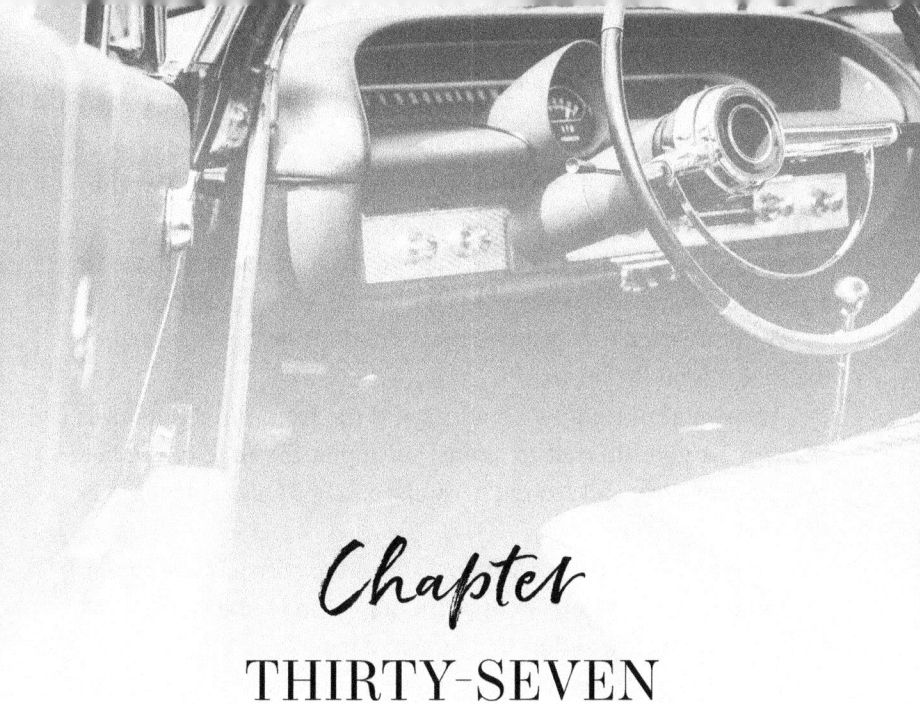

Chapter
THIRTY-SEVEN

Tate

The revelation makes me sick to my stomach, boiling my blood to the point of no return.

Sterling Héroux is an abuser.

A physically violent, vile monster.

The asshole my father competes with.

I don't know how long London and I stay here wrapped on top of her bedsheets, my hand rubbing small circles into her back, but I'm down for staying here forever if it means she's comfortable.

I love her.

I love her so freaking much.

And just the thought of her having to endure so much pain at the hands of somebody that's supposed to love her, breaks me.

It takes me back to years ago, to the night of that AMA award ceremony, where we escaped to the rooftop to talk. I noticed bruises inked on her skin that night. It hadn't been the first. There was also a night in Central Park. But both times London shrugged them off, blaming gymnastics.

London was covering for her father, possibly too scared of what he may do to her if the words ever escaped her lips. But now they have, and there's no fucking way that I'm staying quiet.

My babygirl isn't going to be trapped any longer, I'm going to be right there beside her as she fights for herself, serving justice.

A glimmering orange tinge coats London's bedroom, signaling the sunset is on the horizon.

The sound of shallow breaths spear me from my thoughts as London wriggles herself to sit up. I sit up at the edge of the bed with her, my arms still around her waist and lips pressed against her shoulder.

We glance through her window, out at the mesmerizing sunset. It's sensational with blotches of burnt orange and bubble-gum-pink twirls across the sky, almost in a foreign dance.

It's mesmerizing, evoking a hope we both readily need.

London's stomach grumbles in protest, guilt lodging in my throat when she tells me she hasn't eaten lunch yet.

The next few hours roll past quicker than I'd like. I collect a few items from London's grand pantry and cook a mean omelet with rice. It's nothing gourmet but it's better than nothing. The small smile on London's face when she takes the first taste of dinner will forever be implanted in my mind. She likes it.

I can't keep my hands off hers the entire dinner, my fingers nervously playing with hers, smoothing over her long, red nails and trailing the heart lines in her palms.

Later, London doesn't want to watch a film or go out, she just wants to be in my arms, and I wouldn't want it any other way.

Being under the covers with London unlocks a new intimacy I've never explored before. Just holding her and hearing her heartbeat tightens my heartstrings.

London could be with anybody tonight, or in fact, she could be alone, but she wants me.

She's so beautiful, so fucking beautiful as she glances up at me, twirling the ends of her towel-dried curls. She had a shower not too long ago, while I stayed in her room. It made her skin even smoother, that fragrance of strawberries and cream even more prominent.

"Can you stay the night?" she whispers against my lips when the silvery moonlight cascades across her face, creating darkened shadows of the night. "With me?"

It's not even a question for me, it's instant. "Babe, I ain't going anywhere."

I don't care if her parents are set to come back on Monday and not tonight, I'm not leaving her alone.

Happiness floods London's eyes.

They speak to me, thanking me, without her ever uttering a word.

After a few more moments of silence, I'm grateful she begins to open up, explaining the details of her father's ordeal and all she had to endure. I lost my breath when she got up to the part of further explaining why she never met up with me on that New Year's Eve.

Sterling, Ramona, and London were at Victor LéVont's New Year's Eve party.

Her father made a mockery out of London, adding to her social anxiety.

He cornered her in the elevator and hit her, repeatedly, to '*teach her a lesson.*' In utter rage, he slammed her against the mirrored wall, resulting in a mild concussion, stitches, and yet another cover-up story.

London decided she couldn't do it anymore. She couldn't endure the pain of her father while looking me in the eye and pretending she was okay. So, she was forced to walk away.

If she told anybody about the abuse, her father would kill her. The only reason her text to me was unfinished was because her father stepped into her room, and she had to quickly send it.

It's all beginning to add up now.

The fact she still has a small smile planted on her lips after it is beyond me. She's so strong. So strong, fierce, and beautiful. I can't stop staring at her right now, hating myself for not being man enough to ignore my perspective and understand hers sooner.

I've grown so much since I first met her, we both have.

We've matured.

Come into the people we'll forever be.

But most of all, we've learned the hard way that being a part of the elite isn't worth it. The only thing that's worth it in this life is having a person that understands you through and through, unconditionally.

And London is *my person.*

There's so much vulnerability in our deep conversation. So much comfort and warmth that it wraps me up. It's the most emotion we've ever shared as London feels comfortable enough to share more of her story.

There's a bit of hesitancy when I ask her about the journals. The ones she used to write about me. When I finally have the pink leather-bound journal in my hands, I almost feel guilty. I know London wrote every single one of these entries with the intention of them never been read by anybody else.

Almost like a piece of therapy.

But London tells me it's okay, pecking my cheek when preoccupation floods me.

"I want you to read it." She nods, caressing the journals spine. "It's for your eyes only."

And London's right.

I read over every single one of her entries, from when she was ten years old to two years ago, when she stopped.

It's flooded with our past, timestamped with our greatest memories, and pinned with emotions of a lovesick ten-year-old girl who crushed hard for the little boy who gave her his coat so she could be warm in exchange for a mangled teddy bear.

That very teddy—Mr. Bunny—lies between us now as I glance over the journals, London's head resting on my chest.

Reading the entries revives me in ways I never knew existed, bringing tears to my eyes that prick my vision.

Fuck.

I never wanted London to feel this alone.

I never wanted her to be broken.

I never wanted the emptiness.

But there's no emptiness in her hopeful eyes when I finish the last entry, feeling as if I was reading an extension of her mind.

"You see, Tate," she brushes away my salty tears with her thumb, "I've loved you since we were ten years old too."

I hold her tight, never wanting to let go.

Our hands interlace in the air, my fingers tracing over hers and creating small circles.

"Will you tell me about your parents?" London whispers into the silence. "Your mom?"

"What do you want to know, baby?"

"Everything."

I gulp down. "Are you sure?"

"Of course. Your pain is mine."

My heart clenches. *That means everything to me.*

"When I was eight years old, my mother was diagnosed with Frontotemporal dementia," I explain. "I never knew that would be the last day I'd see her for the next ten years. You see, my mother's dementia was already aggressive when the diagnosis was made. My father never loved my mother. He loved her money, but not the person she was underneath. He refused to take care of her, and when she became aggressive, he locked her in a psychiatric hospital, forbidding me from seeing her until the day I turned eighteen. He wanted to make her suffer and made me suffer the aftereffects."

I feel so liberated by the end of telling her everything, and it feels like a weight dislodging.

"Oh my gosh, Tate, that's horrible. I'm so sorry." Her hands, which have somehow found themselves against my broad, bare chest, slow. She fingers the thin gold chain of my necklace. "Why would your father do that to you?"

I clench my jaw. "Because he's an egotistical bastard. Always has been. When he saw the first opportunity to get my mom out of the picture, he did. He was drowning in so much debt and whiskey that greed made him use all the money my mother saved for me one day. She had a small fortune saved following a family tragedy. He used her money and took advantage of her condition."

"I hate Mirko so much."

"You're not alone in that feeling."

"Is your mother still alive?"

"Yes."

London presses a kiss over my heart, hearing every reckless heartbeat. "What's she like?"

"Beautiful. Charismatic. She used to be so witty. You'll like her so much." I shut my eyes, getting lost in her warmth. "Her name is Elizabeth and she used to be an artist, had such an eye for masterpieces. She loved art so much; it was her everything." I suck in a breath, preparing myself. "The day I turned eighteen, I went to visit her. I found the hospital and visited her and…"

"Yes, darling?"

"She didn't remember me…"

Between my voice breaking and the gasp that escapes London's lips, I pierce my eyes open, only to find they've become a blurry mess. I don't even realize hot tears are streaking down my cheeks until London kisses them away.

She's all glassy-eyed too, her empathy to my misery soothing me in ways only she knows how.

"That must have been so hard, Tate."

"My heart broke. She was telling me to leave, that I wasn't her son, and all I wanted to do was scream. Not at her, but at the world. I hate that it's like this, that it can be so unfair."

London vigorously nods against the pillow, knowing my exact pain. "It's debilitating."

"So much so, yeah."

"Will you see her again?"

I softly shrug, the question toying my mind ever since I stepped out of that chain-link fence. "I don't know. I don't think I can take it again. It's too painful, looking into the eyes of somebody you adore so much and them staring back in complete terror. I hated the way it made me feel."

"Often times…" London sniffles, smoothing her thumb over my chain, "I wonder if all this pain in our lives is here for a reason, you know? Like, if I was happy, would I still appreciate the moonlight as much I do? Would the sun kissing my skin still make me smile? Would I be obsessed with the nostalgic crackle of a vinyl, as opposed to the lyrics? Would I still like the little things?"

"No, you would be too into life to notice them."

"Exactly," London says. "Maybe tragedies happen to keep life in focus. To realize the importance. To learn to heal with the people who are also tangled in melancholy."

"Well, then life really fucked us over, huh?" I tiredly smile, attempting to lighten the mood.

It's a beautiful butterfly effect when she finds the courage to smile back. "Ditto."

"But no, you're right, London. We wouldn't understand each other as deeply if we hadn't met on that park bench, laced in heartache.

We're each other's anchors now, for life. Just two damaged hearts trying to heal each other..."

"In love," she adds.

My throat closes. "Two damaged hearts trying to heal each other in love."

"I like that."

"I like you more."

London's cheeks flame as she quietly yawns, her tired eyes reddening by the second.

"You should get some rest, baby girl."

"But I want to talk."

"I know, but it's been a big afternoon. Besides, I'm not going anywhere."

London gives in, but it's only because if she doesn't, the sandman would haunt her anyway.

"Sweet dreams, my babygirl."

London falls asleep to the sound of rain softly pelting against the window, her legs wrapped around mine, a heavenly scent. She dozes off instantly in my arms, but I can't sleep, just like the night before.

My mind is working too hard, spiraling, figuring out a fast-track way out of this city.

Because I wasn't lying.

If we want to survive, we need to leave Manhattan.

We need to leave this shit and heal with new memories. *Better* memories.

Those embedded with her and me, and this time, destined to never be forgotten.

Chapter

THIRTY-EIGHT

Tate

I wake to the aroma of sugary cookie dough flooding my lungs.
Huh?

It takes me a moment to adjust from the daylight, and a heavenly golden glow blinds my eyes. *Ahhh God.* Once all the tiny little dots invading my vision fade, I glance around the bedroom flooded with pink, and frills, and that lingering whiff of cookie dough.

London.

I'm in London's room.

Everything begins to come back.

Our sworn truce not to hate each other anymore.

The physical and psychological abuse Sterling Héroux inflicts on London.

The emotion lodged inside my wildly beating heart is almost overbearing as I spear my fingers across the crisp bedsheets, over her silky pink pillow, yet coldness webs my fingers.

She's not here.

She's not in this bed.

"London?" I call out, sitting up to glance around the bedroom better, the thin sheets slipping farther down my hardened abs as I rub my eyes. "Baby? You here?"

Nothing.

There's no trickling water coming through the ensuite door either, so I kick off the sheets and stride out of the room, into the fancy fucking marble hallway, where that whiff of cookies gets stronger.

Only now, there's a soft hum of music that laces the air too.

The smile burning up my lips reaches my eyes the moment I find London in the kitchen, moving around and swaying her hips as she pulls heart-shaped cookies from the baking paper tray. From where I'm standing, they seem to be chocolate chip and smell fucking delicious too.

But just seeing London happy, dancing around the kitchen in her favorite silk pink pajamas with no reservations erupts fireworks in my chest. It's as if she's trying to fight her demons, to show the darkened monsters she won't let them win, and that strength is one of the things I love most about her.

Her thrive to fight.

To the death.

Literally.

London still hasn't noticed me yet as she spins around from the kitchen island to the sink, washing mixing bowls.

With her back to me and Lana Del Rey blaring from her Alexa, my smirk only deepens as I tippytoe behind her.

"When were you going to invite me to the party, hmmm?" I muse in her ear, the second I snake my arms around her from behind, pinning my body against hers.

A jolt rushes through London's body that subsides at the sound of my voice.

"Jesus, Tate." She softly giggles, that laughter brightening my soul. "You scared the shit out of me."

"Sorry." I chuckle, nestling my head into her neck and closing my eyes so I focus on her warmth and solace, and her lingering body wash. "Just wanted to say good morning to my favorite girl."

Switching off the faucet, London turns in my hold, the heat in her cheeks obvious. "Good morning, stalker."

Hmmm.

I can't help but take in her natural beauty. Those big, doe eyes, the gorgeous blue seeming a little warmer than last night. Her heart-shaped lips are still all swollen because of me, reddened by my intensity.

"Morning." I smolder, unable to resist slamming my lips against hers. The hot, morning kiss is everything I need to begin my morning as she moans in my mouth, her hardened nipples grazing through the silk, caressing my bare chest.

A bashfulness consumes London when we pull apart.

That flirty, girly, woman I know coming back to me in all forms.

For a few seconds, we do nothing but gaze at each other as the world goes by with Lana's singing a psychedelic remedy.

We're trapped in a moment.

A moment.

I think we're both still getting used to the fact that I'm standing in front of her, in her kitchen, weeks out from graduating.

The world is going to be ours soon.

We can have these mornings every morning.

"I made cookies." She blushes, cutely sashaying out of my hold to attend to her baking tray. "Choc-chip with strawberry jam. Want to try?"

I don't even know if I nod, I'm too ensnared by her radiating glee and how it takes me completely off guard.

"I like seeing you smile," I say as she breaks the cookie in half, strawberry-colored jam gushing out. She feeds it to me and *goddamn.* I roll my eyes back in pleasure, savoring the warm taste. "Fuccck ye-ahhh! This is *so* good."

"Aww, thank you!"

"You're happy this morning, baby."

"Mmhmmmm."

My hands find her hips, the pads of my thumbs caressing the delicate bones. "Wanna tell me why?"

"Because you're here." There's a sparkle in her eyes as she finishes off her half of the cookie and rubs the crumbs off her hands. "Last night was the first time I actually slept in ages. I realized I wasn't going to let my father win, that I deserve happiness too, and I feel happy every time I look at you."

"I'm proud of you, you know that, right?"

London shyly nods.

"I'm also happy to hear you say you deserve happiness, because you do, London, a whole lot of it. It isn't selfish to put yourself first, not if it means surviving. You're beautiful, babe, every single part of you is beautiful to me. You're my anchor, and just know, I'll never let you go."

"You're my anchor too. I appreciate that more than you know. I…also think I know where we should run to."

"Oh yeah?"

"Yeah, and I think it makes perfect sense."

"Where, LonLon?"

London grins, flashing me her pearly whites. "Seattle!"

Seattle

I know I'm supposed to smile.

I know I'm supposed to tell her yes, that I'll look for a place right now.

I know I'm supposed to do anything but remain frozen in the middle of her modern kitchen, the front part of my brain, not working with the rest of me.

Seattle.

Seattle.

Henley.

HenleyKing17 *is from Seattle.*

London was so open to me last night. So raw. How can I not do the same?

How can I continue hiding *HenleyKing17* from her like this?

She deserves to know the truth, before it's too late.

I clear my throat, nerves bubbling. "Seattle?"

"Yes, I just think it's so lively. I did some research and there's really cool vintage stores there and a lot of indie record shops too."

Research…

Research because of Henley?

God, dude, why are you thinking about it so hard? You ARE Henley.

London enthusiastically keeps going, "The entire Seattle scene still has remnants of those punk and soft rock vibes of the '90s. It was actually the capital of rock, think Nirvana. It's northwestern enough, the farthest we can escape to, right? I mean, any farther and we're in the Pacific!"

London's laughter should subdue the ache in my chest, but it doesn't. I actually begin to freak out when my tongue numbs and muscles tighten so much so, I can't even part my lips to get the words out.

I'm just in distress.

Panic-stricken.

Agitated.

And guilty, because I don't want this to be the end of us, but it very much could be. I don't know how she'll take it. What if she hates me? What if she never wants to see me again?

My eyes involuntarily shut as I pinch the bridge of my nose. *God. I can't live with that.*

I can't live with never seeing her again.

"Tate...Are you okay?"

The devil shakes my head for me.

"No," I choke out. "There's something...there's something I..."

"Yes?"

"Something I..."

Come on, Tate. Tell her. Come. On.

Inhaling a sharp breath, I swallow my pride and reopen my eyes.

I'm a fool for those baby blue eyes, which are pooling with concern.

"Do you know who else would love Seattle, London?"

"No." Her eyebrows faintly knit together. "Who?"

Well, here goes nothing.

"Henley," I gulp. "Or, rather, me. *Me*, LonLon. I'm *HenleyKing17*."

London instantly breaks out of my hold, eyes wide and bulging out of their sockets.

"What the fuc—" She stares up at me. "WHAT?"

My heartbeat slows.

Shit.

Shit.

Shit.

I reach out a hand for her. "Baby, I can explain—"

"NO! Don't fucking touch me!" she seethes, it's finally sinking in. "Don't!"

London's breathing so hard, her hair all tangled as she looks at me like I'm the enemy again. Her glassy eyes bravely hold mine, her lips pursed as she bawls her fists by her sides.

"How could you do that to me? How could you lie to me this entire time? You're *Henley*? *Henley?!* No, no it can't be…" She thinks about it for a minute. "Is that why you were so nice to me yesterday? Because *Rose* sent *Henley* that text?"

I stare at my feet, not knowing what to say.

"TELL ME, TATE!" she roars, slamming her fist against the marble island blindly, crumbling a couple cookies and having the strawberry jam splutter everywhere. "GO ON!"

"*Fuck*," I murmur under my breath, smoothing a tense hand over my stubble.

This isn't good. Not at all.

My jaw ticks. "I wasn't nice to you for charity, I was just done being the bad guy."

"So you pretended to be a different guy to get close to me?"

"No!" I gasp. "God, no. That's not what happened at all."

Planting her hands on her hips, London shakes her head. "It's not what it feels like."

"My intent with Henley was never to be malicious, it was coincidental. I didn't even know you were on *Enticed*! I had already been on it for some time as a voyeur. Levi introduced me. He knows all the fucking tricks, including manipulating location pins. I never played you. I didn't fool you." My gaze softens, aching to reach out and touch her. "It was all real, London. Every chat we had *was real*. Every single sentiment—*real*. It's just that you were *Rose Heartache Mila*, and I was *HenleyKing17*. That's all that was different."

Silence paves the space between us.

I hate it.

I hate that we're like this.

I hate I did this to us. *Me.*

"So you've…you've seen me? Naked?"

The question shoots daggers into my chest.

I can't even look at London, feeling so ashamed and dirty. "Yes, I…"

"Did you get off on me?"

Fuck.

I squeeze my eyes shut. "London, I…"

"Answer me, Tate," she grits, her voice a stormy mess.

"Yes."

"Were you ever going to tell me you were Henley?"

"Yes."

"If you still hated me and none of *this* happened, would you have ever told me?"

Her question stumps me, having me blow out a sharp breath. "I don't know."

"So, you would have just continued being Henley until *what*?"

"I…" I shake my head, "I don't know, London."

"Why didn't you tell me?"

"Because I was scared," I admit, a frown on my lips. "You hated me as Tate, so I thought Henley could be different. Seeing you on *Enticed* was therapy. Therapy, I didn't even know I needed. I'm not even talking orgasms. They were nothing compared to the emotional pull I felt to you. The moment I saw you, in that lilac wig, I couldn't look at any other women. You see, London, two nights ago…" I clear my throat, that throb capsizing, greedily, "…I deleted my account. *HenelyKing17* doesn't exist anymore. Not in that way anymore. He's gone. Forever."

I open my eyes to London's glassy blue-eyed stare.

Something's…*changed.*

There's no more darkness clouded in them, no melancholic desolation, just hope.

Hope.

"*Rose Heartache Mila*'s gone too," she whispers, all hoarse and weary.

"Huh?"

"I deleted my *Enticed* account the moment I woke up. That's why I was so happy, because I thought it entailed new beginnings, no matter how deeply my heart shattered for Henley."

"You didn't want to say goodbye?"

"I tried. He deleted his account. You deleted it…*God*," she cries, rushing a hand over her face when it gets too much. Her fingertips tremble, pinching the bridge of her nose, so she doesn't cry. "I was drawn to him because he was so real, now I know it's because it was you."

My pulse thrums against my neck.

I hate seeing her like this. It destroys me.

"I'm so sorry, LonLon. I wish I said it sooner." I lower my voice. "What are you thinking?"

London glances up at me, a beautiful mess.

She chokes out her words. "I don't know if I should hate or love my heart right now."

"Why?"

"Because it's telling me to trust you."

Nodding, I step forward. She doesn't tell me no, her conflicted gaze just stares at me.

"London," I whisper, "I was so scared to tell you. I've been sick to my stomach."

My knees grow weak the longer I stand here.

"I hate you so much. I hate you so much because you're saving my life." London painfully gasps, the cords in her neck heaving. "I was going to plummet into that Central Park lake two nights ago, Tate. I was going to drown a silent death, if you hadn't messaged me back as Henley."

My heart breaks, shattering piece by piece.

"No, baby. *No. No. No.*"

"I hate you so much that I love you." Tears flood her eyes. "I'm so glad it was you."

Shockwaves slam into me as London jumps into my arms, squeezing me hard, because I don't expect it. Not. *At all.* I thought she would reject me, just like everyone does, but she didn't.

She isn't.

I can trust in her.

I can trust in her to never leave because our love is stronger than any barrier.

"I wouldn't want anybody else to be Henley." She sniffles in my neck. "Nobody but you."

Dear god.

Relief attacks my lungs, making me hold her tighter, thanking the heavens she exists.

"I'm going to show you the beauty of life, my angel. We'll learn it together."

"Please." London sobs. "Show me."

With all my heart.

I nod. "I promise. The moon never fades, LonLon, and neither will we."

And for the first time in my life, I know everything's going to be okay.

Because she's in it.

With me.

We remain wrapped like this, in the solace of each other's arms till I carry London to her pink-obsessed bedroom, the warm sunlight stroking her creamy skin as I lay her on the tangled sheets.

Her grip finds my wrist, silently begging me not to go…

So I don't.

London's lingering coconut and rosy vanilla scent is my second home, strumming my tightening heartstrings when I steady my weight on top of her, nestling my muscular body between her thighs. It's almost instant, the way her lean long legs snake around my waist, her locked ankles digging into my curved spine, urging me closer.

She's absolutely breathtaking. Nothing less than a vision. The kind that only exists in iron-hearted poetry, and yet, she's real.

Wet tears stain the glossy silk of her coral pink pajamas, but those by her light eyes have dried, leaving a reddened brim laced in deliverance.

I know, deep down, London forgives me for being *HenleyKing17*, but I can't explain this relentless fire in my lungs, longing to scream out all the reasons I love her, yet I fear it's not enough.

I fear I've broken us.

Beyond repair.

"London, I'm so sor—"

Her mouth hungrily steals the words from my tongue, melting my lips with an insatiable kiss, so intense, it hurts. It's all-consuming, fiery, and sensual, her glistening strawberry-flavored tongue lapping mine, possessing me as she pushes her tits into me, making me feel the pebbled buds.

It's evident she isn't wearing a bra underneath her pajama top, the more her greedy nipples stab through the thin silk, gliding against my bare chest.

God.

I mold her ample tits and London mewls into my mouth. They're perky yet soft in my hands, almost stretching my entire grip. I squeeze them tight before flicking her nipples with my thumbs. She likes that, grinding herself against me, her drenched pussy soaking my boxer briefs.

Fuccck.

I haven't been more aware than in this moment of how I've effectively seen her naked on *Enticed*, but physically feeling her hot skin against mine is on another level. It evokes a part of me I'm unable to ignore any longer.

I want London.

So. Fucking. Badly.

I wanna fuck her, mercifully.

Giving her enough control, I regain my power, dominating the kiss with one hand on her neck, my thumb rhythmically caressing her throbbing pulse. I show her who she's playing with, sexily sucking her tongue, while my hips pin her deeper into the soft mattress. A relentless hunger feeds my soul as I grind my hardening cock against her shorts, heat rushing up my spine.

I break the kiss to stare down at her with unblinking eyes.

"Tell me, are you still mine, babygirl?" I huskily growl.

"Yes." London's baby blue eyes hold me in a devil's prayer, pacifying me. I gawk at her swollen heart-shaped lips and how they break into a smile, a saving grace. "I'm yours, Tatum."

Tatum.

She rarely calls me by my actual first name, if ever, so not only is it a shock to the system, but it also has my cock throbbing, arousal evident in the way she said my name. All raspy and breathy, a tease.

"Always mine?"

"Always yours, Tatum."

There she goes again.

My groan is hot against her bare throat, dragging my lips down until I softly bite the first pearly button on her pajama shirt. "Does that mean you'll let me fuck you like a good little girl?"

The amber blush on her cheeks deepens. "I…"

"LonLon," I rasp out, undoing the last three buttons of her pink pajama top with my teeth. The luxurious material slithers apart, exposing her taut core and the teasing underside of her breasts that remain covered due to one final button, straining their ampleness. "Answer me."

"*Oh, God*! Yes!"

I blow hot air on the underside of her breast until she's writhing in need. "Yes, *what*?"

"Yes, I want you to fuck me," London pants, uncontrollably rubbing against me.

Good girl.

"Touch you?"

"Yes, more than anything."

"Make you cum?"

London moans, tipping her head back against her silk pillow as she rocks her wet pussy over my covered cock, so hard that the materials begin gliding together. "Ye...*Fuck*."

"I need the consent now because soon all I'll be hearing is you screaming my name."

"Yes. When I was on *Enticed*, I'd always make myself cum to the thought of you."

Smirking, I wander a hand to her inner thighs, watching desire pool in London's eyes, the moment my fingers teasingly brush over her silk-covered sex. She's scorching, so wet the tight material by her crotch is darkening, completely drenched, and transferring onto my dark Armani boxers and seeping onto my hard-as-steel dick.

Deciding I need to taste her sooner rather than later, I pop the last buttons on her pajama shirt, my mouth watering at the sight of her plump tits with the prettiest light pink nipples. I curse, throwing the shirt across the room as London proudly smolders up at me.

I attack her left nipple first with my swirling tongue, sucking and rolling before nipping on it with my teeth until she tugs my hair, her moans heavy with need.

"*Lower*," London begs. "I need you lower."

"Be patient, little one, or I won't fuck you at all," I growl.

London moans in protest, bucking her hips against mine in rebellion as I move to her right nipple. Like the other one, I suck on it roughly until it swells and it's as cherry-red and sensitive as her flustered cheeks.

Taunting her longer, I roll my tongue over the crease between her heavy breasts, devouring her sweet skin with hot, opened-mouth kisses, her heart beating wildly against my ministrations.

Fuck me.

With one hand, I cup her heated sex over her pajama shorts, her dripping arousal instantly soaking the pads of my fingers as I curve them over her pooling entrance. London gasps when I grind the heel of my palm against her clit, the silk becoming slick around her, outlining the detailing of her evident lace panties and swollen clit in ways that make my heart flutter harder.

"Has anybody else ever fucked your pretty pussy, baby?"

London shakes her head, her waves sprawling over the pillow.

"*Good.*" I grin darkly. "Because nobody's ever rode this cock either."

"You're a…" Her eyes sparkle. "You waited on this first for me?"

"Of course I did, LonLon. I only want to sink into you."

Then I became a savage beast, hooking my thumbs into the waistband of both her pajama shorts and lace panties, giving us what we both desperately crave as I roughly rip them off her.

Oh.

My.

Fucking.

God.

London Héroux lies before me, entirely naked, and I swear to fucking God, I lose my breath.

"*Holy fuck.*" I slowly stalk my gaze down her petite body. "You're a masterpiece."

London looks at me in such awe and, *fuck*, it's like I'm the only one who has ever told her that before.

It's true. She's so beautiful, even though the faded white cuts on her skin, alongside some darker pigmentation that I associate with the abuse twist at my heart. There's a constellation of soft beauty spots by one prominent hipbone that I can't help but roam my tongue over, humming in satisfaction.

My spiky stubble grazes the juncture of her hip, her smooth skin driving me crazy. Then, a little lower, my eyes darken at the sight of her almost bare, glistening wet pussy. It's the most perfect shade of pink, ripe and calling my name with a thin landing strip. Clear arousal dripped from her, glazing her inner thighs and an erotic drop remains stretched from one thigh to the other.

"Please," London gasps when I spread her legs wider and circle my tongue over her inner thighs, licking up her sweet arousal with a groan and sucking on her skin until it reddens with flowery hickeys marking my love. "Please, I want to come on your cock, Tatum."

My cock pulses at her words, precum sliding down my shaft and into my boxers.

Desperately needing her, I roam my fingers on either side of her pussy, spreading her lips, and salivate over her slick pink flesh. I meet her hooded gaze, aching for heaven as I take one slow lick through her folds.

"OH GOD!" London breathes out, her grip on the ends of my hair tightening. "*More!*"

I smirk up at her like a bastard settled between her thighs. "As if I'm going to stop now, baby girl."

I'm in love with her sweet strawberry taste as I stroke my tongue faster inside her, lapping up her wetness and having her convulse with pleasure. I go crazy, vigorously flicking my tongue up and down, side to side, gripping her thighs as I fuck her even deeper.

Her legs wrap around my neck, smothering me in her throbbing pussy, my stubble scrapping her inner thighs, and *goddamn*, there's no place I'd rather be.

London screams, over and over, thrashing around so I lash her swollen clit recklessly with my widened tongue, sucking it slow before growing wild, vigorously circling it with no mercy.

I don't stop, my heated gaze never leaving hers as my pace increases, her juices splashing around my lips, becoming wetter. I slow and hasten my pace accordingly, teasing her in ways only I know how. Her pleasure is becoming mine as she rolls her eyes back, so close to giving into it.

"Tate, I—*oh fuck!*"

I roughly slip three fingers inside her, shutting her up with my tongue still on her clit, while I pump inside her so intensely, her legs shake around my neck as the bed slams against the wall. She's not as tight as I expected, all the vibrators and dildos she used for *Enticed* stretching her out.

Her walls tighten around me, uncontrollably pulsing as she attempts to hold on, but I finger her too erratically, my bicep continuously tensing. I only continue to pump her deeper until I'm hitting that sweet spot, over and over again, having her clit throb against my skillful tongue.

London's losing her religion, her mouth hanging open as she rolls her head against the headboard, the double penetration making her face the reddest I've ever seen it.

Mmhmmm.

Come on, baby, come for me.

I strum my fingers inside her like my favorite song, so intensely that her heaving breaths become scattered pants, her eyes all frantic in complete ecstasy, switching between rolling back, widening, and slamming shut.

Her thick wetness drips down my fingers, and I know she's close.

"Oh my god, you're going to make me squirt." London whimpers, her ass lifting up to ride my hand like a good girl. "Right now, Tate, you're going to make me squirt *right now.*"

Unable to help myself, I quickly dive my tongue back inside her warm pussy, replacing my arousal-coated fingers. I'm in heaven, fucking heaven when with one final pump and lick, she comes undone, orgasming hard around me, her flavor exploding on my tongue.

London cums violently, screaming out my name with her legs trembling, her pussy gripping my tongue tight through the orgasmic waves that have her gushing out, my tongue twirling over her entrance as she squirts down my throat, her juices dripping down my stubble and neck.

"Such a good fucking girl." I groan, widening my tongue even more, so I can collect every drop of her, mauling her pussy like it's my fucking oxygen, which only makes her squirt harder.

The cords on her neck frantically tighten and loosen as her orgasm settles.

"I'm so proud of you," I smile against her mouth, loving the sated grin that stretches her face before I kiss her, parting her lips with my tongue. I kinkily let her taste her sweetness on my tongue and get glazed in the cum dripping from my chin. "You ready for me, baby?"

London can't stop nodding, eagerly reaching for my boxer briefs. "Take them off for me, LonLon."

London quickly fumbles them off, gasping in awe with wide eyes as my cock springs free, slapping against my abs. "Whoa, you're so big. You have the prettiest cock I've ever seen."

Knowing that the other guy she could be referring to is Nicandro, I clench my jaw, but karma has the anger subsiding, the moment London wraps both hands around my thick cock, softly stroking me into hell. The palm of her hands twist against my swollen head, achingly slow by my underside, before gliding down my shaft again, the precum rolling down it.

"That feels so good, baby." I bite my tongue when she presses my reddened cock head over her velvety pussy, softly rubbing the tip over her entrance, which has us both moaning.

The longer she does it, the more the juices of her orgasm flow out, coating my cock, making it throb wickedly. *Fuck, I'm so close. I need her.*

I need her right fucking now.

"I hope you're on the pill because I don't have a condom and there's no fucking way I'm stopping now."

London flashes me a Cheshire grin. "I'm not on the pill."

My heart sinks. "You're joking?"

"I…" The grin remains as she softly bites her lip. "No. I'm not joking."

"Fuck."

This is my fault.

I should have…well, I don't know, at least thought this through half an hour ago.

"Stop freaking out, you won't get me pregnant, Tate."

I playfully deadpan her. "I don't like the odds."

"Well, that's a shame…" London hums, continuously rubbing herself against my dick, but never letting me slip inside her yet, causing a fire to burn up my spine that won't let go until I'm inside her, fucking her. Those warm baby blues eyes find mine. "I want this with you so much."

"I want this with you too. So badly."

"Do you love me, Tatum?"

"Yes." A pang of vulnerability hits me. "With all my fucking heart, I love you, LonLon."

"Then let's do it, and if the odds really do hate us, then just imagine our merged hearts."

Creating a heartbeat.

A baby.

A baby with her.

The possibility does the opposite of what it should, bringing butterflies to my chest.

Our heated stares never falter.

"Fuck it." I groan, taking my slick cock and stroking it a few times before lining it up with her entrance. Here we are, just two soulmates who waited eight years for our souls to physically unite, as I start off slow, gently rocking my cock between her folds, sinking into her weeping pussy.

Well, halfway in.

Contrary to earlier, I should have fucking bit my tongue because London's so damn tight. I'm trying to do everything to make it feel better for her, using my thumb to softly circle her sensitive clit, but it pains me so much watching her cry pretty tears, wetting those curved lashes.

"You okay, London?"

"Yeah, I just…*Owww*."

"Sorry. Do you want me to stop?"

A breath that's a mix between a gasp and a moan escapes London's throat. "God, no."

"Maybe circle your hips a bit, yeah, that's it, baby. Now I'm filling you more. *Fuck*."

London wriggles her hips like I told her to and I tenderly kiss her tears away, telling her just how special she is to me as I pump my cock deeper inside her. We're both moaning when the base of my cock slaps against her skin, indicating I'm stretching her deep and hitting her womb.

I slowly slip out of her, before filling her again, repeating it two more times before I give into the desire swallowing me up and pin her hands above her head, then recklessly pound into her like it's the freaking end of the world.

"Fuck, you feel so good, LonLon."

London takes the pain like a fucking dream. She moans, and wriggles, and cries, begging me to go faster. "Like that, *yes*, Fuck me just like that."

I frantically rock into her, grunting with every pump as the bed slams against the wall. London's heavy tits shake against my chest, meeting my every thrust like we were born to be together. And when I frantically rub her delicate clit between our perspiring bodies, her lips bite down on the thin gold chain around my neck, eyes sexily rolling back in erotic desire.

I'm making love to London Héroux in the same childhood bedroom where we first gave each other hickeys, where I taught her guitar, where she let me in on all of her battle scars.

This wave of heavenly pleasure shoots across my body, something I've never felt before. I feel so light. So free. I'm floating.

I switch between fucking her hard and making love to the same rhythm as our scattered heartbeats, and I fucking love it.

We're sweaty messes, reaching heaven together, as she screams out my name, making the entirety of Manhattan know I'm in love with my childhood rival. She claws my back, her nails digging into my skin as her pussy grips my dick like a vise, all while telling me how much she loves me.

London's blonde hair is everywhere, whipping over my face when I bury my head into her neck, smiling against it as I hold her tight, and make love to her harder.

"I'm going to give you the entire world and more," I murmur, hot against her neck.

My abs tense with every raw fuck, relentless in devouring her as my dick throbs with more urgency than ever before.

"I'm going to give you every single thing you deserve. The ring, the white picket-fence house, the kids. Everything." I bite my tongue, so fucking close to coming. "I hope they look like you, London. I hope they have your heart. I hope they have your beauty and grace, and your soul."

Her hands rush to cup my stubbled jaw, pulling my face back to look me in the eyes.

London's tender glassy eyes will forever be my nirvana. "I hope they love their mommy and daddy."

My heart explodes.

Our sex slows, back to passionately making love, as I kiss her nose and whisper my truth. "They'll love us so much, baby girl, because we'll always put them first, just like I'll always put you first. I'm going to love you for the rest of my life, you understand, LonLon?"

"Tatum?"

"Yes, my darling?"

"I'd be the luckiest woman in the world if I were the mother of your children."

Oh, my sweet girl.

Squeezing London's ass beneath the sheets, I let loose, pounding her so hard and fast that all of my pants become grunts, merging with her loud moans and beautiful screams.

There's tears in both of our eyes as our bruised lips tangle together, nestled with our love.

We're there, right *there*, as a flash of heat rushes up my back and my balls tense up. London tightens around me, pulsing in euphoria, and we reach heaven at the. *Exact. Same. Time.* I keep fucking her, roaring as I shoot jets of hot cum inside her, continually, even as her pussy milks me.

London chants my name like an angelic devil, her cum a warm solace on my fulfilled dick.

We come down from our high in echoing pants, still tangled in each other, exhaustion dimming our elated smiles. *I want to feel that high again, over and over only with her.*

The scent of sex, candy, and a tinge of distant metal laces the air, my cock a virgin mess, certainly smeared with her blood, but I don't mind.

All I care about is *her.*

All I care about is London as the sunlight kisses our flushed skin.

All I care about is London as I wrap her in my arms and feel like I love her even more, my softening cock still inside her, overflowing cum leaking down her thighs.

All I care about is London as she lulls into a deep, exhausted sleep, that dreamy smile never fading from her lips, and I murmur, "I'd be the luckiest man in the world if you were my wife."

Chapter
THIRTY-NINE

London

I opt to wait in Tate's car when he comes to a halt in front of his red-brick brownstone, desperate for a change of clothes other than his Glorsin St. Claire uniform.

After all, it's early Saturday morning, which calls for something less constricting.

"I won't be long, baby," Tate tells me with a gentle smile, popping open the driver side door. "My dad's car isn't here, meaning I won't get roped into doing something I don't want to."

I grin. "Okay. I'll be right here."

After slipping his backpack on his shoulders, Tate rests his hands against the hood of his Mustang and crouches down to look through the open window. His sexy blue eyes pin mine, a real-life James Dean.

"Sure you don't want to come in?"

I swallow, playing with my hands over my bare thighs. "No, I'm okay."

Tate nods, lingering for a few seconds before he pushes off the hood with a knock.

Metal clashing together drums my ears as he rattles his house keys. "Back in five."

And then he's off.

I watch Tate with my head tilted against the leather headrest as he climbs the stairs of his brownstone, two steps at a time.

My fingers weave over my yellow polka dot sundress, nervously awaiting his return when he closes the grand door behind him. The absence of Tate fucks with my mind. He hasn't left my side in almost twenty-four hours, giving me everything I didn't know I needed.

I can't believe I opened up to him and told him about my father, but it needed to be said and a weight has been lifted from my chest because of it. I feel stronger for it.

Happier.

I know what I want to do about my father.

I want him to pay for everything he did to me.

I want him to rot in jail, for years. I want him to suffer, just like he made me.

But it's something I don't want to think about right now. I'm with Tate.

Tate.

Not my destroyer.

Since Tate told me the truth this morning and we made love, things have been stronger than ever between us. Despite my initial reaction, I'm truly grateful Henley turned out to be Tate. I feel secure knowing that it was him and that his intentions weren't to hurt me, they were to simply keep me breathing.

We've learned so much about each other in these past twenty-four hours, and I don't take that lightly. The fact that he felt comfortable enough to shine a light on his unloving father and his mother's tragic diagnosis speaks volumes to the type of man he's grown up to become.

What I've realized, the more time we spend together, is that although we both come from materialistic families who lack love, affection, and validation, when he and I are together, we're always touching. There's always empathy, or devotion.

And I think that's special.

It's special that we're learning from our parents' mistakes.

It's special that two broken halves really do make a whole.

It's been a rollercoaster of emotions between us, a cluster-fuck, but right now, the tempest is settling. The rainbow will come soon. It has to. 'Cause it's my favorite part.

CLICK.

My body jolts as the driver door clicks open, so much so that I have to slam a hand over my chest to calm my rapidity beating heart.

"Oh, God." I gasp. "You scared the hell out of me!"

Slipping back into the driver's seat, I take the time to admire Tate's tight cashmere sweater and cigarette pants. He drips elegance with his dark hair all perfectly slicked-back and that shimmering gold Rolex enclosed around his left wrist.

His signature sandalwood scent is a little stronger than before, and the redness that tinged his eyes, from our restless night of heavy truths, isn't there anymore.

Tate flashes me a gorgeous smirk, so handsome it warms my core. "Sorry, not sorry."

"You can be such a cocky bastard sometimes, you know that, right?"

"Yup," he plays on, popping the 'p'. "But at least I'm hot, so...*ya know*."

I playfully slap his chest, the warm laughter that escapes him prompting my own.

"I'm joking! I'm joking! I'm a modest man, I swear."

"Yeah, we'll see about that..."

Tate arches a cocky brow and clears his throat to perform his best British accent, "Pardon? What do you take me as, woman? An asshat?"

I choke on my saliva, laughing so hard it hurts to breathe. "An *asshat*?"

Tate remains in character, lifting his chin. "You heard me right, me lady."

"You seriously couldn't have picked a more American insult."

"Why, vex my soul! If I shalt be banished for thee, I thou be a fang-toothed serpent."

I mockingly stare at him pointedly, not knowing if I could be any more in love with him as I am right now. The fact that he takes all my hurt and transforms it into waves of warmth, laughter, solace is everything.

"You done?" I ask.

Tate's eyes darken a shade.

"Babygirl," he hotly breathes, "you'll know when I'm done with you. Trust. Me."

Hmmmm.

My cheeks heat and I cross my legs, calming my throbbing sex. Tate. Notices. My. Every. Move.

His hand instantly returns to caressing my knee, just like it did on the way here. It has me craving more, even through all my haze. His display of affection is like a remedy to me, a therapy, every touch inducing butterflies.

"Why are you grinning like a damn fool, Meadows?"

"Because I'm taking you out on a date." Tate playfully wiggles his brows. "And you know what *that* means…"

Seductively biting my lower lip, I fail to hide my smile.

"I'm a third date kinda gal," I joke.

"*Ohhh.* Is that why you've never had a boyfriend?"

Smartass.

"If this were my car, I'd kick you out."

"Yeah, you'd kick my ass." He cockily nods. "But you wouldn't *kick me out.*"

I play on. "I won't be touching your ass or any other parts, Mr…"

"Parts?"

"Parts."

"Name them."

"Nope, I ain't that vulgar."

"Bullshit."

I raise two fingers. "Scout's honor."

His darkly chuckles. "I think we're past the modesty, darling."

"*Oh,*" I tease. "Are we now?"

"Mmhmmm, and my aching cock thinks so too."

Oh…*my God.*

We share a heated stare, glazed over with desire.

Air becomes trapped in my lungs, and everything becomes heavier.

I want him to fuck me again so badly.

"Checkmate," I whisper, raking my eyes down to the bulge in his cigarette slacks.

I'm not ashamed of the way I gawk at his erection and cup his thick cock, his heat scorching my skin. Memories of this morning spiral in my mind, the enthralling pleasure hardening my breaths and nipples. My hand barely covers any of him, as I teasingly stroke him over the Italian fabric.

"*Fuck.*" Tate hisses in gratification. "What happened to being a 'three dates kinda girl?'"

I flash him my pearly whites. "Changed my mind."

"*Oh*, you're trouble, London."

"Mhmmm."

Groaning, he fists my long French braid, pulling me so close that our hot lips almost collide. "You really know how to ruin plans, little one."

"What plans?"

"Our date."

A date!

"I'd prefer you'd fuck me instead," I purr, looking up through my lashes, devilishly.

"Didn't know my girlfriend was so eager to get fucked hard again while her taste is still on my tongue…"

My heart thumps in my chest. "*Girlfriend?*"

"I said what I said."

I like the sound of that.

Biting my lip, I pull my hand away from his cock. "Drive, before I jump you instead."

"My girlfriend…" He smirks. "*The predator.*"

"We're here!"

I glance around, realizing we're parked in front of a cool indie record store on 10th Ave.

WHOA!

"Wow!" I beam, excited eyes finding his. "Is this the store you mentioned yesterday?"

"Damn straight it is. Wait until you see inside. It's fucking epic!"

Tate wasn't kidding. Not one bit. This place is incredible. Huge. There are four separate levels, each filled with that vintage kinda loving vibes. There are records, cassettes, and CDs everywhere, each tucked away in alphabetic order.

Vibrant band posters line every inch of the walls like wallpaper. There are millions.

Nirvana.

Sex Pistols.

Arctic Monkeys.

"Hi there!" The grunge-like guy sitting behind the front desk smiles. "Welcome to Rockers. Shout if you need anything."

I smile softly at him, wishing I had known about this place sooner, because I would have totally loved to work here.

"Will do." Tate nods. "Thanks, man."

I'm a little kid in a candy store, drooling over every single artist I see, adoring that iconic lived-in smell.

My heart explodes in happiness.

I turn to Tate, honored he'd bring me some place like this. Honored that he knows me so well. Honored that, just like that, all my preoccupation fades because I see just how hard he's trying to be everything I need. But that's the thing, he doesn't need to try; he's already perfect on his own.

"Tate Meadows, I think you just scored some points," I purr, lifting to my toes. "A lot of them."

That infamous smolder edges up the left side of his face. "Am I back in the good books?"

"Maybe."

"Maybe she says."

"Shut up."

Tate takes my hands and gestures toward a nearby never-ending wooden staircase. "The good shit we like is at the very top floor."

We take the stairs two at a time until we're on the fourth level. I like it here. There isn't anybody on this level as Nirvana's "Come As You Are" softly echoes through the coffee-colored retro speakers.

"What did you want to show me?"

Tate's mischievous smirk never falters. "You'll see soon enough…"

He guides me through the huge space, weaving between hip-hop record assortments until we reach the back wall and…

Whoa.

Spray painted over the band posters in neon pink is the chorus of Pink Floyd's "Wish You Were Here." That fateful song that seems to follow Tate and me everywhere.

"Oh my gosh, Tate! This was made for us!"

"You're telling me. I freaked when I saw it for the first time. This place couldn't be more for us, Shortcake."

I turn to him, stunned. "Did you just call me, Shortcake?"

"Mmhmmm."

"Why?" I shriek.

"Cause you're short, are obsessed with strawberries, and I have no idea why I didn't think of it sooner."

"Well," I playfully pout, "I hate it."

"You once hated the nickname *LonLon* too…" Tate's low, gravelly voice rasps. "So what'cha gonna do about it, huh, *Shortcake*?"

I kiss his stupid face, dying a satisfied death when he bunches my hair and pins me hard against the wall. I can feel just how turned on he is, his hard erection pressing against my lower stomach, tempting me in ways I can't control.

Ever since this morning, when we had sex for the first time (ever), I haven't been able to stop looking at him without this bursting in my chest. The feelings have always been there, but there's just something about connecting with him on such an intimate level that has my heart singing.

Tate Meadows is perfect.

He's so perfectly perfect for me.

And I hope he never stops loving me.

"You're such fucking trouble, *Shortcake*," is all he growls the second we pull away, his eyes dark and hungry.

Taking my hand, Tate guides me around the endless sections of records, until we stop in front of Pink Floyd. My heart twirls in psychedelic pink as we go through rock artists, laughing and having the time of our lives with our quirky rock knowledge and lingering gazes.

It specifically squeezes my heart when we pass The Beatles' section and Tate points toward their *Strawberry Fields Forever* record and smiles.

He remembers.

He remembers when I mentioned I like heart-shaped candy called strawberry fields.

We just make sense.

So much sense.

My heart feels so full and happy. Safe.

I feel safe with Tate. I know he'll never hurt me like my father.

It's as if Tate is highly aware of it, with his gentle touches and in-fectious smile. He's doing everything he can to heal my hurt. Even though my father is my monster, I've never felt hesitant with men, but I've always been wary.

There's always a tension is my shoulders that travels down my spine whenever I talk to one, even Nicandro, because I just never knew. I was always on high-alert of being hurt. Not my true self.

But with Tate…

Gosh. I've never felt that.

Not when we were kids.

Not with his demons.

Not now.

I feel free. I can be myself, wholeheartedly. I know he'll love me in all my forms.

Tate Meadows is everything to me. *Everything.* And I think I'm finally realizing the impact of that right here in this indie record shop, as I catch a glance of Tate, all candid. His head is tilted down toward the records, passionately flicking through them, the warm sunlight beaming through the industrial-styled steel windows.

It sun-kisses his face, edging a glimmering golden glow over those long, onyx lashes, his beautifully chiseled jaw, and deepening that dim-ple on his skin. The light skims over his dark stubble, casting shadows of lightened streaks over his whiskers and slicked-back hair, making him even more irresistibly handsome.

When Tate catches me staring, the cutest look of confusion crosses his face mixed with fascination. "Is there…something on my face?"

Smirking, I bite my lip while shaking my head. "No."

He stares.

And stares.

And stares.

And then…

Tate's gorgeous light eyes warm and he turns to me with a hand on his hip, ankles locked, and elbow leaning against a punk-rock *Ramones* vinyl.

"*Ohhh,*" he smolders, uber-confident. "You're checking me out, aren't you? Like what you see, *hmm*? Do you have serial killer tendencies, baby? 'Cause, well, you're letting it show."

I playfully roll my eyes.

Tate tips his head back in laughter, his Adam's apple bobbing up and down, and I can't stop staring at the darkening hickeys aligning his neck. Those *I* made. Those he wears with pride.

His laughter comes to a screeching halt when karma bites him in the ass. Somehow, the *Ramones* vinyl he's leaning his elbow against slips, and he almost loses his balance, stumbling back a bit.

That's when my giggles escape. "Serves you right, idiot."

Chuckling, Tate playfully flips me off.

I don't know how long we spend in this indie record shop, but it becomes my oasis. I can't help but scan every level we cross, impressed that there's also cool retro furniture here, as well as record players.

Record players.

I'm enticed by them, well, most specifically by the record player that we're standing directly in front of. It's a vintage olive colored, the same make and model as the one I used to own before my father broke it to pieces. I haven't been able to replace it since he destroyed it because I'm scared he'll do it again.

"I just realized I bought you a vinyl, but you don't have a record player…do you?"

"I *used* to." I gulp down. "My father, he…broke it a little while ago."

"I'm sorry." Sadness shoots through him and he kisses my forehead. "I'll buy you one in Seattle, baby."

Seattle.

My heart flips.

My Converse come to a screeching halt just before the last flight of stairs to the ground floor. There's a gorgeous green-eyed woman with the most flawless blonde waves grinning up at a familiar man who looks full-on punk rock.

He's tall, inked in dark tattoos and has the most melancholic onyx-eyes. He cheekily grins at something she says, spanking her ass, which has her jokingly shoving him back. He doesn't flinch, remaining planted beside her, except for the metal safety pins lining the edges of his leather jacket that are clinging together.

The familiarity of him suddenly clicks as a soft gasp escapes my lips.

I subtly nudge Tate beside me. "Oh my god, *look*! Is that Elijah Diesel?"

As in Elijah Diesel, the stunning and equally terrifying rockstar: lead vocalist and lyricist of alternative rock band, Diesel Rose. They're beyond famous, breaking records with songs that are always tangled with raw, melancholic poetry that send shockwaves through millions of hearts.

"Shit, yeah. You're right. That's him!"

"*Wow.*"

I soon also recognize the woman as Rosalia Philips, his beautiful prima ballerina fiancée. I remember when they first began dating and all of the sizzling headlines that labelled it *forbidden*, due to their diverse worlds and age gap. But love is love. Who's anyone to change that?

"Should we go up to them?"

I turn to Tate as if he's crazy. "No! He's a famous rockstar!"

"*So…?*"

"If you were a rockstar, would you like people *always* coming up to you?"

"If that person was you, fuck yeah."

"Cliché."

"*Chivalry*, baby." Tate smirks. "*C'est le* chivalry."

"You're gonna fail your French exam, aren't you?"

He groans. "Yeah, pretty much…Hey, can we study for finals together?"

"Sure, but…you've already started studying, right?"

"Ummm…" Tate nonchalantly scratches his jaw. "Yeah, sure. Totally have."

Liar!!!

My eyes widen in horror.

Something tells me he's one of those guys who never studies, yet aces all of them, but *still*!

"TATE!" I gasp, mortified. "Finals literally begin next week! You haven't even begun?"

"I have a photographic memory."

"Bullshit."

"No, it's true. For example…" His lips find mine, "Your pretty face when you come for me, baby, that visual will never leave my mind. You're so beautiful it hurts."

And suddenly, I don't care about studying, the heat between my thighs growing.

We spend the entire day exploring the hidden parts of Manhattan, savoring the beauty outside of the cute and quirky stores for when we escape to Seattle, after finals and graduation.

For dinner, Tate takes me to this cool retro diner, mimicking the '50s and '60s with its vibrant neon lights, black and white diamond-patterned tiles, and servers on roller skates. The red leather booth we sit in during dinner feels so nostalgic of a time before us.

We dance like crazy to Elvis, The Temptations, and Chuck Berry on the jukebox, laughing, and perfecting our rock 'n' roll twist. A little later on, Tate serenades me with *"My Girl,"* mid-dance, his voice a raspy delight. Blushing, I joined the singing but change it to *"My boy."*

Despite my initial shyness, we slow dance to Patsy Cline's *"Crazy"* in the middle of the diner, his hands around my waist and my head against his chest, hearing every symphonic heartbeat. It is such a beautiful, tender moment.

So raw and vulnerable, just like our deep talks.

Patsy Cline's smooth, heavenly voice is almost haunting in the most romantic way.

And when Tate Meadows glances down at me at the end of the song, his fond Atlantic blues spark as he murmurs the lyrics, *"I'm crazy for loving you,"* against my lips with a smile.

Happy tears flood my eyes, throbbing the back of my throat, because *gosh*. I want this moment to last forever and a day. I want to return to 1961, just so we could have authentically slow danced to this song every single night, just a blue-eyed dreamboat and his doll.

I love everything about it and melt in pure adoration when Tate orders us two strawberry milkshakes for dessert with whipped cream, without even asking. He knows me *that* well.

Now, the silvery glint of the moon kisses over Manhattan's

darkened night sky, draping over the twinkling stars, glimmering pavement, and illuminated night sky.

With a few new records tucked under his arms, Tate slows in front of a vintage movie theater on the corner of West 54th Street. It's stunning, replicating the golden age of Hollywood with the ninety-degree lightbox with movie names on the white panel above the revolving doors.

"I've never seen this place before in my life!"

"Well, that's a shame," he hotly teases. "I work here."

My jaw hits the pavement. "Say *what?*"

"This is the theater I work at."

"I mean, I knew you worked at a movie theater, I just didn't think…" I eye the gorgeous brass architecture and vintage flare, drooling. "DAMN! Why didn't you take me here sooner?"

"Umm, not sure if you remember, but we just came off hating each other's guts…"

Our thundery past makes me buoyantly grin now. "Shhhh. So, is this an extension of our date?"

Tate smiles. "Someone's eager."

"I can't help it!" I bounce on the balls of my feet. "I'm just so happy!"

"I'm only joking, LonLon, I wouldn't want it any other way. Trust me."

Tate Meadows truly makes me feel like sunshine on a cloudy day as he intertwines our hands and we step inside the movie theater. It's stunning, with art-deco features that would make anybody stop and ogle in fascination. Vintage film posters line the wall, iconic black-and-white.

Casablanca.

Sunset Boulevard.

And my personal favorite, Hitchcock's *Psycho.*

The instant aroma of buttery popcorn and sweetened candy has me salivating.

Holy cow!

I can't believe Tate works here!

"You're going to miss this place."

Tate squeezes my hand. "It'll be worth it."

He's right. It will.

Tate introduces me to his boss, an older man with a three-piece suit, waistcoat chained pocket watch, and a slight lisp. He has kind eyes, a little set back, and an aged-lobsided smile thanks to the pipe lodged between his thin lips.

"Mr. Charlton," Tate says. "I'd like you to meet my girlfriend, London."

Girlfriend.

He just introduced me as his GIRLFRIEND.

I bashfully wave at his boss. "Hi!"

"Pleasure to meet you." Mr. Charlton tips his head, pushing back his thick black glasses. "I've heard a lot about you, London, why, you've been the talk of the city round this place."

"*Oh.*" I grin. "Have I?"

An amber flush crawls over Tate's cheeks. "Mr. Charlton!"

His boss casually shrugs. "So you're real gone, big deal. It's time I get a kick out of you anyway. Besides, if you didn't want me to rat you out, you shoulda gone to a passion pit."

Passion pit?

Tate's blush only deepens. "God, help me." He turns to me, and I'm amused with just how pink his ears have become. "He basically said I'm head over heels for you and that if I didn't want him to admit it, then I should have taken you to a drive-in movie theater instead."

"Wait, so a *passion pit* is '50s slang for a *drive-in movie theater*?"

"Mmhmmm."

"Why?"

Tate arches a seductive brow. "Why'd you think, doll?"

I think about it for a second...*Ohhh.*

"Gottcha."

Frisky make-out sesh.

Mr. Charlton talks with us for a little longer before an employee interrupts us, saying there's somebody on the phone asking for him.

Mr. Charlton bids us a final goodbye before attending to the call.

"He seems like a real cool guy."

"Yeah, he's such a character." Tate chuckles. "Any film preferences?"

I was so excited to be here that I didn't even read the films playing, only the strips spelling *sold out*. "I thought they were all sold out...no?"

Tate flashes me a sly smile. "I have an idea."

Minutes later, we're walking to the back of the theater holding snacks. Tonight is definitely making up for all the skipped meals because of my father. Tate's holding the butter popcorn and a cherry-flavored soda pop, while I'm a glutton for the candy.

It's a sweet tooth's (*and dentist's*) paradise.

I've got all the goodies in a white paper bag. Chocolate mint swirls, jujyfruits, and my personal favorite, strawberry heart-shaped suckers.

It feels like we're spies or something, the way Tate punches in a code by the cinema's side door, and it buzzes open. New York's breezy coldness kisses my skin as Tate unclips a chain, prohibiting access to the spiraling steel stairwell of an industrial fire escape.

A sign attached to the chain reads, **STRICTLY NO ACCESS UNLESS FIRE.**

But, of course, my rebel boyfriend nods toward the stairs. "After you, my gal."

I get vertigo staring up at the monstrosity. "You sure we're allowed to?"

Before I can ponder more, Tate bolts up the stairs, and I shriek, following him because there's no way I'm chickening out. Adrenalin flips my stomach as we reach the third exit and step off the stairs onto the narrow metal railing surrounding the building.

Shit.

Terrified I'll accidentally slip off the thin edge and plummet to my death, my grip nearly snaps all his carved muscles as I fist his cashmere sweater, my nails clawing his innocent bicep.

"Don't worry," Tate lulls, walking in front of me. "I've got you, okay?"

"Promise?"

"Promise."

My breathing eases. This thrill is worth it the moment we slowly turn the building's corner, the clicking of a rolling projector grabbing my attention…

Oh. My.

Gosh.

I gasp at the beauty staring back at me.

A little farther away, on a tall white wall is a projection of a countdown in infamous black and white. Below us is the cinema's courtyard, full of people on beanbags and fold-out chairs.

A stunning outdoor cinema.

Fairy lights surround transparent canopies, glowing like the sparkle of fireflies warming the almost midnight sky. Nobody's ever taken me anywhere this special before. Nobody but him.

The ledge is wider here, securer, a good two feet—the perfect hide-out spot. We get comfortable on the ledge, setting out all of the snacks with the projector a good distance from us.

I turn to Tate, just in time for the opening credits of *Rebel Without A Cause*.

"Tate?"

"London."

"This is the best day of my life," I admit.

Tate tenderly grabs the front of my neck, possessively, before slamming my mouth to his. He kisses me with a burning desire, groaning the second our tongues collide. My heart's on fire, love our oxygen as our tongues swirl, tasting and exploring every inch like an erotic tempest.

He has the softest lips ever.

"You're the best *part* of my *life*," Tate murmurs into our kiss. "You always will be."

And then, Tate Meadows holds me in the solace of his arms as the moon shines brightly above us, baptizing our tangled limbs. He keeps gazing at me during James Dean's riveting performance with an amorous smile, and through all my happy tears, I thank God he's real.

That he's alive.

That he's *my anchor.*

Without him, I'd die, because he'll forever be the best part of me too.

Chapter
FORTY

Tate

The moment London and I sneak back inside my bedroom hours later, an oasis of pleasure follows. Nobody else is home, just us. I can't keep my hands off her, devouring every inch of her skin, loving on her until all my tangled heartstrings explode inside my chest.

London moans against my lips as I pin her against the shower tiles, her long nails skimming my back as water trickles down it.

We're wrapped in steamy mist, her heartbeat rippling against mine, my kryptonite, as I fuck her against the shower wall, so passionately in love.

With her legs wrapped around my waist, I squeeze her ass, loving the way London breaks the kiss to grin at me so beautifully, I'd happily die here.

Her hips rock against me with my every thrust, her greedy pussy riding my cock. There's so much I want to say to her as tears baptize her cheeks, but nothing comes out but, "*I love you.*"

Over and over again.

I love her.

I love how she throbs around me, biting my neck as she comes undone.

I love how she falls to her knees and fists my pulsing cock.

I love how she swallows my cum, grinning in love.

But, most importantly, I love the way her body finds mine when I lift her up and we embrace each other so tightly. I love the way her heart beats in sync with mine. I love the way emotion etches in her eyes, while a tightness forms in my throat, and I know exactly why…

We're happy to be alive.

In the same universe.

Together.

After we have an *actual* shower, London slips into one of my gray *Nirvana* hoodies. It's extremely oversized on her, grazing just above her knee with sleeves that continuously need to be rolled up. But I'm not gonna lie, it's kinda cute. *Okay, it's a hell of a lot cute.*

London pokes out her tongue at me when she catches me staring.

I like that we're like *this*. Spontaneous enough that we don't even pack an overnight bag. I mean, yeah, our parents don't know shit about our relationship, and this is probably the calm before the storm, but still, I savor it like it's all I have. Because in retrospect, it is.

When London lays on my chest in bed, her silky blonde waves smelling like my sandalwood wash, I realize something about our love…

Our naked truth is we don't always need sex to define our love; intimacy is equally valid.

The intimacy of honesty.

The intimacy of feeling alive.

The intimacy of vulnerability.

Of being heard. Healing. Tender devotion.

The intimacy of being truly loved, through it all.

The intimacy of being the person you always needed.

The intimacy of being fucking respected. Understood. Patient.

These are all things I learned because of London.

Before her, every part of my life was battered and scared. There wasn't a piece of me that made sense. Not a piece I clearly understood. Not a piece I truly wanted to be.

Not one.

And then she stepped into my life, at ten years old, and gave me air.

Air that hasn't stopped flooding my lungs since that moment.

It's not just oxygen, it's her.

Her.

Always her.

I could stare at her for a lifetime, like a work of art, and still find new pieces of her I adore.

I love her.

I love her so much.

And nobody can take that away from me.

Not my alcoholic dad.

Not my devious stepmom.

Not my real mom's heartache.

I've suffered through a lifetime of rejection, but with her, after everything we've been through, I know she'll never let me down. She's here. To stay. For the long haul.

"What's going on in that wicked mind of yours, Mr.?" London says, breaking me from my trance.

I raise a brow. "*Wicked?*"

She flashes me a Cheshire grin.

"No, nothing. I guess I'm just thinking through how I got this lucky."

"I'm the lucky one."

"Disputed." I chuckle, holding her close. "You keep on saying I'm saving you, but in my mind, it's the opposite, LonLon. I've never felt more myself than when I am with you."

"What do you mean?"

"Well…" I sigh. "I guess nobody in my life has every made me feel so stable."

"But you have your friend, Levi."

"Yeah, I know I have him and I love him like a brother, but it's…"

London fills in the silence. "Different."

"Exactly. You…" I glance down, studying her beauty. "You turn my scars into stars."

And the way she's looking at me…

Fuck.

"Tate, can I ask you a question?"

I nod, too lost in everything that she is to speak.

"I was wondering if you have any pictures of your mother?"

The question takes me off guard, and it takes a couple of moments to prepare myself.

My mother.

With a fog in my throat, I untangle myself from London and slip off my king-sized bed in silence. I can feel her eyes burning into the back of my neck as I cross the room, to the chest of drawers, and pull open the third to the bottom. Beside an aged cigar box, there's a silver photo frame, face down.

I know the exact day I turned it over.

Months ago, when I visited my mother in the psychiatric hospital.

Something comes over me when I return to bed and silently hand London the cold frame.

It's almost too painful to look at the photograph in London's grip, but I push through anyway because this is my *mother.*

It's a bittersweet photograph of her and me when I was younger, five or six years old. I'm sitting in her lap, my arms around her neck with a goofy, boyish smirk. My mother's gazing down at me with nothing but adoration etched in her bright, blue eyes. She's grinning. *Joyful.*

I don't know who took the photograph, only that it wasn't my father.

Years ago, my father drunkenly destroyed everything that remotely associated her to us. The only thing I was able to salvage was this crinkled photograph.

Ache.

Ache.

Ache.

"She's so beautiful," London sadly whispers, tracing her fingers along the detailed frame. "You have her eyes, Tate."

I swallow harshly, the tempest brewing in my tense shoulders overbearing.

"She...doesn't remember you at all?"

"No, nothing."

"It's not her fault."

"I know, it's my father's."

"Your father couldn't control the dementia."

"No, but he treated her like the gum on his shoe. He stole

everything she had. He prevented me from seeing her as much as I possibly could before she reached this stage."

"What do you mean by stage?"

"My mother's in stage seven of her diagnosis. Severe cognitive decline. Little to no communication. Agitation."

"How many stages are there?" London asks, concern coating her face.

I shut my eyes. "Seven."

"*Shit.*"

"Yeah."

"It's okay if you don't want to answer, but why is she in a psychiatric hospital as opposed to a care home?"

I suck in a breath. "She's had suicidal tendencies since she was fourteen. She didn't…grow up in the best family and saw a lot of things that nobody should see. She's…"

London lets go of the photo frame to caress my ticking jaw.

"She's attempted to kill herself before." I sniffle. "That psychiatric hospital specializes in mental health and there's also a suicide watch program, so she's safe in there, I guess."

White noise trickles through the silence for a few minutes.

London turns to me, hope flooding her eyes. "Thank you for being so vulnerable with me, Tate, for letting me in. I can see how much you love her, and it pains me this happened. But what if…What if you don't settle for rejection, Tate? I know it's frustrating her not remembering you, so instead, what if you make her learn to love you again? It doesn't have to be as a son, it can be as a friend, if that's easier for her. Deep down, you know she loves you, in all forms."

"It's too painful."

"Baby steps."

"Like?"

London rolls her lips together. "You said she loves painting, yes?"

"Yeah."

"Then paint with her. Listen to her hurt through every splatter and mend it through colors. Earn her trust by doing activities that can bring you closer. You can't force her love, but with time, hopefully, she will show a glimmer of it. A little glimmer is all you need from her, Tate."

I've never thought of it from that perspective.

"If it'll make you feel better..." she pauses, "I could come with you."

Time.

Just.

Slows.

I think I want to cry.

I think I want to smile.

I think I want to marry her.

She'll come with me.

She wants to be a part of my life.

In goodness and in gloom, she's here for me.

"Yes," I shyly tell my dazzling dream, my heart bleeding out her name, "I'd like that."

I've never been this nervous in my life.

The chain-link fence buzzes open, the security guard gesturing for us to step through.

My clammy palms are burning as London and I tread the same eerie corridor I was strolling down four months ago. Back then, the anticipation killed me; now, expectation kills me instead.

I've been mentally preparing myself for months, but in the end, I don't think anything could truly prepare me from witnessing my mother wilt right before my eyes. I've been toying with the possibility that maybe, just maybe, this second visit will do me good. Perhaps I'll find some peace, some confidence that keeps me going, perhaps she'll look me in the eyes and there won't be pain.

I'm fucking praying for it.

Miss Nail-Tapper isn't in today. It's just the younger redhead chick that flirted with me last time.

She couldn't stop staring London down as she typed away on her computer before giving us clearance to my mother's floor, but London didn't notice her. She didn't notice a single thing because she was focused on me, rubbing comforting circles on my back, her smooth hand constantly grazing against the duffle bag I'm holding with paints, and crafts, and faith.

There is a part of me that still can't believe London is right here. That she wants to be *here*, to see me at my worst. I've always prided myself on never letting anybody see the cracks beneath me, but *fuck*, it feels so good not to have that mask up with her.

Tears dust my gaze when we step out of the elevator, in front of my mother's door.

505.

"What's going on, baby boy?"

"I'm scared," I whisper, chaotic tears descending my flushed cheeks. "I'm sorry, I don't know why I'm crying. I just…I'm so fucking *scared*."

London finds my lips, the achingly tender kiss so persuasive, it lulls me, like a lullaby. I fall upon it like ecstasy. I'm so numb and fragile that I let her control it, let her mouth ravish mine, and haunt me like a phantom bride when she pulls away, framing my face with her touch.

"It's okay to be scared, Tate. It's okay because it makes you human."

It's strange, the way Nurse Paige smiles at us when London knocks on that fated door, almost as if she was expecting me. I don't know why, but it brings me a modicum of comfort.

"Good morning! It's nice to see you, Tate. It's been a while."

I wish I could smile.

I wish I could do more than just stare, but I can't.

I need the initial hurt that comes with *her* emerging lavender perfume to subside.

"Hi, I'm London, Tate's girlfriend. We bought some art supplies for Elizabeth; they were cleared by security. We were hoping to keep her company and paint with her, I hope that's okay?"

"Perfectly okay." Nurse Paige nods. "That's so kind, London. Elizabeth will love that."

"That's what we hoped."

"Follow me."

I can't do it.

I can't do this.

London strides forward, following Nurse Paige when she sees me still planted here.

"Babe? Come on, let's see your mom."

I can't move.

I can't fucking move.

But with London's hand laced in mine, it feels better, and slowly, slowly, I inch inside.

It doesn't last long.

The moment I see my mother, my feet come to a screeching halt.

She's sitting in the middle of that infamous floral couch, and Nurse Paige is also there, quietly feeding her a diced boiled egg with a silicone spoon. My mother's eyes are slammed shut, but the soft thumping of London's Doc Martens has those piercing baby blue eyes snapping open.

A breath escapes London under my mother's observation, her gaze roaming up my girlfriend's white floral sundress, glossy pink lips, and then, her blonde twisted side braid.

Frantically wide-eyed, my mother feels for a charcoal pencil, which has rolled to the end of the couch. Chewing the last of her boiled egg, she grips the pencil and eagerly points beside me.

I turn, a drawing pad the only item set on the long, oak recreation table.

Holding it up, I whisper to my mother, "*This?* Would you like *this?*"

She can't stop nodding.

I can't describe what her fingers brushing against mine does as I hand her the drawing pad, only that it warms a piece of my heart that's been dormant for years. The piece reserved for her.

My mother works tiredly, skillfully edging the charcoal against the paper, every rough scrape an indication of her first love flooding back to her. She doesn't stop until she's breathless, wiping away perspiration from the center of her pitched eyebrows as she observes her work.

"Wow!" Nurse Paige gasps, leaning closer to my mom to catch a glimpse. "What a masterpiece that is, Elizabeth! Do you want to show Tate and London?"

A frown overtakes her thin lips. "I…"

"Yes?"

"I…"

A smiling Nurse Paige points toward my girlfriend and me. "Here, I'll show you, Elizabeth. This is Tate…and this is London. They have come to spend some time with you."

"With me?" Her dry voice grazes the silence.

"Yes, Elizabeth, *you*. Aren't you lucky!"

My mother continues gazing at London for the longest time, almost pondering something, before flicking her gaze to me for the first time. Instantly, her sockets narrow like a part of the puzzle in her mind is missing, because it is.

The cruelness of life rips me at the seams.

My mother's no longer the joyful woman with light in her eyes like that photograph I showed London last night. Instead, it's as if she's trapped inside herself, the exterior a familiar heartache, yet all the fragments inside that used to unite us are sinking, never to be found again.

It's out of both our control.

It's only up to God now.

London's hand crawls up my leather jacket, squeezing my tense bicep in comfort.

My mother witnesses the move, and for a fraction of a second, her eyes warm, nostalgia catching them.

"Okay." Nurse Paige stands, collecting the eating tray. "I'll be back soon."

I don't expect her to slow down as she passes me.

"Just so you know…" she whispers close to my ear, "your mother hasn't felt inclined to draw like that for a very long time. Your girlfriend inspired something within her, became her muse. You should find comfort in that, because it's a very big step. Trust me, Tate. It is."

Nurse Paige then steps out of the room.

I'll never forget the adoration in London's eyes when she sits on the floral couch beside my mother, her fond smile making my heart flip.

"Hi there, Elizabeth, do you mind if I see what you drew?"

Surprisingly, my mother slides the drawing pad to her.

Another big step.

A baby step, but a step, nonetheless.

"Oh my goodness, Elizabeth! This is…*magic!*" London gasps, observing the drawing, her focus darting everywhere. "Oh, Tate! Tate, come here and look at this!"

I round London's side, unsure of how my mom will react if I sit next to her because of last time.

I lose my breath as I observe the art.

Whoa.

A dark shiver blasts up my spine.

It isn't fear.

It's awe.

It's a stunning charcoal sketch of London, perfected with textured shading, flawlessly capturing every detail. It's so realistic and deserving of an entire art gallery dedicated to it.

I clear my throat. "I love everything about it, Elizabeth."

I love everything about it, Mom.

She gives me an approving nod.

When silence fills the space between us, this time, it's comfortable. The air isn't thick and depressing, I don't feel like suffocating, for some reason, the tension lifts from my shoulders.

"Do you want to do some more? Maybe on a canvas with paints?" I encourage, unzipping the duffle bag. "Look! They're all yours now. We even bought you some nice oil paints."

My mom's eyes widen, swirling in absolute desire. "Yes!"

The excitement in her voice...*God.*

Relieved, I find it in me to smile.

I help my mother to the table and slide in her chair, while London takes out all of the art supplies, laying them out in organized piles. Small canvases. Watercolors. Brushes. Paper.

"I think you'll have to teach me how to draw, Elizabeth, art has never been my strength. Let's compare, shall we?" London laughs to herself and grabs a sheet of loose paper. "Look at this..." She draws a marginally fucked-up stick figure. "Okay, so that's how *I* draw people."

She then slides Elizabeth's drawing pad beside it and gestures to my mother's drawing. "And this is how *you* draw people. See what I mean? I'm a fool and ashamed to even be here!"

A sweet giggle rumbles up my mother's throat.

It's the first time in ten years I've heard it. *Ten. Years.*

I don't realize how much I've missed it until it grips my heart.

My girlfriend just made my mom laugh.

London's warm gaze finds mine, as if she knows.

"I love you," she mouths.

I. Melt.

My mother snatches a small canvas, doing what she does best to prepare herself by laying out all of the oil paints. Then, she sets one canvas in front of me, and another in front of London.

"No dark colors," she instructs, practically flinging all of the darker shades off the table.

A smirk burns up my lips that I suppress with a hand.

"No dark colors, okay, got it." London nods, eyeing the remaining tubes. "Which one?"

My mother sorts out the paint palettes for each of us as follows.

Her: Oranges, yellows, and white.

London: Reds, pinks, and lavender.

Me: Blues, greens, and copper.

I blankly stare down at my canvas, not knowing what the fuck to do, but it's okay.

It's okay because London was right about this.

It's okay because I'm tranquil here with my mother.

It's okay because anxiety fizzles in exchange for courage.

We spend the next couple hours creating art in silence, well, with the occasional humming of my mother's unnamed tune, a repeated melody of the streaks of sunshine during a stormy day, hot cocoa, and a mother's embrace.

Seeing the light come back in my mother's eyes is something I never thought I would see. This is the closest I've ever been to her in my life, post-diagnosis. It's therapeutic. Healing.

London's right.

I know my mother loves me, even if she doesn't know it. Deep down, imprinted on her heart is me, even if she doesn't remember. There's a beat in her heart dedicated to me that now I understand Frontotemporal Dementia can never smother.

It didn't smother *me.*

It just hid me away, but that doesn't mean I'm faded.

It's finally all making sense.

I deserve to be happy.

To be loved. To be free.

I *deserve* to be sitting here, painting the shittiest oil painting, sitting right here beside my mom.

It doesn't matter that I'm not familiar to her, all that matters is her closeness.

Her willingness to trust me.

If art is that avenue, then so be it. I would hire a fucking art studio just so she could find solace in *that*, find solace in *me*, without any restrictions.

My father wasn't protecting me, he was silencing me. He was trying to make that heartstring of hers snap.

But he didn't.

He never will.

Because now I know my place, and it's *here*. With *her*.

The abundance of joy in my chest replaces the lack of love I grew up with since my mom was taken away. But now she's back. Right in front of me. And I'll never take that for granted.

Then, in the same breath, something takes over me. A realization dawning on me that I hadn't thought of until now...

Seattle.

London and I plan to run away to Seattle after graduation.

It means we're leaving the toxicity of our lives here.

But it also means another thing...

Leaving my mom.

Fuck.

An ache lodges in my throat because I know how much London needs this. I know just how deeply she craves moving away and restarting our lives, because I yearn for it too.

Fuck, I do.

But...How can I leave my mom?

How can I leave her now that I just found her?

The dilemma circles my mind during the rest of our painting, clouding my thoughts and rattling my premature happiness.

The weight in my chest taunts me. It gets heavier with every breath.

I can't choose.

I can't choose between my mother and the love of my life, London.

I let out an unsolicited sigh.

Fuck.

What the hell am I going to do?

Chapter

FORTY-ONE

London

Something's wrong.
S   I instantly feel it.

Tate's quiet the entire five-hour drive home to Manhattan, and it's killing me. His thumb hasn't stopped meticulously rubbing over his thin, vintage driver's wheel, grazing over the edge.

I know, deep down, he was trying to do everything to hide it from me, after all, he couldn't stop glancing my way every red light, tangling my fingers through his, kissing that hot, sensitive skin and the back of my hand, but he did it all with a smile.

The long, exasperated sighs were also a dead giveaway, showing more than he probably thought he was with his thumb strumming over his bottom lip, deep in thought.

For the first two hours, I did my best to convince myself it had nothing to do with me. Perhaps it was his mother he was thinking of; after all, the successful visit we had today was extremely bitter-sweet. She's such a beautiful woman, talented in her own ways, and it still makes my heart soar that Tate was open enough to let us meet.

I love his mom.

I love him.

And that's all the family we need.

But after our Rochester to Manhattan drive ticked over to hour three and all the gorgeous hues of dusty pink and flaming orange colored the sky, shifting together like watercolor to create one of the prettiest sunsets I've ever seen, the overthinking begins.

What if...

What if I'm the thing going through his mind?

What if he thinks me meeting his mother was a mistake?

What if the sex is getting to him, the fact that we didn't use a condom the first time, and now he's stuck on the possibility?

That has to be it.

There isn't any other explanation.

Perhaps seeing his mother questioned what he'd be like as a father one day. I've thought about it, and if it's one thing my diabolic relationship with my parents has taught me, it's that I, without a doubt, want to be the opposite of them.

"My beautiful boy," I murmur, leaning against the headrest as my hand roams up his leather jacket, curving by the carved muscles of his biceps. They're strong and firm like valleys beneath the leather. "What's kidnapped your mind?"

Tate remains silent for the longest time, chewing his lip. "I'm fine."

Liar.

"You're not okay, Tate, you've barely spoken a word to me since we left your mom."

The moment he hears the last two words in that sentence, the muscles in his jaw tick, working over his sexy dark stubble, which catches on the sunset, warming his whiskers. "Said I'm fine."

My eyebrows furrow. "Apparently not."

"London." Another heavy sigh escapes Tate as he rubs his temple. "My mind's just in a real mushy place right now and I don't really want to talk about it. Maybe I'll feel like it later, but for now, I can't."

I swallow thickly, giving into his words.

If the roles were reversed, I'd want him to give me some space too.

"Okay." I hesitantly nod. "I respect that."

"Thank you."

The crackle of the vintage AM radio floods Nirvana, the first few guitar drifts capturing my heart. The drums surface, mere seconds before Kurt's pained poetry licks all my open wounds.

My fingers fan over my flat stomach, seeping into my white floral sundress. "Tate?"

"Yeah?"

"I can take a pregnancy test soon, if that's what's stressing you out."

Tate slows by a stop sign and simultaneously glances at me with that familiar allusive glint, so piercingly blue, his eyes remind me of Paul Newman's.

He slowly strokes his tongue along his lower lip. "You really think you're pregnant?"

"I don't know." I nervously gulp. "The possibility is there."

"How soon can we buy a pregnancy test?"

"A week or two, I'd say."

"Okay."

Tate is still pensive as he gives way to a car before pumping the accelerator, constantly flickering his gaze between me and the road. "When are you supposed to get your period?"

My cheeks heat. "Tate…"

"*What?*" he says all dumbfounded, and I appreciate the smirk that burns his lips. "Babe, I'm not some random psycho asking you, I'm your boyfriend."

Fair point.

A month ago, I was so trapped in a spiral of stress that I can't even remember when I got my last period. Groaning, I pull out my phone from my pink velvet crossbody bag with diamond-buttoned studs.

Tate's gaze narrows. "Are you avoiding my question?"

"No, you idiot. I'm looking at my period tracker."

"You have an app with a tracker for that stuff?"

"Yeah." I laugh. "Me and every other woman in the world."

"Oh, I…" Tate cutely opens and closes his mouth like a fish. "Didn't know that."

I can't help playfully rolling my eyes.

The period tracker finally loads.

"In two weeks." I click my tongue. "Start of June. That's when it's expected."

He hums in approval.

Seconds later, we coincidentally pass a supermarket that's still open, neon sign flickering.

Tate turns to me. "How about we buy a test now? We'll be swarmed with finals shit soon, well, not that we already aren't, so at least we'll have it there at the ready."

Butterflies bloom in my stomach, swirling at his keenness.

"Yeah, okay."

Inside the supermarket, I can't stop glancing between three plausible pregnancy test kits, trying to compare the brands and result times, all while Tate eyes the condoms, snatching two packs from the shelf in record time, while I'm still here, deciding.

Tate throws the condoms in our basket before his arms snake around my waist from behind, nestling me in a big, bear hug with his lips on my neck. "Baby girl, at this rate just get all of them. One of them has to be accurate."

It's exactly what I do.

The girl at the checkout, a little younger than us, can't stop blushing as she scans our items. Her acne-flushed face drowns in rosiness as she fumbles with the pregnancy tests and even worse, the condoms.

Tate and I share an amused smirk.

Yeah, probably not the best combination.

When I offer to pay, Tate refuses, slapping a few bills on the counter in exchange for the brown paper bag containing our purchases. I've noticed that about him. He likes being a gentleman around me. He never lets me pay, even at that record store yesterday, but I still like to offer.

Tate clasps my hand, confidence in his stride as we step out of the supermarket, not an inch of nervousness written across his face, even though our lives will change depending on the results inside of that fateful brown paper bag.

Right now, I'm not fazed that I'm only eighteen and that my life up until this point has been so volatile, all I care about is the way my heart sings at the possibility of carrying Tate's child. I know how happy he'll be if I'm pregnant, how happy I'll be for it.

We can finally restart our lives in Seattle, just how we wanted with one more addition to our small little family—a combined heartbeat.

Tate Meadows is the best thing that's ever happened *to me*, but a baby could be the best thing to ever happen *to us*.

"I wasn't stressed about the possibility of you being pregnant, you know that, right?" Tate admits, once we're back on the road, two more hours to kill.

Wait...

I stare at him, perplexed. "You weren't?"

"No, in fact, the thought makes me so fucking happy." Tate's thumb grazes over my knuckles, ironing over my skin as I lean closer to him, our shoulder blades kissing. "Besides..." His gaze flickers to me, heating. "You'll be an incredible mother, LonLon, I just know it."

If I knew I was pregnant, I'd blame the hormones for the tears that blur my eyes.

Happy tears.

So freaking happy.

"You're gonna be such a beautiful daddy 'cause I know you'll love her with all your heart."

His eyebrows boyishly perk up. "*Her?*"

"Him, her, it doesn't bother me because it's our missing piece."

My heavy truth has Tate kissing the side of my head, his affection lingering, and when he pulls away, there's tears in his eyes too.

We don't talk the rest of the drive because we don't need to, our persistent thoughts overtaking our minds, filling in the strumming music flooding the space between us.

When we finally make it back to Manhattan, just after 10 p.m., Tate slows in front of his red-brick brownstone.

"I know we have school tomorrow, but do you want to come in for a bit before I drop you home?" Tate asks, looking like he desperately needs *this*. Like he'd crumble apart if he isn't with me for a little while longer.

I nod.

Before I know it, he's rattling his keys into his front door, that tick in his jaw returning.

What's going on, baby boy?

Before the words can roll out my mouth, Tate pushes the door open and the sight before us has me losing my breath.

His father, Mirko Meadows, is drunkenly perched on a metal barstool in the kitchen, his reddened eyes glazed over, a beer bottle so tightly gripped in his fist that his knuckles whiten, possibly numb.

Tate slows in front of me and holds out a protective arm, keeping me back.

But Mirko's hellbent eyes aren't on his son, they're on me as he sleazily roams his gaze down my body, slowing by my sweetheart neck-line, glossy lips, and long, lean legs. Consciously, I edge down my sundress, mindful of how it barely brushes my mid-thigh when he flashes me a warped, lopsided smirk.

"Take your fucking eyes off her, Mirko." Tate growls.

Ignoring his every word, his father's smirk only deepens. "Hmmm, want me to put those lips of yours to work, blondie? I'll teach Sterling's slut daughter something she'll never forget."

Oh.

My.

God.

Fucking asshole!

I fist Tate's leather jacket seconds before he launches forward, tugging him back in place.

I can fight my own battles, I always have.

"Excuse *you*? You don't get to talk to me like that, Mirko Meadows," I spit.

"Now, now," he slurs, clicking his tongue. "Don't be like ya daddy."

My heart plunges deep into the Atlantic.

"She'll never be like her fucking father!" Tate roars, breaking out of my grip and storming at Mirko, roughly fisting his white t-shirt so forcefully, it drags him to standing. "*Understood*?"

Mirko drunkenly laughs in his son's face, so far gone with the world.

"What 'cha gonna do 'bout it, son, huh?"

"Fuck you up so hard you won't breathe," Tate chillingly whispers with a straight face.

The admission rushes chills up my spine, and I don't know if it's good or bad.

I know just how badly Tate rightfully hates his father after everything he's done to him, but hearing him speak the words that must have been crowding his mind for a long time feels…

"Think I don't know where you've been?" Mirko scoffs, tipping back the rest of the beer, the glass almost shattering the second he slams it against the kitchen counter, jolting my heart.

"You're drunk."

"Yep, drunk ol' man again, but as I said, I know where you've been. Get emails 'bout it."

He tracks his adult son's visitations with his mother?

Tate's nostrils flare, fuming. "Of course you do."

"You've gotta stop seeing her."

"Don't."

Mirko doesn't listen.

"You've gotta stop seeing that bitch! She don't deserve a second of your goddamn time!"

"And *you do*?" Tate scoffs.

Mirko's face twitches, anger shining through. "I am *your father!*"

"SHE IS *MY MOTHER!*"

"You have another mother. Your stepmom!"

"Stop. Fucking. Talking."

"Your real mother don't love you, son, she doesn't even *remember* you!"

"SHE LOVES ME MORE THAN YOU EVER COULD!" Tate screams, his chest racing up and down, as he closes the gap between them, glaring down at his father. "So don't you even fucking dare try, you hear me? You stole the best years of my life with her, keeping her caged in there, preventing me from seeing her like a son should. I missed out on so much, Mirko. *So. Damn. Much.* Because of your greed. Your sickened heart. *You.* All you do, all you've *ever done*, is blame other people. Guess what? It's time to take accountability for your own actions."

His father cockily smirks. "Nope!"

My heart bruises when Tate slams his fists against the counter.

"You're disgusting," I spit out at Mirko Meadows. "Tate's right about you, all you're good for is destroying things. You should be ashamed of yourself. Of everything that you've done. For stealing her money. For making her suffer, living the past ten years in crippling loneliness *because of you*."

"She deserves it."

"Elizabeth. Could. Never," I grit, stepping closer and mentally ignoring his wandering eyes. "You could have had a beautiful son. You could have loved him right. You could have been addicted to him instead of the expensive liquor, invested in his life, his dreams. But no, you could never do that, instead, all you've ever done is treated Tate like the piece of gum on your fucking expensive shoes. You don't deserve Tatum, Mr. Meadows, you deserve to be swallowed up in a pit of the devastation that *you are*." My voice hardens in confidence. "That you *will always be*."

My words hit him harder than anything, evidently twisting his mind.

"*Bitch!*" he spits, launching at me. "Wanna get hit till you're black and fucking blue?"

Before the gasp even falls from my lips, Tate's solid fist collides with his jaw, over and over again, with a lethal snarl. His scary eyes are laser focused, a famished wolf and his prey.

"I'm gonna fucking kill you," my boyfriend seethes, striking him repeatedly, in a frenzy of hits. "*Kill. You.*"

Mirko attempts to protect his face, but the hits collide so hard and fast, jabbing at his blooded jaw, which eventually pops and shakes, having him scream out in mercy. But Tate isn't having any of that, viciously bunching his shirt and tossing him to the floor, crimson blood spraying everywhere.

My boyfriend is relentless against his father's dehumanizing screams and pleas, puncturing his chest and face with his fists, all while I remain standing here, frozen in place, paralyzed.

No.

No. No. No.

My eyes are wide, dryness coating my throat as fear ruptures my heart.

Tate doesn't stop laying his assault.

Not as Mirko's body stiffens, or when his eyes roll back with a heavy grunt.

Not as I rush up to Tate, begging him to stop, but it's like he's in his own world.

Not as his stepmom and Maddie speed down the stairs, screaming and crying to no avail.

Mirko Meadows isn't moving, shallow breaths the only indication he's still alive.

Eventually, Tate pulls back with one final hard hit, his fist a bloodied mess as he staggers back, breathless, and the dark look in his soulless eyes when they meet mine is debilitating.

It breaks me.

Piece by piece.

Reminding me of my father's, after his rage.

Oh my God.

That's when fear lodges in those baby blues eyes that are usually so expressive, but right now, only hold agony. Tate sees my hurt while I stare back, tears of heartache stinging my cheeks. He realizes, exactly, in this moment, why my trembling hands cast over my mouth, dazed.

"SHIT! What did you do?" His stepmom sobs. "What the hell did you do to him?"

"Taught him a lesson he'll never forget because I'm *done*," Tate grits, gesturing to her and Maddie. "After everything you three destroyed in my life, I'm done with all of you."

"All I ever wanted to do was help you! You never gave me a chance!"

"Because you think you're my damn mother when you're not. When you can never be."

"Tate Lee Meadows," she snaps. "I will not tolerate you talking to me like that!"

Maddie joins in, clicking her fingers. "Lay off my mom or you'll fucking deal with me."

Tate scoffs, shaking his head as he turns back to his stepmom. "You have no authority to tell me what to do when you haven't stopped disrespecting my mother since the moment you walked into my life! You think Mirko loves you? You think Mirko truly *cares*?" he hisses. "He *doesn't*. He never could. It's why he's drowning in liquor and cheating on you, and there's nothing you can do to stop it. He'll keep going until he's fuckin' dead, so I might as well help him. You married a liar, Sabrina, a fraud, a cheat. *You* should have run a long time ago, but you didn't."

Whoa.

"Tatum—"

"You don't have the right to call me that." There's pain in his eyes. Pain I so desperately want to take away as he taps his heart. "He hurt me. He hurt me right *here*. He's killing my mom."

The fragments of my fear fall away, and in its place, my empathy for Tate brightens.

Tatum Lee Meadows isn't my father.

He's a man breaking free from his caged demons.

One, who in a heartbeat, would protect me from this world.

Maddie hasn't stopped glaring at me. I have far more pride than to stoop to her level. I don't want anything to do with her. I've moved on, not even caring about her lack of apology.

Mirko stirs on the floor, coughing up blood as he comes to, eyes springing open.

Sobs don't stop stifling Tate's stepmom. "He's not cheating on me."

"He is. Her name's Lolita. Just ask him about her."

"GET OUT!" she screams. "GET OUT OF THIS FUCKING HOUSE! *NOW!*"

The wickedest smile carves Tate's lips. "Gladly."

Tate throws his house keys to her and then quickly runs upstairs, returning seconds later with a barely-closed suitcase.

Without looking back, he strides pass them, his bloody hand nestling in mine and I meet his stepmom's bitter stare, just before Tate Meadows slams the door on his life as he knew it.

The silence is deafening.

We've been parked in front of my apartment for a good ten minutes, the brown paper bag sealing our fate pressed against my chest.

I want to say something.

I want to fucking say anything.

But nothing rolls off my tongue.

I want to comfort Tate, I want to be angry at him, I want to love him till the dawn breaks over this heartbreak city, but I don't know how. It's just me, myself, and I, trapped in my echoing mind, praying he says something to me before I let myself out.

Tate hasn't stopped staring at his tense hands on the steering wheel, laced in the crimson blood of the man who made him. The one I know he'll forever despise, as will I.

Sighing, Tate reaches across to the glovebox, leather scraping my thigh as he pulls out a pack of cigarettes and a lighter. The amber flame is mesmerizing, licking the soft breeze of his cracked open window.

He slips the death stick between his full lips, a real '50s rockstar when those dim blue eyes meet mine, and then lower to my flat stomach. Something flashes in his eyes, something close to hope, prompting him to flick the lighter off and yank out the unlit cigarette with a thick swallow.

"Sorry," he murmurs into the night, his croaky voice fading, "I wasn't thinking."

"We have school tomorrow so I should…go up to my apartment now an—"

"I want to do the same to your father, LonLon, except I want him dead."

Tate's look is deadly.

He's serious.

"Baby…" I gulp down. "We should say goodnight."

"I don't like that your father's going to be there when you wake up tomorrow."

My heart pangs. "I know."

"Can I come in?"

"I think we both need some rest; it's been a long night."

Tate slowly nods, returning to the glovebox compartment, only to pull out an aged cigar box, stained in a chestnut-colored finish.

My heart thumps in my ears when he opens the box, my eyes growing wide at the deadly silver pistol inside.

A gun.

"Tate…" I gasp, feeling like I'm suffocating when he places the lethal weapon in the palm of my hands. Its coldness radiates chills, the gun heavy and a glint of moonlight licking the metal barrel. The handle is wrapped in a sangria red leather, the trigger the shiniest shade of argent.

"I'm not forcing you to use it," he breathes, "but in the case that you do…"

For the next few minutes, Tate goes on to explain every detail of the gun: the right way to hold it, how to uncock it, the hand pressure around the grip seconds before aiming and hitting the trigger. All his words blur into one, and at one point, I just look at him, terrified yet intrigued.

"Is this yours?" I ask.

"My father's."

"Does he know you have it?"

Tate keeps his eyes on the gun. "He's not in the right state of mind to operate one."

"Where are you staying?"

"Levi will have me."

"What if I miss him?"

The question makes Tate look at me through his beautifully-long lashes. "There's seventeen rounds in it, baby girl, you won't miss. Sterling won't have a chance against your self-defense."

Self-defense.

This pistol is my self-defense.

All my father's inflicted pain floods my mind, every single slap, hit, and concussion, which snapped the remaining threads of my childhood. But I'm far from that little girl who hated the color blue because it reminded her of the bruises Daddy left on her. I'm far from being his punching bag anymore. I'm far from being so traumatized from the pain that I didn't want to live.

Now I'm eighteen, a woman with pride, who refuses to be haunted by my father's sins.

I want this pistol.

I want it to lull me to sleep.

I want it to save me from the nightcrawlers.

From him—Sterling Héroux—my antagonist.

It's why I embrace Tate with every single ounce of strength in me and tell him just how brave he was with his father, just how much I love him, and just how desperate I am for *it.*

He listens.

He listens to me.

He listens with a smile before leaving.

And when I fall asleep in my bed, his lingering kiss forever chained to my lips and the pistol submerged beneath my silk pillow, I dream of my index finger kissing the shiny trigger.

Boom.

Chapter
FORTY-TWO

London

I wake to my father's venomous shouts echoing around my bedroom walls.

Shit.

His murmured shouts are quick, sharp, with that familiar edge I know too well. My heartbeat skips as his voice jolts, a mixture of "*kill*" and "*bitch*" swirling the air.

Through my broken, sleepy fog, adrenalin pumps through my veins as I slither my fingers beneath my silk pillow, clasping the cool metal pistol. The one Tate gave to me in self-defense, *should I need it.*

The neon red light of my alarm clock flickers *5:43a.m.*, its glow radiating.

My father's booming voice continues echoing against the ridge of the cold gun, numbness falling over me when I hear shattering glass and my mother's screams.

Possibilities overtake my mind. Possibilities, as to why they're fighting, but I, more than anyone, know that Sterling Héroux's reasons don't always have to be sufficient.

Before Tate sped off in his vintage 1969 Ford Mustang, he told me to call him if it got to be too much and that he'd be here in a second, a heartbeat. This probably would be the time to call him, but my ego resists it. I want to fight this battle. On my own. To the death.

I've never, not for one second, had anybody in my life to hold the shield up for me. I've had to grip it myself for eight excruciating years, through all of the physical abuse, emotional torment, and constant unlove.

And it ends now.

I'm adamant.

As I slither out of my warm bedsheets at the second booming sound of breaking glass.

"Sterling, you need to calm the hell down!" my mother pleads as I descend the dark hallway, my bare feet kissing against the marble floor.

There's a fear in her voice that I've never heard before. A sense of vulnerability and weakness. It's not like her.

At all.

Something must have happened—*something bad*—when they were in Los Angeles, meeting their potential client.

At the end of the hallway, when I quietly turn right, the warm glow of the kitchen chandeliers shine down on the Italian marble, caressing the tips of my bubblegum pink painted toenails.

I don't have the gun with me. *Not yet.*

But I know where it is if I need it.

My breath hitches at the sight in front of me. My father pinning my mother against the kitchen countertop, his back to me, and their leather walnut brown Louis Vuitton suitcases scattered by the private elevator doors.

"You don't get to tell me what to do, Ramona!" My father hisses. "Do you love him?"

"Get. Off. Me."

"DO YOU LOVE HIM?"

Him.

It all sinks in, suddenly making sense.

Victor.

Victor LéVont.

This all has to be about him.

My suspicions are confirmed seconds later. My mom slams her plump lips closed, fear crawling up into her eyes as she rubs a hand over her face. Her usually perfect bouncy curls are the opposite, disheveled and messily pulled back in a bun. Dark smudges under her eyes and the white mini dress outlining her figure comes second to the blotchy, blue bruises circling her left bicep, each a fingertip apart, as if my father gripped her there for too long in a fit of rage in Los Angeles.

"Fucking answer me!" My father growls, viciously slamming his fists against the countertop behind her, his hips pinning her roughly against the marble. "*Bitch*!"

"I don't love him."

"Bullshit."

My mother anxiously gulps. "It meant nothing."

"So it *happened*, right?"

"Sterling," she exhaustingly whispers, her arms craving peace when they slither around his reddening neck. "Baby, I don't love anybody else but you."

"You're lying by the skin of your teeth, you fucking bitch. What is it about Victor that I don't have, hmmm?"

"I'm not with Victor. H-He only said that on the call because we sometimes joke around abou—"

"Is it his money?" my father rasps, shaking his head. "No. No, that motherfucker can't have more than me, and that wouldn't satisfy you because all you are is a money whore."

Sadness coats her eyes, and for the first time in my entire life, empathy pangs my heart.

My father's so cruel.

So cruel it hurts.

"Don't you remember, Ramona? Don't you remember the way you were so fucking obsessed with me, yeah? How you selfishly manipulated me to get you pregnant so you could escape your shitty parents and be with me."

Oh…*God*.

My jaw hangs open at his words.

I was just an act of selfishness. Rebellion. I was made with manipulation. Deceit.

"Are you obsessed with Victor LéVont, like you were obsessed with me?"

"Sterling, stop."

"Don't tell me to stop."

"I'm telling you to fucking sto—"

The words aren't even out before the loud slap zaps the air, echoing inside me like a hurricane.

Tears glaze my mother's eyes as she rushes a hand to her left cheek, cupping the instant amber flush.

"You…You *hit me*," she whispers.

"No, you fucking asked for it."

"I freaking hate you! I hate you so much."

Sterling Héroux lets out a cold, mocking laugh. "Oh please, darling, what's that going to do? Hurt my feelings, hmm? Try again."

In an instant, Sterling yanks my mom around, forcing her to bend over the counter as he yanks a fistful of her hair. "I'm going to fuck you into submission. Fuck you so hard, you won't ever remember Victor again."

"No, I don't want it." A pained cry escapes her as she desperately wriggles around, attempting to break away from him, but she can't. She does everything she possibly can to escape the monster, all while he angrily pulls up her dress, exposing her transparent Chanel stockings. "Get off me! PLEASE, GET OFF ME!"

"Why don't you call your fucking boyfriend to come save you, hmm?"

"Stop! I don't want you to touch me!"

My eyes shoot daggers into the back of his head when he slams my mother's face into the marble. "You don't have a choice."

The excruciating metal ricochet of his slack's zipper rolling down ruins me.

I need to stop this.

I need to stop this right now.

My bare feet inch forward, but then stall when my mother's anguished confession halts me in place, practically throwing cold water all over me.

"Sterling, *please*, don't do this. I…I'm…" her voice softens, "I'm pregnant."

My eyes practically bulge out of their sockets.

What?

"What the fuck are you talking about Ramona?"

"I'm…pregnant. It's early. Two months."

Two months.

"By him?" My father growls.

"Sterling, please."

"BY *HIM*?"

A gulp, and then… "Yes. It's Victor's."

My head is spinning, over and over again, comprehending what this means for us.

My thirty-five-year-old mother is pregnant.

Pregnant.

By a man who isn't her fifty-two-year-old husband.

Oh my God.

My heartbeats slow, paralyzed.

"You're fucking dead to me, Ramona!"

And then he lays his attack, vile and sickening as he spins my mother around, and before she can gasp for air, his fists collide with her face. It happens in seconds. *Seconds.* He hits her over and over again, until she's a gory mess with crimson blood dripping from her busted lip.

She's sobbing and struggling to fight back against my father's strength.

My mother's hands frantically spread over her flat stomach, almost instinctively. Her shaky fingers sprawl over the expensive white minidress, staining it in blood, and my father takes advantage of that, addressing his strong blows to her womb instead, never stopping through his grunts.

Through her cries.

Through my screams as I bolt up to them, attempting to pull him away from her, my fingers digging into his clenched fists, to no avail.

"DAD!" The shout is out before I know it, sharp and explosive, just like him. "*STOP IT!*"

His shoulders physically tense beneath his crisp white dress shirt and a strangled breath escapes my mother, something close to relief. "Go to your fucking room, London!"

"*No.*"

That's all it takes for Sterling Heroux's assault on his wife to slow, his fury pinning me. "What did you just say to me?"

I stand tall, defiant. "I said *no.*"

"London," my mother whimpers, her terrified eyes meeting mine, pleading, "listen to him."

She's scared.

She's so scared of what he may do if I don't.

"And make him kill the baby?" I motion to her stomach. "*No.* I'm not freaking leaving."

"I said go to your bedroom before I start on you." My father towers over me, pathetically attempting to manipulate me with all his tall-and-scary vibes, but it doesn't intimidate me.

Not anymore.

I'm stronger than this.

I'm so much stronger than him.

Jaw clenched, I lift my chin and stare him down. "I'm not five, *Sterling.*"

"You have school in a few hours."

"*Oh,*" I tease with a cocky smirk. "How nice of you to remember you have a daughter!"

The words hit him like a lightning bolt, and it isn't long before he stalks toward me, gripping my throat and slamming me against the French-doored fridge as he does. He does it all while I remain smirking, because I'm not his little bitch anymore.

I deserve to be loved.

I deserve to be treated right.

I deserve everything but his touch.

"Becoming just like your bitch mother, aren't you, huh?" Sterling Héroux grits, then nods to her. She's slumped against the counter, catching her breath. "A fucking gold-digging slut is all your mother is, London. So, did you know?"

"Know *what*?" I spit.

"That she's in love with that damn Victor LéVont?"

Well...

"I'm not in love with him!" My mother gasps, failing to soften his hardened soul.

"QUIET! I WASN'T FUCKING TALKING TO YOU!"

Those devilish eyes find mine again. "*Did you know?*"

"No."

He squeezes my throat tighter. "Fucking liar."

My stinging slap against his cheek rings out, emitting silence.

The flush on his cheek reddens, feeding the vein popping in his forehead. "You don't know what you just did, *hündin.*"

"Get. Off. Me."

"Or *what?*"

I inhale sharply, making the younger me proud. "Or I'll call the police."

His eyes drip down to my body. "Not a scratch on you, London. Not from me, anyway."

"I have pictures," I spit. "I took one every single time you hit me. It's *over* for *you.*"

Sterling's face instantly darkens, scrunching up. "You're playing the card of the victim."

"No, I'm a survivor."

"The only thing you are is pathetic." My father's coarse thumb slowly strums against a tender spot on my neck. I know *exactly* what he's outlining. "Think I wouldn't find out about this? Want me to break this pretty neck, hmmm? The one all peppered with Tate's marks. Because I will. I'll break it. I'll do it *right now* for going against me. You won't even make it to your finals!"

"You can do whatever you want, but it doesn't change how deeply I hate you," I manage to choke out. "You say I'm pathetic, but your abuse made me anything but. Your torment made me stronger. Made me finally understand myself. Made me realize I'm worth loving and being loved, and Tate Meadows loves me more than you ever could. You won't *ever* be able to take that away from me."

My father's pressure around my neck intensifies, and as adamant as I am to remain strong, his firm fingers begin to dig into my pulse, breaking the barrier between tolerance and destruction.

It feels like I'm sinking, falling, uncontrollable tears pricking my eyes the longer it feels as if I'm suffocating within myself. *Sinking.*

Sinking.

Sinking.

Further into the Atlantic.

My lungs burn, desperate for an escape, but I refuse to plead with Sterling Héroux.

I *refuse* to give him any leverage over me as I bravely stare up at him, eyes wide, enduring the monsters which continue to crawl into his soulless eyes. And in this moment, as his lips numb to whiteness from just how intensely he's pursing his thin lips, I...*wish he were dead.*

I wish he didn't exist.

I wish there was nothing tying him to me.

It would be so much easier, for all of us, if he were gone.

He's caused too much pain, too much torment. It's irreversible.

There's no saving him.

He's a lost cause.

He'll always be.

He'll always be, because as long as he's still breathing, he'll always be Sterling Héroux.

The abuser.

My abuser.

"Don't talk to her like that."

It's my mother.

"Defending this bitch?" my father scoffs.

"She's my *daughter!*" Her voice is all husky and groggy. "And I *love her.*"

Thump.

Thump.

Thump.

My heart kicks into overdrive.

My mother has never, not even once, told me she loves me.

Never.

My eyes find hers and they're peppered in regret, so much so, it tugs at my heart and triggers the tears coating my eyes to fall, making her face a blurry, crimson kaleidoscope of devastation.

Oh God, my heart, it hurts too much.

I'm so conflicted, because I never thought I'd feel these bubbling loads of emotions sizzling inside me. Conflicted that in this moment, I actually care. It hurts me seeing her like this.

"As your *husband*, Ramona, I can rightfully say you don't love anybody but *yourself.*"

A flash of strength floods my mother.

"You're right," she spits. "I *don't* love you, Sterling Héroux, in fact, I don't think I ever did."

Silence.

Something shifts in him as he eyes my mom—the equivalent of an ominous kiss of death.

All it takes is a few seconds, laced with my gasping breaths, which subside the moment my father's grip weakens before entirely slipping off. The gravity of his faded strength has me dipping, my knees smashing against the marble floor so hard, I'm in ruins.

But that doesn't stop me from thinking, from scheming, from running into my bedroom when my father returns his attack on my mother, hitting her harder than ever before, while recklessly searching kitchen drawers, clanging metals spiking my anxiety until he produces a knife.

A sharp butcher's knife, catching a glint of light.

He's going to murder her, right in front of me.

The commotion deepens when I scramble inside my bedroom in the dark, the sob rippling through me aching my throat. My vision's a blurry mess as I overturn my pillow and fist the gun, doing my best to remember everything Tate told me as I sprint back into the kitchen, petrified.

Once again, my father's back is to me. He has the knife pierced against my mother's throat, on standby, heedlessly urging her to choose between *him* or *London* as she wheezes for air.

I'm so conflicted because I never thought I'd feel these emotions sizzling inside me. I never thought there'd be a moment where I actually care about her. It hurts me seeing her like this.

"Choose, Ramona! *Me* or *her*?"

"I can't breathe!"

"*ME* or *LONDON*?"

My mother's gaze jolts toward me, widening at the gun, which trembles in my firm grip.

I can't believe I'm doing this.

I can't believe I'm doing this.

I'm…I'm *doing* this.

"London! I choose *London*! I always will!"

The butcher's knife is seconds from puncturing her throat when…

Sterling Héroux tenses at the cocking of the gun, but it's too late.

Boom.

Boom!

BOOM!

The silver pistol heats in my hands with every fired bullet, the loud gunshots ricocheting. A terrified grunt escapes my father as he slumps over, bullets peppering his back, all while my mother screams in horror. His once crisp white shirt is now painted red as I exert all of my pent-up anger, defending my mother and saving myself from the monster whose blood flows in my veins.

Releasing my grip, I concentrate and aim, licking the trigger with my index finger. *Do it.* And with a steady breath, I pull the trigger, firing into the back of his head, brain mass exploding.

Sterling Héroux, my destroyer, collapses to the marble floor, face-first, lifeless.

Ohmygod.

Breathless, my mother rushes down to press two fingers against his neck.

It feels like the longest two seconds, my heart thrashing inside me.

"He's dead…" she whispers.

Dead.

A weight lifts from my chest, alleviating the ruckus and filling it with freedom instead.

Before I can comprehend what's happening, Ramona Héroux is rushing to me and tightly pulling me into the first hug of our lives. Through my tears, I let go of the gun and hold onto her, her affection so foreign. She's sobbing in my arms, her thin body shaking uncontrollably.

Then, my mother softly cups my cheeks, her dimmed light eyes widening in realization. Her beautiful curls are smeared in death, sticking to her bloodied face as she weakly smiles at me.

Smiles.

Through the ache.

Through the bedlam.

Through our melting hate.

She. Smiles. At. Me.

"You saved *us*, London," she gasps, crying harder. "Thank you for saving my life."

Suddenly, I don't feel trapped anymore.

I don't feel so scared, or alone, or unloved.

For the first time, since I was nine, I can breathe again.

Here, in my mother's shaky foreign embrace, I finally feel safe.

Tate's therapeutic kiss is one I didn't know I needed when he rushes into my hospital room, the most beautiful misty pink roses in his hand and now scattered across the thin bedsheets.

"Baby girl, I love you," he rasps against my lips. "I'm so proud of your courage."

Tate Meadows is here to cure my aching cries, the shock coursing through my bones, the relief taking over me. He's *here* as he lies down on the bed with me, kissing my honey blonde waves and the darkening blotches on my neck, and continues whispering that *it's all over now.*

Tate revives me, over and over again, just by having his warm touch caressing me.

My mother and I were brought here for observation after the police took our statements at the apartment, whilst my father, Sterling Héroux, was pronounced dead at the scene.

My father's dead and I finally feel alive.

When the doctor is happy with my results and discharges me, I tell Tate there's somebody I need to see. He waits outside my mother's door, giving us privacy.

Piercing gray-green eyes dart my way.

Victor's.

Victor LéVont is seated by my mother's bedside, fretfully rubbing his salt-and-pepper stubble. His black running shorts and tight black workout long sleeve top carving his masculine physique.

"London," he whispers, warmth kidnapping his eyes as he stretches out his long legs and stands tall. "Hello, London."

The successful Frenchman has me frozen in place as my mind wanders to the fact that my mother is pregnant. By him.

I swallow thickly. "Hi."

It's the only word that escapes me.

My mother is asleep on the bed, curled to her side with IV tubes connected to her hands and her blonde waves, that are still dipped in redness, pulled back, exposing her face and all of her husband's torment.

"Is she going to be okay?"

Clenching his jaw, Victor nods. "The doctor says she's extremely lucky with all of the blunt trauma she received. The fucking bastard was inches from causing internal bleeding."

"Is the…" I gulp down. "Is the baby okay?"

Emotion consumes him.

"She told you about that?"

"She was pleading for her baby's life."

"Jesus Christ." Victor shakes his head, choking on his breath and he slowly rushes a hand over his face, ending by tugging his dark wavy hair, even more silvery strands than when I saw him last. "They did a lot of scans and tests, and everything seems to be okay. Baby's a trooper."

Relief.

It's all that floods me.

"Wow," I manage a smile. "I'm so happy to hear that, Victor. Genuinely, I am."

"Thank you."

I nod.

"I'm so sorry for everything you've endured, London. I'm sorry this happened to you."

"It's not your fault."

"No, it is. Three years ago, at the New Year's Eve party I hosted, I sensed something was wrong with how your father was treating you but didn't push it. I feel so guilty that I didn't do more for you, London. I should have stood up to him. I should have announced my love for your mother right then and there, not continued to hide it like we did. Perhaps then you and your mother could have lived with me, happily, and you wouldn't have suffered so much of his pain."

The knot continues to tighten at the back of my throat. "You don't know if that would have happened."

"You're right, I don't, but I know that you would have been happier."

When his guilt-filled gaze becomes too much, I gaze down at my hands. The same hands that only hours before silenced my father's life forever in an act of self-defense.

The panicked grunt that he made before his death will forever haunt me, but he deserved it, and I hope now, wherever he may be, his soul catches fire and burns a slow, torturous death.

"I am happy now, Victor. I'm *healing*. Piece by piece. In the ways I know how."

Victor outstretches his arms. "Is it okay if I...?"

A gravitational pull has me running into his embrace before I can entirely register it. It was something, years ago, I would have never done. Victor holds me securely in his solace, his expensive cologne merging with the reek of death, and for some reason, I don't feel any of the tension I thought I would. I feel safe in his arms, just like I did my mother's, and I've only ever felt that way with Tate.

"London, I don't want to be the villain in your life," Victor breathes by my ear, his thick French-accent rooted in verity. "I love your mother so much and I would never hurt her. I would never hurt *you*. I'm not a violent man, my *mére*—mother—taught me better. Your mom cares about you, she's just scared and insecure because she knows her faults, but she wants to do and be better, believe me. We're having a baby now, so I'm open to being the stability your dad never gave you. I'm not saying we have to be best friends, or that you have to call me *papa*, what I'm saying is that I'm here for you now, London, okay? I'm *here*, and I'll never allow any repeats of the pain you've tolerated."

I squeeze Victor till I can't no more. "That means a lot to me. Thank you."

"Of course."

When my mother wakes, Victor kisses her softly before giving us some time alone.

"I know I haven't been the best mother, in fact, I've been awful," is her first croaky admission. "I subjected you to so many years of torment. I would just stand there while Sterling... *God*, I'm so ashamed of it, London. I hate myself for it, you have to believe me." She sucks in a breath, letting that unfamiliar hint of her vulnerability expand my lungs. "I really do care about you, even if I've had a fucked-up way of showing it. I've never known how to be a mother, but I'm open to trying. I was seventeen when I had you. I was so scared to tell my father, and when I did, he told me either I have an abortion, or I leave their house. I didn't want to lose my baby, so I moved in with Sterling, and my family disowned me that very night. I came from a family of coldness and no affection, I craved it more than anything, but I couldn't. It's not a reflection of you. It's of me. I created such a hardened shell around me that I forgot who I was."

She takes another breath, continuing, "You saved my life, London. I was so scared. I thought I was going to die when he had that knife pressed up against me. All I kept thinking of, in those moments, was you. It wasn't until the beauty of life was about to be snatched from me that I realized, in the end, all I have is you, London. I've never had something worth being proud of. *Ever*. You're my only beauty through the pain, and I'm so sorry I overlooked it for so long.

"I'm proud of you, London, for following your heart. Of the strong woman you've become. Of finding somebody like Tate who loves you. I don't give a shit about the fucking rivalry with the Meadows, *you* do what makes *you* happy, because it's something I should have done a long time ago. I know you need time to heal and accept it, but I'm sorry. I'm so sorry *for everything*." My mother gives me her best amorous smile, with hope in her eyes. "I love you, darling."

I love you, darling.

God. *I'm supposed to hate* her, but I can't, not with these revelations.

I'm beginning to realize that my mother's life was truly tarnished growing up. That love wasn't in her vocabulary by choice, it was by association. Sometimes people do bad things. People like my father, for example, who don't have moral compasses or care about the human condition.

Then there's those like my mom, who perhaps aren't actually *bad*, they've just had bad things happen to them, which casted a shadow over their goodness, trapping them in themselves.

My mom just needed a way out.

And whether that be through my father being dead, or loving Victor, or having a baby, perhaps now, I can finally see her for who she is. I can't forget what she's done, but I can forgive.

I reach out to her. Her eyes sparkle as she swiftly tangles her fingers through mine.

"Someday, I hope..." I confess, witnessing her smile deepen, "I can love you too."

We don't need to say anything else.

Because maybe, just maybe, we'll reach the other side of hell together.

Chapter

FORTY-THREE

Tate

Two weeks later…
JUNE.

The following two weeks were challenging, filled with finals, graduation prep, and endless articles outlining the man, Manhattan elite, Sterling Héroux, truly was behind closed door before his merited death.

NYPD labelled the act as lawful self-defense, and the investigation promptly closed.

London didn't want to go to the funeral, and I stood by her. There's no reason a man so cruel deserved a daughter so beautiful to have any part of it. We were in the middle of finals anyway, and rumor had it that not even her mother, Ramona, or Victor attended it.

The fact that Ramona Héroux is pregnant comes as the biggest shock of my life, to London as well. I still despise her for all the hurt she placed on London's shoulders, but after their heart-to-heart conversation in her hospital room, London tells me she feels closure with her mom. But their relationship isn't perfect, it needs time to heal and mend and strengthen.

The day of Sterling's funeral was an ominous stormy ruin of a day, the kind of cold in the air that matched his cruel motionless heart. London wanted to do nothing but stay in bed all day, in the king-sized bed of the hotel we'd been staying at since we're both technically homeless. London just wanted me close, wanted me to hold her and feel my wildly beating heart and I let her, because there was nothing more I wanted to do.

The tempest brewed outside, pelting down on our panoramic floor-to-ceilings windows, and with every rumbling roar of thunder, London buried her face deeper into my neck. It was only after a glorious rainbow blanketed the sky, did a tired smile form on her lips, coated in hope.

Coated in a renewal from her tainted start.

The rainbow didn't only signal new beginnings, it also brought peace. *So much of it.*

That night, I made love to London until dusk twirled around the stars.

I made love to every single inch of her, slow and sensually, with her aching lips on mine.

There was a point where I was getting tired of changing condoms, just wanting to love on her all night without stopping, but we both knew it was the right thing to do. During the fog of it all, London hadn't taken a pregnancy test, nor had she gotten her period yet, but the latter could be due to stress. After all, it had been an anxious couple of weeks.

London wasn't grieving the loss of her father for the man that he was, she was grieving that part of herself she lost sight of years ago. She was grieving that nine-year-old girl she used to be, saying goodbye to her old life, and beginning her new life. With me.

With strength.

London saved herself.

She fucking saved herself.

And I'll forever be proud of her for that.

We both graduated high school with flying colors.

My stepmother, Sabrina, attended, but it was only for her daughter, Maddie. They didn't even glance my way, and I'm glad. I don't need them in my life. I don't need anybody else but London. I haven't spoken to my father since the night my life changed for good. Which brings me to right now, three days post-graduation. London and I are sitting on the hexagon-tiled hotel bathroom floor, the entire world in our hands, with a loading pregnancy test above us on the vanity countertop. *Well,* three pregnancy tests *to be exact. This has been the longest three minutes of my life.*

"What if I really am pregnant?" London whispers, cradling her knees to her chest.

"Simple. I'd ask you to marry me."

London's pretty baby blues brighten. "I didn't know you were an old school romantic."

"Only for you. I want you to be a Meadows, even if it's everything I detest."

She's quiet for a moment. "What was your mother's maiden name?"

"Holloway, why?"

"Well, we could always change our last names to that, right?"

Whoa.

"You mean…" My heart pangs in awe. "You'd really do that for me?"

London nods. "In a heartbeat, babe. From the first moment I saw her, I instantly loved your mother. I think she's beautiful and kindhearted, and I'd really like to honor her in this way. Besides, I want to give our baby a new beginning, we can't do that with Héroux or Meadows."

She's right.

Our baby.

"London and Tate Holloway…" I murmur, testing the names on my tongue. "I like it."

"Me too."

"What did I do to deserve you?"

"You promised me the moon."

Our heated stare only continues when London's phone vibrates on the tiles between us, signaling three minutes is over. She blindly grips all three pregnancy tests, my heart in my throat as she glances down at them with the widest pearly-tooth smile, and then…

Her baby blues dim.

The smile fades.

Shit.

"I'm…not pregnant, Tate."

My heart jolts, in shambles, as I take the tests from her and try to make sense of the mixture of single lines and **Not Pregnant** staring at me. But on one of the tests…it seems like there's a second faint one to me. Like a madman, I inch closer to the window, seeing if the cloudy rays of sunshine will clear up my anticipation, but London's already lost hope.

"I'm not pregnant, baby."

"But I swear to God, this really looks like…"

"I know, I know, but faint lines can be confused with false positives."

I turn to her, devastated when I see just how broken down she's become. Her head is in her hands and the desolation kills me. I instinctively cradle her to me, kissing away the heartache etched across her face.

"We're going to have a beautiful family one day, Shortcake, I promise."

"I know, but…"

"I get it. I really do, because there was nothing more I wanted than a baby Holloway, but our time will come, angel, and when it does, it'll be the best thing to ever happen to us."

"Why are you so good to me?" London sniffles.

"Because you're worth it, LonLon."

"In Seattle…there it'll all be different, and everything will begin to go our way."

I kiss her forehead, my lips lingering. "We'll become a family in Seattle, my girl."

And in this moment, more than ever, do I know that I can't live without her. The question has been spiraling inside my mind for weeks, but now I finally know the answer.

I love my mother, I love her with all my heart, but I'm an adult now, and with that comes sacrifice, no matter how much it sucks. London and I need Seattle. We need it more than oxygen.

"When can we leave?" she softly asks.

"Whenever you're ready to, Shortcake."

London chews her lower lip. "Tomorrow?"

Tomorrow.

"Tomorrow," I smile, my heart flipping. "There's just something I need to do first…"

My mother's in the sensory music room when we arrive to the psychiatric hospital, wearing the same turquoise poplin dress that I remember she used to wear all summer when I was a kid. The fabric is embedded in my mind, working like a *rewind* button on my favorite tape recorder.

Summer beach days.

Late summer nights at the drive-ins.

Those early summer mornings playing piano.

Turquoise.

Turquoise.

Turquoise.

And here my mother is now, seated at a glossy, ebony-colored Bechstein piano, heavily focused and playing the same repeated chords of the beginning of a song that once was our entire world.

D – A – E

To Build A Home.

To Build A Home by The Cinematic Orchestra and Patrick Watson.

The repeated melody sparks something inside me, clasping a memory of my past I've stripped away and attempted to hide from my mind for ten excruciating years.

Why?

Because I'd thought I'd never hear my mother play this song again…*I was wrong.*

I once read that dementia patients benefit a lot from sensory activities, including exploring music, almost as a type of therapy that activates the enduring cognitive functions in the brain.

Music therapy.

Brain function.

To Build A Home was a song only we knew.

The thought of never hearing her play it again was excruciating, debilitating. I didn't know that there was still a fragment of the song that remained. Seven seconds. The most precious seven seconds of my life. It takes me back to being that eight-year-old kid before tragedy happened, when I would beg my mother to play this song one more time before bed, just so I could see the stars twinkling in her eyes, a hushed lullaby only she and I knew existed.

"Elizabeth," I smile, sliding onto the polished piano bench next to her, "I'm back."

It hurts so much that I can't call her *Mom* like I crave, but that, with time, will come.

Her slender fingers slow by the long piano keys, and she snaps her head to me, something inside me dying and then coming back to life again when I notice a little sparkle in her eyes. The sparkle that was there whenever the warm, sultry breeze tangled through her lovely blonde curls.

"Hello," my mother whispers, before trickling her gaze up to London, who props against the piano. "No smile?"

My eyebrows knit as I glance to my girlfriend, realizing my mother's right.

She remembers.

The last time London was here, a permanent smile fixated her lips. She was so brazen and cheery. Today, she's a little defeated with a cloudy smile, and I know exactly why. A lot has happened since we last were here. But we'll get through it, I know we will. *We'll take care of each other.*

During the five-hour drive here, I explained to London the entire war in my head I was having regarding leaving my mother here in Rochester, New York. She understood it perfectly, with empathetic tears in her eyes, offering for Elizabeth to move with us to Seattle, but I've thought about it too and logically, it wouldn't work.

Elizabeth has a system here and Nurse Paige is so compassionate; besides, my mother isn't fit to move and I wouldn't forgive myself if something happened as a result of it. We decided on visits. A fuck load of them. And it mended the sting.

"Always a smile for you, Elizabeth." London grins, but I see straight through it.

She's sad to say goodbye to my mother too.

"We have something to say to you, mo-Elizabeth." I clear my

throat, kicking myself for almost slipping up because I know the effect it would have had on her. "Some real big news."

My mother slowly nods, glancing between us.

"We're moving to Seattle."

Her eyebrows knit, and before I can say anything else, London holds out her phone. She shows her a map of America, pointing to New York and then all the way over to the west side of the country, to Seattle.

"That's where we're heading tomorrow," I continue. "But we promise to be back soon, to visit you, that way we can paint with you again. Would you like that?"

A frown forms on her lips. "You…go?"

Dear God, my heart's aching.

"Just for a little while."

"Why?"

Why?

I freeze.

"Because…" A shaky breath escapes me. "We need to build a life there. A safer one."

"*To build a home…*" she whispers to herself, shutting her eyes and I know exactly why.

Our song.

It's the song she used to play on the piano, and I used to sing. Simultaneously. Therapy.

My mother once had a grand piano, exactly like this Bechstein model. So sleek and elegant with long piano keys and an open-hinged lid. My father destroyed it right in front of me.

Like a bittersweet tempest, my fingers stretch over the keys, isolating them across the familiar chords I know will flutter something inside her. It's my only bid of saying goodbye in a way that may open up the heart-shaped box inside her. The one riddled with fuzzy nostalgia.

I begin playing The Cinematic Orchestra and Patrick Watson's *To Build A Home* on the piano, memories fueling me as the hauntingly beautiful chords purr, reminding me of heaven.

We return back to the people we were, to the people I crave to somehow revert to as I softly sing the lyrics, my voice raspy and a little edged in a bittersweet heartache I can't shake off.

My eyes are closed, but I feel my mother's hot stare, her heavy breathing, the way she cups my knee over my jean-clad thigh, just like she always used to when I was younger. Back then, she was the phenomenon on the piano, and I was the words; today, I'm both.

The lyrics stab out of me, consoling me in the darkness, emotion wrapping every single word because this song couldn't relate more to my mother and me if it tried. It's so her and me. *It's us.*

"When the gusts came around to blow me down
I held on as tightly as you held on to me
I held on as tightly as you held on to me"

The chords begin to speed up, upsurging, and the pad of my fingers kiss them like crazy. I need to swallow emotion to continue singing.

"And, I built a home
For you
For me

Until it disappeared
From me
From you

And now,
It's time to leave and turn
To dust"

My voice cracks at the last word, but I push on, continuing to play my heart out, until the softening brings me back to the shore and everything becomes slower, more intimate, too familiar.

I slip my fingers off the piano and my blurry gaze moves to my mother, only to find tears glazing those blue eyes I'll always love. I witness the moment a piece of the puzzle unlocks in them.

A single tear rolls down her cheek.

And then, a million more.

My chest heaves, finally freed.

My mother's shaky hand nestles by my stubbled jaw, her

warmth my oasis, the longer she studies me with that alluring gaze. There are fragments of us still left in her, I just know it.

"You're too beautiful to cry, Mom," I murmur, gently wiping her tears. "Please, don't."

Mom.

I just called her *mom.*

Her perplexed eyes widen a fraction, and then…

"Tatum?"

Everything.

Inside.

Me.

Stops.

Functioning.

I can't feel my heart, or my hands, or my damn feet.

Everything feels so numb, yet completely awake and alive.

She just called me Tatum. I missed it so much.

"Yes," I adamantly nod, nestling my hand over hers on my jaw, "I'm Tatum."

"Tatum," she murmurs once more, this time with a lingering smile, her eyes flooding with so much warmth before fear ripples over her, as if she's comprehending what's happening to her. "Baby boy."

I may be a grown ass fucking man, but I can't help the way it begins sinking in and it all just explodes for me, hot tears sliding down my throat and sobs rippling out of me as I hold onto her, tightly, just like the song says.

"*Mommy,*" I whisper, savoring the way she embraces me back. "I love you so much."

I know she may not remember this in ten seconds; tomorrow she may wake up and forget this day ever existed; the next time I see her I could simply be a cloudy figment of her imagination, so for right now, I'm selfish and take in her lavender scent until it lulls me into a state of tranquility.

My mother still loves me.

She loves me with every single breath.

And now, I finally understand, that *she always will.*

We make it back to Manhattan in record speed, stopping by London's place, so she can pack her belongings for Seattle. We don't know how long we'll stay there, only that, for now, it's the place we want to run away to.

I feel reborn after seeing my mother—*revived*.

I'll never forget the look in London's eyes when we made it to my car, just as the moon began flirting with the darkening sky, and she wrapped me in her solace. It's there where I couldn't stop sobbing, feeling like every single aspect of my life was finally blooming into beauty and it was all because of my sweet girl.

I help London bubble wrap all her vinyl, while she sorts through her clothes, adamant that a capsule wardrobe is what she's aiming for. I could tell she was going fast because she didn't want to bump into her mother, but we did, just as we were leaving. Ramona Héroux stepped out of the private elevator, just as we were about to step in, a hand innately clutched to her stomach.

She was beginning to show.

Ramona became emotional when London revealed our plans, but also told us that this would be the best thing for us. She said that she'd be here, with open arms, should we ever need her.

I had booked us an 8 a.m. flight out of Manhattan and quit my job at the movie cinema earlier this morning, so now, the only thing left to do was bid good riddance to the city that held us hostage for eighteen years. That begins with the one person I know I'll miss like fucking crazy...

My best friend, Levi Prescott, is ever-so-casually sitting on his brownstone steps in the dark, puffing on a cigarette when I pull into park, my headlights gleaming the *residential parking only* sign.

"You're totally not allowed to park here." London smirks, sorting through her stash of strawberry field candy in a heart-shaped jar, those I'm yet to taste.

"You're such a pain in my ass."

"Welcome back, Tatum Lee."

Snickering, I gesture to my best friend through our rolled-up windows. "Come out with me for five minutes, Shortcake, I wanna introduce you guys properly."

Even with just the silvery moonshine, I witness the heat crawl up her cheeks. "Okay."

What's supposed to be five minutes ends up being an entire hour when Levi invites us inside. He's such a nice guy and he treats London well too, I'm going to miss him a fuck of a lot, and I feel it in the way he squeezes my shoulder tightly before I slip back inside my car.

"You better keep in contact, bro," he teases with that telling smirk. "Or I'll find you."

"Stalker much?"

"Shut the fuck up." He bursts out laughing, before turning to my girlfriend. "And for the record, London, I was always rooting for you. Sorry I was looking at your tits on New Year's Eve."

God, that seems like a lifetime ago now.

Giggling, London playfully rolls her eyes. "It's forgiven."

Levi glances back at me with those cocky wiggling eyebrows of his.

"Such an asshole," I jokingly shove my best friend out the way. "Bye. I hate you."

"Awww, I *love you too*, man!"

I chuckle. "Love ya!"

Our next goodbye? The place where it all began...

London and I sink onto our fated Central Park bench, our memories merging into a beautiful remedy to everything we've endured. This is where it happened, where I fell in love with the love of my life. And it's here, *now*, as we etch an *L* and *T* inside a love-heart into the aged, burgundy-colored metal bench with my car keys, where I finally feel like I'm home with her in this city.

This is healing.

This is us healing, under the very twinkling stars and glinting moon I once promised we'd escape to...*and now, we are.*

Our love will forever be engraved on this bench in a love-hearted reminder.

Back inside my car, I stupidly smile at Central Park, until it fades in my circular side mirror.

London's frowning when I turn to her, softly rolling a red,

strawberry field candy in her mouth. "I feel like you're sacrificing more than I am by leaving and it makes me feel bad."

Adamantly shaking my head, I smooth my lips over her knuckles. "LonLon, you've sacrificed *your life* to keep breathing after your father's abuse, so don't for one second think that. Levi and my mother will always be here. There's nowhere else I want to be than with you."

"Forever?"

My grin reaches my eyes. "Forever and a day, Shortcake."

London's sweet strawberry candy taste explodes in my mouth when I sensually kiss her at the next red light, her moans melting in my mouth. Our tongues growing wild as she transfers the heart-shaped candy to my mouth. It's tastes like heaven, an allusive kiss personally made for us.

Oh fuck, yes.

I suck on it slow as she cages it between her teeth, feeling my lips bruise when we continue kissing with the candy rolling between our tongues. Passion intoxicates us, diminishing her worries.

I hit the accelerator with the strawberry field in my mouth, rolling it around like my very own sugary dream. London sexily pops another in her mouth, smirking at me while I zoom through Manhattan at eleven o'clock at night, back-lit billboards, shiny skyscrapers, and glowing office windows lighting up the city.

At one point, London unbuckles herself and somewhat leans out her window, flashing me the lilac lace of her panties beneath her white tennis skirt as her silky honey blonde waves angelically flutter through the rapid wind. She knows *exactly* what she's doing to me.

I take in her movements, Red Hot Chili Pepper's *"Can't Stop"* rushing through the radio. My cock hardens just from watching her. I'm going to have my Mustang flown into Washington State, so this being my final memory of our last night in this car in Manhattan means *everything* to me.

It's heavenly, the way her baby blues pool in such desire when she slithers back to her seat, unspoken words filling in the adoration provoking me. London seems happy, so fucking happy. It's three seconds before I roll into a parking spot on a dark street, isolated by overhanging trees.

London's lips pepper my throat, moaning against me as she undoes my belt, pops the buttons on my jeans, and recklessly pulls down my boxer briefs. My breaths scatter the moment she pulls out my aching, hard cock. She slowly wets her lips, those darkening eyes on me, when she fists my base, my fingers spearing through her sun-kissed hair.

"I know you want this, baby girl," I pant, feeding into desire. "Make me come."

London purrs against my mouth, the heart-shaped candy still in her mouth as she seductively rolls it across my crown, continuously swirling her tongue around me as I moan out her name.

Fuccck.

She lavishes my cock with her heated touch, French-kissing down to my base, before pumping solid strokes against my shaft. She's here, *right here*, licking up my leaking pre-cum with that fucking strawberry candy gliding against my cock, taunting me in its transferring pinkness.

The candy melts against my cock and I push back in my seat, giving her more headroom.

This woman's gonna be the death of me.

"You taste like strawberries," she hums, vibrating around me as she sucks on my pulsing crown, slurping and circling me until I can't help but nudge her head lower. My baby takes me good, taking my length so deep, I hit the back of her throat and I groan as she stays there for a while before bobbing her head up and down, sucking me hard, like the good little girl she is.

She works me so fast, her tongue reckless in her pursuit to drive me wild. Heat licks my spine, making me stop checking around for pedestrians and return my gaze to her, watching as those gorgeous baby blue eyes find mine, her ass up in the air. In the moonlight, a smile curving on her lips around my cock.

"You look so pretty there, smiling around my cock like that, LonLon." I begin to rock my hips against her hot mouth, having her gag a few times because of my reckless intensity. "Relax that throat, baby girl, a little more and I'll let you ride my cock right here in this Mustang."

London's eyes light up, taking me slower this time, her hand back to jerking my base, hard and rough, just how I like it. I'm panting, thrusting myself deeper in her mouth, desire ruining me.

Needing more, I slither my free hand down her spine and unclip her tennis skirt, smirking devilishly as it slips to the car floor. My fingers frantically squeeze her peachy ass before blindly stroking my fingers over her lace panties, right by her sex, feeling just how drenched she is.

London moans against my cock as I flicker her swollen clit before rubbing it slow.

She's so fucking ready for me.

My cock pulses in her mouth, greedily, all while my body is coated in the need of feeling her again. It's why I selfishly pull her off my cock, and London does the rest. Catching her breath, she straddles my waist and pushes the scrap of her lace panties to the side, sexily waiting for me.

Her pebbled nipples brush against my shirt, stabbing through her tight white camisole.

"Ride my cock, LonLon," I whisper in her ear as I slip inside her warm, dripping sex.

Our moans merge together, our very own oasis, as I let London ride my cock for a little while, her eager hips restlessly rocking in circles. She screams in my arms, squirming in pleasure, and she tips her head back, her blonde waves sprawling over the wheel as she fucks me faster.

We're in such close proximity, that rippling sex of hers squeezing around my cock rhythmically, virtually jerking me with every thrust. Her lips find mine, stealing searing kisses.

Fuck. Fuck. Fuck.

That's when I take over, fucking her so hard and deep that our skin viciously slaps together. My abdominal muscles tense as I pound into her, our sex on fucking fire with how it ruins us.

My groans rumble through our kiss and I love the way she wraps an arm around my shoulders, the other hand slamming against my foggy window, groaning and gasping against my lips, her hot breath taunting me. That strawberry taste on her tongue as I swirl it with mine has me moaning against her again, tasting my salty pre-cum on her tongue.

London sinfully grins against me, her throat straining with every fast pump, her ample tits shaking against my chest, making it obvious that she isn't wearing a bra. I get lost in her. In our erotic sounds, in our perspiring sweat, in the way we're illegally having sex in public, making my Mustang shake.

"Oh God, Tate!"

Our faces press together, her face nuzzling into my chest the harder we go.

When she pulls back, I see that her glittery pink eyeshadow has exploded, causing glitter to coat her face, sparkling in the moonlight like a fucking dream I seductively devour.

"I'm gonna come inside you so deeply, London, give you a baby made of nothing but love."

"Oh, Tate, *yes*," she whimpers. "I want it. I want it so badly with you."

London's legs tremble around me and she sexily thrashes against me, biting down on my shoulder as she explodes. I feel her clench around me, gushing against my cock in ways that make me dizzy.

Her orgasm slides down my base, pooling by my spread thighs, having my cock glide in and out of her even smoother.

Godddd, London.

Growling, I fuck her even harder, this time, my thumb strumming her clit in a ruthless pattern that has her throwing her head back, her thighs squeezing my obliques. Still on a high from her first orgasm, London comes again in loud pants and whimpers, her pussy lost in tremors, prolonging her climax, and sparking my own.

I spill inside her with a groan against her parted, heart-shaped lips, my orgasm shooting through her warmth, hard and deep, so good it has her eyes rolling back with a sexy, sated smile.

London slumps against me, our sweaty half-naked bodies tangled together and in a complete state of nirvana. I can't stop caressing her warm skin, smiling.

One more sleep, and we'll be living the first day of the rest of our lives...*together*.

"I love you," I say softly. "I love you to the moon and back, Shortcake, and nobody will take that away from us. Not even the heavens. I'll die in every lifetime, just to find you again."

Chapter
FORTY-FOUR

London

My jaw drops the moment the Uber slows down in front of an absolutely stunning duplex in the middle of Pioneer Square, Seattle, my eyes savoring the home before turning to him.

Tate Meadows sits still beside me on the jet-black leather seat, doing a shit job at keeping the goofy, boyish smile from his lips.

"Tatum Lee, what did you do?" I gasp.

"I don't know what you're talking about…"

My heart warms as I turn back to the duplex, drinking in its striking brick features: steel-framed windows and cute little flowerpots alongside the upstairs Juliet balcony.

"Do you like it, baby?" Tate whispers in my ear, the hot rasp emitting shivers down my spine.

The good kind.

"I don't like it, I love it."

"Good. Because it's ours."

My gasp is so loud that the driver scolds my way, but I don't care, I'm too ecstatic, squealing as I hold onto Tate tightly. "Are you serious? This place is ours? But how? Don't leases take forever?"

"It isn't a lease. I bought it for us. It's ours, babygirl, for however long we want it."

Oh my gosh.

Tears swell in my eyes because for the first time ever, life has given me something worth cherishing forever—him.

"Wow! That's so sweet of you, Tate. Whoa…How much was it? Would you like me to pay for half of it? I've got some money saved up from *Enticed* and could always use that to go toward our place, or the furniture, or—"

"LonLon," Tate darkly smirks at me, "I got us, okay? So just shut up."

Giggling, I bite my lip, knowing just how annoying I must be. "You're right. I'm sorry."

We literally just arrived in Seattle. Our six-hour flight from JFK to SeaTac was so therapeutic for me that, at one point, I had to pinch myself to ensure I was still alive. I adore this Seattle neighborhood. Pioneer Square, it's right in the heart of Seattle, filled with vintage stores, pretty tree-lined streets, and quirky boutiques.

The duplex is even more stunning inside, a gorgeous two-bedroom with a spacious living room and the coolest mid-century kitchen I've ever seen. I love the entire feel of this house, how it's bright with natural earthy tones like the cream backsplash and beige bamboo floorboards.

I love that there's no fucking marble. I love that it's so different from our old life in Manhattan, because this is our new life, *mine* with *him*. And I'm going to adore it with everything I have.

It's unfurnished, aside from something wrapped in pink wrapping paper on top of the oak kitchen countertop.

"What's this?" I muse, tracing my finger over the edges of what seems to be a box.

Tate smolders, stepping away from sorting out our scattered suitcases by the front door to stride my way, all sexy and shit. "I don't know, what could it be…?"

I arch an impressed brow. "Did you…get this shipped from Manhattan ahead of time?"

"Half right." He clicks his tongue, playfully pulling me to him by the belt loops of my jeans. "Got it shipped ahead from LA."

"LA?"

"Mmhmmm."

"Oh my God, Tate! What is it? What is it?"

Tate's warm chuckle echoes through me as he nuzzles his face into my neck, peppering slow, sexy kisses down it. "Can't we baptize every room first, kitten?"

"Nope."

"Why?"

"Because I want to know what's inside!"

"Fineee," he groans, hotly cupping my sex through my jeans, "but tonight, you're mine."

"You're such a horny bastard."

Tate narrows his gaze, his look a famished wolf starving for his prey. "*Ahem*?"

I flash him a toothy grin. "I said you're *my* horny bastard."

"That's better, Shortcake."

Laughing, I dig into unwrapping the gift, excitement building in my bones.

Tate fondly smiles at me, leaning against the countertop with his head cutely propped on his hands.

I sort through the envelope on top of the wrapped gift first, sparks sizzling inside me at the adorable card with a vintage red moving truck and the words, ***To building our lives together!*** imprinted on the top in cursive, and then a little lower and smaller in brackets, ***and sex, a lot of it***.

I pointedly smirk over at Tate.

He smirks right back at me. "Open it."

I do, and *gosh*, his words are everything…

LonLon,

At this point, we're in Seattle. You're reading this card while I'm probably staring at you like a creep (I'm sorry, it's just I'm in love with everything that you are and don't want to spend a second without you) but we did it. We fucking did it. We moved in together!!!! And I can proudly say, wholeheartedly, that it's the best decision we've ever made.

I can't wait to wake up to you every morning. For you to get angry at me when I accidentally buy the wrong milk. To wash the dishes, while you dry them. It's the mundane things, babygirl, that make my heart skip. What kind of furniture will we buy? Will you establish a favorite room? Will I ever remember to empty the vacuum cleaner? I don't fucking know, but I look forward to finding out, with you.

I look forward to doing everything on this earth with you.

So thank you, for trusting me this deep. You know I'll never take advantage of that. Ever, darling. It's you and I till the end, till we reach the moon, and then, all over again.

I hope you like your housewarming gift from yours truly.

Love you to the moon and back,
Forever your Tatum x

I'm left bawling like a damn baby at his heartfelt letter.

"Wow, that was so beautiful, babe. I feel the exact same way." I sniffle, kissing his stubbled cheek. "By the way, it's almond milk, but not the unsweetened one 'cause I hate it, okay?"

Tate chuckles through the emotion surrounding us. "Sweetened almond milk, got it."

The moment I unwrap the gift and open the plain cardboard box, I gasp… No.

No.

No.

YES!

A vintage bubblegum-pink record player stares right back at me.

Tate bought me a record player.

Just like the one I always wanted.

"OH MY GOD, TATE! THANK YOU! I FREAKING LOVE YOU!"

Tate can't stop laughing when I bounce up and down, my eyes probably stars as he sets it up, all while I run to my luggage and snatch the one vinyl record I've been dying to hear ever since he bought it for me.

Pink Floyd's *The Dark Side of The Moon*.

Once again, I'm crying my eyes out like a damn romantic fool as we beautifully slow dance in the kitchen to the crisp sound of our favorite band. We dance around like crazy, swaying our hips, twisting, and giggling. We're hopeless romantics, tenderly dancing around in our new kitchen with only a few items to our name, and yet, I'm the safest I've ever felt because I have him.

And when I glance up at my very own knight in shining armor, mid-slow-dancing, I whisper twelve words that have him becoming that damn romantic fool this time...

"I look forward to doing everything on this earth with you too."

"Yeah?"

"Mmhmmm." I hum.

"*Everything?*"

"*Everything.*"

Eyes still on me, Tate slowly pulls something from his pocket and waves it around.

It's a pink velvet jewelry box, anxious streaks of permanent strokes brushing over the soft fabric.

My heart slows. "Tate...?"

"Don't worry," he smirks, "I'm not proposing."

Tate ends my curiosity when he opens the small jewelry box, revealing a sparkling gold necklace with *LonLon* written in the prettiest cursive. "That New Year's Eve, when you didn't show because of your father, I sat on that bench for ages with this gripped in my hands. That year, on our fifteenth birthday, I wanted to make you mine. I was going to give you this, kiss you and probably do something corny like ask you to be my girlfriend, but that never happened. So, this is yours, London, three years overdue, but the sentiment remains, *well*, it's stronger than ever."

It feels like a breath of new air when Tate puts the personalized necklace on me and I dust my fingers over the expensive gold, glancing down at it in awe.

"*LonLon*," I murmur to myself with a smile. "It's so beautiful, thank y—"

Thump.

My heart kicks into overdrive as the kitchen slants, stopping my words as I grip the countertop for support. Something drills inside my mind, unsteadying my grip, and it's only when Tate holds onto me with panic in his blue eyes that I realize it's not the world spinning, *it's me.*

His words blur as my vision fizzles out of focus. Again and again and again.

I go to speak, but I can't. Everything feels distorted. Pink Floyd fades in exchange for Tate's anxious hollers, asking me if I'm okay, but I can't feel his touch.

No, I…I can't feel anything at all.

A numbness I've never felt before overtakes me, restraining me until it all just fades…

Out of focus.

Out of this world.

Into the darkness.

A vicious bright light blinds me, pulling me back to life.

What is going on?

My gaze focuses on the dark eyes staring down at me, an older woman draped in a white coat and a silver stethoscope around her neck.

A doctor.

A doctor?

A doctor flashing a bright light in my eyes, which she dims once she sees I've come to.

But before she can say anything…

"Baby girl," Tate murmurs, appearing beside me and framing my face with his big hands. "Oh, thank god, you're okay. You scared the shit out of me."

"What…What happened?" I whisper, my voice drier than usual for some reason.

"You fainted in my arms, London."

It all comes back to me, shaking me to the core.

Tate inches closer to the hospital bed, gently resting his forehead against mine.

"I prayed to so many fucking gods, you have no idea, LonLon." His sad eyes find mine, all hallow and red, like he's been crying. "I don't know what I'd do without you."

Awww.

I smile. "You can't get rid of me that easy."

"Yeah, thank fuck."

The doctor clears her throat, snapping our attention to her on my right side. "Hello there, London, I'm Dr. Stanwyck, how are you feeling?"

"I feel…okay. A little confused."

"Oh, well that's perfectly normal. With Tate's consent, I've taken a few tests and observations, and I'm here to tell you everything's come back beyond satisfactory."

Satisfactory.

I'm *okay.*

Tate's brows narrow. "If everything's satisfactory, then why did she faint, Dr.?"

"Again." Dr. Stanwyck smiles. "Perfectly normal."

Why does she keep on saying that?

Tate and I turn to each other, perplexed.

Dr. Stanwyck glances between us, like we're supposed to know something, but we don't.

"I, uh…" I clear my throat, thanking Tate when he hands me some water. "Sorry, I don't think we understand what you're alluding to, Dr. Stanwyck?"

Her face falls. "*Oh.* You don't?"

I shake my head.

"Your bloodwork returned and it's apparent to me that…"

"Yes?"

"Well, London, you're pregnant."

My heartbeat flutters.

Pregnant.

"Congratulations to you both!" Dr. Stanwyck again smiles at us, and then walks out.

I'm pregnant. It wasn't a false positive after all...

Tears blur my vision, happy tears, which only intensify when Tate's eyes widen, speckled in adoration. He slides on the bed, embracing me like I'm the only tangible thing in this life.

"Sweetheart," he breathes, "we're going to have a baby."

"Our missing piece."

"Our forever piece." Tate's hands gently stretches over my flat stomach. "*Wow.*"

The thrill inside me doesn't let go as I fan my fingers over Tate's hand, until those Atlantic blue eyes I'll always love pin mine.

"Do you remember what I told you that night?" he asks.

"Yes," I murmur, all flustered by his warm caresses. "You said you were going to give me the entire world. Said you hoped our baby had my heart, my beauty, grace, and soul. You said they'll always love us because we'll always put them first. You said you were going to love me for the rest of your life, that you'd be the luckiest man if, someday, I was your wife."

"I meant every word. I'll love you and baby Holloway forever." He gulps down thickly, and with a nervous breath and a raspy voice, he utters words that'll forever change my life. "Marry me, LonLon?"

Oh my God. My eyes widen.

Tate mistakes it as panic. "I know, I'm sorry I don't have the ring but th—"

"YES!" I squeal, playfully shoving his chest with a reassuring grin. "I'll marry you!"

Our slow kiss tangles with emotion, a reminder of all we've become, that we're healing together.

"I have the perfect name if it's a girl...*Luna.*" My voice breaks, even more tears spilling because I can't believe this is my life, with him—so happy and free. "It means *moon* in Italian."

"*Luna* Holloway..." Tate grins. "I like it."

"Luna *Elizabeth* Holloway."

"I love it more." His glassy eyes warm. "Did we reach the moon, babygirl?"

"We flew beyond the moon, my darling, to our very own planet. Forever ours."

Tate Meadows kisses me again, this time even longer, and I know we'll make it.

I love him and all our kisses in heartache, because they led us two-thousand-four-hundred miles away to a new city, a new life, and by next spring, a new bloom to our unconditional love.

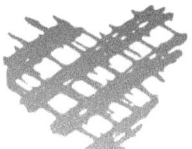  

Epilogue

London

Five Years later...
JUNE.
Tate and London are 23.

Luna Elizabeth Holloway flashes me a mischievous smirk, her adorable dimples sinking in, the spitting image of her father's.

"Luna," I warn, biting my tongue to hide my smile. "That's not a very nice thing to call your brother."

"But Mommy, Mommy! He really looks like a flamingo!"

I softly cup her little chin, grinning as I gaze into her wondrous electric blue eyes. "*You* look like a flamingo, Little Miss Pink."

It's safe to say my four-year-old daughter is the perfect combination of Tate and me. She's beautiful, cheeky, and compassionate, just like her daddy, and is obsessed with pink, like me. Her honeyed blonde waves are pulled back in a French braid that I literally redid twenty minutes ago, but with all of the summersaults and dancing around to Pink Floyd, strands messily hang out.

Luna bursts into a fit of giggles. "Yeah, but I am a *cool* flamingo!" She points to her newborn brother's rosy cheeks, happily cradled in my arms, and playfully rolls her eyes. "All he do is drink Mommy milk!"

"He's a little boy and has to grow up to be just as tall as Daddy, my dear."

That makes my tutu-loving daughter gasp. "*This flamingo* is gonna be tall like Daddy?"

"That's right, beautiful."

"WOWWWWW!"

Luna's girlish squeal has Maxwell stirring awake in my arms, aggravating him as he wriggles around and screams, having me softly rock him against my hip.

"Oh, my sweet boy," I murmur with a smile, brushing my lips against his smooth forehead, loving his baby smell. "It's okay, you're okay, your sister just got very excited, that's all."

His screams don't fade until I unbutton my sundress, his little mouth sucking my nipple.

Luna flashes me a toothy smile. "Ooops."

Exactly.

Like.

Her.

Daddy.

A lot has changed in the past five years.

For one, Tate and I co-founded our very own record label, after graduating college right here in Seattle. We named it *Silver Moon Records*, with the intention of signing indie bands. It's going so well. Working together is a brand-new step in our relationship, but I wouldn't want it any other way. Being our own bosses is a dream.

We've already signed a few alternative rock bands who have placed their trust in us, and the future of *Silver Moon Records* truly is looking bright. Even though I'm technically still on maternity leave, I always find a way to appear in our 6th Ave modern office, an eight-minute drive.

As for my mother and Victor, they're happily married with an adorable baby boy in the South of France. She truly is trying, making an effort to be a part of my life with regular calls and visits, and while the tension of our past still hasn't healed all our wounds, I'm open to these baby steps.

Tate hasn't spoken to his father, Mirko, since the night they fought. I had stumbled across a few articles that outlined Mirko Meadow's brutal divorce with Sabrina, his spiraling alcoholism, and then the rapid downfall of his real estate company, coming under fire for their crooked business. His company was declared bankrupt five years ago, while Héroux Real Estate was taken over by another Manhattan hot-shot and renamed, ending the twenty-year feud between the rivaling firms.

Then, there's Tate's mother, our sweet Elizabeth. We lost her last year; it's been one of the hardest pills to swallow. Even as our business bloomed and our family grew, our visits to her in Rochester, New York, increased as well. The last time we saw her, she was happy, smiling, playing with Luna who couldn't stop dancing around. While she didn't know who we were, or that Luna was her very own grandchild, seeing them together tugged at my heartstrings.

Elizabeth had severely declined in the past few years, to the point where she didn't speak anymore, nor play the piano, and painting became too taxing on her aging bones, but we still spent time with her, happily, because she was the crux of our little family.

Losing Tate's mother couldn't have come at a worse time because two days later, I found out I was pregnant with Maxwell, and I didn't want that to take away from his grief journey. I wanted this to be about Tate, not us, but when I finally told him the news, hope bloomed in his solemn eyes, reviving him.

Every day I wake up and thank God that I'm alive, that I didn't plummet to my death in that Central Park lake, because then, I wouldn't have ever been able to see all of the beauty Tate and I created from the tragedies.

Tatum Lee Holloway (*yes, we made that official name change*) is my everything.

He's my home.

My savior.

Mine.

The moment the front door unlocks, and that familiar metal clang of keys hits the entryway table, life floods my lungs.

Tate is home.

My husband rounds the corner in the most irresistible navy tailored suit that has me salivating. He's a handsome stud with those sparkling blue eyes, dark stubbled jaw, and the sexy crow's feet at the corners of his eyes, telling of all the days and night drowned in laughter and smiles.

Tate's eyes hold mine, as he rounds the corner, his slow, sexy smolder inciting butterflies inside me.

I feel my cheeks heat.

Yes, heat.

It doesn't matter how long I've known this man; he still gives me butterflies.

"DADDYYYYY!" Luna cheerfully rushes up to him, executing their usual routine as Tate lifts her up into his strong arms and plants kisses all over her face. "DADDY, I WOVE YA!"

"I love you more, my sweet girl. Were you a good girl for Mommy today?"

"Oh yeah! And I've GOT A NEW FLAMINGO SONG. WANNA HEAR IT?"

Before Tate can respond, Luna begins singing while bouncing in her father's arms, the happiest little girl in the entire world.

"MY BROTHER'S A FLAMINGO*OOOO*, HE'S PINK AND REALLY CUTE. BUT HE GOT NO BEAK, SO INSTEAD HE EATS ALL OF MOMMY'S MILK*KKK*!"

At those lyrics, my husband's darkened gaze meets mine and his smolder deepens.

"Hiiii, Mommy," he sexily mouths.

Feeling hot all over, I grin and softly bite my lower lip.

"MY BROTHER'S A FLAMINGO*OOO*! AND HE LIVES INSIDE A ZOO! ALL THE OTHER BIRDS JUST FLY AWAY, 'CAUSE THEY WANNA STEAL HIS SHOES." Luna keeps going, so high-pitched and off-key, but it's the most adorable thing, seeing her confidence shine. "MY BROTHER'S A FLAMINGO*OOOO*, HE GOT BLOND WAVY HAIR, WHEN MY DADDY GOES TO WORK, I EAT CANDY AND SAY IT WAS MY BROTHER THE FLAMINGO*OOO*! *YEAH*!"

We erupt in applause with Tate even whistling, prompting Luna to cutely curtsey as we continue to chant: "*Go Luna! Go Luna! Go Luna!*"

She can't stop bouncing up and down. "Again? Again?"

Tate can't help but cave for his little girl. "Okay, but can I kiss Mommy hello first?"

"Fineeeeee."

Tate attends to Maxwell first, gently kissing his forehead and dramatically fist-pumping him. His fascinated gaze roams to my nipple our son is happily feeding from. "Lucky little boy."

His fingers spear over the back of my head, fisting my blonde waves. "Fuck, baby, I missed you."

"DADDY YOU SAID A BAD WORD. I JUST GOT A DOLLARRR!"

Tate glances back at her, that gorgeous lopsided smirk piercing through the stubble. "Now, now, Luna, what did Daddy tell you about eavesdropping?"

"Eaves...*what*?"

He playfully rolls his eyes. "Never mind."

Mimicking him, she rolls hers too. "Whatever."

"You're making her a little troublemaker, Mister." I smirk at him, pecking his lips again.

The deep rumble in his voice emits all his love for our family. "Says you, Shortcake."

Within seconds, Tate's right by our daughter's side again, prepared for a repeat of the performance of her life.

This time, we all join in on the catchy song as they goofily dance around the living room, cheerfully.

Seeing them together swells my throat.

I'm so happy Luna loves her daddy.

I'm so happy Luna will never endure what I did.

I'm so happy it ends with me and begins with Tate.

At one point, Tate takes my hand, and I do my best to salsa around them while still breastfeeding. We don't stop until we're all sweaty, panting messes, heads tipped back in laughter.

And, gosh, I'm so grateful for it.

For everything Tatum promised me.

Because now, *this* will forever be our lives.

Desperate to know more about hot rockstar, Elijah Diesel and Rosalia?

Read on for the first Chapter
of Vanessa Luisa's emotional, angsty age gap and enemies-to-lovers, steamy rockstar romance, *Remember I'm Yours* and *Diesel Rose*.

Remember I'm Yours is the prequel novella to the standalone novel, *Diesel Rose.*

* Available to buy now on Amazon & FREE in KINDLE UNLIMITED!

DIESEL ROSE: AN ENEMIES-TO-LOVERS ROCKSTAR
ROMANCE STANDALONE

**Rosalia Philips isn't only the muse laced into every lyric I write.
She's my cure.**
The reason I'm still breathing.

Four years ago, I let her go. Now, I'd do anything to make her mine.
One night, while my famed alternative rock band is on a world-
wide tour, our fate collides, and I become addicted to her.

I told her I'd ruin her life. That I wanted nothing to do with her. *I
lied.*

I'm the poetically tragic rock star.
She's the beautifully broken ballerina.
Together, we're the cruelest of enemies…and the messiest lovers.

Our attraction is chaotic like nineteenth-century Brontë.
Unpredictable like a psychopath's lullaby.
Diabolic like the Joker and his queen.

And yet, we won't stop till we unravel what we crave most…to be
loved.
Whatever that freaking means.

But just like every addiction, her love could be the very thing that
kills me…
And these are the reasons why…

**NOTE: This full-length book is a standalone and INCLUDES the
prequel, Remember I'm Yours.**

Chapter
ONE

Rosalia

I think I have a boy crush. Okay, let me rephrase that, I *do* have a boy crush.

One of my favorite things to do at a quarter to midnight whenever I can't sleep is scrapbook. My mom is a hairdresser downtown and always brings home old magazines clients flick through so I can cut out whatever I like. At first, it gave me the heebie-jeebies touching magazines a dozen other women (and possibly men too) had touched, but now I guess I'm over it.

Tonight was supposed to be like any other night. Flip through the magazines, cut out aesthetically pleasing vintage pieces with my pink diamanté scissors, and slap them in my scrapbook. Except, tonight *isn't* like any other night, it's different, because my mom didn't only bring home old editions of *Vogue* and *Harper's Bazaar* in a white plastic bag that's laced with holes. There's also something else.

Rolling Stone magazine.

And the good thing is, it's the latest edition.

May.

She's never brought a *Rolling Stone* magazine home for me before, and I wonder if she accidentally got it from the barber section at her work. I wasn't going to look through it, but I did, and *God*, how grateful I am that I did.

It's the first page I randomly opened on.

Page twelve.

And I haven't dared look away since.

Dark-gray eyes, the lightest shade of onyx stare back at me. They're the kind of eyes that are so cold, they should scare you. Instead, they have a sense of sugary thrill flooding my body. They're devilish. Wolfish. Everything my parents warned me about. *And everything I crave.*

My heart skips a beat because he's the most beautiful man I've seen, in a dark and edgy kind of way. A deadly piercing gaze. Perfectly high cheekbones. Thin full lips that remind me of James Dean's.

Everything about the black-and-white picture of this man leaning against a barbed-wire fence intrigues me. His punk-inspired leather jacket with silvery spikes around his shoulders and safety pins by the edges. The destroyed white tee underneath. His distressed black jeans. Those unlaced black Doc Martens with a single white broken love heart on the side of the left one, almost as if it's been stitched.

It feels like there's a story behind those white Band-Aids wrapped around some of his fingers that he has looped above his head in the wire. I'm fascinated by the ink on his hands, the ones more visible like the skull, serpent, and roman numerals, and I instantly wonder if he has more.

Why is he making my heart go so funny?

I like the way he's looking at the camera with furrowed brows, a mixture between broody and motionless, making it seem like he just doesn't give a damn. Like life has done a number on him.

I stare a little too long at the thin black eyeliner around his eyes. I always thought eyeliner was for girls, but seeing it on him, I know I've been wrong… *wow, it's really hot.*

I brush the pad of my finger over his face, almost intimidated at first, as I wonder if his eyes are really that dark or are instead a dark cocoa brown. Maybe it's just the dark ink of the page tricking me? Maybe.

Beneath his photo, a white cursive font reads:

The true hatesick up-and-coming sinner of Manhattan; Elijah Diesel.

Elijah.

"Elijah," I murmur to myself, wanting to get used to the name on my tongue. "Elijah Diesel."

He seems a few years older than me, okay, *a lot* older. Ten years my senior at the least, and although I so desperately want to read all of the little text surrounding the picture, I kind of want to make my own impression of the guy.

After chewing my bottom lip for the longest time, I cut out his picture, being careful to make it perfect, and stick it on a new page in my scrapbook.

Elijah Diesel

I write in permanent marker as a title on the page, and then I draw four little black hearts.

A little lower down, toward the bottom of my page, I write all my feelings out with my heart beating a million miles per second.

Right now I'm looking at you for the first time, and I think I'm going to get addicted to you. I want to know everything about you, Elijah. Or should I call you Diesel?

Butterflies take over my stomach and I can't help just how deeply my cheeks burn. I roll over on my bed to my back and cover my mouth, softening my giddy giggles while New York's silvery moonlight merges with my warm yellow wall sconces.

"Stop being so foolish, Rosalia Philips," I whisper to myself. "He's just some hot rocker."

But I know he's much more than that.

He's the first person who's managed to make me crack a smile through my midnight blues.

The first man who makes me feel a funny type of way just staring at his picture.

The only one I think I'll get lost in forever, until he's staring right back at me.

Whoa.

I settle down and stare up at my ceiling, a seventeen-year-old girl trying to rebel from the world as she knows it, second by second.

Who are you, Elijah Diesel?

Exactly where can I find you?

And why does my heart beat so crazy for you?

It's been a month, and my mom hasn't brought home the next edition of *Rolling Stone* magazine for me.

I tried buying the latest edition before school this morning, but the damn newsagent had just sold out. I knew a couple more in the area, but I would have been late for the last day of eleventh grade before summer, so I promised myself I'd check out the other newsstands after school.

The anticipation has been killing me all day because as much as I know I can just search up Elijah Diesel on my phone, there's so much more thrill in turning a page and seeing him instead.

It's just after three o'clock when I step into the convenience store by my school.

The older guy behind the counter takes one look at my wavy blonde hair, my cropped white shirt, and pink-and-white plaid skirt and scoffs, "Kids these days."

With a clenched jaw, I ball my fists but continue walking to the section of the store I know all the hotshot magazines are, no matter how deeply the man's words hurt me.

I'm not even the worst of my generation. I swear, I'm not. First, I don't relate to my generation. At all. Second, I've never had a sip of alcohol. Never smoked. Done drugs in the bathroom. Hell, I've never even kissed a guy in my entire life.

I'm just a seventeen-year-old virgin who loves short plaid skirts and knee-high socks. I'm not hurting anybody, so to hell with this guy.

Why don't you fix your flickering lightbulbs, popcorn ceiling, and grossly stained carpet instead, dude?

I almost do a happy dance on the spot when the new edition of *Rolling Stone* stares back at me. It's the last one left. I grin and snatch it from the stand at record speed, then I actually start bouncing.

Yes. Yes. Yes.

Just as I begin flipping through it, wanting to see if I can see a glimpse of Elijah Diesel before I buy it, the man behind the counter clears his throat.

My breath slows and I don't like the glare he shoots my way. "Aye, blondie, this isn't a library. You want to read the magazine, you buy it and you get the hell out of my store."

Rude.

Narrowing my eyes, I slap a twenty-dollar bill on the counter and practically run out of the store, not caring about the change. My mom would kill me if she knew, but once won't make a difference, *right*?

Rushing down the street, I wait until I'm on the next block before I come to a slow by my bus stop. Even though I live in Brooklyn, I go to school in Manhattan. Don't ask me why, but my father—one of the most respected neurosurgeons in the city—wanted it that way. And that way it is.

Leaning against the bus shelter, I couldn't be more ecstatic as I slip my schoolbag between my feet and carefully turn each page of the magazine. New York's slightly warm breeze kisses my skin and blows my waves, giving me hope of a beautiful summer approaching.

But that hope slowly shrivels up when I go through the entire magazine, never seeing a photo of Elijah Diesel once.

My heart drops.

No.

No. No. No.

He has to be in here. *He's got to!*

I go over the magazine a second time, then a third, and by the fourth time I'm groaning. I seriously feel like slamming it right in the trash can, so devastated that I waited an entire month for nothing.

"It can't be." I sigh, shutting my eyes just as the bus pulls up. "How can he not be in it?"

It's just my luck. Something like this was bound to happen to me.

I just wasted twenty dollars. That idiot back in the store will probably wipe his mouth with it after devouring a greasy cheeseburger.

Ickkk.

For me, it isn't just false hope, it's giving in to the fantasy of Elijah Diesel slipping away from my very fingers. I so desperately craved another photo of him to put in my scrapbook. One I can stare at whenever I don't feel all right, just like I did for the past month, but now I feel like a fool for doing so.

You're the foolest of fools, Philips.

And yes, I'm hyperaware 'foolest' isn't even a word, but let's just pretend it is.

I flicker my eyes open, ready to take the bus all the way home with my head hung low, when something stops me. I don't know why, but my breath halts in my throat at the dark Doc Martens somebody stepping off the bus is wearing. I haven't glanced up yet, but those shoes look awfully familiar.

Doc Martens…

Unlaced…

A stitched white broken love heart on the side of the left one…

I swear I've seen them before but where?

Where? Where? Where?

And when it finally hits me, I internally gasp.

The picture! They were in that picture last month.

Wait, that would mean… No, no, it couldn't be. It can't.

As my gaze flickers higher, at the person descending the bus right in front of me, I slow by their studded leather jacket. And the moment those familiar melancholic onyx eyes bore into mine, I forget how to breathe.

Holy sweet Jesus, it's him.

Him.

Elijah Diesel.

And he's even more beautiful in person.

My mouth gets all dry and my hands become so sweaty holding *Rolling Stone* magazine that it slips from my grip. I cringe as it slides across the sidewalk like it's on skates. And I don't know if the timing could be any worse, but just as it slows, Elijah unintentionally stomps his feet right on the magazine.

Oops.

Almost on instinct, he picks up the magazine, stares at the cover, and then his eyes slowly flicker to the gap of sidewalk between us until they meet my pink platform sneakers.

Ever so slowly, his gaze rakes up my body with a sexily clenched jaw, and I'm happy to confirm his eyes are really that dark. It feels like a lifetime passes the way he's checking out my long, lean legs, my short skirt, and cropped white shirt with little floral-patterned peaches, some midriff exposed.

He stays there for a little while, and the longer his hot stare lingers, the more my chest heaves. My breaths are rushed and all frantic-like. I feel my nipples harden in arousal, stabbing through my lacy bra and outlining my shirt.

He does this to me.

He does this *all* to me.

And when those dreamy dark onyx eyes finally meet my face, my knees buckle.

The bus moves off behind him with a hiss, and it feels like we're in a slow-motion movie with the way his dark hair softly blows in the wind, the ends so wavy.

Arching a brow, Elijah gestures toward the magazine he's holding. "I think you dropped something, *Peaches*," he calls out to me, and *dear God*, his voice…

It's the perfect combination of a sexy raspiness and a murmur, as if he can disguise himself in them both, ready to pounce at any minute now.

Striding up to me, he extends the magazine out to me. Our fingers brush when I take it from him, and sizzling electricity shoots down my arm.

Gosh, this guy is a dream.

It feels so weird seeing Elijah up close after spending the past month looking at his picture all alone in my bedroom. *This is so much better.* I can't get over his musky, sandalwood scent with a hint of tobacco. It's a scent I've never smelled so up close before, and instantly I wish I could smell it forever.

Wow. He's so tall and I'm even wearing platform sneakers. He's easily six-two, six-three.

Wait a minute, did he just call me "Peaches?"

I nervously smile, an obvious blush crawling up my cheeks. "Umm, thank you."

Elijah nods, his broody gaze flickering between my eyes and my plump lips, which I can't help but softly bite.

He stares for a second longer, and just as his hot breath hits my lip, he steps back and begins walking away with such a swagger that his leather jacket sways from side to side.

Despite my fingers continuing to fizzle, a hollowness takes over my body and I don't know why. This was it, my chance to tell him whatever, and I just blew it. *Ugh!*

Chewing my lower lip, I watch as Elijah keeps on walking in the opposite direction of the convenience store. He must have lit up a cigarette in the seconds he walked away because now clouds of thick white smoke lace the air around him every so often.

He smokes.

Mama always tells me how bad smoking is. That neither me nor my older sister, Maya, should ever touch a cigarette. For the past years, I've believed her, thought it was such a dirty thing, but knowing *he* smokes changes everything.

He doesn't make it seem dirty as he looks both ways before jogging across the street, Elijah Diesel makes smoking look like it's heaven's cure to all the chaos here on earth. And perhaps it's that reason alone, (or the fact that I'm still astonished that he was right in front of me), but I do the unexpected.

Quickly stuffing the magazine in my schoolbag, I sling the backpack over my shoulder and wait for the lights before running across the Tribeca street.

Even though Elijah's several feet ahead of me, his studded leather jacket is still in view, and I use it as my guide while I weave through people, apologizing and jogging faster until I'm mere inches away.

The damn guy keeps on walking faster, and here I am treading along behind him, not even knowing what I'd say if he turns around. All I do know is that his scent makes me feel like home, and I could get used to the cigarette smoke hitting me from ahead.

"Hey, watch where you're going!" A lady pushing a stroller growls when I almost run into her as I turn a corner five feet behind Elijah.

I turn to her, mortified. "Oh my God, I'm so sorry, please forgive me, I'm just…"

She comes to a halt with a glare. "I don't care what you're '*just*' doing, be careful around corners!"

I feel bad right to my core, but she walks off with her stroller before I can say anything else.

Breathing out a strangled breath, I vow to forget it completely and focus on Elijah, but when I turn back around and there's no sign of him or any leather jacket, I begin to panic.

No. No. No.

I did not just lose him!

Where could he have gone?

He didn't cross the street again and there's no way he could have entered the cafés a little farther down unless he bolted, which is... highly unlikely.

Damn.

I glance around, frustrated with myself this too was all for nothing.

Stuff it, I'm going home.

Spinning on my heels, I'm adamant to call it a day when I unexpectedly slam into a solid chest and tumble back, almost losing my balance.

My schoolbag slips and falls to the ground with a thud.

What the hell...?

The second I crane my head up and glance at my victim, I'm pretty sure I'm about to piss my pants. It's Elijah, and unlike before, there's a deadly look in his steel-black-eyed stare.

"Are you following me?" Elijah growls ever so wickedly, stepping forward until we're only inches apart. "Because if you are, it ain't gonna be good for you, *Peaches*, believe me."

He continues to stare me down, awaiting my response, all while my mouth dries up and I wish I could just disappear. It doesn't matter how badly I've had a crush on him, right now if looks could kill... I'd be gone. Long gone.

Jerk.

I don't like the soullessness in his death glare or the way he clenches his jaw when I part my lips before closing them. I don't know this guy. At all. Which is why I do the only logical thing in my head during this current moment...

I take one last glance at my dark, edgy sinner, and then bolt in the other direction.

I run all the way home, (and yes, through the Brooklyn Bridge too) like I'm some sort of freak. It takes me over an hour, and by the end of it, I'm slow walking like I just won a marathon.

Or just came last.

But I keep on going until I lock myself in my bedroom, panting. And it's only then, as my breaths finally begin to stabilize, that I realize I no longer have my schoolbag. In fact, I don't think I ran home with it at all. It slipped from my shoulder when I slammed into Elijah's chest, and I never picked it up.

Oh. My. God.

He's with it. He has it.

And the worst part of all? I have a keyring on it with all of my information in case of an emergency.

My *name.*

My *number.*

My *home address.*

It's all at his fingertips.

Groaning, I dive onto my bed and bury my face into my silk pillow.

Ohhh no!

I'm so screwed.

Elijah Diesel is going to kill me!

Want to continue reading *Diesel Rose*?

Read Elijah and Rosalia's angsty age gap, enemies-to-lovers rockstar romance today! *Diesel Rose* is available and FREE on Kindle Unlimited!

Acknowlegments

Tate and London's meet cue lived rent-free in my mind for months before their bittersweet love sprawled out like ink across my keyboard. There's something about the innocence of their start that truly became an addiction for me to write. I really wanted to highlight their tenderness, fondness, and emotional solace from the moment they met. Even through all their angst, trauma, and hate, in one prologued gaze, they could return to the rich little boy and the broken little girl they were on wintry Central Park bench, and everything would be okay. I loved writing Tate and London and will truly miss them. Thank you for trusting me with their journey, even the raw parts, because they too matter in order to heal.

Mamma, I love you more than words exists. *Grazie di cuore. Ti amo per sempre.*

Nonno and Nonna, *vi amo entrambi per sempre. Grazie.*

Daniela, my beautiful PA, you're incredible! Thank you for everything that you do for me. I truly appreciate it and cherish you so much. Thanks for always believing in me, babe.

Emily, Becca, and Kelly, thank you all for perfecting the manuscript!

Gemma, you're always my cheerleader. Thank you for feeling their heartache!

Lori, you're incredible and your talent always takes my breath away. Thank you!

Daniel, thank you for the stunning photograph, your assistance and all the kindness!

Stacey, you're beautiful. Thank you for the gorgeous formatting & making me smile!

My street team. You girls rock. I'm so grateful for you!

My author and blogger friends for always being by my side and giving my work so much looove. My wonderful babes over in my

Facebook Reader Group: *Vanessa Luisa's Lovelies*—I adore all of you too. Thank you to my PR team too for all of the assistance!

And last but not least, big thank you to all my beautiful readers, because without you all this wouldn't be possible. Thank you for adoring my words and all your love. Love you!

Vanessa Luisa xo

ALSO BY VANESSA LUISA

The Giannotti World:
An interconnected series of bittersweet romance
standalones set in Seattle.

Merciful Vows (#1)

DIESEL ROSE:
The poetically tragic rock star and his muse…

Remember I'm Yours (#0.5)

Diesel Rose (#1)

STANDALONES:

Oceans of Us

Kisses in Heartache

Happy reading!
Vanessa Luisa xo

About the
AUTHOR

Vanessa Luisa is a contemporary romance author. She resides in Melbourne, Australia, with her army of current reads, sassy cat, and Tom Hardy…the latter is purely all in her mind, but shh don't tell her!

She loves writing angsty, emotionally gripping, sexy romance with passionate alphas and strong-willed women. Her love of reading and writing have always been with her, and while she has a background in certified personal styling, nowadays she's turning her dream of being an author into reality.

She adores all things from the Golden Age of Hollywood, Seinfeld and believes tea is a writing essential. When she isn't writing, she's busy running her own business and spending time with loved ones.

Vanessa loves interacting with readers so please feel free to reach out to her via socials, subscribe to her newsletter, and/or contact her at vanessaluisaauthor@gmail.com for any questions or comments.

Connect With
VANESSA LUISA

Join my Facebook Reader's Group: www.facebook.com/groups/
vanessaluisaslovelies

**Subscribe to my MAILING LIST/NEWSLETTER to be notified
of new releases, behind the scenes, and receive exclusive bonus
material:** www.vanessaluisa.com/contact

Instagram: @thevanessaluisa
www.instagram.com/thevanessaluisa

Facebook: www.facebook.com/vanessaluisaauthor/

TikTok: @thevanessaluisa
www.tiktok.com/@thevanessaluisa

Twitter: @thevanessaluisa
www.twitter.com/thevanessaluisa

Follow me on Goodreads:
www.goodreads.com/author/show/21142369.Vanessa_Luisa

Website/Blog: vanessaluisa.com